SHADOW

OF THE

LORDS

ALSO BY SIMON LEVACK

Demon of the Air

SHADOW
OF THE
LORDS

Simon Levack

THOMAS DUNNE BOOKS

ST. MARTIN'S MINOTAUR ⚜ NEW YORK

THOMAS DUNNE BOOKS.
An imprint of St. Martin's Press.

Extracts from *Fifteen Poets of the Aztec World* by Miguel Leon-Portilla are reproduced
by kind permission of the publishers, University of Oklahoma Press.

Extracts from Bernadino de Sahagun, *The Florentine Codex, A General History of the
Things of New Spain,* translated and edited by Arthur J. O. Anderson and Charles E.
Dibble, are reproduced by kind permission of the University of Utah Press and the
School of American Research.

www.thomasdunnebooks.com
www.minotaurbooks.com

ISBN-13: 978-0-312-34841-0
ISBN-10: 0-312-34841-X

First published in Great Britain by Simon & Schuster UK Ltd

First U.S. Edition: September 2006

10 9 8 7 6 5 4 3 2 1

For Sarah and Isaac, with love

Thanks . . .

To Jane Gregory, Broo Doherty and everyone else at Gregory & Co for your patience, encouragement and advice.

To Kate Lyall-Grant and your colleagues at Simon & Schuster for your enthusiasm and suggestions – not to mention buying this book in the first place!

And to Sarah for your love, support, merciless criticism and gruesome ideas.

Author's Note

The featherwork was the shadow of the lords and kings.

Fray Diego Durán, *Book of the Gods and Rites*

Like its predecessor, *Demon of the Air*, this book is set in Central America in the early sixteenth century, shortly before the coming of the Europeans.

At this time the region was dominated by the warlike nation we call the Aztecs. When they first appeared at some time in the thirteenth century they were just one of a number of nomadic tribes with a common language and history, but over the next two hundred years or so they fought their way to the top. Forced to settle on a desolate, marshy island in the middle of a briny lake, they turned it into a fortress, surrounded it with fertile fields built upon artificial islands, and used it as a base from which to cow most of their neighbours into submission.

The Aztecs' own name for themselves was *Mexica*; they gave this name to the city they founded, calling it Mexico. The southern part of the city was called Tenochtitlan, and the northern part Tlatelolco. Modern Mexico City stands on the same site.

At its zenith, under Emperor Montezuma II, Aztec Mexico

was probably the largest city in the world, outside Asia. It was the capital of an empire that stretched as far east and west as the coasts of the Caribbean and the Pacific and as far south as modern Guatemala. Like any city it was a crowded and colourful place, home to merchants, artisans, warriors, priests, lords, beggars and thieves.

We are most familiar with the warriors and priests, owing to the Aztecs' notorious practice of sacrificing prisoners of war, along with other victims. Nobody writing about the period can afford to ignore them, but in this book they yield centre stage to the merchants and artisans, and in particular the practitioners of an art form with no parallel elsewhere: featherwork.

I was lucky enough to see a tiny example of the Aztec featherworkers' craft at the exhibition at London's Royal Academy between November 2002 and April 2003. Even after five hundred years, I was able to marvel at the painstaking care and exuberant sense of colour that had gone into producing it, and wonder what combination of inspiration, religious fervour and technique might have guided the maker's hand.

Some of the answers I dreamed up found their way into this novel – along, of course, with the usual mayhem . . .

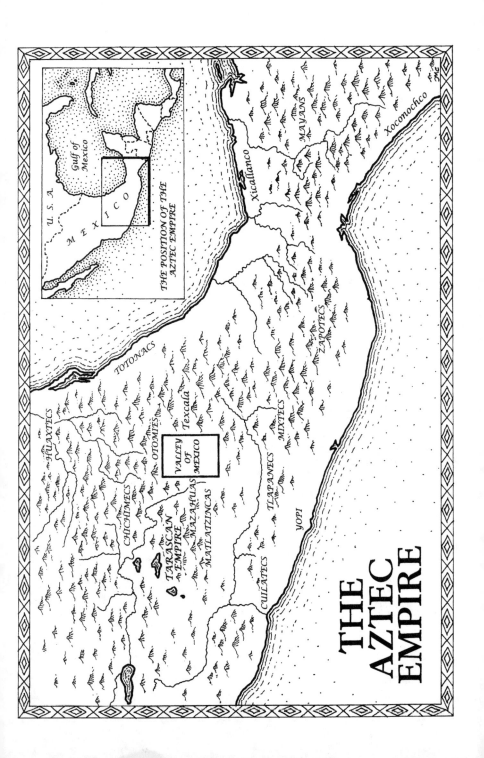

THE AZTEC EMPIRE

THE POSITION OF THE AZTEC EMPIRE

U.S.A.

MEXICO

Gulf of Mexico

TOTONACS

HUAXTECS

CHICHIMECS

OTOMIES

Valley OF MEXICO

Texcala

TARASCAN EMPIRE

MAZAHUAS

MATLATZINCAS

TLAPANECS

MIXTECS

ZAPOTECS

MAYANS

Xicallanco

Xoconochco

YOPI

CUITLATECS

VALLEY OF MEXICO

Citlaltepec

Zompanco

LAKE
ZOMPANCO

Xaltocan

Tepotzotlan

LAKE
XALTOCAN

Teotihuacan

Cuauhtitlan

Tepexpan

Papalotla

Tenayuca

Tlalnepantla

LAKE
TETZCOCO

Tetzcoco

Azcapotzalco

Huexotla

Tlacopan

Tlatelolco

Tenochtitlan

Coatlichan

Chapultepec

Chimalhuacan

Mixoac

Iztapalapan

Coatepec

Tepepolco

Coyoacan
Huitzilopochco

Mexicalizinco
Colhuacan

Iztahuacan

N
W   E
S

LAKE
XOCHIMILCO

LAKE
CHALCO

Chalco

Xochimilco

Cuitlahuac

Mixquic   Ayotzinco

0   5
miles

MC

MEXICO-TENOCHTITLAN

To Tepeyac

Atecocolecan

Sacred precinct and
market of Tlatelolco

Pochtlan and
Amantlan

N
W · E
S

TLATELOLCO

Copolco

TEOPAN

CUEPOPAN

The Heart of
the World

Atlixco

To Tlacopan
& Chapultepec

TENOCHTITLAN

AZTACALCO

MOYOTLAN

Toltenco

To Iztapalapan
& Coyoacán

0   1
miles

════════ Canals
▬▬▬▬ Roads & causeways

MÓ

A Note on Nahuatl

The Aztec language, Nahuatl, is not difficult to pronounce, but is burdened with spellings based on sixteenth-century Castilian. The following note should help:

Spelling	Pronunciation
c	c as in 'Cecil' before e or i; k before a or o
ch	sh
x	sh
hu, uh	w
qu	k as in 'kettle' before e or i; 'qu' as in 'quack' before a
tl	as in English, but where '-tl' occurs at the end of a word the 'l' is hardly sounded.

The stress always falls on the penultimate syllable.

I have used as few Nahuatl words as possible and favoured clarity at the expense of strict accuracy in choosing English equivalents. Hence, for example, I have rendered *Huey Tlatoani* as 'Emperor', *Cihuacoatl* as 'Chief Minister', *calpolli* as 'parish', *octli* as 'sacred wine' and *maquahuitl* as 'sword', and have been similarly cavalier in choosing English replacements for most of the frequently recurring personal names. In referring to the

Emperor at the time when this story is set I have used the most familiar form of his name, Montezuma, although Motecuhzoma would be more accurate. To avoid confusion I have called the people of Mexico-Tenochtitlan 'Aztecs' rather than 'Mexicans'.

The name of the principal character in the novel, Yaotl, is pronounced 'YAH-ot'.

The Aztec Calendar

The Aztecs lived in a world governed by religion and magic, and their rituals and auguries were in turn ordered by the calendar.

The solar year, which began in our February, was divided into eighteen twenty-day periods (often called 'months'). Each month had its own religious observances associated with it; often these involved sacrifices, some of them human, to one or more of the many Aztec gods. At the end of the year were five 'Useless Days' that were considered profoundly unlucky.

Parallel to this ran a divinatory calendar of 260 days divided into twenty groups of thirteen days (sometimes called 'weeks'). The first day in the 'week' would bear the number 1 and one of twenty names – Reed, Jaguar, Eagle, Vulture, and so on. The second day would bear the number 2 and the next name in the sequence. On the fourteenth day the number would revert to 1 but the sequence of names continued seamlessly, with each combination of names and numbers repeating itself every 260 days.

A year was named after the day in the divinatory calendar on which it began. For mathematical reasons these days could bear only one of four names – Reed, Flint Knife, House and Rabbit – combined with a number from 1 to 13. This produced a cycle of fifty-two years at the beginning and end of which the solar and divinatory calendars coincided. The

Aztecs called this period a 'Bundle of Years'.

Every day in a Bundle of Years was the product of a unique combination of year, month and date in the divinatory calendar, and so had, for the Aztecs, its own individual character and religious and magical significance.

The date on which the first chapter of this book opens is 23 December 1517; in other words, One Death, the fourteenth day of the Month of the Coming Down of Water, in the year Twelve House.

ONE DEATH

1

'Listen!' my brother cried. Mamiztli – 'the Mountain Lion' - was staring across the lake towards the island and city of Mexico. 'Yaotl, what was that noise?'

'Daybreak', I said shortly.

For the first time in an eventful night, I noticed that the water surrounding us was no longer black. The lake's surface had caught the deep blue of an early morning sky. It was going to be a crisp winter's day, hailed by a yellow-white radiance spreading through the thin haze that veiled the eastern horizon. Mist blanketed the mountains surrounding the valley, and swirled around the countless temples in front of them, softening their harsh, angular forms.

Birds twittered and flapped among the sedges at the water's edge, but the sound my brother had drawn my attention to had come from one of the temples, and as we gazed towards its source it came again, drifting lazily towards us over the still water: the call of a trumpet, hailing the dawn.

Another followed it, and soon the air around us was alive with them, both from the city itself and the many little towns behind us on the lake's western shore, until it felt as if the boat we stood on was the only place on Earth where priests were not blowing lustily into conch-shells. It was strange to hear them from a distance, over the water. Perhaps that was why my brother had not recognized their sound. It felt as if they were calling to us alone, instead of proclaiming to the World at large their relief and delight that the Sun had come up one more time, and that today at least he would not desert his people.

For us, every morning was a struggle whose outcome could never be known in advance. Every time the Sun rose, he re-enacted the birth of our War-God, Huitzilopochtli, and his terrible battle with his half-sister, the Moon Goddess, and his half-brothers, the Stars. Like the War-God, the Sun always won, but we could never escape the thought that he might not, and that we owed every day to the favour of the gods.

I shivered, and it was not from the chill of the early morning air. After such a night as had just passed, I could well believe that nothing, not even the Sun's rising in the morning, was certain. I had come out expecting to face an old enemy and found instead my own child, a son I had never known I had, and then watched him slip away and vanish, as fugitive as a fiery spirit on the lake.

As the last of the trumpet calls died away I felt an urge to do something that, in the days when I had been a priest, I had done out of habit: to offer the gods my blood, the nourishment the Sun needed for his day's journey.

Finding a sharp edge was easy. There were several slivers of obsidian scattered around my feet. They had been struck off blades set into the wooden shaft of a sword, at the moment when it had been driven into a man's skull. A weeping woman crouched over his prone body. I stepped delicately around her, avoiding the corpse and the other things – some of them human, none of them alive – that were scattered around it. I stooped to pick up one of the hard, glittering shards with one scrawny hand while the other reached up to my temple to tug a mass of long, tangled hair out of the way. Then I quickly cut into one of my earlobes.

With no bowl or paper to collect the blood, I let the warm fluid run down my hollow cheek and the side of my bony jaw, staining and matting the grey-streaked hair that lay over them. I stood and looked towards the city and the glowing sky beyond it and offered up a wordless prayer, remembering how it had once been every morning, the smell of incense and the vain fluttering of the quails we had sacrificed and our voices appealing to the Sun to do his work.

The woman's brittle voice shattered my reverie.

'Haven't you spilled enough blood for one night?'

The woman's name was Oceloxochitl, which meant Tiger Lily. The dead man was her son, a young merchant named Ocotl – the word for a pine torch or, as we thought of it, a Shining Light. A more vicious, treacherous, murderous youth would have been hard to find, although you would not have known it from the way his mother wept over his body, cradling it and shaking it as if to try to wake him up again, while his blood soaked her skirt, blouse and mantle and trickled along her bare arms.

'I didn't kill him, Lily,' I said. 'I told you how it was.' I appealed to my brother. 'Lion, you were here too.'

Lion's name normally suited him. He was a big, muscular man, every inch a warrior, but this morning he looked anything but fierce. He avoided my eyes, fixing his own on the city taking shape in the mist. He scowled. He hated lies and told them badly.

'It all happened like you said, Yaotl,' he said mechanically. 'What do you want me to say? Momaimati here . . .'

'Don't involve me,' growled the fourth person on the boat, a stolid commoner whose name meant One Skilled with His Hands or, in other words, 'Handy'. 'I didn't see anything.'

Which was true, if unhelpful. I looked desperately down at

the bereaved mother, wondering what I could say to her now. The anguished face she turned up towards me had had twenty years' worth of lines etched on it in a single night. I had seen it looking very different once, very close and flushed with passion, black hair with its intriguing silver strands flowing from it like a spray of feathers from a fan as I pressed her down on a sleeping-mat. A lot had happened to us both since then, but I could not help wishing for something – some word of comfort, if not from me then from anyone else – that could make a start at smoothing away those lines. I watched as her hand strayed automatically towards the young man's blood-matted hair, before drawing back sharply as it brushed the blades set into the sword's flat shaft. My own fingers twitched in sympathy. I was about to lean forward, to reach out to her, even though I knew I would almost certainly be rebuffed, when another voice made me freeze.

It was the voice of an ancient man, hoarse with exhaustion and strain, but still clear and powerful. My master, Lord Feathered in Black, had not attempted to climb out of the canoe he had arrived in, and was still reclining in its stern, looking up at us as his craft bobbed gently beside the much larger boat I stood on.

'In case you've all forgotten,' he snarled, 'the man and the boy who did all this are still out there.' His glance swept over the carnage on the bigger craft. 'I want them alive and conscious. They're not getting away with what they've done, do you hear? I'll make an example of them. As soon as we get back to the city I'm sending warriors out here to start searching. Handy and Yaotl, you're to wait here, with the boat, until they arrive.'

Handy was a retainer of my master's – not a slave, but a common man who hired himself out by the day. I had no thought for his position now, though. All I could see was what my master was telling me to do. Then I imagined myself in the midst of his hunting party, and pictured its quarry, seeing the terrified, stricken face of a young man whose real identity the Chief Minister could never have guessed at.

'My Lord! I can't! You can't ask me . . .'

For a moment my master was speechless.

'"Can't"?' He was shrill with indignation. 'What do you mean, "can't"? Who are you to tell me what I can and can't do, slave?'

At that sharp reminder of what I was, I recollected myself, feeling like a man running blindly towards a cliff-edge who realizes only just in time what is in front of him.

'I . . . I am sorry, my Lord. I didn't mean to be impertinent. It's just that . . .'

I could not tell him. It would have meant death for me as well, to admit to Lord Feathered In Black, the *Cihuacoatl*, the Chief Minister, Chief Priest and Chief Justice of the Aztecs, the second-most powerful man in the World, that the boy he blamed for killing Shining Light, and for so many other things besides, was my own son.

I had lied about the night's events, both to Lily, to save her from the truth, and to my master, to save my own skin.

The big boat I was standing on had belonged to Lily's son, Shining Light – the same young man whose corpse she was weeping brokenly over now. He had been a merchant, a member of the class of long-distance traders known as Pochteca, who earned their fortunes and renown through long, often hazardous journeys into distant lands. Shining Light had found an easier path to riches, however. Unknown to the rest of his family, he had hoarded their wealth on this boat and used it to finance an illegal gambling operation, taking secret bets on the sacred Ball Game.

Deceiving and stealing from his own mother and grand-father had not been Shining Light's only crime. He had depraved tastes, particularly when it came to boys. Once, in one of the marketplaces, he had picked up a rootless but resourceful young man, an orphan named Quimatini, or 'Nimble'. Nimble had no place in Aztec society. He had sprung from a brief, illicit liaison I had had with a pleasure-girl. He had been brought up among the Tarascans, beyond the Mountains to the West, and had drifted back into Mexico as a youth. Shining Light had adopted him, in his own per-verted fashion, and the lad had posed as his lover's son while he ran errands and collected bets from his customers.

One of those customers had been my own master, Lord Feathered in Black. Shining Light had double-crossed him, though. Many others were caught up in his treachery, and some of them lay on the boat around us, murdered. My son had been his unwitting accomplice.

Lord Feathered in Black had finally caught up with Shining Light and Nimble on the night that had just passed; but he had not learned the truth about either who they were or what they had done. My master, my brother, Shining Light's mother Lily, the commoner Handy and I had gone in search of them, setting out across the lake in two canoes. As it happened, the canoe with my master and Lily in it had been deliberately run ashore by its boatman, who had panicked and run away, and only Lion and I had confronted the pair. We were the only ones to learn that the man who had betrayed my master was indeed Lily's child, and that the young man he had in his thrall – who was in the end virtually his prisoner – was my own son.

My brother had had to kill Shining Light. We had set Nimble free, and when my master, Lily and Handy finally reached us, we had lied to them. We had let them think Lily's son had been held captive by the man he had pretended to be, and killed by him, and that that man and Nimble had escaped.

They appeared to have believed us; but even so, old Black Feathers was not going to let the matter drop. Nimble and his lover had seen and heard things that could imperil his life if the Emperor learned of them. Moreover, he had been duped. My master's was not a forgiving nature. He wanted revenge.

I was babbling, saying anything that came into my head if I thought it might help persuade Lord Feathered in Black to relent.

'I might let you down. I'm weak, my Lord. I've lost blood, the precious water of life. I might not be able to guide a search party . . .'

My master laughed out loud.

It was a strange noise, a prolonged hoarse cackle, ending in a series of harsh dry coughs. Then he cleared his throat and his ancient face settled into a grin.

'Oh, don't you worry yourself about that, Yaotl. So you might let me down – so what? It'll be so much the worse for you!' He threw a significant glance across the water towards the nearest of the temples. 'Right now you're probably worth more as a sacrifice to the gods than as a slave!'

My heart sank at this further brutal reminder of my position.

'You find the boy and his father,' my master went on relentlessly, 'and no excuses! If you don't, it'll be the worse for you!'

My master had no idea that he was telling me to deliver up my own child, but I knew that if he had known it would have made no difference.

Then Handy spoke up.

'My Lord, I am sorry, but you can't send Yaotl after Telpochtli and the boy.'

I stared at him. Terror made my stomach churn. I wondered

what he had really seen and heard. He had been knocked into the water early in the fight with Shining Light, before Lion and I had found out who he and Nimble really were. Surely, I told myself, Handy could not know?

Then the commoner spoke again and, realizing what he meant, it was as much as I could do not to laugh out loud from sheer relief.

'Have you forgotten what day it is?' he went on wretchedly.

Out of the corner of my eye I saw my master's face, the taut muscles and bulging eyes seeming to collapse inward as his expression changed from fury to comical bemusement.

'Yaotl is a slave,' the commoner reminded him. 'He's sacred to Tezcatlipoca. My Lord, this is Tezcatlipoca's name-day. You can't give Yaotl orders today, it would offend the god. We're in the middle of the lake – what if he stirs up a storm?'

I saw my brother start at that, and then squint suspiciously at the sky. He had always been more god-fearing than I was. 'He's right, my Lord.' He looked down at my master, whose eyes had now closed in an expression of resigned exasperation.

'After all, you're in a little open canoe. It wouldn't do to take the risk – not on a day like One Death.'

Of all the gods there was none we Aztecs feared more than Tezcatlipoca. The Mocker, we called him, the Enemy on Both Hands, He Whose Slaves We Are. All those titles suited his character – untrustworthy, whimsical and dangerous. You could feel his influence whenever your affairs depended on chance. The merchant who set out on a long trip with his canoe richly laden with trade goods and ended up on a mountainside with vultures picking at his bones was a victim of Tezcatlipoca's caprice. So was the Lord who sat down in his reserved seat in the front tier overlooking the Ball-Court, with his stake laid out before him, only to watch helplessly while a

small rubber ball flew and bounced from one player's hip to
another's and reduced him to penury.

I had been no less a victim of the Lord of the Here and
Now. Despite being the son of a commoner, from a poor
family of farmers and paper-makers from one of the meaner
parishes at the southern end of Tenochtitlan, I had found
myself among the privileged few allowed to train for the
priesthood; but I had ended up as a slave.

For a little boy, who just happened to have been born on an
auspicious day, to be thrust into the care of the sinister, black-
robed, bloodstained masters of the school we called the House
of Tears had hardly felt as if a god were smiling upon him.
Twenty years later, though, the man the boy grew into was to
feel Tezcatlipoca's malice even more keenly, when for a minor
and meaningless offence he was thrown out of the Priest
House and trampled into the mud at the lake's edge by the
men who had been his friends and colleagues.

My expulsion from the priesthood was only the start of my
misfortunes. To the misery of knowing what I had lost – not
just my status as a priest, recognizable at once by my long hair
and black face-paint, but also the daily round of penances and
observances that had given my life its meaning – was added the
ignominy of being picked up and taken home by my family.
They had tolerated me, but never let me forget how I had let
them down: how I had thrown away a chance my brothers and
sisters had never had, not to mention whatever it had cost my
father to secure my admittance to the House of Tears.

I had sought refuge from their taunts and reproaches inside
a drinking-gourd. I hoped the sour taste of sacred wine would
take away the bitterness of my loss. Instead it doubled my
humiliation, getting me arrested for the crime of public
drunkenness.

I ought to have died then. For priests and nobles, the

penalty for being found drunk without lawful excuse was to be cudgelled to death. In some ways the alternative was worse. My life was spared, but all my hair was shaved off, in the plaza in front of the Emperor's palace, before a laughing, jeering crowd. How he wore his hair mattered to an Aztec, whether he had it piled up on his head like a pillar of stone to show he was a successful warrior or left it unkempt, bloody and matted as the mark of a priest. Having your head shaved was like being told you were nobody. It was what we did to a war-captive before sacrificing him, as a sign that, whatever he may have done in life, now he was just a corpse.

I had endured it only because I had known I was going to get blind drunk the moment I was set free.

I had paid for my next gourd full of sacred wine, and many more after that, by selling myself into slavery.

Slavery was not all bad. An Aztec could sell himself to cover his debts or provide for his family when times were hard or, as in my case, to keep himself in drink for a little longer. The deal had to be struck openly, in the market, before four witnesses. Then the law allowed the slave his freedom during the time it took to run through the money he was given, before he had to surrender himself to his master and do his bidding.

After that, his master owned his time but not his life. A slave's property was his own, not his master's. His master had no rights over his family or his children. A slave could not be ill treated or killed or even sold without good reason – although once he had given his master cause to get rid of him he might well find himself being bought by the priests as a cheap sacrifice.

There were worse fates than slavery that could befall a man, so long as he had no self-respect. A slave could not glorify and enrich himself by going to war and dragging home captives, or pay his debt to his city by giving his labour to some great public work, as it was not his to give. In the eyes of my people, I counted for nothing more than an extension of the Chief Minister's right arm.

'What's so funny?' my brother demanded.

We were standing on the Tlacopan causeway, the broad road connecting the island of Mexico with the lake's western shore.

Handy had put us all ashore, ferrying us in relays to the small town of Popotla. There my master and the woman had found canoes to take them home, leaving Lion and me to walk. Ordinarily Lion could easily have hired a boat himself, but he had no money with him, and in his present state no one would have taken him for the distinguished and wealthy man he was.

Now he and I found ourselves in the middle of a dense, jostling crowd. In the northern part of the city the great market of Tlatelolco alone drew at least forty thousand men, women and children every day: buyers and sellers of everything from feathers and jewels to slaves, building materials and human dung to spread in the fields. Most of the bulky items, such as hides or tree trunks or stone from the quarries, came in by canoe, but there was enough traffic left over to jam the roads. Lion had just avoided having his eye pecked out by a live turkey slung over a farmer's wife's shoulder, and his snarl as he recoiled and caught my involuntary grin reminded me that this was not what he was used to.

My elder brother's origins had been as humble as mine, naturally, but his career had been no less remarkable. Unlike me, he owed his advancement to his own prowess rather than the day of his birth. Like almost any commoner's child he had gone to the House of Youth as a boy and learned all the skills needed to fit a man or woman for life as an Aztec. In the case of boys that meant rudimentary instruction in song and dance, medicine, history and polite speech, and advanced and intensive training in physical fitness, tactics and weapon handling. Lion had excelled at his studies, and then, when turned loose on our enemies, had fought his way to fame and fortune, dragging home more distinguished captives than he could count himself, and winning one of the highest ranks a commoner could attain: *Atenpanecatl*, Guardian of the Waterfront. With his rank had come the marks of distinction and high office: the yellow cotton cloak with the red border, the cotton ribbons that bound his hair, the distinctive earplugs and the special sandals with oversized straps that he was allowed to wear within the city's limits.

'What's funny?' I echoed his question. 'Why, this. I mean, look around us. Tezcatlipoca has really surpassed himself this time, hasn't he?'

Lion's retort was choked off as he lurched forward involuntarily. Someone had barged into him from behind. He was a porter, probably on the last leg of a long journey from one of our tributary provinces. He had not been looking where he was going, probably because he had his head bowed against the weight of the bale hanging from his brow by a tump-line. From the faintly resinous smell about him I guessed the bale was full of copal incense.

The man muttered something that might have been apologetic in his own language, and my brother's outraged rebuke died in his throat. Lion turned on me instead.

'If you mean having me rub shoulders with peasants and barbarians is Tezcatlipoca's idea of a joke, brother, then perhaps you could tell your patron god that I don't get it!'

If he was trying to sound belligerent then he spoiled the effect by sending a hasty glance skyward, as if anxious that he might have said too much.

'I didn't mean you,' I assured him, although I could easily imagine the god laughing at the picture my brother presented now: the illustrious warrior with his hair hopelessly tangled, his cloak torn and bloody and one of his sandals missing. 'I was being purely selfish. Look at me: I was born on this day, remember? On One Death: Tezcatlipoca's name-day. I was always going to achieve everything or nothing. So our father got me into the priesthood, no doubt expecting me to end up as the Keeper of the God of the Mexicans or something similarly illustrious, and what do I find myself doing? Celebrating the god's name-day, and mine, as one of his own creatures – a slave. You have to admit, that is funny.'

'It was your choice. You didn't have to sell yourself. You could have come back home.'

'And done what? Spend my days with a digging-stick, stirring shit into the soil?'

'Honest labour in the fields was good enough for our father. I suppose you thought all that was beneath you. Well, brother, let me remind you . . .'

'Don't!' I could guess what was coming: a résumé of my downfall, culminating in the moment when I had had my head shaved, and sparing no detail – especially my brother's role in wielding the razor himself, after he had persuaded the judges to spare my life. 'I didn't need your lectures then and I don't need them now. Didn't you think I'd suffered enough?' Seeing a gap in the throng in front of me, I plunged into it, hoping to shake off both my brother and the things he made me remember.

The crowd had parted to make room for a raucous quarrel between two pleasure-girls. No doubt it had begun as a trivial dispute over who was going to ply her trade from what spot in one of the city's many markets, and so far they had not got much beyond cracking chewing-gum in each other's faces, but it had potential. I found myself grinning at the thought of what my stiff-necked, pious brother would run into if he followed me: black hair flying around him, fleshy, tattooed arms, stained pale with yellow ochre, reaching out to him with wickedly long fingernails, the air heavy with the vanilla scent of cheap perfume and ringing with inhuman shrieks from those vivid red mouths . . .

I forgot that there was more to being a great warrior than brute strength. The hand that tugged sharply at my cloak's hem and almost wrenched the garment from my shoulders reminded me that Lion was more agile than I was and there was almost nothing I could get into or out of faster than he could.

'I don't suppose it ever occurred to you,' he shouted, trying to make himself heard over the cries behind us, 'that your family might have helped?'

'I'd had your help,' I said shortly. 'Sorry, brother, but it came at too high a price.'

'And the disgrace? What about the shame you brought on yourself?'

'On you, you mean! Don't try and kid me, Lion. That's what this was always about, isn't it – keeping me busy digging over some weed-infested mud-patch somewhere, safely out of sight, so I wouldn't blight your precious career!'

To my surprise, the mighty warrior did not fly into a rage. He looked briefly, sadly, at our feet – his with the one precious sandal that was what remained of his dignity, mine bare as always – and mumbled: 'No, it's not that.' Then he looked up again, his face wearing as thoughtful an expression as I had seen on it. 'Look, your antics over the years haven't helped – but I've overcome that; all of us have. Except you. Are you really going to be a slave for the rest of your life? No one lives for ever, Yaotl, not even slippery characters like you. The best you can hope for is to leave a good name behind. Maybe it didn't matter before, when you thought you had no children, but now you know you've got a son. Don't you want to leave him anything, beside the knowledge that his father died a slave? If you won't exert yourself for your own sake, what about his?'

It was a long speech for him, delivered softly, with none of the hectoring tone his lectures were usually couched in. In the awkward pause that followed I reflected that it must have cost him a lot of effort. I wondered whether he had been saving it up, rehearsing it.

I turned away from him. The crowd flowing around us suddenly seemed distant. I tried looking into the busy, preoccupied faces that were hurrying past me, but for some reason it was hard to bring them into focus. I wished he had not mentioned Nimble.

Eventually I muttered: 'If my son has any sense, he'll be on the far side of the mountains by nightfall. He'll never know me.'

'Maybe he'll be back, some day.'

I shook my head furiously, to clear it. 'Anybody would think I had a choice!'

'You could run away. It's One Death – you could do it today.'

'Only if I happened to be in the marketplace.' I knew about the custom he was alluding to, the tiniest chink of an opening that was offered to slaves on Tezcatlipoca's special day. 'And then only if I managed to reach the Emperor's palace without being caught first. Oh, and the rule is I have to tread in a turd on the way, remember?' I had always suspected this last twist revealed the custom's true purpose: to give the bystanders a good laugh. What could be funnier than watching a man running through the market with soiled heels, with his cursing master behind him, stumbling in his efforts to avoid stepping in his slave's footprints? 'Do you think I'm likely to be let near the marketplace today? It's a fairy tale, Lion. Nobody ever really escapes that way – not unless he's more trouble than he's worth and his master lets him go just to spare himself the expense of feeding him.'

'Buy your freedom.'

I laughed out loud. Startled faces turned towards me, and even the piercing cries of the girls still squabbling behind us dried up, as if they had realized that their audience's attention had wandered.

'Buy my freedom?' I hissed, abruptly feeling the need to be a little bit discreet. 'You must be joking! With what?'

Lion looked ruefully down at the tattered remains of his cloak. 'I'm still the Guardian of the Waterfront, even if I don't look like it! What did old Black Feathers pay you for your liberty – twenty cloaks? I can double that. I can offer more if it isn't enough.'

'And how would I pay you back?'

His answer caught me unawares. He said nothing. Instead, he lunged at me with both arms outstretched and his palms, held out flat in front of him, slammed into my chest with all of a hefty, muscular warrior's substantial weight behind them.

I was a pace or two from the edge of the causeway, with my back to the water. With a shout of alarm, I staggered back under the force of the blow until there was nothing under my heels but empty space. For a moment my arms whirled frantically as I tried to keep my balance, and then I fell, breaking the surface with so much force that the breath burst from my lungs as a glistening cloud of bubbles.

By the time my head was in the air again, with water streaming from my mouth and nose, I had got the joke. I gathered he had explained it to the bystanders, judging by the laughter that greeted my reappearance.

'Happy birthday!' he cried.

'Very funny,' I gasped, as my fingers sought a purchase among the rough stones lining the causeway's side. 'It would be funnier still if you'd help me up!'

'Going Through the Water', we called it: the traditional ducking your friends and family would give you on your name-day. 'I suppose I'm supposed to provide you with a feast,' I muttered, as I scrambled back on to the road. 'Sorry, Lion, but you're out of luck there!'

'All right,' he replied mildly, 'I'll let you off. But as for paying me back – I'm offering you the chance to buy your freedom as a present, you idiot!'

For a moment I felt light headed with relief.

I had a day ahead of me when I could pretend to be my own man; but that was only because I belonged to Tezcatlipoca, and on his day, that one day in every two hundred and sixty, nobody dared lay a finger on a slave. Tomorrow, I would be returned to my duties, and the first of them would be to hunt down my own son.

Yet my brother was saying that this need not happen. I could be free every day of my life. I could be free of old Black Feathers's arbitrary and often murderous will, with a new beginning that somehow cancelled all the shame and misery I had known since the day I left the Priest House. The prospect was like the best sacred wine I had ever tasted: it made me feel almost giddy but still sharp, and even as I was about to embrace it – as I was about to embrace my brother, for the first time since we were children – I saw the fatal flaw in the scheme.

'Forget it,' I said brusquely, forging ahead into the crowd.

'Forget it?' For a moment Lion could only stand still, echoing my words incredulously. Then he dashed after me, rudely shouldering aside a couple of men who had strayed into his path. 'What do you mean, forget it? Are you mad? Don't be so stubborn, Yaotl. Listen to me!'

I kept looking for gaps between the broad backs blocking the way ahead – anything rather than meet my brother's confused, anxious, angry eyes.

'I'm not being stubborn, brother,' I said at last. 'It's Lord Feathered in Black we're talking about – the Chief Minister. You could offer him twenty times my worth and it wouldn't matter. He's the second-richest man in the World. He doesn't need your money, or anyone else's. If he keeps me on, it's because he still has a use for me – and the moment he doesn't I'm dead, and nothing you can offer will make the slightest difference.'

For a moment Lion looked as hurt as if I had struck him. Then the streak of bloody-mindedness that was possibly the only trait we had in common took over, and I saw his face freeze into an impassive mask.

'If that is how you feel, Yaotl,' he said stiffly, 'then all I can say is, I hope you enjoy your holiday!'

2

Lord Feathered in Black had a splendid palace near the centre of the city, within easy reach of the Heart of the World, the sacred precinct, around whose temples and towering pyramids much of the business of our lives revolved. Also nearby was the still more magnificent palace of my master's cousin: the Emperor Montezuma the Younger.

I returned to my master's house feeling footsore and numb. After a sleepless and violent night followed by a long walk and a quarrel with my brother, I found it hard to think about anything other than the urge to find my own room, shed the clothes I had worn all night in favour of my old cloak, curl up on my reed mat, pull the cloak over my head and fall asleep.

Sleep was long in coming, however. I could not stop dwelling on the task my master had set for me, and my brother's startling offer.

The law was kind to slaves, but my master had shown more than once that he was too strong for the law to bind him. I might be allowed to rest today, but tomorrow he was going to make me look for my son, and if I displeased the old man – if, say, the boy was allowed to get away again – then he would make sure I regretted it. He could find a way of disposing of me if he wanted, I was confident of that.

The prospect of being free of all these fears once and for all was tantalizing, and it kept me awake like an itch I could not reach. It was all the more maddening because, had I belonged to almost anyone else, my brother's scheme would have worked. But I knew my master: if Lion approached him, old Black Feathers would just laugh in his face.

I lay shivering under my cloak, although it was not a particularly cold day, and was still wondering when sleep would come and chase my fears away when the steward shook me awake.

'Yaotl!'

Something was amiss.

It was dark in my room; with the wicker screen that covered the doorway pushed aside it was not quite pitch black, but the pallid grey light of evening falling on my floor told me I must have slept what had remained of the afternoon away. That was not what had confused me, though.

'Yaotl!'

I could hear drums. From somewhere close by came the sharp, shrill call of the two-tone drum and under it the massive, insistent beat of the ground drum. I could hear flutes as well, and the wail of a trumpet, but it was the drums whose voices I fixed on, as they seemed to reverberate through the stucco floor under me, making my sleeping-mat shake in time with their rhythm.

No, it was not the drums either. I was used to the drumming. It must mark a ceremony of some kind, an offering to a god: I would be able to work out which god when I woke up and remembered what day it was.

'Yaotl! Wake up!'

There was something wrong with the voice. I knew it from somewhere: a rough growl made hoarse by years of shouting at people, but its tone was all wrong. It sounded polite, almost deferential, and seemed even more odd when I realized that the shaking was not the drums after all, but the speaker's hand gently pushing at my shoulder, as though he were trying to wake me up but was afraid of succeeding.

It all fell into place when I heard his next words. They were muffled, as if he were speaking into his hand, not wanting to be heard.

'Come on, wake up, you lousy piece of shit! On any other day I'd be kicking your worthless head in!'

Then I remembered what day it was and what the music was for. I nearly laughed out loud. I stopped myself, though, and made do with sitting up as gracefully as I could, gathering my short cloak around my shoulders in what I hoped was a lordly manner.

'What do you want, Huitzic?' I asked coolly.

My master's steward snatched his hand away as if burned. He stepped back hastily, catching the hem of his long three-captive warrior's cloak with his heel as he did so, and all but fell over on his backside.

Huitztic: his name meant something very close to 'Prick', which was exactly how I thought of him.

To earn true renown as an Aztec warrior, you had to have captured at least four of the enemy. Then you were counted among the great: you could bind your hair up with bands with eagle-feather tassels, wear long labrets and leather earplugs and sit in the Eagle House, chatting on equal terms with men like my distinguished brother. All this was yours if you took four captives.

The Prick had taken three, the last of them many years before. In return he had been given a red cotton cape with an orange border, a richly embroidered breechcloth, a few other tokens and a job. The Emperor had graciously allowed him to become the overseer of my master's household and then, since he failed to distinguish himself any further, had forgotten all about him.

For as long as I had known him, the steward had been an embittered, vicious bully. Fortunately, like most bullies, he was terrified of a higher power, be it human or divine. The last time he had touched me it had been to beat me mercilessly for running away, but this was my patron god's name-day. I might pay for it later, but for the moment I was safe with the steward and his superstitious fear. It was said that anyone who chid or beat a slave on One Death would be punished by pustulating sores.

'You have a visitor.' He had retreated to the wall by the doorway, which was as far away from me as he could get without leaving the room. I noticed that he had something draped over one arm.

I scrambled to my feet. 'A visitor?' For a moment I dared to believe it was Lion, come to renew his offer to buy my freedom, and that my master might be disposed to accept it. 'Who is it?'

'No one I know,' he said, dashing my hopes. 'He turned up just now, while his Lordship was preparing to sacrifice to the god. He's in the big courtyard, where they've set the idol up.'

I hugged myself under my cloak and shivered, still chilly from having lain on the cold hard floor. I looked through the doorway into the gathering gloom. 'I'd better go.'

'Wait!'

I turned curiously towards the steward as he stretched his arm towards me. Draped over it was a length of cloth, its colours still bright, freshly laundered if not brand new.

'Master said you were to have this. We didn't have time to give you a bath, but you have to have a new cloak, he said.'

I took it wonderingly, and as I dropped my old, soiled mantle and tied the new one on, I marvelled once again at Tezcatlipoca's bizarre sense of humour. The cloth was only maguey fibre – even on this day I was forbidden cotton – and the arm that had proffered it had been as stiff as a beam; but what a grand joke the Lord of the Here and Now must have thought this, making men who would curse and beat me on one day give me presents on the next.

Silently I followed the steward to the great courtyard in the middle of my master's palace.

I was not going to be able to meet my visitor for a while. The edges of the space were packed with members of the Chief Minister's household and guests, and it was as much as I could do to squeeze in among them to find a place from where I could see what was happening. One or two looked at me curiously, but they made way for me when they recognized me: something else that could have happened on no other day than this.

The middle of the courtyard had been kept clear. Off to one side, the musicians were still playing the accompaniment to a hymn. There were the drummers, trumpeters blowing into conch-shells and the flute players, whose instrument was Tezcatlipoca's favourite. Around me the crowd swayed in time to the beat of the drums and the flutes' thin, nasal piping.

My master stood with his back to me. He held himself upright still and from behind might have passed for a much younger man, but he was recognizable tonight by his regalia: the white cloak with the black feather border that was the mark of his exalted office.

In front of old Black Feathers stood the god.

Tezcatlipoca lived most of the year in a shrine inside the house, close to the principal hearth, but today they had brought him out, the better for us all to see him and pay him his due.

He had been in my master's family for generations, and was beginning to look his age, with his paint chipped and faded in places and cracks opening up in the wood he had been carved from. All the same he had lost none of his power. From the tall white plumes that crowned his head to the black disc of the scrying-glass in his left hand and the deer hoof, symbol of his terrifying swiftness, tied to his right foot, he was a faithful representation of the Lord of the Here and Now. When I looked at the broad dark stripe running across his face, so very like a frown, at the flint-tipped arrows in his right hand and at the very real blood smeared over half his face, I found it hard not to tremble. Men had fashioned this monstrous image, but the power that lived in it belonged to the god, and the tiny eyes boring through the cloud of sweet-smelling, resinous smoke veiling his immobile face held all of Tezcatlipoca's ferocity and malice.

My master had gone to great lengths to appease him today, judging by the fresh flowers heaped in front of the idol and the equally fresh blood, whose reek overpowered the flowers' scent. The headless bodies of sacrificial quails lay on the ground around him, their precious water of life spilling on to the earth-covered floor to make a rich dark paste.

The old man was coming to the end of a song. Old Black Feathers was a priest as well as head of the household, and the words he was intoning must have been so familiar to him that he could have mumbled them in his sleep. Yet there was something in the way he spoke them – a real fervour, such as I had not heard in his voice in years – that told me he genuinely needed Tezcatlipoca's help tonight.

> *'I make offerings*
> *Of Flowers and Feathers*
> *To the Giver of Life.*
> *He puts the eagle shields*
> *On the arms of the men,*
> *There where the war rages,*

In the midst of the plain.
As our sons,
As our flowers,
Thus you, warrior of the shaven head,
Give pleasure to the Giver of Life . . .'

He groaned his way through the verses as if wringing them from within his own heart.

I knew that they had been composed by his own long-dead sister, Macuilxochitl, many years before. Was that a coincidence, I wondered, or was he deliberately setting out to remind the god of everything his family had done to honour him, as if asking him to return the favour?

'Laying it on a bit thick tonight, isn't he?' I muttered.

The man next to me in the crowd looked at me curiously. He was shorter than I was, slightly stooped, and his hair was grey and thinning. He wore a plain cloak that did not quite reach his knees and his hair was loose and unadorned. He looked like a commoner, but I assumed he was a merchant, concealing his wealth as they always did, or perhaps a craftsman – a lapidary or a goldsmith or a featherworker. My master was not given to inviting people to his house unless they were likely to have something he wanted: knowledge or money or a skill he could use.

I noticed he had been giving his blood to the gods; his cheeks and neck were covered with it, and some was still glistening.

'If he is, it's hardly surprising. We all have to appease the gods tonight. Why else do you think we're all standing out here? Haven't you heard?'

'No.'

My reply took him aback. 'Have you been asleep all day or something?'

'Yes.'

'Then you've not heard what happened last night.'

It was my turn to stare. Surely, he could not mean my master was beseeching the god to help him because of what we had been doing the previous night. I could see why he might have done, because our adventures on the lake had added a last twist to the crazy turns his fortunes had taken lately. However, there was no way old Black Feathers would have let that become public knowledge.

'I don't know what you're talking about,' I said carefully.

The man had been whispering, but now he lowered his voice until it was almost inaudible beneath the musicians' thumping and squealing and my master's entreaty to the god.

'You must be the only person in Mexico who hasn't heard! A god has been seen, in the streets, in the north of the city, in Tlatelolco. Several people saw him – I saw him myself! It was Quetzalcoatl, it was the Feathered Serpent!'

He looked at me expectantly.

If he expected me to gasp or groan or cry out or start tearing at my hair and skin or do whatever else people are meant to when seized by fear of the gods and the anticipation of their own doom, he was disappointed.

'Really?' I said.

I had reached my own understanding with the gods many years before. They had given their own blood and bodies to form the first humans and make the Sun and the Moon rise. To sustain them and recompense them for their sacrifice, we offered them the hearts and lives of great and beautiful warriors. Because we did that, we claimed the right to address them on their own terms. Whimpering with fright would not make the crops grow, stop the lake flooding or deflect the spears of our enemies; making sacrifices and demanding that the gods accept them and do as we asked just might.

Which is not to say that I took no notice of omens or that most of the city was not transfixed by them. Almost anything, from seeing a rabbit run into your house to dreaming about your teeth falling out, could be taken as a portent. In recent years, more strange things than ever had been seen: strange lights in the sky, temples bursting into unquenchable flames for no reason, the lake boiling and rising on a day when the air was still. Perhaps that was why everyone was so jittery about this latest apparition. Looking around me, it seemed to me that the crowd in the Chief Minister's courtyard was unusually large, and unusually silent and attentive, even for Aztecs.

'So what happened, exactly?' I asked.

'You're a cool one,' my neighbour grumbled. 'What happened? Why, the god was seen up there, just after midnight. Lots of people saw the same thing. When Lord Feathered in Black heard about it, he summoned us all here.' As Chief Minister my master was ultimately responsible for what went on in the streets of the city, and gods roaming around on the loose were clearly something he had to know about. I wondered whether he had been as sceptical about what he had heard as I was.

'You say lots of people saw it?' The streets of Tenochtitlan and Tlatelolco were usually deserted at night. There were too many malignant spirits about. Nobody wanted to risk seeing an owl, a sure portent of your own death, or meeting the Divine Princesses, the ghosts of mothers dead in childbirth who avenged themselves on men by bringing sickness upon them.

'I think there was a feast,' my neighbour said defensively. 'Maybe some of the guests. . .'

'Maybe some of the guests had had a few too many sacred mushrooms. They might have seen anything!'

'Do you want to hear about this or not?' He took my

silence as assent. 'The god was running – or trying to run. He was staggering along the side of a canal, and shouting – cursing. It was like he was drunk.'

'What made everyone think he was Quetzalcoatl?'

'He looked like him! He had a serpent's face, all smooth and glittery, and the rest of him was covered in feathers – feathers sprouting from his head and down his back and even from his pendant and the shield he was carrying, great long green feathers everywhere. You should have seen it!' he went on, breathlessly. 'The most beautiful quetzal feathers ever, like nothing I've ever seen – and I'm a featherworker!'

I was still cautious. The description sounded too accurate: too much like the images that decorated countless shrines and temples. 'Did you really see all this?'

'I'm telling you, I was there! He was right in front of me – as close as you are now.'

'You weren't a guest at this feast you mentioned, I suppose?' The more I heard, the more convinced I was it was the sacred mushrooms talking.

'No,' he said, plainly nettled. 'Look, I was as sober as I am now, all right?'

I sighed; I had really not meant to start a row. 'All right. I'm sorry, it just sounds incredible. Weren't you scared?'

'Scared? Look,' he said, with a perverse note of pride, 'I'm not ashamed to say it – I was so scared I wet myself!'

'So you were wandering around in Tlatelolco by yourself . . .'

'I was walking by the canal that separates Pochtlan from Amantlan – you know it?' I did: I could picture the broad waterway, edged on both sides by landing stages and the whitewashed walls of houses and courtyards, most of them large and well kept, since Pochtlan and Amantlan were two of the richest parishes in the city. 'I heard the commotion on the other side – someone shouting, and running feet. It was too dark to see much in the way of detail from the other side of the water.' The only light would have been the stars and the flickering glow of the temple fires burning at the tops of nearby pyramids. 'All I could see was someone moving in the same direction as I was. I remember wondering if he was going to cross the bridge in front of me – then he did!' I heard the man swallow nervously. 'I was so frightened I couldn't even run. I just watched him staggering across that little wooden bridge – I don't know if he was drunk but he was definitely unsteady on his feet – and the next thing I knew, I was face to face with a god!'

Face to face with a god. In the man's expression, in his staring eyes and bared teeth, I saw something of the terror he must have felt. He was telling the truth, I had no doubt of that. To have learned from others that they had seen what he had and that it had not been just a bad dream could only have added to his fear.

I was about to ask him what had happened next – where the god had gone, whether he had fainted or run away – when an urgent tugging at the hem of my cloak interrupted me.

'Your visitor, slave,' the Prick hissed.

My visitor would not come into the courtyard. The steward had to lead me out to him. He did so with ill grace, flapping the ground at his heels with the hem of his long cotton cloak in the hope of stirring some dust up into my face as I walked in his footsteps. By the time we got to the foot of the broad flight of steps leading from the terrace at the front of my master's house to the canal that ran by it, he was muttering audibly.

'Not much longer to go. Just you wait till tomorrow, you uppity little sod . . . Here you are.'

In the failing evening light the paved space at the front of the house bore a pale, colourless glow, as did the house opposite. The canal between them was a broad band of pure black. In the middle of it danced a shimmering patch of yellow light, the reflected glow of the fire on top of a nearby pyramid.

My visitor had contrived to stand so that his body was silhouetted against the patch of light, and all I saw of him at first was the angular shape of a tall man half turned towards me.

'Yaotl?'

'Here he is,' the steward said unenthusiastically.

'Thank you,' my visitor said, and then, when the other man showed no sign of going away, added pointedly, 'That will be all.'

I heard the steward's cloak rustle as he turned on his heel and stalked back into the house. The moment he was out of sight I turned to the shadowy figure standing by the canal.

'Thanks very much. Do you have any idea what that is going to cost me in the morning?'

The stranger laughed.

'Shut up!' I snapped. 'You don't have to put up with that oaf every day of your life. He's bad news when he's annoyed – and nothing annoys a flunky like him more than being ordered about by a complete stranger. Who are you, anyway?'

The laughter dried up quickly. 'Sorry, but I thought it was funny – I mean, I should have known better, because we're in the same position – but I have to give you a message, and it's urgent and very private.'

'"The same position"? So you're a slave, too?' I warmed towards him a little. To have seen the steward off as he had took some nerve, even if it was my hide that was likely to pay for it. By now, also, I was intrigued. 'Whose slave? And what are you doing running errands on One Death? Shouldn't you be having a rest?'

'I volunteered. I'm new, you see – only sold myself a little while ago. My name's Chihuicoyo.' It meant 'Partridge'. 'I haven't even spent all the money I was given yet, so by rights I shouldn't be working, but my master needed me in a hurry, and you like to make a good impression, don't you?'

I understood that. A valued slave might be given a position of responsibility, overseeing other slaves, or even get his freedom on easy terms. If he ingratiated himself enough with his master's wife and the old man died off at a convenient time, then of course the possibilities were endless . . .

'So when Icnoyo sent for me to give you a message, I didn't think I ought to refuse.'

I stared at the man.

It was hard to make out any details in the poor light; just a short cloak that hung from his shoulder in the stiff way that cheap maguey fibre cloth does. All I could see of his face was a pair of glittering eyes, narrow like most Aztecs', and some strands of hair. He wore his hair shorter than I did, I realized, but so did most people: I kept mine hanging loose over my shoulders to cover my ears, mutilated as they were by years of penitential bloodletting as a priest.

It was not his appearance which made me stare, though. It was shock.

'Did you say "Icnoyo"?' I asked weakly.

Once, when I was a youngster in the House of Tears, one of the older boys gave me a piece of amber which, it turned out, he had been rubbing with a piece of cloth so as to wake up the spirit inside it. It had given me a shock and him a good laugh.

This slave's words jolted me now as much as that piece of amber had.

Icnoyo, an old merchant with an unlikely name – it meant 'Kindly' – was Lily's father, and the grandfather of Shining Light. To hear from the old man this evening, when I thought

I had done with his household and had only to worry about my own troubles and the horrible dilemma I would be faced with in the morning, was the last thing I would have looked for.

'That's right,' the slave confirmed. 'Kindly was very anxious to get this to you straight away. I had to give it to you in person, nobody else. He said it wouldn't mean anything to anybody else, but you'd know what to do with it.'

'Maybe I would. If it's so urgent why didn't his daughter tell me about it last night, or this morning? He forgets what I am. I might have been able to do something about it today, if I'd known what he wanted, but it's no good now. I think my master has other plans for me.' I sighed regretfully. Now I was getting over the shock I could feel my interest being piqued. What sort of cryptic message could Kindly's slave be bearing?

'Hold your hand out.'

Partridge's voice abruptly dropped to an urgent whisper. Without thinking I did as he asked, and in the darkness I felt rather than saw the heavy cloth-wrapped bundle that fell into my palm. When I looked down I noticed that it was darker than the skin of my hand, and that was also when I registered that it was damp.

'What's this?'

There was no answer.

When I looked up again the slave had vanished.

I looked wildly about me. I took a deep breath, ready to call out, but stopped myself, and stood and listened instead.

The only sound was the soft pad-pad-pad of bare feet running away along the road by the canal.

I perched on the bottom tier of the stairway leading from the canal up to my master's house and stared at the thing in my hand.

The sound of the drums still came to me, but now the musicians my master had hired were competing with those in other nearby houses, so that from where I sat the whole city seemed to echo with their rhythm. Every great house would be full of people praying and making offerings to Tezcatlipoca. For those who did not live in great houses or who could not get themselves invited to them, the priests in all the temples would be intoning hymns to Him Whose Slaves We Are. Everyone, from the most celebrated warrior and the richest merchant to the meanest serf shivering on his waterlogged plot out on the lake, would be demanding the god's favour. The poor man would pray for the stroke of fortune that would make him instantly rich. The rich man would ask the god to stay his hand and let him keep what he had.

Almost alone in the city, I asked for nothing. I had nothing worth keeping, and I had seen too much ever to believe that the god could not make things worse if he chose.

The only thing I did have was a sodden cloth-wrapped bundle. As I hefted it an unpleasant thought occurred to me about why it might be so damp. Then, when I brought the thing up to my nose for a cautious sniff, I almost threw it away in disgust. There is something about the smell of human blood that retains the power to appal even the most accustomed of butchers.

Gingerly, with the bundle held at arm's length, I started picking at its wrapping. As the thin, cheap cloth started to come away in shreds, I promised myself I would throw the nasty thing in the canal and wash my hands the moment I found out what it was.

My fingers, numb with cold and damp, seemed to move more and more slowly the closer they got to the middle of the parcel. There was something about its weight, tugging at my hand like a doomed fish being brought up in a net, about its shape, sleek and full of purpose, about its unemphatic gleam, which I knew well enough to fear.

Then it lay in my hand, with the remains of its cloth binding littering the ground around me like the discarded skins of snakes.

My first impulse was to drop the thing. My second was to wrap my hand around it and clasp it to my chest in a fierce embrace and never let go. My third was to be violently sick.

In the event I did none of those things. I just sat by the canal and stared at what lay in my hand, a bronze knife sticky with congealing blood, and tried to grasp its meaning.

I knew this knife. I had been threatened with it more than once. The last time I had seen it, its blade had been buried in the breast of Kindly's old slave, Nochehuatl. That had been five days ago, and it explained how the merchant had come by the weapon, although I realized with a thrill of horror that some of the blood that coated it now was fresher than the dead slave's would be.

It was a grisly token, but it was more than that. The knife had been the only thing my son owned, his sole memento of his upbringing as an exile among the Tarascans, the barbarians beyond the mountains in the West who alone knew how to make and work bronze.

Why had the old merchant sent it to me now? Was he trying to tell me that my son had come back to claim it?

TWO DEER

1

'Come on. Wake up!'
It was dark and bitterly cold. How typical of my master, I thought, to treat me to a new cloak that was too thin to keep out the cold. Then I realized that there was no cloak over me and I was lying shivering on my sleeping-mat in nothing but my breechcloth.

I must have thrown my cloak off in my sleep, I thought, rolling over and groping for it. My fingers found the rough leather of a sandal, and then the calloused skin of the foot in it just at the moment when the foot left the floor and flew towards my ribs.

It was more of a sharp poke than a blow. I managed to bite back my cry. I realized who the foot must belong to and did not want to give the Prick the satisfaction of hearing me howl.

'Move yourself!' he snapped.

I sat up. 'Where's my cloak?'

'Here. This is yours.'

A heap of cloth was thrown at me out of the darkness. I thought there was something wrong when I unravelled it. It seemed too rough, was frayed at the edges, and smelled.

'What's this? Where's my new one?' I regretted the question straight away.

The steward laughed. 'It's not One Death any more, slave.

You didn't think his Lordship was going to let you keep a brand-new cloak, did you?'

The steward and I passed through a maze of canals out on to the open lake, with me, naturally, plying the paddle of our canoe.

From all around us came the sounds of a city emerging gradually into wakefulness. The dying echoes of the pre-dawn trumpets fell from the temples, drifting through the streets like fog on a still day. From the houses on all sides we heard the swishing noise of courtyards being swept and the gentle splashing sounds made by the women as they laved the faces of household idols. I may have imagined it but I thought I heard an unusual note in these sacred rituals this morning, as though some of the brooms were being wielded more vigorously, the little statues being dowsed more liberally, than usual. I wondered whether rumours of Quetzalcoatl's appearance had something to do with it.

Life went on, however. Along with the other sounds came the wholesome slap of maize dough being thrown on a griddle. A couple of times I heard a baby crying and a woman's voice cooing softly in response. From somewhere nearby came a coarse oath, as a man set out for the fields or the marketplace, realized he had forgotten his lunch and turned back to get it.

Far away in the East, the souls of dead warriors would be practising their songs and dance-steps as they waited to escort the Sun through the sky. Of course, you could never hear their voices and stamping feet, but the sounds they made seemed to my mind to grow and swell beneath the chatter of the Aztecs around us in the way you hear the hum of a hive beneath the buzz of one or two stray bees.

A man who died in battle or on the sacrificial stone spent four years in the Sun's entourage; after that, we believed, he was reborn as a hummingbird or a butterfly.

'Now will the Sun rise
Now will the day dawn
Let all the various firebirds
Sip nectar where the flowers stand erect.'

'What's that? What are you talking about? What do you think you are, some sort of poet?'

My son's bronze knife lay concealed in the folds of my breechcloth, an uncomfortable weight knocking against my hip. The impulse to whip it out and shut the steward up for good was almost overwhelming. I restrained myself, though. What would I do afterwards? I had come face to face with this truth before: if I ran away now, I would not be safe anywhere in Mexico, and in a world full of our enemies, no Aztec was truly safe anywhere else.

One day soon, I realized, thinking about the beatings and humiliations I had suffered at the Prick's hands and about the young man old Black Feathers had ordered me to look for, I might have to raise my hand against my master and his servants, but until then I was better off just doing what I was told. I could not let anything jeopardize the goal I had set myself: to find out why Kindly had sent me the knife.

Besides, I had an answer for the steward.

'It's a hymn,' I said reprovingly. 'Don't you know it? It's the one we sing to the Maize God every eight years . . .'

'Used to sing, in your case,' he sneered. All the same he looked uncomfortable, as if caught in some impious act. He huddled beneath his cloak and kept his eyes fixed on the water around us.

'Where are we going?' I asked. The waterway had broadened and the close-packed houses had given way to small one-room huts half hidden by sedge and willow.

'Back to the merchant's boat. We'll pick up Handy . . .'

'You don't mean to say he's still there?'

'Oh, don't worry about him – he's being well paid!' The steward laughed harshly. 'Then we go after our fugitives. Lord Feathered in Black reckons they won't have got very far. He thinks they'll have holed up somewhere near the lake shore yesterday. They'll have realized we had men out looking for them and they'll have wanted to rest and keep under cover in daylight. They may have moved last night, but if we can pick up their trail and move more quickly than they can, we'll have them!'

'What if we can't?' I asked naively.

The steward leaned towards me so that his face was uncomfortably close to mine and I could smell the chillies and cheap tobacco on his breath.

'If we can't,' he snarled, 'then I'll make sure old Black Feathers knows whose fault it is, and no doubt he'll do to you what he'd do to those two if he could catch them. I think an arrow through the balls was what he had in mind!'

The merchant's boat was as we had left it, except that the bodies that had lain on its deck had gone.

'Shining Light's mother sent a boat to pick him up,' Handy explained when the steward and I hailed him from the canoe.

'And the others?'

'Over the side. Some warriors came out yesterday morning. Tied rocks to their feet and threw them in. Very efficient about it, too – they even brought the rocks with them.'

'Warriors?'

'Otomies. Real hard bastards.'

'Otomies? Are they still here?' the steward asked quickly, glancing nervously at the boat, which was plainly unoccupied except by Handy.

'Yes, they're bobbing about under the water and breathing

through straws,' Handy snapped. 'Of course they're not here! They paddled their boat over to the mainland. I didn't feel like asking them to take me with them!'

I understood his annoyance. It was born of fear.

The Otomies are a race of savages who live in the high, dry, cold lands to the north of the valley of Mexico. They are renowned for being brave, strong and stupid, and for painting their bodies blue. We used to make jokes about them: 'A real Otomi, a miserable Otomi, a green-head, a thick-head, a big tuft of hair over the back of the head, an Otomi blockhead . . .' The joke was that you could say all that to one of these foreign dimwits in a conversational tone and he would nod and smile as if you were asking after his grandmother.

'Otomi' was also the name of some of our most ferocious warriors, the army's elite, berserkers sworn never to take a step backward in battle – and if that sounds reasonable, then you try wrestling a big Texcalan nobleman to the ground without losing your footing once, and see how long you last. These psychopaths resembled their barbarian namesakes in every respect except the blue paint, and the fact that you did not make jokes about them, not if you valued your life.

I had to quell a sudden feeling of panic as I realized they must be engaged in the same search we were. If they got to my son before I did, I thought, he would not stand a chance. If the Chief Minister wanted him alive they would probably cut one of his feet off to stop him running away and then keep the foot as a souvenir.

'The mainland?' said the steward, biting his lip. 'We need to get over there.' He was as nervous about meeting the Otomies as Handy and I were. After all, as a mere three-captive warrior, he was almost as far beneath their contempt. The moment I realized this, I caught the earliest glimmer of a plan, as faint and elusive as the first star in the evening sky.

'We need to get after them,' I said briskly. 'If they're hunting the same people we are, we ought to be joining forces, don't you think?'

'Well, I don't know. . .'

'I'd rather go back to the city,' Handy grumbled. 'You haven't been stuck on this boat for a day and a half. Do you have any idea what my wife's going to do to me when I finally get home?'

'Old Black Feathers isn't going to take kindly to anyone going home before we've looked for these two.' I looked straight at the big commoner to make sure he grasped my meaning. 'All we really have to do is find the Otomies and point them in the right direction . . .'

'"All we have to do"?' the steward spluttered. 'Are you mad? Look, we're not talking about a bunch of little kids out looking for frogs and water-snakes in the marshes. Chasing a couple of runaways is one thing, but this is getting dangerous!'

'And what's our master going to do to us if we go back empty handed?' One look at the steward's face told me I had touched a nerve. Old Black Feathers could easily make life almost as unpleasant for him as for me. 'Let's face it, we've no chance of finding them by ourselves, and if we do, how are we going to get them back alive? If we find the soldiers and tell them where to start looking, they're as likely as not to tell us to get lost – then we can go back to our master and tell him we've done our bit.'

Handy seemed to make up his mind then, scrambling over the side of the merchant's boat and making our canoe rock alarmingly.

'You won't have far to look for the warriors,' the commoner said. 'They camped just beyond that stand of bulrushes over there. They were singing half the night – kept me awake, not that I was about to complain! If our two runaways heard them I should think they'd have taken off pretty quickly.' I thought so too, before remembering that there were not two runaways, only one, and I strongly suspected that he had not run anywhere. Besides, I realized that the singing must have been a feint: while some of the Otomies pretended to carouse noisily, serenading the creatures of the night with boastful warrior songs, others would be creeping quietly through the dense growth of reed and sedge at the shoreline, using the noise as cover. 'I just want to know what you're going to tell them.'

As I dipped the paddle into the water and began to propel our overloaded, suddenly ungainly craft in the direction Handy had indicated, I gestured towards another place at the water's edge, where I could make out a fresh disturbance in the mud and a short trail of flattened plants.

'I'll tell them to look over there,' I said. 'That's where their quarry landed.'

Handy followed my glance. Then he stared at me. He opened his mouth as if to say something and then shut it again.

The place I had pointed out was where my master's boatman had grounded his canoe and run away, two nights before. Handy had witnessed the whole thing. I tried not to let the tension show on my face while he decided whether to mention it or not.

'Over there,' he said at length. 'Right.'

Before I could groan with relief the steward asked: 'Why didn't you tell our master this yesterday?'

'It was too foggy yesterday morning. I couldn't be sure.' I turned quickly to Handy, hoping to change the subject. 'What will happen to this boat?'

'Lily and her father will send someone to fetch it, I expect. There's enough merchandise left on it – bales of feathers, bags of cocoa beans – lots of stuff from the hot lands in the South –

they won't want to leave all that floating around in the middle of the lake!'

'But if it was dark when they escaped . . .' Whatever else you might say about my master's steward, he was persistent.

'What's that over there?' I asked. 'Looks like smoke to me.'

A thin streak of smoke, the sort of thing you might expect to see rising from a pipe that had been packed too tightly, had appeared over the top of the rushes in front of us.

'It is,' Handy confirmed. He looked at me. 'I think that's from the fire the Otomies made.'

We were very close to the bank now: so close that I could see the water below us changing colour, from dark blue to a cloudy green, and hear the buzzing noise of the flies and mosquitoes that lived in the shelter of the tall plants. Ducks paddled listlessly in and out of the reeds, their feet just visible below the water's surface, little dark angular shapes making eddies in the scum around them.

'Where do we go now?' I began to ask, but the question died in my throat before I had finished asking it.

Something whistled through the air. The boat shuddered. Handy, standing up in the bows, cried out in alarm. An instant later came a scream and a loud splash and suddenly there was no sign of the steward.

I grabbed both sides of the canoe and clung to them as the vessel lurched from side to side. The water was in turmoil, with ducks streaking across its surface in all directions and a large shape floundering noisily about just under its surface.

'What's happening?' I cried. 'Where's the steward?'

'He jumped in.' Handy dropped on to one knee and reached out over the water towards the submerged creature splashing about beside us. 'Bet he can't swim.'

For a moment I hoped he was intending to shove the steward under and hold him there until his struggles stopped, but then a hand came up, groped blindly towards one of his arms and seized it with enough force to throttle a dog.

'Help me, won't you?' he grunted as he hauled the sodden, helpless object towards the boat. I did not move. I thought I was doing enough by restraining myself from bashing the steward over the head with the paddle. Instead I looked around for whatever had attacked us. It took only a moment to find it.

'Harpoon.' Handy had seen it at the same time: a short hardwood spear projecting from the boat's side, near the bow. Its flint tip was buried deep in the wood. 'You were lucky, Yaotl – a hand's breadth or so higher and that would have gone through your spleen!'

A length of rope trailed from the spear's shaft. I tugged at it with my fingers, making the rope rise dripping from the water, and then dropped it suddenly when I realized that our assailant must be at the other end of it.

'Who threw this?' I whispered hoarsely. We were floating in plain sight of the bank and had made enough noise already to scare every bird on the western side of the lake, but I still felt the urge to be quiet.

'I'd take a wild guess,' retorted Handy drily, 'and say it was the man standing over there among the rushes. It's the throwing-stick and the rope he's holding. They sort of give it away.'

I had not seen or heard him but that was hardly surprising. An Otomi's favoured tactic when confronted by the enemy was to rush screaming towards him and drag him noisily to the earth by his hair, but that did not mean he would have forgotten all of his hunting skills. Perhaps he had been lying in wait for us all along or perhaps, as soon as he had heard us coming, he had crept towards the shoreline to greet us. Either way here he was, and I felt myself caught off guard.

He was tall and spare, without a sign of any excess flesh under his dark, weather-beaten skin. He wore only a breechcloth, his full warrior costume having presumably been discarded in favour of being able to move about without having it rustle on the ground behind him or against the tall plants on either side. He carried no sword, but that gave me no comfort. One look at his hairstyle – the tall column that crowned his forehead and the loose locks flowing extravagantly over the nape of his neck – assured me that he could probably have killed all of us with his bare hands.

Following Handy's gaze, I took in the throwing-stick, a long plain length of wood with a notch at the end for the spear. The warrior had been hoping to catch his breakfast and we had got in his way.

He watched our antics in silence. While Handy hauled the spluttering, coughing steward over the side, I took up the paddle to propel us towards the bank.

Handy and I jumped into the water, tugged our feet out of the muck beneath it and waded ashore. The steward fell in, got to his knees and began to be violently sick.

Only when he had finished retching and stood up, pulling his waterlogged cloak around him in an effort to restore his dignity, did the Otomi deign to speak.

'Who are you?'

'Lord Feathered in Black is my master,' the steward gasped, 'and this is . . .'

'I didn't ask you!' the stranger snarled. 'I know perfectly well who you are and what your master wants. What's he got to say?' He nodded towards me.

'I'm Yaotl,' I said. 'I'm the Chief Minister's slave, and this here is a retainer of his, Handy. We were just looking for . . .' Suddenly inspiration died on me like a plant withering for lack of water and manure, and I found I was left floundering helplessly. 'Just looking for . . .'

'A man and a boy?'

'Have you found them?' the steward asked eagerly. My stomach lurched fearfully at the thought that the Otomies might already have found their prey, or the boy at least, and my son might even now be on his way back to my master, trussed like a deer, shivering with pain from whatever the warriors had done to him and terror at the tortures the Chief Minister was intending to inflict.

'No,' the Otomi said sourly. He bent down and tugged sharply at his rope. The spear at the other end splashed into the water, making me wonder how much strength it took to pull it free with so little effort. 'Not a trace of them. Spent the whole of yesterday wading through this muck. Nothing. The lads up in the hills behind us haven't done any better, but at least they kept their feet dry!' He scowled at each of us in turn as he reeled in his rope. 'So old Black Feathers decided we needed some help, did he?' There was no need to ask how much help he thought we were likely to be. 'You'd better come with me. You can tell my captain why the duck he was going to have for breakfast is happily paddling away on the wrong side of the valley!'

The steward pursed his lips dubiously at the prospect of meeting a squad of hungry warriors. 'We want to show you something first,' he said hastily.

'Really? What is it – a side of venison?'

'Yaotl thinks he knows where the two you're looking for went.'

The Otomi looked me up and down. 'Experienced tracker, is he?'

'No,' I said, 'it's just that . . .'

'Only we could do with one. Look, we're not used to this sneaking-about stuff, you see? Show me some Texcalan scumbag who thinks he's hard enough to take me on and I'll show you what I can do with him, but following a trail through the marshes isn't my idea of fun, I can tell you!'

Handy, loyal as ever, took up the steward's theme. 'Well then, Yaotl here's your man. He could track a bird through the air!'

'Wait a moment!' I cried, alarmed. I could see my plan to mislead both the steward and the Chief Minister's warriors succeeding altogether too well. What would happen if they expected me to lead them to their quarry and found out that I had no more idea of where to start looking than they had?

The Otomi looked at me. 'Quite right,' he said thoughtfully, 'we can't just go running around on my say-so. We ought to go and see the boss first.' With that, he turned and vanished into the rushes, leaving only a small gap between the tall, swaying plants as a clue to the direction he had gone in.

The steward looked at me. 'What now?' he asked in a disgusted tone.

'Better get after him, I suppose,' I said reluctantly.

'Good idea, smartarse. Where did he go?'

'Follow the smoke smell,' Handy suggested.

It did not take us long to make our way along the trail of broken reeds and churned-up mud to the site where the Otomies had built their fire. Above the rustle of rushes and the slap of mud beneath our feet I could hear urgent, angry whispers being passed back and forth.

'So what did you catch, Cuectli? A deer? A heron? A duck?' The voice had an odd quality, as if the speaker were murmuring asides out of one half of his mouth only.

Cuectli, whose name meant 'Fox', responded with a sad sigh. 'Only idiots.'

I could not quite catch the captain's reply, but plainly it was not an encouraging one, as the next thing I heard was Fox's voice singing my praises. 'One of them's a tracker, though. An expert. Claims he can follow a bird through the air!'

'Let's have a look at him, then!'

The next thing I knew I was being pulled through the tall plants into the clearing, there to stand face to face with one of the ugliest-looking individuals I have ever seen.

If I had needed a reminder of the type of man the Emperor liked to have in the vanguard of the army, in the front row of the battle line, one glance at this one would have been enough.

Unlike Fox, the captain was fully dressed. His torso, arms and legs were tightly wrapped in a suit of bright green cotton, which served only to emphasize the bulging muscles under it. His feet had been thrust into broad, flat sandals that put me in mind of paving slabs. He had bound up his grey-streaked hair in the same way as Fox. I could not see the insignia he would carry on his back when he went into battle – a tall, teardrop-shaped device, crowned with long green feathers, which would make him instantly recognizable to friend and terrified foe alike – or his round, feather-bordered shield, but I guessed they were both close at hand, carefully wrapped up to preserve them from the mud and damp. No doubt they would have impeded his progress through the rushes, but in his case, I thought, they were hardly needed. He would have been fright-ening enough stark naked, because, even though I took all the details of his costume in and grasped their meaning without conscious thought, I forgot all about them when I saw his face.

Someone had taken a sword to it, many years before. Someone had cut through flesh and bone, from brow to jaw-line, and where the left side of his face should have been had left nothing but a glistening slab of scar tissue.

How had he survived a wound like that? I felt a chill when I realized that he must have won the fight in which he got it, since otherwise he would be dead, his heart torn from his breast at the summit of a pyramid in Texcala or Huexotzinco. Perhaps his partner had saved his life, for Otomies always fought in pairs. What was left of his lower lip sagged under the weight of a human wrist-bone that dangled from it, and I suspected that this had belonged to the man who gave him the wound.

Behind him, his comrades were trying to build a fire out of reeds and some kindling they had brought with them. The ground was too damp and all they were getting was clouds of thin smoke, which would be doing nothing to sweeten their tempers, especially once they realized they had nothing to cook on it anyway. Some of the warriors were dressed like their captain, while others wore only their breechcloths. I wondered briefly why any of them had bothered to put their uniforms on, since they were not going to war, but then I realized that the answer was all too obvious. It must be so long since any of these blood-glutted veterans had met anyone equal to him in battle that a fight scarcely meant anything to them any more. Their business was killing and maiming men who were already paralysed with fear. That was what they had come here to do, and they had dressed accordingly. And they were hunting my son.

The captain interrupted my thoughts in the crudest manner possible, by stretching out an arm, seizing my jaw and dragging my face close to his. He tilted my chin up towards his face and let his sole eye rove lewdly over my features.

'Name?' he snarled.

I should have been meek, but his examination reminded me of the slave market, of strangers looking into my mouth, feeling my muscles and measuring my worth in lengths of cloth and bags of cocoa beans, and I could not help answering him back.

'I can't tell you when you're holding my jaw,' I pointed out unintelligibly.

'What?'

Fox said: 'I think he wants you to let go.'

'Oh, I'm so sorry.' Suddenly the pressure on both sides of my face doubled, forcing my mouth open and stretching the skin of my cheeks over my teeth. It was impossible to scream but the pain made me squirm. My head was wrenched from side to side so hard that the motion made me dizzy, and then the captain shoved me backward and let go, making my knees buckle and sending me sprawling on to the ground. My head hit Handy's chest on the way down, driving the breath from his lungs with a loud grunt.

'Funny man,' the captain sneered. I rubbed my jaw as I glared resentfully up at him.

'I think his name's Yaotl,' Fox offered.

'"The Enemy", eh? Well, he's the first enemy we've seen today. What about it, lads? Do we show the runt what it feels like to meet the Otomies?'

There was a stirring among the shadowy figures behind him. I sat up quickly, knowing the captain's followers would tear me to pieces on command.

'I'm the Chief Minister's slave. I was sent here after the same two men you're looking for. We're all here to do the same job and we're none of us here because we want to be . . .'

'I wouldn't be too sure of that! Nice and quiet here – no one about – we could have some fun. How about a game where you all pretend to run away and we hunt you down like wild pigs?'

'No . . .Ya . . .Yaotl's right.'

To my amazement, it was the steward who spoke up. His voice shook so much that I could barely make out the words, but plainly his fear of being caught up in the Otomi's sadistic fantasy was enough to loosen his tongue.

'Lord Feathered in Black sent us. Yaotl can tell you where the man and the boy went – can't you, Yaotl?'

I got up slowly, too nervous myself to appreciate the wheedling note in the steward's words to me. I spat blood out of my mouth, carefully avoiding the Otomi's feet.

'I think so,' I said slowly. 'I saw where they landed. I can try to pick up the trail from there.'

The captain turned his eye on Fox. 'What's he talking about?'

'I expect he means that spot where the ground's all churned up – where we thought someone must have run a canoe ashore, going quite fast.' He gave me a hard stare. He was right, of course, and I tried to hide my dismay. These men were going to be more difficult to fool than I had thought, and the consequences if they thought I was leading them astray on purpose did not bear thinking about. 'We checked that place out yesterday,' Fox added, 'and there's nothing. Someone ran off into the rushes, all right, but there's only one set of prints and they disappear as soon as you get up into the fields. What makes you think you're going to find anything else?'

'Yaotl's an expert tracker,' my master's steward put in maliciously. He had little idea what we were looking for but would be happy to let me take the blame for not finding it.

I had no choice but to play along with this. Even if it cost me my life, I had to keep these brutal killers from picking up my son's trail.

'Let's at least go and have a look.' I sighed. 'It's not as if any of us has anything better to do!'

2

'Are you going to tell me what's going on now, Yaotl?' Handy and I were pushing the canoe ashore. We and the steward had gone by water to the place I had pointed out earlier, where churned-up mud and trampled rushes showed that someone had landed a boat. The Otomies had been happy to walk; I could hear them approaching us, crashing through the reeds, their joyful shouts accompanied by the flapping and splashing of birds and animals scared from their nests and hiding places. The steward had gone on ahead, keen to get his feet on relatively dry land. Since I could no longer hear his teeth chattering I judged he must be out of earshot, provided we whispered.

'We have to lose those bastards.'

'Well, I agree with that. What do you want to bring them here for, though? Isn't this where old Black Feathers' own boat ended up? The Otomies are right, you know – one man went up this trail, not two. We both saw what happened – your master's boatman grounded his canoe on purpose and ran away. You don't have to be a skilled tracker to work out which way he went, but it's not him we're looking for, is it? So what's the idea?'

I had no choice but to let Handy into my confidence. In any event he had seen enough of what had happened two nights before to piece the rest together for himself.

'We're not looking for two men. We're only looking for one, and he's not who you think he is.'

Handy and I grasped the canoe's slippery sides and heaved it in among the rushes. We leaned over it, breathing heavily, and stared at each other. The big commoner's face looked troubled, his brows pinched together in a frown, but then abruptly it relaxed.

'I see,' he said heavily.

'You do?'

'No, not really. But nothing with you is ever straightforward, I've learned that much! Who are we really looking for, then?'

I told him quickly.

'So your master thinks he's looking for two men, but actually one of them never existed and the other one is really your son, and you want to convince the Otomies that these two imaginary characters went this way so that they don't pick up Nimble's trail and find out where he really went – have I got it?'

'More or less.'

'And then you have to lose them afterwards – before they find out you've been lying to them?'

'Yes.'

'And the knife . . .'

'Nimble's knife, yes. I have to find out why Kindly sent it to me.'

He stood up. 'Well, you've excelled yourself this time! How are you going to do all this?'

'I don't know, but I've got to manage it somehow. You can see how important this is. If the Otomies get to Nimble first, either they'll kill him or they'll make him wish he was dead already. You understand – you've got sons yourself.'

'Yes, and I'd like to live long enough to see them again!'

Handy looked sick. 'On the other hand, I suppose we're stuck with these lunatics, at least until they think they've found what they're after. All right, show off your hunting skills! Just remember who's going to get the blame when it all goes wrong!'

I was spared having to decide whether to thank him for that or not by the sight and sound of the steward as he burst out of the rushes, panting like a man running from a pack of coyotes. A moment later his pursuers appeared: two breechcloth-clad Otomies, whooping like excited children as they closed on their prey. They would probably have thrown themselves on him if the grotesque features of their captain had not appeared behind them, his voice barking at them to come to order.

He strode towards us, his green-clad arms and legs swinging carelessly, keeping up with his men with no apparent effort. He still carried no shield, but I noticed that he was armed now. From his right hand dangled the most evil-looking sword I had ever seen. Instead of a flat shaft edged with obsidian, this was a long round club whose blades stuck out four ways. I felt sick when I saw it. You could not cut cleanly through anything with a weapon like that: it had been made to crush bones and shred flesh, to maim, not to kill.

As Fox and the other warriors stumbled into view behind him, he turned his eye on me.

'Well?' he rasped.

'A footprint.'

'I can see that.'

I knelt in the mud with the captain standing over me. I could feel his breath on my neck.

'Barefoot,' I said.

'I can see that too. What does it prove?'

'The two we're after weren't wearing sandals.'

'Most people don't wear sandals. Not everyone who does would keep them on in this mire, either, if they didn't want to spoil them.' His own, along with the legs of his suit, were splattered with mud, and the ends of their long floppy straps were black from where they had been trailing in it. I assumed he did not mind as he could afford to throw them away. Successful warriors like him were richly rewarded.

'When are you going to tell me something I can't see for myself?' he growled.

That was when I saw where I had been going wrong, and how I might come out of this alive, after all.

The captain wanted me to tell him about something he could not see. What did it matter if I could not see it either? I had only to lie convincingly and I had been doing that all my life.

I tried to remember how the more patient and long-suffering of our instructors at the House of Tears might have behaved when confronted with a particularly doltish novice wilfully refusing to grasp the obvious – me, perhaps, craning my neck and squinting at the night sky and for the twentieth time getting the Celestial Marketplace mixed up with the Ball-Court of the Stars. Imitating him, I uttered a long, weary sigh. 'Very well. Let's look at this print again, shall we? Does anything strike you as odd?'

'No.'

'Lift your foot up.'

The captain gave me a suspicious look but did as he was told. His leather-shod sole hung uncertainly in the air for a moment, making him look as if he had been frozen in the act of kicking me in the face.

'Now, look at your own footprint. You're not exactly little, are you? How come your footprint's so much shallower than this one?'

He put his foot down again. 'Is it?' He bent forward. 'Hmm. I suppose so', he added reluctantly. 'What of it?'

I had to bite my lip to stop myself breathing a loud sigh of relief. The difference in depth between the two prints, if there was any, was imperceptible, but if he convinced himself he could see it and accepted my explanation, I knew I might live through the rest of the morning, at least.

'Well, obviously there was more weight on this foot.'

'You mean whoever made this print was bigger than I am? Interesting.' He stood upright again, rubbing his chin speculatively. 'This could be more fun than I thought it was going to be!'

I twisted my neck to look up at the towering, brawny figure. 'That's unlikely,' I pointed out. 'What I think is, this was made by two men. One of them was carrying the other!'

With the Sun peering at me over his shoulder it was hard to make out the man's expression. I found myself holding my breath while he thought about what I had said.

The thoughtful silence went on and on. The muscles in my chest were taut and straining. I started to feel slightly dizzy. The longer I knelt in front of the captain, looking up at him, the more he seemed like a statue, a great, crudely carved block of granite about to topple over on to my head.

'Fox!'

I let my breath out in an explosive gasp as the line of men behind the captain stirred. Fox came forward.

'See these prints? See the difference between them?' The captain lifted his foot again.

The breechcloth-clad warrior looked uncertainly from one indentation to the other. 'I see them,' he said at last.

'You're an idiot!' his captain roared suddenly. 'Can't you see how much deeper that one is? Obviously made by a man carrying someone else on his back. How many times did you go over this ground yesterday? A child could have spotted this. Even this slave saw it, almost the moment I did!'

Fox stepped back hastily, his eyes wide with terror. 'Sir, I'm . . . I'm sorry, sir. I should have seen it . . . I just couldn't see . . . I mean, why . . .'

'You're as blind as you are stupid, that's why!'

The man swallowed nervously; but when he glanced at me, I saw that much of his terror was feigned. His eyes were clear and unblinking, and even though he quailed visibly before his captain's sudden rages, I could see from the way he curled the corner of his mouth and his swift, shrewd appraisal as he looked me up and down that he was not the one in real danger here.

'I couldn't . . . Sir, I just couldn't see why one of them would have been carrying the other.'

'Well, it's obvious, isn't it?' the captain shouted. He prodded me hard with his upraised foot. 'You tell him, slave!'

I stood up carefully. 'Could be any number of reasons. Perhaps one of them was lame. Twisted his ankle getting out of the boat, maybe.'

'You see?' The captain sneered.

Fox lowered his head.

'Now take us up on to dry land, before we all get foot rot! I want to see this slave pick up the trail where you lost it!'

I stood aside as the line of warriors shouldered their way through the rushes. My master's steward and Handy brought up the rear of the column. The steward passed me without a glance, casually swinging his elbow so that it all but connected with my chin. Behind him, Handy stopped by me for a moment.

'I heard that,' he muttered. 'It's crap, isn't it?'

'Of course it is,' I whispered back. 'If that idiot's footprint is shallower than the other one it's because he's wearing sandals and they spread his weight. Also the boatman was running, so of course his print was heavier. But it worked!'

'Can't wait to find out what your next trick is!'

'Neither can I,' I murmured ruefully, as I set off after the rest of the line.

Beyond the rushes the ground became firmer and started to slope steeply towards the wooded hill called Chapultepec.

The maize fields around the base of the hill were bare at this time of year. They formed short terraces, bordered by bushes and broad, low, fleshy-leaved maguey plants; apart from these and a few scattered huts there was nothing to obstruct our view of the countryside. I looked up at the hill, conscious that everyone else was staring at me.

'No footprints at all,' Fox said. 'There was a frost two nights ago, and it's exposed here, so the ground would have been too firm.' He shot me a challenging look. 'So where did they go next?'

I lowered my eyes. Fox was, as usual, right: the earth here offered neither a clue nor, which was more to the point, anything I could manufacture a clue out of. I thought about the trees on the hill above us. The idea of leading these men into the woods and losing them there was tempting, until I imagined myself treed among them, perched on a high bough, a helpless target for Fox's throwing-stick and spear.

'Your men have already searched the woods,' I said to the captain. He grunted his agreement. 'Well, it wouldn't have been the first place I'd have looked. Maybe they rested up there for the night, or maybe not – but either way they'd have moved on. Now the question is, where?' I was aware of my fingers rubbing one of my torn earlobes, an old nervous habit. I was trying to look like a man concentrating fiercely, while in reality my mind had suddenly gone blank.

The man we were really following, my master's errant boatman – where had he gone? Where would I have gone, in his
position?

The captain grinned at me. 'You're going to tell us where –
aren't you?'

I glanced helplessly at Handy, just because his was the least
unfriendly face I could see. The muscles of his jaw were oddly
contorted: if our situation had not been so desperate, I might
have thought he was trying not to laugh. Then he saw me
looking at him. His expression froze for a moment. The corners of his mouth drooped dejectedly. Then he seemed to
make up his mind about something, and, with his voice faltering only a little, he spoke up.

I might have wept with relief. He was my friend, after all. At
the very least, however afraid he was of the Otomies and however annoyed he was with me for getting him involved with
them, the stubborn commoner was probably more angry
about being bullied by the captain.

'They wouldn't be out here at all,' Handy said. 'If they
stayed in the open you'd hunt them down in no time. It
wouldn't take a squad of warriors much longer to flush them
out of the trees if they tried hiding out on the hill. They both
know what old Black Feathers is like, don't they?'

'They do.' I picked up his train of thought. 'They'd be
expecting a regiment to come after them, and they'd know the
warriors would chop the whole forest down if they had to
before they stopped looking. So they can't be hiding here.'
When I saw the solution, I had to suppress a grin: it was so
elegant I almost believed it myself. 'On the other hand, they
can't have run very far, can they? Not with one of them carrying the other. So . . .'

The captain twisted his sword threateningly. The shards of
obsidian sunk in its shaft flashed as the sunlight caught them,

and his own eyes glittered as he watched them. When he spoke he seemed to be talking to the weapon, as though reassuring it that it would have work to do yet.

'So what you are telling me is that the men we're after can't be running away and they can't be hiding either. What, then? They just vanished? Are they sorcerers? Did they turn themselves into moles and burrow into the soil? Are they down there now, laughing at us?'

He drove the blunt end of the shaft into the ground. It struck the earth with a 'thump' that seemed to reverberate in the open field's empty silence, and when he let the weapon go, it stood upright unsupported.

'Somebody,' he reminded me, 'is going to pay for all this. If these men are lost. . .'

'They're not sorcerers,' I assured him hastily. 'I didn't say they weren't hiding. I just said they would not be hiding out here.' I glanced quickly at Handy again: he was looking at his feet, no doubt wondering whether he had been right to take my side.

I took a deep breath. I might live or die by my next few words. But I saw what I had to do. I could not fight the Otomies, nor could I run away from them. I had to take them somewhere where they could not hurt me no matter how angry and frustrated they got and where I would not need legs like a roadrunner's to outpace them. I had to lure them on to my own ground. I thought wistfully of the city I could not see, out on the lake, hidden by the tall rushes. I imagined its vast, bustling crowds, its networks of narrow streets and canals, the baffling mazes of its marketplaces, the refined manners of its people, most of whom could admire a man like the captain from afar but would go out of their way to avoid talking to him. I could have lost the warriors there in no time.

My own city was beyond my reach, but there were others. 'Where's the nearest large town?' I asked innocently.

The captain got Fox to draw a rough map in the dirt with the point of his harpoon.

'Say this is Chapultepec,' he began, digging a small hole.

'Don't bother putting the little villages in,' I said helpfully. 'They wouldn't go near those. Everybody knows everybody else, so they'd spot strangers straight away, and they'd tell you about them as soon as you asked just to get rid of you. Telpochtli and the boy would know that.' I knew there was no point in my trying to hide in a village either, for the same reason.

Fox glowered at me. 'Right. Here's the lake . . .'

'I think the shoreline should come out further west than that . . .'

'Shut up. This is a map, not a work of bloody art. How far could they have gone? I need to know how big an area to cover.'

I thought about that: the bigger the better, as far as I was concerned, since it meant the Otomies would have to divide themselves between more towns. 'Hard to say . . .'

'You told us they rested up the first night and we know one of them was too lame to walk.' The captain's voice was subdued, for him. He was clearly thinking about how he was going to keep control over his men if he had to disperse them widely over the countryside. 'Even if he was walking by yesterday morning he won't have been going very fast. He won't be up for a climb either, so we can forget anywhere very high up. They certainly haven't left the valley.'

Fox drove his harpoon repeatedly into the ground, reciting the name of a town with every blow. 'Coyoacan, Mixcoa, Atlacuihuayan, Popotla, Tlacopan, Otoncalpolco, Azcatpotzalco . . .'

'We have to search all of them?' the captain asked in a disgusted voice.

'I would,' I said, 'but if you go into any of them mob handed you'll just attract attention and frighten your quarry off. Send a couple of men to each . . .'

He looked at me suspiciously. 'And if you were our runaways, which town would you pick?'

'The biggest,' I said honestly.

'Right.' He looked briefly down at Fox's map. 'You and I are off to Tlacopan, then. They,' he added with a glance at Handy and the steward, 'can come with us. So can Fox. The rest of you split up how you like: two to each town and a couple to stay here in reserve. Let's go!'

3

So we set off for Tlacopan – the captain, Fox, Handy, the steward and I.

It was going to take us the best part of the afternoon to reach it, but as I kept assuring my companions, it was the largest and most important town on the western side of the valley, and so easily the best prospect as our quarry's hiding place.

Most of the journey was undertaken in silence. We had little to say to each other in any case, and every reason to keep our voices down. Although we avoided towns and there were not many people about in the fields, no part of the valley was ever quite empty and there was always the possibility that rumours of our approach would run ahead of us. It did not help that we all so obviously came from the great city at the centre of the lake.

The people who lived in these parts, the Tepanecs, were not barbarians. They spoke our language, and we thought of them as allies. Their ancestors had sprung from the womb of the World at the Seven Caves at the same time as ours. However, that did not mean they loved us.

Once, long before, the Aztecs had been the subjects of a Tepanec city, Azcapotzalco, which in those days had been so populous that it was known as the Anthill. It had been my master's father, the great Lord Tlacaelel, who had persuaded the Aztecs to rise against their masters, and when the revolt was over the city of Mexico had been freed and Azcapotzalco reduced to a small tributary town whose only claim to distinction was a big slave market.

Only one Tepanec city had sided with the Aztecs in the revolt. As a result of its help, Tlacopan was grudgingly admitted into an alliance with Mexico, but the Aztecs did not treat the Tepanecs as equals. Tlacopan got the smallest share of the spoils of war, and our Emperor treated its king as a subject in all but name. There were plenty of people living on the western side of the lake who had grown up with stories from their fathers and grandfathers of how Tepanecs had once ruled the World and made even the Emperor of Mexico do their bidding. Who could blame them if, from time to time – such as when they visited Mexico during one of the great festivals, when the tribute was distributed, and saw how meagre their shares were in comparison with the Aztecs'– they wondered how it might be if the old order were restored?

'So watch what you say and who you say it to,' growled the captain, reminding us all of this history. 'These people won't try to kill you on sight, but if they see a chance to put one over on you, they'll grab it!'

He set a brisk pace, driving us towards the town at a steady trot during the warmest part of the day. He barely broke into a sweat, despite being clad in quilted cotton from head to foot, and if Fox was finding the going any harder he was not about to show it. Handy, used to hard work in the fields in all weathers, ran on without complaint, the effort he was making showing only on his glistening brow and in the firm, determined set of his jaw.

As for me, I had been trained to manage feats of endurance and bear great pain without a murmur. In my time as a priest, I had been pierced all over with maguey spines, had slit open my tongue and drawn ropes through it, had bathed naked in the lake at midnight and had fasted till I was faint with hunger. I ran now until my thighs and calves burned like raw flesh, my chest felt too weak even for shallow gasps and my tongue was a strip of dried meat dangling limply in my parched mouth, like a freshly skinned pelt hung up in the Sun. Then I kept running, with my discomfort set aside, my legs left to work by themselves, and the knowledge that when I was allowed to rest, that was when the real agony would set in.

Not long afterwards, the steward fell over.

'I don't believe this!' the captain roared. He turned back, still running, towards the gasping, twitching heap by the roadside. 'Don't either of you sit down!' he warned Handy and me as he passed us. 'We'll be off again as soon as he's back on his feet. What's the matter with you?'

Handy was doubled over, trying to massage some life back into his legs, while I kept mine straight in an effort to stop them buckling at the knee. 'He hasn't done this for a few years,' I offered, between deep, painful breaths. 'Not really part of his duties now.'

'And he calls himself a warrior? Can't stand a man who lets himself go soft. Come on, you, up!'

I felt dizzy, as if I had taken a very mild dose of sacred mushrooms. It made the spectacle of the mighty, one-eyed warrior jabbing my master's steward roughly with his foot seem all the more unreal. Part of me wanted to summon up the last of my breath to cheer the captain on and urge him to kick the fallen man harder. The rest of me felt something like awe. Here was my tormentor, the Chief Minister's steward, a man who treated me worse than a dog, suddenly made another man's helpless victim. The sight made me wonder what the Otomi might do to a mere slave, if he thought he had cause.

'Can't go on,' the steward gasped. 'Have to rest.' When he looked up at the captain his face was puce.

'Bugger.' The captain pivoted sharply on one foot and kicked a stone across the road with the other, no doubt wishing it was the steward's head. 'Nearly there, too!'

His brutal, ravaged face swung in my direction. I blinked the sweat out of my eyes and turned to follow his gaze.

I had been too caught up with putting one foot in front of the other to take much notice of the countryside, but now I saw that we were leaving the open fields. Just ahead of us the road was flanked by a long, low wall. Plum trees reached over it with naked, frost-stripped boughs. I glimpsed a house deep within the orchard, its whitewashed walls gleaming behind the dark cage-work of the branches.

Taller trees reared up beyond the orchard, the green of cypress and fir catching the sunlight and flashing brilliantly among the bare black skeletons of oak and ash. Farther away still, towering over the tallest of the trees, were the squared-off humps of Tlacopan's pyramids.

'We've made good time, you know,' I told the captain. 'It won't hurt to rest a while.'

He spared a glance for the steward, who had now made it on to his hands and knees, although the sound of his breathing reminded me of an angry rattlesnake. 'And what then?'

'You could send me on ahead,' I suggested hopefully. By now, I thought, when the heat of the afternoon was over, the townspeople would have come out of their houses and the place would be bustling again. There would not be much of a crowd compared with the vast numbers that filled Mexico's sacred precincts during a festival, but there should still be plenty of opportunities for an undistinguished-looking slave to slip quietly out of sight.

The captain snorted derisively. 'No chance! You think

you're leaving me in charge of this?' His foot twitched in the steward's direction again. 'No, I'll tell you what we'll do. Fox and I will go on ahead. We'll start making some discreet enquiries in the marketplace.' The mobile half of his face grinned, showing a broken row of blackened teeth. Plainly he was looking forward to scaring information out of Tepanecs. I found this strangely reassuring: this man would have no trouble persuading people to talk, but getting them to tell the truth would be entirely beyond him.

'You three will follow us. We'll meet up in the sacred precinct, under that temple.' He gestured with his ugly sword towards the tall pyramid beyond the trees. 'Be there before nightfall.' Then, waving the weapon in my direction, he added softly: 'I don't have to tell you what will happen if you're not!'

Handy and I watched the two warriors as they trotted away to bring terror and uproar to Tlacopan.

The big commoner let out a long sigh. 'It's a relief to get rid of those two, isn't it? If that captain of theirs had made us run any further I'd be in the same state as him!'

We both glanced behind us, towards where the steward was slowly getting to his feet.

'He probably runs twice around the lake before dawn,' I said, with a nod towards the cloud of dust the warriors had kicked up. 'Now, I don't know about you, Handy, but I think I'm getting too old for this sort of sport! Why don't we rest here for a while and then see if the Tepanecs can find us something to eat?'

I gathered from the smile that began to form on Handy's face that he had no more enthusiasm for what we were up to than I did. 'Now there's an idea,' he replied. 'Come to think of it, one of my brothers-in-law was here once, and he told me there was an old woman in the corner of the marketplace who sold the best gophers in chilli sauce he'd ever tasted.'

The hopeful look on his face froze at the sound of the steward's voice.

'Rest? Eat? What are you two talking about?'

The Prick was breathing heavily and his face was still dark, but he was on his feet and no longer the wreck of a man the Otomi captain had been kicking a little while earlier. As he glowered impatiently at us both I realized that he must have feigned his exhaustion, at least in part. His was not the sort of pride that would flinch at a childish trick like that. He had felt humiliated and belittled by the Otomi, but had been prepared to suffer a little more abuse just to get rid of him. Now his tormentor was gone, and he was his own man again, and free to show it in the only way he knew how.

'Thought you were going to bunk off, did you, Yaotl? Thought you'd have a nice, quiet afternoon, taking your ease in the shade of the fruit trees before a gentle stroll into Tlacopan and maybe a light snack to round off the day? Is that what you thought?' He took two steps towards me and thrust his face close to mine. Out of the corners of my eyes I could see his fists balling, as if he was about to hit me, although they remained at his sides, no doubt because Handy was there. The commoner was not my master's possession, and if he chose to intervene the steward could not be sure of winning either the fight or the court case that would follow.

'We'll see what Lord Feathered in Black has to say about your idea of obedience later,' the steward crooned, 'but first I think we'd better make a start, hadn't we? Why don't we go to the market, like your friend here said, and try asking a few questions?'

I hung my head submissively. 'All right,' I mumbled, 'you're in charge.'

I comforted myself by reflecting that the steward had no

more chance than the Otomies of getting a useful answer out of anyone here. On the other hand, I thought gloomily, as I trudged after him along the road leading into the centre of the town, I still had no idea how I was going to get away.

Get away I must, though. As I walked, my son's knife bounced against my hip, reminding me that I had urgent business elsewhere.

To an Aztec born and raised in Mexico, Tlacopan was a strange place.

Mexico was a city of whitewashed adobe houses and courtyards, more than anyone had ever been able to count, crammed together so tightly that from the outside it was hard to tell one from another, and almost every one of them was served by a canal. We spent so much of our lives on the water that some of our children learned to paddle a canoe before they could walk. Apart from the great, broad avenues that spread out from the Heart of the World in each of the Four Directions, most of our roads were narrow paths. Our fields lay on the outskirts of the city, on artificial islands made of mud dredged from the bottom of the lake, and they throbbed with activity all year round because their permanently damp soil could bear fruit even at the height of the dry season.

How different were the towns on the mainland! We found ourselves sauntering along wide, dusty streets, between expansive plots that would be full of maize, amaranth, beans, squash, sage or chillies by the end of summer but which now lay largely empty. In the middle of each plot stood a house, its walls stouter than we were used to, since the people here had no bridges they could pull up in the event of an attack.

'What's that smell?' Handy wrinkled his nose. 'Don't they empty their privies around here?'

'What do you expect?' the steward rasped. 'Barbarian scum!'

'They can't help it,' I said indulgently. 'They don't have boats to take it away, like us. They have to spread it straight on to the fields or carry it all the way down to the lake.'

The steward made a dismissive noise in the back of his throat.

I found myself looking anxiously at the few people we passed, and then at my companions, in case the steward's obvious contempt for the locals somehow showed. I need not have worried, however, since after a day wandering around in the marshes, we looked less like the all-conquering masters of the One World than a little party of bedraggled peasants.

'I suppose the market must be near the sacred precinct,' the steward said. 'So we'll make for that pyramid.' He gestured towards the tallest building in Tlacopan, which now reared up above the trees in front of us. We would be in its shadow soon.

'And what then?' Handy asked.

'We do what we were told, of course – ask around, find out if the man and boy have been seen. It wouldn't hurt to get to them before the Otomi does!'

Handy looked enquiringly at me. I returned his gaze impassively. So far as I knew my son had never been near Tlacopan. If the steward wanted to waste his time searching for him here, that was fine by me.

'Let's go, then,' I said. 'We might even find your old woman and her gophers on the way!'

The pyramid loomed ever taller as we approached it. Soon we found ourselves looking up at it between the branches of the trees around us, its bulk like a great shadow thrown across half the sky, blotting out the Sun.

'Nearly there,' said Handy to no one in particular. 'Where's the royal palace, though? I thought that faced the sacred precinct.'

'You're looking at it, I think,' I told him. 'They don't build on the sort of scale we're used to here.'

In front of us stood a low wall with a building beyond it. It was the sort of house a well-to-do family from Tenochtitlan or Tlatelolco might have lived in, a long, single-storey affair with a low thatched roof. It sprawled over more ground than the houses we were used to but to our eyes it had little else to distinguish it. Homely sounds came from behind the walls: women's voices, children chanting a nursery rhyme, the repetitive clacking of weavers using back-strap looms.

'What do you expect?' I asked, as Handy and the steward gaped. 'We take the spoils of war and the king in there, he gets whatever Montezuma thinks he can spare him. Tlacopan is supposed to get a fifth of the proceeds of the Empire, but I bet if you looked in a tribute warehouse here you'd find it was half empty.'

'So they probably don't like us very much,' muttered the steward. 'So what? Who does? Where's the marketplace?'

'Follow the road round the corner of the wall,' I suggested. 'Everybody seems to be coming from that direction. I suppose trading's over for the day.' I looked quickly up at the sky and frowned. 'Funny, it's early yet.'

'They're not going home,' Handy said. 'They're running away from something!'

Perhaps forty people were coming along the road straight towards us. They were women, their brightly patterned skirts bunched in their hands as their knees flashed beneath their hems, their blouses flapping like paper streamers in the wind, and children, naked under their billowing cloaks, and a few men wearing only breechcloths, their untrimmed hair streaming wildly behind them.

'Off the road!' I snapped. 'They'll mow us down!'

We darted out of the way just in time to let the little group surge past. None of them spared us a glance.

'What's going on?' asked the steward.

'Here come some more,' Handy said. 'Why don't you stop one and ask?'

The steward looked at us both indecisively, as a second wave of fugitives bore down on us. Then, with a sudden access of courage, he darted into the streaming crowd and hauled out the smallest child he could find.

'You!' he barked at the kicking, squealing infant. 'What's all this? What are you running from?'

'Aztecs!'

The cry of alarm seemed to convulse the crowd. It recoiled as one person, shrinking away from us like a coyote threatened with a blazing torch. One woman alone threw herself at the steward, screaming abuse and slapping his face so hard that he staggered back, before she snatched the child and ran on.

'Funny.' Handy stared after them while the steward, clearly dumbfounded, rubbed his cheek. 'They all ran when they heard your voice. It must have been your accent, but I didn't know we were that frightening!'

'We're not,' I said wonderingly. 'Something's happening up ahead.'

I looked around me. The wall of the little palace hid the sacred precinct and the marketplace from view, and gave no clue as to what might be going on beyond it. The voices we had heard a few moments before were silent, and I imagined the women, hearing the commotion outside, abandoning their work to snatch up the children and usher them hastily indoors.

Nearby grew a small silk cotton tree: a native of the hot lands in the South, no doubt planted here as an ornament and to shade the courtyard on the far side of the wall. I glanced speculatively up at its widespread branches. If I could climb high enough, I thought, I might be able to see what had stirred the townsfolk up without having to get too close to it.

I stripped off my cloak and passed it to Handy. 'Give me a leg up.'

The boughs creaked and bowed alarmingly under my weight, making me thankful for my slight build and the meagre diet that kept me from accumulating much in the way of fat. I climbed as high as I thought I could, and perched there uncomfortably while I surveyed the ground around me.

'Well?' the steward demanded. 'What can you see?'

'I can see the marketplace. The sacred precinct is just beyond it. All the traders' merchandise is still laid out on mats on the ground, but there's hardly anyone about. Strange. All the people there are standing around in one corner. There's a little crowd there – all men. Some of them are armed but they're not doing anything. That's where the trouble is, in the middle of the crowd.'

'What trouble?'

'I can't see.'

Then I caught it: a telltale flash of green, vivid against the brown flesh colour of the men surrounding it. The spectators had formed a ring around two figures in their midst. I knew one of them at once, even though it was too far away to see his face. 'It's the captain! And he looks as if he's caught someone!'

Then, as the implications of what I was seeing dawned on me, I cried out, unthinkingly: 'But that's impossible! The boy can't have come here, he just can't . . .'

Fortunately neither Handy nor the steward heard me. A new arrival had distracted them.

'There you are! What's the slave doing up in that tree?'

I looked down to see Fox's face staring up at me.

'He's watching your captain,' replied Handy.

'Well, he can come down now,' Fox said, 'because we've got the bastards!'

The steward let out a whoop of joy, of relief at the thought that the search was over and he could go home.

My head swam. Despair overwhelmed me, making me feel dizzy and sick and short of breath, as if my lungs suddenly saw no point in continuing to work.

Since we had in reality been pursuing one person, not two, there could be no doubt who the warriors had laid hands on. Who else could it be but Nimble?

'You stupid boy,' I groaned softly. 'Why did you have to come here? Why here, of all places?'

Starting down the tree, I groped blindly for a handhold, missed and fell.

Branches lashed my back, arms and legs as I crashed to the ground, but they broke my fall, so that instead of killing myself I ended up in a bruised, shaken, dusty heap at the foot of the tree, with the steward's and Fox's laughter ringing in my ears.

'Don't just lie there, you lazy turd! Get up!'

I took no notice of the steward. I could not bear to look at his grinning, gloating face. It would not make much difference to my fate whether I obeyed him now or not, so I kept my eyes on the earth, shaded and shielded by my forearm.

'You didn't fall that far!'

Someone touched me. I flinched, expecting a blow, but the touch was gentler than that: a hand under my shoulder, making as if to lift me off the ground.

'Come on, Yaotl.' Handy's voice growled in my ear. 'We've got to go. Here's your cloak.'

I wanted to shrug him off, tell him to leave me alone, but then I heard the steward snarling again.

'How sweet,' he sneered. 'There's no coming between you two, is there?'

I felt the commoner's grip on my shoulder tighten. He was about to lose his temper, which would do him no good at all. I forced myself to remember that he did not have to help me and that if he were just to stand by and watch the steward and Fox kick me to death he might save himself a deal of trouble.

I hauled myself to my feet, accepted my cloak and glowered at the steward.

Handy asked the question I could not bear to voice.

'So which one did you get, then?'

I shut my eyes to stop the tears from flowing. I would have clapped my hands over my ears too, if I could have done it without it being obvious.

'The older one. No sign of the boy yet.'

'What?'

My eyes sprang open. I stared at Fox, open mouthed but mute because I could not trust myself to speak.

My son was not the man at the centre of that crowd, being dragged about by the green-suited warrior. I could only thank the gods for that, and wonder who the captain's victim really was.

'But . . . but . . .' Handy stammered.

'Come and see,' Fox cried, turning towards the market-place. 'I think the captain's enjoying himself!'

As he and the steward set off, I could see Handy's mouth working and realized he was about to blurt something out that we would both regret. I moved swiftly to one side and planted a foot firmly on top of one of his, converting his next words into a muffled oath.

'Quiet!' I hissed. 'I need to think.' Aloud I said: 'How did you catch him?'

'Oh, easy,' Fox called out over his shoulder. 'The captain's good at this sort of thing. It's just like collecting tribute from barbarians, really. You just march into the middle of the marketplace, knock over one or two pitches to get their attention – starting with the potters is best, it makes a good noise, though breaking up a few turkey pens works just as well – and tell everybody exactly what you're looking for. Once they saw the captain's costume they couldn't move fast enough!' He laughed. 'What was really funny was how apologetic they were that they couldn't bring us both of them. Someone produced this pathetic specimen and told us he was the only runaway Aztec they'd seen. I think the captain's trying to make him tell us where the boy is now.'

We rounded the corner and were at the edge of the almost empty marketplace. I stared across the rows of pitches, the straw mats strewn with merchandise, obviously hastily abandoned, judging by the refuse that lay about them: small change in the form of open bags of cocoa beans, half-eaten tortillas with a couple of bewildered-looking turkeys pecking at them, a water-seller's gourd spilling its contents on to the dusty floor. In the far corner stood the crowd: the bravest of the local youths, or at least the keenest to show off, no doubt unable to tear themselves away from the spectacle of one Aztec torturing another. Everybody with any sense had run away as soon as they thought the warriors had found what they wanted.

'Come on!' cried the steward. 'We'll miss the fun!'

He trotted forward, leaving the rest of us behind in his eagerness to watch another man suffering. I wondered whether he was hoping to pick up some tips.

Then I forgot his state of mind as an appalling thought occurred to me.

The captain and his victim were hidden from me by the backs of their spectators and at this distance I could only just hear the familiar bark of the Otomi's battle-trained voice, but I suddenly knew who his victim was.

What Aztec had run away two nights before, presumably to seek shelter on the western side of the lake?

It could only be my master's boatman, the one who had abandoned the Chief Minister and his canoe two nights before. He must have gone to ground in the middle of the largest nearby town – just where I had told the warriors to search.

'The idiot,' I muttered. 'Why didn't he keep running?'

How long did I have, I wondered, before the captain beat the truth out of him? How long before he learned that I had laid a false trail?

An unnaturally high-pitched wail from within the crowd seemed to be my answer.

The steward quickened his pace. I could almost hear him salivating. Fox was close behind him. Soon they were pushing their way into the crowd, elbowing aside young men whose backs parted meekly before them while their eyes remained glued to the fascinating spectacle in their midst. Handy and I, too, found ourselves drawn towards the horror at the centre of the circle of men. We two stopped short of the clear space around the captain, keeping close to the edge of the crowd of his spectators, although Fox and the steward were soon standing next to him, looking down admiringly at his handiwork.

I noticed the blood before I saw the man.

The earth in front of me was covered in it. It lay in streaks and dapples and little puddles, as if jerked out of its victim a little at a time. Here and there among the dark red spots and splashes lay tiny fragments of something hard and white that I struggled to identify until I turned my eyes towards the boatman.

If I had not already worked out who the pathetic figure lying with his legs drawn up to his chest and shivering at the captain's feet was, I would not have recognized him. He had turned his face upward, perhaps in a vain appeal for mercy, but it did not look like his face any more. It was a mask of congealing blood with a hideous, jagged hole at its centre, for the white fragments that lay on the ground around him were pieces of his teeth.

Before he had started working on the man's mouth the captain had obviously lavished attention on the rest of his face, as the boatman's nose was broken, his ears were shapeless rags and the flesh around his eyes was a mass of pulp, but it was the teeth which were the worst. He was using a small flint knife, no doubt looted from a nearby stall, to chip away at them, reducing them one by one to jagged, bloody stumps.

'Now,' he said conversationally, 'let's try again. I haven't cut your ears off yet, so I know you can hear me. Where's the boy hiding?'

'Yaotl, I don't like this.' Handy's voice rumbled close to my ear.

'Yaotl?' The captain caught my name and looked up. 'Good, you caught up with us! You were right, you see? You led us right there. Now I was just showing these Tepanecs how we Aztecs treat people who let us down – do you want to join in?'

I felt the crowd around me shuffle uneasily, and suddenly there was a little space around me and Handy, as if the men nearest to us had realized who we were and decided not to stay too close.

The shattered face turned towards me. The eyes, the only part of it that seemed to have been left mostly intact, rolled in my direction. A movement of the hand holding the captain's flint knife distracted them for a moment, but they were soon back, thin, pale ellipses fixed unwaveringly on me. The boatman let out a small keening sound, as if he were trying to say something. I did not know whether he was speaking to me or about me but he plainly knew who I was, and if I did not think of a way of preventing him from telling the captain, I was likely to feel the edge of that bloody little knife myself.

The steward unwittingly saved me.

'Let me!' he cried, almost dancing across the space in the middle of the crowd in his eagerness to join in. 'We'll show these Tepanec scum what we're made of!'

The spectators did not like that. I heard muttering and shuffling feet.

The captain glared at the steward. 'Save your breath,' he sneered, gesturing angrily with the knife. A drop of blood fell on the steward's arm. 'You might need it if you have to run anywhere!'

The Prick looked down at the splash of blood, dark against his skin. He was suddenly very still.

Somebody in the little group of men around me made a low noise at the back of his throat. Fox, who had been standing next to the captain and looking uncertainly from him to his victim to the steward, gave a nervous cough. He could see the spectators getting more and more restive. Whatever they might think about Aztecs, seeing us quarrelling with each other would not make them any more biddable.

'You can slip away, can't you?' I muttered to Handy, out of the corner of my mouth.

'Why? What are you going to do?'

'I'm going to start a riot. I want you to get a message to my brother. Get him back here with a squad of warriors.'

He glanced over his shoulder, considering the distance to the shore of the lake. 'If I can get to the causeway, I can be back in the city by nightfall,' he said, 'but I still don't understand . . .'

'Go on, then!' I urged him. 'There's no time to lose!'

He gave the pitiful creature on the ground one lingering

glance, just as the captain took a step towards it and raised his knife again. Then Handy reached out, slapped me once on the arm, and ran.

'Where's he going?' snapped Fox.

'Thought he saw something,' I said. 'Might have been the boy. He'll be back in a moment.'

'Ah!' The captain bent towards his victim. 'Did you hear that? Now we can really start to have some fun!'

Then he drove the knife one more time into the already ruined mouth. The boatman let out a bubbling scream and writhed and jerked like a stranded fish.

'How did this happen?' I asked quietly.

Standing next to me was a young man. His head was shaved, and I guessed that meant that he had lost the tuft of hair that he would have borne throughout his years at the House of Youth, or wherever boys from Tlacopan did their training. So he had been to war and taken a captive, but judging by his nervousness and the way his eyes followed the captain, constantly flicking from the man's villainous face to the flint knife and back again, he was no seasoned veteran.

'Someone told me they found the man hiding in a granary,' he said. 'They could tell he was an Aztec, of course, so they had him locked up in the palace and sent a messenger to Mexico. Then the Otomi came. He said the Aztec Chief Minister had sent him. He ordered us to hand over any Aztec runaways to him, so we brought the man out.'

'And you let him get away with it?' I said, raising my voice provocatively.

I glanced quickly at the men in the middle of the crowd but they were concentrating on the boatman, who was coughing and spitting blood and fragments of teeth out on the ground. How long did I have before he started to speak?

'What kind of warriors do you have here, anyway? Two

men start terrorizing your women and children and breaking up your marketplace, and you just do what they tell you? Didn't anyone think to stop them, or ask them why they were doing this?'

Fox looked up, frowning, and took a step towards his captain, as if he wanted to warn him of something. He must have heard me, I thought desperately, but then the boatman reached up to grab the hem of the captain's cloak, tugging at it as if he were trying to haul himself upright, and I realized that he was trying to speak as well and that whatever time I had was fast running out.

'Call yourselves men?' I cried out at last, letting as many of the crowd as possible hear the scorn and incredulity in my voice, and no longer caring whether or not the captain, Fox and the steward realized what I was up to. 'Why, it's no wonder we Aztecs rule the whole World!'

'No wonder at all, when your Emperor keeps our King as a hostage in his palace and all our seasoned warriors are sent abroad while yours squat at home with nothing to do except drink chocolate and torture their neighbours!'

I turned, as did the men around me, to look at the speaker.

He was a priest. I could tell that immediately, by looking at his face, which was stained black with soot, streaked with blood drawn from his earlobes, and framed by a mass of lank, tangled hair. He wore a long robe, of cotton rather than maguey fibre, and the tobacco pouch that hung from his neck was no mere shapeless bag but a miniature jaguar, complete with jaws, four paws and a tail, exquisitely fashioned from real ocelot skin. He must, I realized, be a man of some standing. Perhaps he was from the city's chief temple. I looked up at the summit of the pyramid that loomed over the sacred precinct and the marketplace and understood: he had been standing up there, watching the captain's and Fox's activities, and having seen the disturbance in the marketplace and realized that nothing was being done to quell it, he had come down to take a hand.

I looked at him and laughed deliberately. I was still trying to sound scornful; moreover I wanted to keep the relief out of my voice.

'Tell me, O Wise One,' I said sarcastically, 'just how many Tepanecs does it take to subdue two Aztecs, then?'

'Here . . .!' One of the young men next to me put a hand on my arm, warning me to show more respect, but the priest quelled us both with a look.

'One,' he assured me, before stepping through the crowd into the space at its centre.

He walked straight up to the captain. The Otomi glared at him with his sole eye.

'What's the meaning of this?' demanded the priest.

'Who wants to know?'

'A servant of Tezcatlipoca.'

The captain's answer was to stoop briefly to pick up his cruel-looking sword and then bring himself up to his full height, with the weapon raised so that its blades flashed in the evening sunlight.

'A servant of Tezcatlipoca, eh? Well, the warriors of Huitzilopochtli tell you to mind your own business!' he roared, shoving the priest in the chest with his free hand.

It was not a hard blow, merely a warning. The Tepanec stumbled back but kept his balance. Nonetheless, it was too much for the spectators. Men surged forward, baying and growling. Elbows and knees barged me aside, almost knocking me over as the youths around me, their pride wounded by my taunts, rushed in to defend their priest.

For a moment there was so much shouting and scuffling that I could not work out what was going on. I heard hoarse cries, the thump and slap of feet and fists striking flesh and the sharper sound they made upon bone, and yelps of pain. Out of the corner of my eye I saw the flash of sunlight on the blades of the captain's sword. A jet of red liquid shot through the air, droplets falling hot on my cheeks, and someone squealed in pain.

After that there came a long, despairing wail, a cry of sheer terror in a voice that reminded me of my master's steward's. Then, gradually, all became quiet again.

Standing on tiptoe, staring between heads and over hunched, tense shoulders, I was able to make out just enough to establish what had happened.

The Otomi had the priest by the throat. He seemed to have forgotten the boatman, at least for now. He was not holding his sword: someone must have managed to wrench it from his grasp.

Fox stood with his back pressed against his captain's. If they were not a pair, they were prepared to fight as one now, defending each other to the death and taking as many of the enemy with them as they could. There was still a small space around them, no man daring to come within arm's length.

The steward was easier to see because three of the Tepanecs were holding him up like a trophy. His eyes and mouth were wide open with terror.

'Well?' The captain's voice was tense but steady. He jerked his terrible head towards the steward. 'Never mind him. He's nothing. Which of you is going to be first? You'll have this priest's blood on your hands!'

A kind of shudder went through the crowd, but nobody moved.

Then the priest spoke, his voice hoarse through being forced out past the Otomi's almost lethal grip.

'Nothing lives for ever on Earth,' he gasped. 'You can kill

me, and my ashes will be buried with a dog to guide me through the Nine Hells, and I'll find my resting place in the Land of the Dead. But then you'll just be torn to pieces, and the pieces dumped outside the city like garbage, for the vultures and coyotes to pick over. You'll never rest, and your families will never be able to stop mourning you.'

The captain had no answer to that that I heard. I did not see the grip on the priest's throat slacken, but I did not see any of the men around him move either.

I was not looking at them any more. Before the priest had finished speaking, I was running as fast as I could towards the shore of the lake and the causeway that would take me back to the city.

4

It was dark by the time I reached Pochtlan. I ran much of the way. In my anxiety to put as much distance between myself and the Otomies I did not stop even to urinate. When I finally stumbled, gasping, to a halt, beside the canal that skirted the merchants' parish, I was desperate.

I might simply have used the canal, but Aztec modesty prevented me. For a moment I hesitated, shifting my weight uncomfortably from one foot to the other, until I saw the solution. A wooden bridge spanned the waterway and at the far end of the bridge, in the featherworkers' parish of Amantlan, stood a wicker shelter.

I trotted towards it. Others might have hesitated, mindful of tales of demons that caught men during night-time trips to the latrines, hideous female dwarfs whose appearance heralded sickness and death, but my need was urgent enough to overcome such fears.

The frost had made the bridge's planks slippery and treacherous, forcing me to take short, shuffling steps across it, with my eyes fixed on my feet.

The bridge shook. A tremor ran up both my calves and told me I was not alone. I looked up and the next moment was fighting to keep my footing as my legs shot out from under me.

A god glared silently at me from the far end of the bridge.

I cried out in shock and dread. Even while the rational part of my mind was telling me that what I saw was easy to explain, something older was shouting it down: the terror I had known as a little child, staring up at the fearsome idols in their niches in my parents' house, and the lore drilled into me in the House of Tears, when I had learned the harsh ways of the gods while sacrificial blood streamed from my tongue and earlobes and shins and penis.

Smoke or steam wreathed the god's face. Glittering scales fell one over another across his skin. Long, blue-green plumes, each as stiff and sharp as a spear-point, crowned his headdress and towered over his conical fur cap. His eyes were perfect black circles, whose gaze seemed to pass over and through me as indifferently as if I were a thing so insignificant as to have no meaning in his world. Savage fangs, curved like the young Moon, guarded his yawning, ravenous mouth. There was no tongue but I thought I saw something moving inside that dark maw, something that threatened to uncoil and snap out at me with the speed of a lash.

He came towards me through a cloud that thickened and swirled as he spoke.

'Who are you? What are you doing here?' he cried. His voice was muffled, as though coming from inside a cave.

My legs finally gave way and I toppled backward, crashing on to the hard wood with a shout of pain and fear. The bridge bucked under me. For a moment I lay staring straight up at the stars, with my arms spread out and my palms flat on the floor.

Whimpering with fright, I struggled to get to my feet, falling backward twice before my hands and heels got any sort of a purchase on the slippery wood. I sat bolt upright and stared wide eyed at the empty bridge ahead of me and the entirely empty road beyond it.

I blinked several times to clear my vision.

There was nothing to see.

I hauled myself to my feet, slipping over more than once, and half ran, half slid to the end of the bridge, careless of the fact that a false step could send me tumbling into the canal's icy water. I staggered on to dry land.

The waters of the canal, hidden from view by its high banks, lapped loudly. I wondered at the splashing sound for a moment, as there was no wind and nothing to disturb the water's surface, but then I thought that in the empty silence of the night all noises would be magnified, and concentrated on what I could see.

I was in Amantlan now. The featherworkers' homes stood in a single uninterrupted row in front of me. None showed any sign of wakefulness and there were no dark passageways between them that a man or a god could be hiding in.

I let out a long breath and watched it cloud the air in front of me and slowly disperse.

'Vanished into thin air,' I grunted. I felt a renewed jab of fear. I had no difficulty recognizing what I had seen. No Aztec could have mistaken it.

'Nonsense,' I told myself. 'He must be around here some-where. He's hiding, that's all. If I wait long enough I'll see the bastard.'

But it sounded hollow. However hard I tried, I could not convince myself that I had not seen what others had seen: the Feathered Serpent, the Precious Twin, the Lord of the Wind.

'Quetzalcoatl?' I whispered. 'Why?'

If the god of wisdom, the god who had created mankind by mixing his own blood with ground-up bones he had stolen from the Lord of the Underworld, was abroad in the city, what could this mean? The god bore the same name as the last king of the Toltecs, Topiltzin Quetzalcoatl, our own Emperor Montezuma's predecessor. It had long been rumoured that the

Toltec king had never died, but had fled his realm vowing one day to return and reclaim what was his. Did what I had just seen somehow portend the end of Montezuma's reign? If it did, what would come after it?

I let out a long, shuddering breath, and looked down, feeling a chill about my loins. I realized wryly that I no longer needed the latrine after all.

I discarded my breechcloth, replacing it with a strip of maguey fibre ripped from the bottom of my old cloak. Then, feeling naked and chilly but with my modesty still essentially preserved, I crossed the bridge again and went to meet the old man who had sent me the knife.

Kindly's was the only house in Pochtlan that I knew well. Until recently he had lived here with Lily and Shining Light. Lily had lost her husband many years before on a trading venture. Since then she had run the household more or less alone. Her son had grown up, despite all her care, into a dissolute monster, and her father, the household's nominal head, was an old man close to senility who made full use of the licence the law gave him to drink all the sacred wine he could hold.

Once, briefly, Lily and I had slaked each other's despair and loneliness. The moment had passed, swept away like leaves on a flooding river by a tide of feelings – her care for her son, mine for my own survival – but it had left its mark. Now I found it hard to approach this house without thinking of its mistress as she had been then, and afterwards: coolly courageous in her determination to find her worthless boy, utterly broken in her grief over his body.

I swallowed once. I had no need to be nervous, I told myself. I was not entering this house as a trespasser, as I had once before. I had been summoned here. I gripped the bronze knife and stepped over the threshold, with my head darting to left and right as if I expected to be ambushed.

Nothing moved in the shadows around me. I allowed myself to relax, until a querulous old man's voice snapped at me out of the darkness.

'There you are! Took your bloody time, didn't you?'

I started. After everything I had seen and done that day, culminating in the apparition on the bridge, it was as much as I could do not to turn and run. I made myself stand still, while my breathing slowed and the pounding in my chest settled down to a normal rhythm, before I replied.

'Kindly? Is that you?'

I was answered by a shuffling noise, a harsh growl as of someone clearing his throat and about to spit, and a shadowy movement that gradually became a little, bent figure coming into the starlight in the middle of the courtyard. It was hard to make his face out in the gloom, but even if I had not known his voice, I could have guessed who he was from the sour reek of his breath.

'Of course it's me. Who else would it be?'

'What are you doing out here at this time of night?' I demanded suspiciously. 'Aren't you cold?'

'Freezing! But I don't sleep much at night now. I heard you scampering about out here and thought I'd better take a look before you woke the rest of the household. You picked a funny time to call.'

'You sent for me,' I said shortly. 'Your slave gave me this. I came as soon as I could.'

I held out the bronze knife. He waved it away.

'I'm sorry it had to be so theatrical, but I needed to get your attention!'

I tucked the weapon back into the scrap of cloth tied around my waist. 'You got it. Now what do you want from me?'

I heard shuffling footsteps moving slowly away.

'Come into the kitchen.'

I followed the old man into the most important room in the house: the kitchen, the room with the hearth, whose flickering yellow flames cast deep shadows across the faces of the idols surrounding it, throwing them into stark, grotesque relief.

I had looked into this room once before, but a few things had changed. The long, tall merchant's staff that had stood in one corner, propped up and wrapped in bloodied strips of paper – offerings against its owner's safe return, from whatever remote corner of the World his calling might send him to – was missing. Then I remembered that the staff had belonged to Shining Light and his mother would have had it burned with his remains. Where it had stood were neat piles of goods: tobacco tubes, cocoa beans and spices, cups and plates, enough wood for a huge fire. They must have been bought for the young man's wake.

'Where's Lily?' My question came out as a croak, because my mouth had suddenly gone dry at the thought that I might see her again, that she might be sleeping or stirring just a few paces away.

'Away,' he said shortly. 'Now we've got our merchandise back, we need to shift some of it quickly, to get some capital back into the business. She's in Tetzcoco, for the market. She went straight there, as soon as she'd finished washing her son's body.'

I sighed, although whether it was with disappointment or relief I could not have said myself.

'Now, there are things I have to show you.'

The old man was pushing something into the fire. A moment later the room was filled with the bright flames and acrid, resinous fumes of a pine torch.

'Follow me.'

He led the way slowly across the courtyard: a little man, lurching along, with the flickering torchlight catching his silver hair, and his head bowed like a hunchback's.

As I fell into step behind him, a sharp cry sounded from somewhere near by.

It was stifled in an instant, as if someone had clapped a hand over the caller's mouth, but it seemed to hang in the air: a shout of pain or terror, the sort of sound a very young child might make waking from a nightmare. However, the voice that uttered it had not been a child's.

'What was that?' I asked in a hushed voice.

The old man did not break his stride. He had turned his head sharply in the direction of the cry but his only response was the sharp hiss of an indrawn breath, a sound of irritation rather than fear.

'Nothing,' he snapped, hurrying on.

I looked over my shoulder, towards where the sound had come from. I stared at the opposite corner of the courtyard, where doorways were pools of absolute blackness opening out into the surrounding gloom. Peering at them told me nothing. 'It must have been something. Listen, I saw something tonight . . .'

Kindly did not answer me, and when I turned back towards him I saw that he had gone, but the light of his torch flickered inside a nearby room and spilled out of the doorway, as faint as moonlight reflected off the surface of a canal.

I followed him.

'What's this all about?'

The old man carefully set the torch into a bracket on the wall. Then he gestured silently at something in the middle of the room.

I looked around me briefly. I had been in here before, and

recognized the peculiar decorations. The walls and ceiling in one half of the room were immaculately whitewashed and adorned with neatly executed, if not elaborate, paintings of the gods. By contrast the rear of the room had been left bare, covered only with a thin, uneven coating of brown plaster. There had once been a false wall dividing the two halves of the room, as there often was in merchants' houses, to conceal hoarded wealth.

Now the room was empty except for a wicker chest in the middle of the floor. There were some brown stains around it.

The chest lay open. I walked towards it and stooped to look inside.

'It's an empty box.' I straightened up and faced Kindly. 'Stop playing games with me, old man. I want to know about this!' I brandished the knife in front of his face. 'Why did you send it to me?'

'Just look again.'

The lid was not merely open. Someone had wrenched it off, ripping its leather hinges. One side of the box was crushed and bent, as if it had been kicked or thrown, and some of the reeds it had been woven from were torn. When I looked at it more closely, I saw that it was soiled: something had splashed on to it, the same brown stuff that had stained the floor, and although it was not sticky any more I had no difficulty, even in the poor flickering light of Kindly's torch, in recognizing blood.

Then I looked in the box again and saw that it was not empty after all. Something lay in the bottom, curled against its sides in a smooth, perfect curve, as still and natural as a snake contentedly sleeping off a meal. It was a frail thing, hard to spot in the deep shadows cast by the box's sides, although I recognized it as soon as I knew it was there.

I reached inside the box, fingered the thing, stroked it

reverently and gently lifted it out. As I held it up to the light it uncurled itself to its full length, greater than one of my arms. It seemed to glow in the torchlight, shimmering as my breath disturbed it, its colours changing from green to blue to turquoise to something else that was none of them and all three at the same time.

'A quetzal tail feather,' I breathed. I could not remember having handled anything so precious. For an Aztec this represented true wealth, far more than gold or shiny stones. It was beautiful, iridescent, and the colour of the young maize stalks on which our hopes rested every summer; it was hard to get, for it had to be plucked intact from the living bird; and it was fragile, like life itself.

And I had seen others just like it only that night. I stared at Kindly in disbelief. Surely, I thought, it must be coincidence. How could this old man be connected with the apparition that had confronted me on the bridge? 'Where did this come from?'

'Off the arse of one of those funny-looking birds that fly around in the forests down in the South, of course. Where do you think? It's not where it came from that I care about – it's where the rest of it went!'

'I don't understand.'

'Look at the base of the feather.'

Instead of a sharp quill, the plume ended in a jagged stump. 'It's been broken. It looks as if it was torn off something.'

'It was.' The old man sighed wearily. 'Didn't you think that was rather a big box to hold one feather, even a very special one? Until the night before last there was some important property of mine in there – more or less all I had, at least until you found that boat with all the stuff my grandson stole from us. Now this is all that's left.'

'This wasn't one of a bundle of loose feathers,' I said. 'It was broken off a finished work.' I looked at the old man suspiciously. 'What was it, a fan, a banner, a costume?'

'Something like that,' he mumbled, as though he felt embarrassed.

'How did it get broken?'

His shoulders sagged even more than usual. 'Someone stole it – all but this feather!'

'When?'

'Two nights ago. The night we held the banquet.'

'But your house was full of people – lords, merchants, warriors . . .' I had been at that banquet, attending my master, who had been among the guests.

'Yes, exactly. Full of lords, merchants and warriors, most of them out of their heads on sacred mushrooms. What better time to for someone to sneak in and steal a priceless work of art, eh?'

Another voice interrupted him: the one that had sounded across the courtyard earlier.

'There it is again,' I said, but the old man's reaction was the same as before, his head turned sharply aside and a look of annoyance on his face.

'Nothing,' he muttered nonchalantly. 'Probably an urban fox. We get them around here, rummaging around in people's middens. If the parish police did their job it wouldn't happen.'

'Didn't sound like a fox to me,' I began, but he had already changed the subject.

'Now, whoever stole this piece must have got in here very late – not long before dawn, in fact.' Kindly spoke briskly. 'We had guards on the doorway. We didn't release them until long after midnight, when everyone had either left or gone to sleep. You were long gone. I didn't notice anything was amiss until the morning.'

'And what did you find then?'

'Why, just exactly what you see. Nothing but this one feather and the box it was stored in!'

'So what was it?'

The old man squinted at me thoughtfully. He cleared his throat noisily. He seemed reluctant to speak, and his silence endured until I could not stand it any longer.

'Look,' I snapped, 'you brought me here so that you could show me something. I came all the way from the western shore of the lake, at no small risk to my own life, let me tell you, especially if my master and his steward get to know where I've gone. Now I'm tired and hungry and very tempted to go and throw myself at my master's feet and beg his pardon just for the sake of a few hours curled up on my own sleeping-mat. So if you want me to know what was in that box, then tell me now. Otherwise I'm going!'

Kindly let out a deep sigh that tailed off into a dry rattle. 'All right,' he said wearily. 'But this is a secret, do you understand?'

'Yes,' I agreed doubtfully.

'You've heard of Pitzauhqui?'

'Pitzauhqui? The craftsman?' Of course I had heard of him. He was famous, although he had obviously not shown much potential as a child, since his name meant 'Skinny'.

'Who else?' He clucked in exasperation. 'Skinny, the featherworker.'

'You're not serious?' I stared down at him. 'It's really by him? Why, it must be worth . . . it must be priceless! How did you get your hands on it?'

If feathers were our most precious commodity, featherwork was our most elevated art form. To the skill of the scribe or the embroiderer were added the dexterity and judgement of the featherworker who chose, trimmed and placed feathers whose shape and natural colour could bring to vivid life the most extravagant design. Featherworkers created mosaics, costumes, fans whose plumes seemed to radiate from their settings like petals from the heart of a flower. A skilled practitioner of the craft was a man of standing, not as high as a warrior's but as high as a merchant's and with none of the envy and bitterness that attended a merchant's wealth. The featherworkers made the most of this status: like most craftsmen, they passed their skills down from father to son and mother to daughter. I did not know either the featherworkers or their parish, Amantlan, very well: the Amanteca, as they were called, guarded their secrets jealously.

Among the featherworkers there were perhaps a couple of craftsmen as renowned as Skinny, whose skill was such that he was said to be a sorcerer, with the power to make the plumes fly into place and even change colour at a word of command. I had seen one of his pieces once. It was a small thing, just a fan made of roseate spoonbill feathers, but I had never forgotten it. The craftsman had contrived to set and layer the plumes so that no two caught the light in the same way. They were all red, but just to glance at them was to see so many colours: orange, chocolate, scarlet, a pink that put me in mind of a magnolia in flower, and blood at every stage from freshly spilled to three days old and cracking.

Skinny's work was legendary, and would command what-ever price the seller asked. I could not begin to guess how Kindly had been able to afford one of his pieces or who might have been so desperate as to sell it to him. All the same, if I had had to guess, the last name that would have occurred to me was the one Kindly gave, answering my question.

'I got it from Skinny himself.'

'I thought he was dead.'

'I can assure you he isn't.'

I stared at the feather in my hands: it was waving wildly,

picking up my own agitation, and as it caught the torchlight its blue and green colours chased each other like waves along its length from stem to tip. I looked at the broken end, and tried to imagine the work of art it had been wrenched from. I thought of the man who had made it, and felt something like awe at the thought that the feather I was holding had been part of it, that the great craftsman himself had selected it, handled it and found it its rightful place, gluing it there with turkey fat that he applied himself because no one else could be trusted to do it properly.

'I heard that he never replaced a feather. He always chose the perfect plume and placed it perfectly, first time. My master tried to commission something from him and couldn't get it – and people don't usually say "No" to the Chief Minister! That's why I thought he was dead. He hasn't been heard from in years, anyway, and there was a rumour that he'd gone out of his head on sacred mushrooms.' I frowned at the old man suspiciously. 'How do you know it was really something of his?'

'I told you, he gave it to me himself!'

I bent down and carefully laid the feather back in the bottom of its box. It weighed nothing, and I was afraid that if I just dropped it it would blow away. It might even drift up into the torch flame and be ruined, and that would never do. I felt an urge to preserve the thing, against the day when it might be reunited with the rest of whatever peerless creation it had once been part of.

I did not stand up again at once, because I wanted to think. I stared into the dark space inside the box and thought about what I was going to do next. I knew what I ought to do: turn around, walk straight past Kindly and step out of the room, out of the courtyard and into the night. I did not know where I might go after that, but I could already see that the alternative was likely to bring even more trouble down on my head than I was already in.

However, I had my son's knife. It had been sent to me for a reason, and until I found out what the reason was, I could never rest. And so, in spite of everything, I stood up and faced the old man and asked him the question he knew I had to ask, to which I already knew the answer.

'So somebody stole a piece of featherwork from you. I'm sorry to hear about it, but what's it got to do with me?'

Kindly looked at his feet. At least he had the good grace to appear embarrassed.

'Well,' he mumbled, 'you see, I rather hoped you might find it for me.'

'And why would I do any such thing?'

He looked up again. In the torchlight his eyes glinted like polished jade. He pursed his lips, as if in thought, before answering: 'Because . . . It's like this, Yaotl. The featherwork wasn't the only thing in that box. There was something else – something I left in here for safe-keeping because, to be honest, I couldn't decide where else to put it.' He nodded towards the angular shape on my hip. 'I'd wrapped the knife up in several thicknesses of maguey fibre cloth to stop any blood getting on the costume. It was just a shapeless lump of material, but someone found it and took the trouble to unwrap it.'

'And used it, too.' I took the knife out once more and examined it. It was valuable in itself, since it was made of bronze, that dull, hard metal that only the Tarascans in the West knew how to work and which was almost unknown in Mexico, but its material worth was not what Kindly had been thinking of.

'Let me guess,' I said. 'You think whoever came here the other night knew the knife was in this room. . .'

'In the house, at least. This was the only empty room, and the rest of the house was full of people, so it would have been the first place a thief would look anyway.'

'And then, having taken the knife, he decided to lift this costume as well?'

'It can't have been that simple. For one thing, there was some sort of struggle over the costume, because that feather was broken off. For another . . .'

'The knife was used.'

'Yes.'

'And you don't know who was injured?'

His frown turned the lines on the old man's face into ravines. 'I don't. Nobody in my household, and I think one of the guests would have complained if he'd woken up with stab wounds, don't you? But there was a trail of blood from here out into the courtyard.'

'There were two of them.' In spite of myself I was curious. 'What happened – did they fall out?'

'It looks like it, doesn't it? What else could it have been – two men burgling my house in the same night, both of whom just happened to know exactly what they were looking for and where to find it, and one of them deciding to stick a knife in the other? I think that sounds unlikely.'

'Where did you find the knife?'

'In the courtyard.'

I stared at the knife again. It occurred to me that it ought to be cleaned up, but then I thought that was not my task. It was my son's. Mine was to return his knife to him.

'What I thought,' Kindly was saying, 'was that maybe whichever of them stabbed the other changed his mind and carried his friend home. Of course, they had my property with them. And if you found either of our thieves, you see, then you'd find my property. But at least one of them came here looking for that knife. And you want to know who that was, and why, don't you?'

'So that's why I'm here,' I said dully. I kept looking at the weapon. Suddenly I was seeing it with fresh eyes. It was valuable, to be sure: but what might it be worth to someone who had never owned anything else?

My grip on the thing tightened until it shook and my knuckles turned white.

'I was right, wasn't I?' the old man said softly. 'You'll do anything to get this back to its owner.'

'How did you know?'

'Call it a lucky guess. Lily told me what happened on the lake, the other night, and all the things you'd said to her about yourself while you and she were . . . while you were here before. It wasn't too difficult to work out that that boy must be yours. And if you thought he'd been here, instead of running away from the city and putting a safe distance between himself and the Chief Minister, you'd be desperate to find out where he was, and what he was up to.'

I remembered the effort and heartache it had cost me, learning that Nimble was my child. How had Kindly discovered it? I shivered at the thought that if this feeble-minded old man could manage to deduce the truth so easily, in spite of the lies I had told his daughter, others might be able to as well – my master among them.

'So you think my son came looking for his knife,' I replied in a low voice, 'and that I'm bound to go looking for him, and if I find out what happened to him, I'm bound to find your precious featherwork.'

He clapped his hands together delightedly. 'I knew you'd understand! Of course, I'll pay you if you bring it back in one piece. When can you start?'

My jaw dropped so fast and so far that it hurt. 'I don't

believe you! You somehow manage to get hold of a fabulously valuable piece of featherwork. You keep it here, in a house full of mushroomed-up warriors who everyone knows have no love for you merchants – not to mention the other merchants you invited as your guests, all of them rivals of yours who would cheerfully steal from you out of spite. Then when it gets stolen – big surprise, that! – you expect me to go and get it back from you? Are you mad?'

Anyone else might have accepted what I said. I might have expected a different man's face to darken or turn pale, according to whether he felt embarrassed at his own foolishness or angry at my reproof, or perhaps to crumple dejectedly when he realized he was not getting his own way. Indeed, I watched Kindly's face as I finished speaking, but I saw none of these things, and it quickly dawned on me that I was not going to.

The Kindly I had known was a broken old man, good for nothing except lounging against the wall of his courtyard, swilling sacred wine and talking idly with anyone who still had the patience to listen to him. The steady, unremitting stare with which he returned my gaze belonged on another, still older face than his: the face of a merchant who had once journeyed through hot lands, frozen lands and steamy swamps, who had seen friends die, his son-in-law among them, who had burned his fellow merchants' travelling-staffs with their bodies and then fought and beaten the barbarians who had killed them. No words of mine were ever going to touch this old man.

'You know I'm not,' he said stonily. 'And I know you'll do what I'm asking, Yaotl, because it's the only way you'll find out what happened to your son.'

I was still gripping the knife. It would have been ridiculously easy to stretch out my arm and sink the blade in this vile old man's chest. Nobody could have known my hand was behind it: nobody except Kindly himself knew I was there. For a moment there was nothing I would rather have done, but my arm seemed to have gone dead.

I dropped the arm with a sigh, letting the weapon dangle loosely from my limp fingers.

'All right. You win, you old bastard. You'd better tell me just what this wonderful piece was. A headdress, a warrior's back device, a mosaic?'

'Oh, no. Nothing so mundane.'

'Well, what, then?'

'It was the raiment of a god.'

5

'The raiment of a god.'

It was so obvious, I thought, and it explained so much. I cursed myself for an idiot, for the terror I had felt on the bridge, confronting what I had thought was an omen. 'I bet I can guess which one.'

'You've heard the stories, then.'

'About the vision? I can do better than that, Kindly. I saw him myself!'

He stared at me. 'You?' he spluttered. 'When?'

'Just before I got here.' Suddenly I felt the urge to laugh, remembering my own incredulity at hearing the feather-worker's account at my master's house. Of course neither of us had seen a god. We had both met a man in a stolen costume, although what he was doing haunting the canal between Pochtlan and Amantlan, and how he had managed to vanish so completely, were still a mystery.

Kindly stared at me dumbly while I told him what had happened to me. 'So it's still in this parish,' he muttered when I had finished. 'Maybe it'll be all right after all.'

'Just how did you get hold of this thing? It must be worth . . .' My voice tailed off as I tried vainly to imagine what you could barter for something so valuable.

He laughed. 'It's priceless, Yaotl! It's not even as if Skinny was the only craftsman whose work went into it. Naturally as a featherworker he was the last to handle it, since the feathers are the most fragile part, but . . . well, you saw the mask? The serpent's head? The scales are turquoises, and so's the spear-thrower the god was given to carry.'

'His sandals were made of obsidian,' I recalled.

'That's right, and the front of his shield was striped with gold and seashells, and there was a bloody great emerald set into his cap that would have bought you twenty times over.' I had to grit my teeth at this callous reference to my status. 'I tell you, the lapidaries had a field day! But it's the feathers you would really have noticed. I've never seen anything like them.'

'Me neither.' Nor, I remembered, had the featherworker I had spoken to at the Chief Minister's house. 'So how did you manage to get hold of this thing? For that matter, why? It surely wasn't Skinny's to sell!'

'Skinny and I go back a long way, you see,' he replied care-lessly. 'His father and some of his uncles used to work for me. Our families helped one another out, from time to time.'

I looked at him coolly. I thought I could work out what came next. The featherworker obviously knew Kindly was broke, and that his grandson had made off with everything his family had. He obviously assumed the old merchant would do anything to make money, and if offered what looked like a bar-gain would snap it up with no questions asked. 'I don't suppose you stopped to think that maybe whoever originally commis-sioned this fabulous costume might want to get his hands on it?'

'Of course I did! But we had our story ready.' He grinned ruefully. 'We were going to say it had been stolen from his workshop.'

And no doubt, I thought, by the time the costume's owner started making serious enquiries, it would already have been sold.

I thought about what Kindly had described to me, the fabulous wealth that the gold, the stones, the feathers, even the seashells, each one picked out and placed with such care in its setting, must represent, the unique craftsmanship that must show in every facet and every plume. I wondered where he could possibly hope to sell something like that, and who would dare buy anything that distinctive. Surely nobody in the city, or in any of the other towns in the valley of Mexico. Perhaps, I thought, Kindly had meant to send it abroad. I knew his family dealt in feathers, importing them from the hot lands in the South and the East, and that they must trade with the barbarians who lived there. Was he hoping to exchange the god's costume for feathers, for working capital to replace what his grandson had taken?

I thought then that I understood what he had been up to. However dangerous it might have been, to Kindly it would have been worth everything he staked on the venture, to have the prospect of being able to trade in his own right again. For so long, he and his daughter had been impoverished, their business crippled by his grandson's cheating. The sacred wine Kindly drank so freely may have dulled his judgement, but it had not blunted his pride. He had seen a chance to free himself, to exercise once again the independence that set his merchant class apart from the rest of us Aztecs, and he had seized it without a second's thought.

How ironic it was that, with his grandson dead and the boat with all the family's wealth on it recovered, that independence had become his and Lily's for the taking, without his having to lift a finger.

'So, to sum up,' I said sourly, 'you think I am going to go and look for this costume – or rather, for the man wearing it – in the hope that I might find out what became of my son on the way?'

'That's right,' Kindly said blandly. 'Of course, I'm sure we could negotiate a finder's fee. . .'

'Oh, don't bother!' I cried, suddenly overwhelmed by a feeling of disgust. I had no choice in the matter, of course, as I had known full well from the moment I had been given my son's knife, but I did not have to like it. 'If you can think of a way of telling my master where I've been and what I've been doing that won't get me killed out of hand, than I'll settle for that!'

'Really?' he replied brightly. 'Is that all? That's a deal, then!' Then, seeing my scowl, he added: 'Oh, come on, Yaotl – I'm joking! Look, I don't know what you're going to tell your master, but I guess if you were really worried about that you'd be sitting obediently at the old man's feet instead of squatting there talking to me. Let's face it, each of us needs to find something and the chances are the things we both want are in the same place. I can't very well go running around after them – I'm too old and too well known. So it has to be down to you. Now what about it?'

All my exhaustion, a day and most of a night of unceasing activity and strain, seemed to descend on me then, and I bowed my head, cradling it on my knees, within my folded arms. 'All right. You win. I'll look for your precious featherwork.'

'Excellent!' he chortled. 'Now, I think we ought to seal our bargain with a drink, don't you? There's a gourd of sacred wine in the kitchen. I won't be a moment.'

Before I could stammer out an answer the old man was out of the room and padding across the courtyard. A moment later he was back, thrusting a gourd full of sloshing liquid in my direction. I recoiled silently.

'Oh, come on, Yaotl. You can't pretend you're not partial to a drop. This isn't the usual rotgut, either. It's pure maguey sap, not some rubbish made out of spit and honey!'

'I don't want it,' I said, looking down.

He had pulled out the maize cob that served as the gourd's stopper, letting out the sharp smell of the stuff inside. 'Why not? Used to be meat and drink to you, this stuff, didn't it? Oh, suit yourself.'

He tipped the gourd up to his own face. I found I could listen to the liquid inside it with more detachment than I would have thought I was capable of. Was this because what I was looking for was so important to me that it cut through the old craving? I clung to that thought: I told myself that if I ever felt that way again, so desperately in need of a drink that I would do anything to get one, steal, betray the people closest to me and abase myself in ways unthinkable to an Aztec, then perhaps I only had to remember that I had a son, and the yearning would pass.

Eventually I managed to say: 'Just find me a blanket and a clean breechcloth and let me stay here for the night, won't you?'

There was no answer.

After a moment or two I looked up, surprised.

Kindly had put the gourd down. He was shuffling his feet awkwardly, shifting his weight from side to side and sending nervous glances out through the doorway.

'What's the matter?' I could barely keep my eyes open by now. In my imagination I was already swaddling my aching limbs in a rabbit's-fur blanket, with my head cradled on my rolled-up cloak and no intention of waking up until long after daybreak, but a glance at the old man's face was enough to dispel all that. I moaned, realizing that I was not likely to get any sleep that night after all, and feeling like a runner who has just topped what he thought was the last ridge before home only to see that, on the far side of the valley below him, there is a steeper slope than ever for him to climb.

'I'm sorry, Yaotl.' His tone was too distant and distracted to be apologetic. 'I can't let you stay here. This is the only empty room and I need it – all the stuff off that boat is coming back before dawn, you see, and it'll have to go in here. You know we merchants always move our merchandise by night. I can lend you a blanket, though, and give you some water and something to eat.'

There was not much of the night left by the time I left Kindly's house, with an old, patched blanket wrapped against my shoulders and my hands clutching a tortilla and a drinking-gourd that the old man had generously pressed into them at the last moment.

'Do your best, Yaotl,' he said, as he all but pushed me into the street. 'I'm relying on you! And so's your son!'

He seemed keen to be rid of me after I had declined his offer of a drink. I wondered about that, as I stood by the whitewashed stone wall of his house and watched its pale reflection catch ripples on the surface of the canal at my feet, making each one gleam fleetingly. I wondered about his air of distraction, of something like embarrassment. I wondered too about the odd cries I had heard. They seemed to come from close by, but I had not heard them again and there was nothing to see.

Then I sighed, telling myself that these were minor mysteries compared to the others I had got caught up in of late. Wrapping myself more tightly in the blanket, I turned and walked on, back towards the bridge that led across the canal to Amantlan. If I was going to look for old Kindly's precious feathered costume, I thought, then I might as well start by talking to the man who had made it.

It was as I was padding back across the bridge that I first noticed the trail of blood.

It caught my eye as a thin dark smear, glistening with reflected starlight. I knelt and ran my finger through it and sniffed it. It was fresh.

I got up and looked back and forth along the short bridge. To my surprise the trail started about where I was standing, and ran on to the far shore. Had there been a fight here, with the wounded man staggering off in the direction of Amantlan? I looked down again. There were a few marks in the frost that coated the bridge's planks. I could see my own footprints, melted into the frost by my bare soles. There were other, less distinct marks, streaks that might have marked the passage of something heavy, being dragged across the canal, and the bloody smear was in their midst. I could not see anything that suggested a struggle.

Frowning, I walked slowly over the bridge, following the trail until I saw where it was going to take me. That was when I hesitated, stopping to sniff the air, and feeling the first spasm of nausea as I realized what must lie beyond the wicker screen at the bridge's far end, the one I had been making for when I thought I saw the god.

My sense of smell may have been more acute than most. As a priest, I had spent much of my life in darkness – in the niches at the backs of temples where the Sun's rays were never allowed to penetrate, surveying the stars from the summit of a pyramid, or patrolling by night the hills around the lake our city stood on, seeing nothing but alive to the scents the wind brought, of pine and sage and briny water. His eyes sometimes mattered less to a priest than his nose, and the old instincts still served me when I needed them.

I stood by the wicker screen. I watched as the foggy cloud my breath made dispersed in the cold, still night air, and then took a slow, deep, deliberate sniff.

I fought back the gorge rising in my throat as each of the smells pressed its claim to recognition. They were all foul: piss and ordure and, underlying the others but unmistakable, an odour no priest or former priest could ever forget – the reek of fresh human blood.

I looked down. There was no doubt that this was where the short trail I had followed led. The smell came from behind the screen, and there was nothing I could do now but go and look for its source.

I knew something of what I would find. There would be pots into which passers-by could relieve themselves, and which would be taken away by boat for sale in the markets as dyestuff or manure. Sure enough, I found several large, squat, plain clay vessels, their outsides streaked, spattered and darkly stained by years of careless use. I peered at the unsavoury things as closely as I could in the darkness, but could see nothing out of the ordinary. Then I took a step forward, and felt my stomach lurch.

My bare feet stuck to the ground.

I did not need to look down. The smell rising from all around me was enough to tell me what I was standing in. The space around the pots was awash with it. Enough blood had been spilt here to satisfy even Cihuacoatl, our most ravenous goddess, if it had been offered as a sacrifice.

My head spun. I was tempted to lean against the screen for support but stopped myself just in time, as the flimsy structure would surely have collapsed. I looked around wildly, probing each dark corner for some sign of a body, desperate to assure myself that the dead man had not ended up where I could see he almost certainly had.

Groaning, I accepted the evidence of my eyes and ventured towards the nearest pot. I pushed it nervously with the heel of my hand. It was too heavy to fall over, and merely rocked back on to its base. I tried to upset it again, failed again and finally, howling with frustration and disgust, got both my hands on its slippery rim and shoved.

I jumped back as a stream of vile sludge slopped across the ground at my feet. Mercifully, there was not enough light to see what colour it was, but there was no mistaking either its smell or the pale thing that flowed out on the dark, stinking stream. It was part of a human arm. The hand was turned up towards me, as if in supplication, although its fingers were closed around something, a small, hard, gleaming object, with an irregular shape, like a carving in jade or obsidian.

I bent towards the hand for a closer look, but at that point nausea finally got the better of me. I ran to the edge of the canal and vomited, voiding my almost empty stomach and heaving drily and painfully until I scarcely had the strength to draw breath. For a long time after that I just knelt by the water's edge, watching the gathering pre-dawn light catch the ripples on its surface until the moisture in my own eyes turned them first into vague ghostly shapes and then into a feeble, pale flickering, like a blanket being shaken out on a dull day.

A long time passed after I had fled from the horror I found behind the screen, during which I did nothing but crouch wretchedly beside the canal. When my stomach had stopped heaving I wept, and when my tears had dried up I merely stared at the water.

I ought to have gone back, to tip up all the other pots and confront their secrets. I shifted my weight from my heels to the balls of my feet twice, meaning to get up and look behind the screen again, but both times I stayed where I was. I thought I could guess what had happened, and I could not bear to have it confirmed.

My son had gone to Kindly's house, looking for his knife. I

wondered whether he had surprised another thief, whoever had stolen Kindly's costume, or whether, as Kindly himself believed, the two of them had been in it together and had fallen out. One of them had stabbed the other, and the victim had ended up here. I looked back along the bridge and tried, in spite of myself, to visualize what had happened: the killer carrying the body as far as the middle of the bridge, perhaps, and then dropping it and dragging it the rest of the way before cutting it up and concealing it hastily in a public privy.

Could Nimble have done such a thing? I closed my eyes and tried to imagine the boy I had known all too briefly killing a man for the sake of a bronze knife and a feathered costume. It was difficult. Nimble had been the lover of a vicious, cold-blooded and sadistic murderer, but he was no killer himself. Yet the alternative explanation was worse: that it was my son's body that lay in pieces, just a few paces away.

I had to know.

Swallowing once, I forced myself to my feet, and then realized that the matter was out of my hands and my chance had been lost.

It was almost dawn and the city was coming to life. Canoes began gliding by, and one or two of their boatmen glanced curiously at the miserable creature standing by the canal, his face pale from retching, his eyes raw and his clothes reduced to rags. I knew that I had better move on quickly before somebody else discovered what I had seen and connected it with me.

With one last brief glance at the screen, I went on my way.

THREE RABBIT

1

I had no difficulty in memorizing the directions Kindly had given me. Still I managed to get lost four times. The horrifying discovery I had just made kept forcing itself into my thoughts, making it hard to concentrate. It was not until late in the morning that I found myself where I wanted to be, and even then I was not certain I had got it right.

The route Kindly had given me took me among the sturdy, respectable houses of the featherworkers, and past them. It led me down narrow, overgrown, silted-up canals whose stagnant waters reeked even on a cool winter's morning, among wretched hovels, some of them little more than one-room huts, some of them obviously long abandoned and others with their roofs coated with moss and their sides piled high with stinking garbage, and into what I was convinced must be another parish altogether.

Eventually I asked a water seller to confirm that I was where I thought I was. He was standing up in a canoe, using his paddle to hack his way through the reeds in his path while lumps of green scum swirled and coagulated in his wake. The canoe was laden with pots that I presumed were full of fresh water from the spring at Chapultepec, on the mainland. Every morning the water sellers drew it from the aqueduct that had been built over the lake in Emperor Ahuitzotl's time, and filled their pots with it for sale to countless thirsty households in the city. Of course, Mexico was riddled with canals, but nobody in his right mind would ever drink out of them.

My question made him laugh. 'Amantlan? You must be joking!' His voice had a nasal tone, the result of trying to avoid breathing through his nose. 'Amantlan's back there.' He jerked his head to indicate the way I had come. 'This is Atecocolecan.'

I stared about me, bewildered. I had not realized I had walked so far, but as I took in my surroundings it began to make sense. Atecocolecan: the Place of the Angry Water. I had walked all the way to the edge of Mexico's island, close to where the northern causeway linked the city to Tepeyac on the mainland. 'It's a dump! Look – there isn't even a path over there. It's just a marsh – you can't tell where the canal ends and the ground starts. These houses must be waterlogged all the time.' The name of this place was no accident. After a serious flood many of the hovels around me would be drift-wood.

He dipped his paddle in the water. 'Afraid so,' he acknowl-edged.

'Do you know where Skinny lives?' I called after him, as his canoe at last got under way through the gap he had hacked through the foliage. 'Only I was looking for him, but I got lost.'

'Skinny?' He laughed shortly without looking around. 'You're not lost. He lives right here!' He waved his paddle at a house just a few paces away. 'Doesn't owe you any money, does he?'

'No.'

'Good for you! If you catch him, mention me, eh? Tell him I'll settle for a nice plump turkey hen, as long as she's a good layer. Otherwise he can drink his own piss!'

The paddle hit the water with an emphatic splash, throwing

up a jet of green and brown muck. It did not propel the canoe
forward with any great speed, but it probably felt good.

Skinny's house was not one of the meanest in this part of the
city. It was in better condition than the dwellings on either
side. On the other hand, they were both ruins, evidently
deserted, unless you counted the rats. The featherworker's
property looked sturdy enough, but its walls were in desperate
need of rendering and all that remained of the garden on its
roof was a few bedraggled brown leaves trailing over its edge.

A gang of men driving wooden piles into the bed of the
swamp at the back of the house, shaking the ground with
their hammering and tormenting the air with their tuneless
singing, did nothing for the neighbourhood. The water seller's
parting remark came back to me. Here was the home of a
family down on its luck.

I wondered how a featherworker could possibly have ended
up here, especially one as eminent as Skinny. Amantlan was
like many parishes in Mexico, in that its people were a close-
knit community, bound together by ties of kinship, whose
sons and daughters rarely married outside and were expected
to carry on a family business that they had in common with all
their friends and relations. Put two Aztecs together and there
would be rivalry, and the Amanteca were no exception to
this, but something extraordinary must have happened to allow
a great craftsman to fall so far, without his peers doing anything to stop it.

Considering the state of his home, I began to wonder
whether it would, after all, be so surprising if Skinny had sold
the god's costume to Kindly. He might well have been desperate enough.

A low square doorway, leading straight into a room, broke
the clean white expanse of the wall in front of me. There was

no screen but the interior was too dark to give anything away. The glare of a sunlit courtyard, visible through another doorway directly opposite the street entrance, made it look darker. By squinting I was just able to make out a few features in the courtyard: the domed shape of a sweat bath against the rear wall, another doorway off to one side.

There was no one in the first room and I went straight through into the courtyard. That was deserted too. This puzzled me, because most dwellings in Mexico were home to more than one household and were consequently crowded, even during the day with the men away in the fields.

I stopped wondering about that when I saw the idols.

Every house in Mexico had them. In most a ledge near the hearth served as a shrine, a home for the household's patron deities, who might be feared or adored but were always cherished and often treated as if they were members of the family.

Here, it seemed, things were done differently. Two of the courtyard's four walls, the ones that were not lined with rooms, were richly decorated with statuettes of the gods. Some were new, some old. The biggest was half my height and I could have closed my fist around the smallest. They were made of everything from brilliantly polished greenstone to crudely carved wood, ash or fir or something similarly cheap and plentiful. I saw Tezcatlipoca, Xipe Totec with his mask of human skin, Tlaloc with his protruding, goggle eyes and his consort Chalcihuitlicue, She of the Jade Skirt, Ohmacatl, the vain and importunate lord of the feast, several other gods I knew and a few I did not know. I supposed the particular gods of the featherworkers – Coyotl Inahual and the women Xilo and Xiuhtlati – must be here, and I recognized Yacatecuhtli, the merchants' god, whom the featherworkers honoured as well.

There was something odd about these figures, apart from their number and variety. All of them, despite having been placed so carefully in niches that had been lovingly prepared for them, were coated in a fine layer of dust, and some were stained, smeared, defaced with dried muck. One of the idols had even been broken. It was impossible to tell which god it represented, because all that was left was a jagged greenstone stump.

Clay flower pots stood on the floor of the courtyard. One of them had fallen over and cracked, leaving the floor around it strewn with soil. That made me frown, for sweeping was a sacred duty and for a pious Aztec to neglect it altogether was all but unthinkable.

When I looked up again I saw I was no longer alone.

Although the wall to my right stretched the whole length of the courtyard, there was only one opening in it, the one I had caught sight of from the front of the house. A short, grubby cloth screen had been hung across it. This still shivered, as it would if it had been tugged aside and jerked back into place. A man stood in front of it.

'Who are you? What are you doing here? This is a private house. Whatever you're selling, we don't want any. Get out!'

I took a step back, astonished. It was not the sort of greeting I would have expected to get anywhere in Mexico, where visitors could normally expect to be received with almost ceremonial courtesy. I stared at the stranger, taking in as much of his appearance as I could while I tried to think of a suitable reply.

He was about my height and, like me, perhaps forty years old. He was thin and gaunt, with his ribs showing plainly where his cloak parted. Dark hollows around his eyes added to my impression that he was in need of a square meal. Their lids were heavy as well, and he kept blinking as he stared at me, in the slow, stupid manner of someone who has just been roused from a deep sleep.

A long scratch ran down one of his cheeks. It was a recent wound, and I doubted that it was deep enough to leave a scar, but it might easily have been much worse, since it began a hair's breadth from the corner of his left eye.

I cleared my throat uncertainly. 'You must be Skinny. Is that any way for a great craftsman to greet a customer?'

The eyebrows shot up to the top of his forehead and fluttered down again. 'A customer?' He gaped at me.

The screen behind him rustled and was pulled aside. He jerked his head around quickly, and I saw one of his hands clench and loosen nervously as I peered over his shoulder to see who was following him into the courtyard.

A woman's voice cooed: 'Skinny? Who's this?'

Aztec children learned at an early age that it was rude to stare openly at someone. If my father could have seen me at that moment he would probably have had me hanging upside down over burning chillies, grown man or not, until he judged that seared lungs and streaming eyes had reminded me firmly enough of my manners.

She slipped from the room as silently and gracefully as an ocelot stalking a sparrow along the branch of a tree, and stood next to the man, so close that her bare arm brushed against his, all the time keeping her eyes fixed on me with a stare as frank as mine. Perfect ellipses, those eyes were, wide and glistening, their irises pure black, matching the hair that fell loose about her face and cascaded like molten tar over her shoulders. No doubt its dark sheen owed something to indigo dye, but a man would have to have been made of marble to care about that. I was not, which was why I could not help noticing, beneath her plain skirt and shift, the curve of the woman's thigh and the swell of breasts tipped by nipples as small and sharp as arrowheads.

'Says he's a customer.'

Skinny's voice snatched me out of my reverie. Hastily I forced my eyes back to the woman's face. It was a perfect oval of clear, unblemished skin, with an interesting pallor that might have been natural but was more likely the result of staining with yellow ochre. I wondered how old she was, thinking she must be much younger than the man, perhaps not yet twenty.

'Madam, I am sorry to have troubled you,' I mumbled, 'but I was looking for Skinny the craftsman. . .'

She yawned. A hand flew upward to cover her mouth, and dropped again to reveal a weary smile.

'I beg your pardon. You must think we're very rude, but neither of us slept very well. You must have come far, you'll be tired. Have a rest and something to eat.' It was merely the conventional way to greet visitors but she managed to make it sound as if she was truly concerned. Detaching herself from the man, she began walking towards a doorway in the wall behind me.

I forced myself to take my eyes off her and turn back towards the man. 'You are Skinny, the featherworker? I have got the right house?'

He looked hastily from me to the girl and back again. 'Yes,' he admitted gruffly. 'And this is Papalotl, my wife.' Her name suited her. It meant 'Butterfly'. 'We weren't expecting visitors. Who did you say you were?'

'I'm Moquequeloa,' I said, on the spur of the moment, and instantly regretted it. It was one of the names we used for Tezcatlipoca, and meant 'Joker'. 'I was looking to buy a piece of featherwork for my master.' I could not resist a quick look over my shoulder, but all I could see of the girl was the sheen of her long hair in the dark room beyond the doorway she had gone through.

'You want to buy a piece of featherwork?' The man's hollow

eyes widened and then narrowed suspiciously. 'What kind of piece, exactly? What made you come here?'

That seemed like an odd question, coming from a renowned master of his craft, but I was spared the need to answer it straight away by his wife's reappearance.

'I can't offer you very much, I'm afraid,' she said. She had a drinking-gourd in her hand which she proffered, this time with modestly downcast eyes. 'Here is some water. All we have to eat are some cakes of stone dung.'

'Thank you.' I took the stopper off the gourd and raised it. I took a cautious sniff before pressing it to my lips, and decided I was not thirsty after all. It must have been a long while since Skinny's credit with the water seller had run out. I passed the gourd to Skinny, who took it and drank without hesitation, as if he no longer noticed what the contents tasted like.

'It's very kind of you,' I added politely, 'but I ate and drank before I came here.' Stone dung was what we called scum skimmed off the surface of the lake, which was dried and sold in the markets as crumbly cakes. It was nourishing enough, provided nobody had been emptying pots of whitewash into the water while it was being harvested, but scarcely appetizing. During one of the lowest periods in my life I had made a living collecting the stuff, and so I was even less fond of it than most Aztecs.

Skinny gave the gourd back to his wife. 'The man says he wants to buy a piece of featherwork,' he muttered.

Her frown etched a single straight line in the exact centre of her forehead, and was almost as pretty as her smile.

'We had better sit down and talk about this. Can you bring some mats out, darling?'

Wordlessly he turned and went back into the room, emerging a moment later with three reed mats that he threw on the floor at our feet. As each one struck the earth it raised a little cloud of dust whose motes spiralled lazily in the bright still air. Again the slovenliness of the household puzzled me. In almost any other courtyard in Mexico the mats would not have been needed, unless it had been raining, because the ground would have been swept so clean you could have eaten off it. As I squatted and tried to make myself comfortable, I wondered what the gods, looking down from their niches in the walls, could possibly make of it all.

Skinny rested his buttocks on the mat next to mine. Butterfly knelt facing us.

'You must think us very impolite,' she said. 'We're in a terrible mess at the moment.'

I did not comment.

'We live here with Skinny's brother, Tlatziuhqui. He and his wife have that room over there. Her name's Cempoalxochitl.' Tlatziuhqui was a curious name: it meant 'Idle'. Obviously he had shown even less promise as a little boy than his brother. Cempoalxochitl meant 'Marigold'.

I followed her glance towards the doorway she and her husband had first emerged from, and then looked back at her, letting my expression pose the obvious question for me.

'They aren't here. They. . .' For the first time she seemed unsure of herself, faltering and looking at Skinny for help.

'Disappeared,' he said shortly. 'That's why we aren't doing any business at the moment. Too much to sort out. This house is really my brother's, so we need to make sure the parish will let us keep it. Sorry you've had a wasted journey.' A smile formed on his mouth but his eyes were still glowering at me. He was not sorry about my wasted journey and did not mind if I knew it. He wanted me in his house the way a gardener wants slugs, and he did not mind my knowing that too.

'Disappeared?' I echoed. 'What do you mean?'

'One day they're here, the next they're not. Don't ask me why.'

I turned to the girl. 'When did this happen?'

She gave me her discomfitingly sensuous smile. 'Three nights ago, on Thirteen Snake.'

I frowned. Thirteen Snake was the night the costume had been stolen from Kindly's house. 'And they simply walked out? Your husband said this was Idle's own house.'

She fidgeted on her mat. I kept my eyes at about the level of her chin to avoid becoming fixated by those slender brown knees.

'We've been asking ourselves Why? ever since – haven't we, love? But we can't think of an answer. Nobody has seen them. We thought they might be with Marigold's father, but he doesn't know any more than we do.

'We can only hope,' she added, catching her breath, 'that they haven't met with an accident.'

It was difficult to imagine what sort of accident might befall two people at once, unless they were caught out on the lake in a canoe and swamped by a storm, or their house fell on their heads in an earthquake. If there had been any storms or earthquakes in the valley in the last few days, then I had slept through them.

Skinny said: 'Joker isn't interested in our troubles. We've already told him we can't help him. Let's not waste any more of the man's time.'

'You're not.' I was not sure that the featherworker's brother's disappearance had anything to do with what I was looking for but I was curious, to say the least. I glanced around quickly, to remind myself of my surroundings. The house was not large, but with just four adults living in it, it would not have been overcrowded. Aztecs were used to living on top of one another. I dismissed the idea that the vanished couple might just have wanted some space.

'Does anyone else live here?'

'No.'

I hesitated before asking my next question. Skinny clearly did not have the most even of tempers and I was not anxious to provoke him, but I could not leave without satisfying my curiosity on one point. 'Forgive me, but . . . why are you here? This isn't the featherworkers' parish, it's not even close. How come you ended up . . .' I nearly concluded 'in this hovel?' but changed it at the last moment to 'in Atecocolecan?'

'I was born here.' Not even Skinny's lips were smiling at me now. 'I think we've talked long enough. Thank you for coming. Sorry we can't help. The street,' he added pointedly, with a significant look towards the doorway I had first come through, 'is over there!'

I did not move. His answer was as astonishing as anything I had heard. I thought about probing further, but in the meantime I found myself staring speculatively at his cheek, not troubling to hide my interest.

'There was a fight, wasn't there?'

'What?'

'How did you get that scratch?'

'It was an accident,' the woman snapped. She dropped her sultry tone for a moment and her voice suddenly had a shrill, nervous edge. 'And it's none of your business anyway!'

'What sort of accident?'

They both started to get up. For a moment I wondered whether they were going to attack me. I tensed, ready to defend myself if they made a move to throw me bodily into the canal outside. I could probably have taken on the man, I thought, and I assumed the woman would be of no account in a fight by herself, but I was not sure about both of them together, and there had been a dangerous quality in her voice, a hint of something she had kept hidden, a reminder that I did not know for sure what she might be capable of.

Their eyes met, and some sort of unspoken signal seemed to pass between them. They both froze for an instant, and then relaxed. As quickly as it had come the danger seemed to pass and they resumed their former attitudes, he glowering at me from his mat, she smiling at me from hers.

The man let out a long sigh while the woman said: 'Forgive us. We don't mean to be discourteous but we're both under a lot of strain at the moment.'

'It was a copper knife,' Skinny added. 'It slipped while I was trimming a pattern on the cutting-board. Happens all the time. Look, here's another one.' He held up his hand. Across the palm was an ugly gash, a much deeper wound than the one on his cheek, but no older; the edges had been stitched together with hair and the stitches were still there.

'There was no fight,' the woman said earnestly. 'If there had been, and Idle and Marigold had run away, they'd have gone to her father, but I told you, he hasn't seen them.'

'Who's he?'

'Cuehmoliuhtoc,' said Skinny, rubbing his wounded hand absently. A corner of his mouth twitched as though at a private joke. 'My chief rival, the great featherworker. There's no love lost between us, anyone will tell you that.' This was only to be expected if the man's disposition matched his name, since Cuehmoliuhtoc meant 'Angry'. 'Of course, he'd be the first person his daughter and my brother would run to if there were a problem between us – but there isn't!'

I decided to drop the subject for the time being. If the costume had disappeared with the vanished couple then I would have to look elsewhere for it. If it had not, then I still had some bargaining to do. 'Listen, you still don't know what I came here for.' I looked from one to the other, finally settling on the man, because I thought his face was more likely to give something away when I told them my story. 'Kindly the merchant sent me.'

Skinny had been on the point of picking up the water gourd again. It lay neglected on the ground beside him, while his hand froze in the air above it. His eyes narrowed.

'Go on,' he said eventually.

I glanced slyly at the woman. Her face was impassive, but the last trace of the flush had left her cheeks.

'He bought something from you recently. A costume of Quetzalcoatl. He has, um, mislaid it.' I laid as much emphasis on 'mislaid' as I dared and paused to let the words sink in. 'Now he would like to replace it. He would like very much to get another one, exactly the same. Exactly the same.'

I had given a good deal of thought to this. Somebody had come to Kindly's house knowing that he had something of great value, and meaning to steal it. The person most likely to have that knowledge was the person he had got it from. I might well be looking at the thief, and if all I had wanted was to find the merchant's stolen goods, it seemed to me that my task could not be much simpler. I had no assurance that Kindly would pay a ransom to get his property back but I was certain he would. It was not as if he could not afford to. I did not much care whether he could afford to or not, anyway: compared to my own plight, the knowledge of what had almost certainly happened to my son, I thought the old merchant's troubles were trifling.

I sat back and waited for Skinny to name his price.

The man glared at me more fiercely than ever.

'I have no idea what you're talking about,' he growled dangerously.

I sighed wearily. 'Yes you do. All Kindly's asking is, how much do you want?'

'To make a feather costume? I told you, we aren't in business at the moment. I'm sorry to disappoint you and your master, but I can't help!'

I was beginning to feel uncomfortable. I looked at the woman again. She was watching her husband intently and did not seem to be paying any attention to me.

'I suppose you expect me to make you an offer,' I said at last. 'Very well. We will give you what Kindly paid you the first time. That's in return for not reporting the matter to the chief of your parish, not to mention the featherworkers' elders.'

'Reporting what?'

'The theft of the bloody costume!'

In the silence that followed, my exasperated cry seemed to bounce back at me off the walls of the courtyard.

Skinny and his wife both stared at me, their expressions as cold and unmoving as those of the idols on the walls around us. I began to wonder whether I might be wrong, and whether it was possible that the featherworker had not stolen the costume from Kindly after all.

It was the woman who spoke.

'I really think you ought to leave now, Joker.' She hissed the words at me between clenched teeth, but followed them with a deep sigh and a reminder of her smile. 'I'm sorry, but you've made a mistake. Things are hard for us. You must understand.'

Skinny scowled at me. I scowled back, but plainly pulling faces was not going to do me any good.

I got to my feet. 'You know where to come if you change your mind!'

I spoke to the man, but I let my eyes linger for a moment on the woman. I did not care if it seemed ill mannered. I had had enough of playing games with the two of them, and besides, she was beautiful, and I did not expect to see her like again soon.

2

My son's knife jarred against my hip as I walked back towards Amantlan. Each time the hard smooth metal knocked against my skin it reminded me of him. Each jolt was like a faint cry, a distant sound of despair and pain and fear which I could never answer, and each imagined cry seemed fainter and more plaintive than the last.

I felt an impulse to take the knife out and look at it, to talk to it even, as if it were the only thing I had left of its owner. I fumbled inside my breechcloth for it but came to my senses just in time. There were too many people about, any of whom might have noticed a thin, ragged slave clutching a unique bronze knife. Boatmen poled their canoes nonchalantly through canals that, here at least, were regularly cleaned and dredged by work details made up of the parish's common folk. Little children, their cloaks flapping over their naked loins, followed their mothers from house to house, the women bearing food or hot coals to light a failed hearth or just going to gossip. A small group of men was working its way along the canal towards me, their calf-length cloaks, stone-pillar hairstyles, cudgels and set, determined expressions giving them the look of a war party.

I peered at the soldiers, looking nervously among them for a green uniform or the peculiar glitter of sunlight on the blades of the captain's vicious club. I tensed, with my fingers curled

tightly around the hilt of the knife. If the Otomies had managed to extricate themselves from the chaos I had left behind
me in Tlacopan, they might well be after me, to punish me for
misleading them.

These were not the captain's warriors, however. From the
casual way they spoke to passers-by, they seemed to be locals,
and it was easy enough to guess what they were about.
Somebody must long since have gone behind that screen by
the canal and found the remains among the stinking pots there,
and these men were making routine enquiries.

I let go of the knife, pulling my hand out of my breechcloth
just as a young woman, a passenger in a canoe, shot me a disgusted look.

I lowered my eyes self-consciously before turning quickly
away.

I dared not go back across the bridge between Amantlan
and Pochtlan. Anyone seen near where the body had been
found was liable to be stopped and questioned, and as a runaway slave I could not contemplate that.

I wanted to go back to Kindly, to tell him what had tran-
spired at Skinny's house, and to question him about it too.
Kindly had told me that Skinny's father and brothers had
worked for him. At the time that had not made sense, because
I had assumed that Skinny was from the featherworkers' parish.
What kind of labour could a family of featherworkers provide
for a merchant? Atecocolecan, on the other hand, was the
sort of impoverished place that would breed field hands, day-
labourers and porters. I could have understood Kindly hiring
men from there. But then how had Skinny become a featherworker in the first place? How had he gained admittance to a
trade so jealously guarded by the families that had practised its
secret arts for generations?

However, I would have to postpone my conversation with

Kindly. It would mean a long detour through the neighbouring parishes. In any event, I thought a call on Skinny's rival would be just as valuable, especially if his daughter and son-in-law had run off with the stolen costume. If there was any chance that Idle was the thief, then I had to find him. He might know what had happened to my son.

I had no trouble finding Angry's house. In the parish of the featherworkers everybody knew where their chief craftsmen lived, and the first person I asked, an old beggar pretending to sell withered-looking chillies out of a broken basket, pointed the place out to me straight away. He wished me better luck than he had had, which I took as a reflection on my appearance.

'What is it now? Not that bloody chilli seller again? I thought we'd kicked his arse into the canal!'

Angry's voice was as loud as it was fierce. He was shouting over his shoulder at the man who had let me into his house, a wizened little man with an undistinguished commoner's short cloak and tonsured head, probably a needy relative whom the master featherworker employed as a favour. This servant stumbled meekly after the craftsman, mumbling and plucking at his cloak, while the great man strutted about his busy courtyard like a turkey cock surveying his hens.

Angry himself was a tall, portly man, whose cloak hung limply about him with the air of having despaired of ever being able to conceal his stomach. His hair was white and his face deeply lined. He was older than his rival, Skinny, perhaps as much as a bundle of years old. As he walked his arms waved clumsily. They seemed to move independently of each other and the rest of his body. I had always thought of featherworkers as artists, whose delicate fingers manipulated the materials in their grasp as carefully and tenderly as a midwife washing a newborn's face. It was hard to reconcile this image with Angry, whose hands ended in tuberous growths that looked like rolls of dough.

He was the kind who could draw the eye to him irresistibly, so that at first I barely noticed what else was going on in his courtyard. Only when his servant finally managed to attract his attention again and get him to pause, stooping and frowning, while the little man explained who I was and why I had come, did I think to look around and take in my surroundings. They were remarkable.

The courtyard had a bare look. It was clear of anything that was ornamental or that did not obviously serve an immediate practical purpose. Even the idols were fewer in number than usual, although there clearly had been many more, for the walls were covered with bare plinths and empty niches. Curious though these were, I barely spared them a glance before gaping at the people. The place was crowded. It throbbed with so much activity it put me in mind of a bee-hive.

In one corner, boys stirred steaming pots of glue: liquid turkey fat whose vile smell suffused the whole space. They doled the stuff out into wide tortoiseshell bowls, which smaller boys carried to the women pasting freshly carded cotton on to maguey leaves, to the men who stuck broad, coarse heron and parrot and molted spoonbill feathers together to form the bases of patterns, and to a little group in the far corner who sat apart from everyone else. These last were the true craftsmen, whose task it was to select and place the most precious plumes, those plucked from the green trogon, the red spoonbill and the hummingbird, and the most prized and coveted of all, the long, shimmering tail feathers of the resplendent quetzal.

There were others whom the boys ran straight past, because their part of the process did not require glue: the women who

carded the cotton, creating layers so thin that a picture could
be traced through them; the men who laid the cotton over the
pictures the scribes had drawn, to trace their designs on to it;
and those who carefully peeled the painted and glued cotton
away from the leaves that had been used as backing.

From all this industry would emerge the fabulous, radiant,
shimmering feather mosaics that were Angry the craftsman's
speciality.

He was striding in my direction now, his face dark and his
brow creased in a frown that matched his name.
Incongruously, two small, fat dogs trotted silently at his heels.
They came and danced around my legs, growling at one
another and sniffing and pawing at a loose thread hanging
from the remains of my cloak while their master glared down
at me.

'What do you want?' he demanded, adding, before I had
time to answer, 'I hear you know something about my daughter and my son-in-law. Tell me about it!'

I eyed his pets suspiciously, having always thought myself
that the only place for dogs was in a nice hot bubbling stew
with beans and chillies. 'I went to see Skinny and his wife
today . . .'

Angry interrupted me with a loud snort.

'They told me you weren't the best of friends.'

'Did they, now?' His face darkened. He glanced down at the
dogs, as if noticing they were there for the first time.

'Acamapichtli! Ahuitzotl! Come here!'

As the beasts trotted, whimpering, towards him, he bent
down and scooped them up in a fold of his cloak. Then he
turned away again, but only for as long as it took to catch the
eye of his elderly servant.

'I'm busy. Look after these two.' He handed the beasts over
with more tenderness than I would have thought him capable

of. His servant held them at arm's length as though he thought they were about to defecate all over him.

'You must be fond of dogs,' I observed.

Still looking away, the big man grunted. 'My wife was. She bought a couple to breed from with the cloaks I gave her when we were married, and got quite successful at it, but for some reason none of hers ever ended up in the pot. Whenever we ate dog it always came from the market. I keep those two you saw for her sake. They're the last of their line.'

'I'm sorry,' I said. 'When did you lose her?'

'Three years ago. It's none of your business. Tell me about my daughter.'

I told him about my meeting with Skinny and Butterfly, repeating the story I had offered them: that I was Kindly's slave, sent by the old merchant to retrieve his property. 'They said Marigold and her husband disappeared on the night the costume went missing. Of course, I don't know that your daughter had anything to do with the theft, but it would help if I could find her. Kindly is very keen to sort this out as quietly as possible.'

'So you think I'll help you find my daughter, do you?'

'Or I could help you find her,' I said coolly. 'Skinny and Butterfly said she hadn't come here. So I thought you might be anxious to know where she was, as well.'

There was a long, dangerous silence while he thought about what I had said. Then, surprisingly, he uttered a harsh, mirthless laugh.

'I see what you're about! I must be desperate to find my daughter and that wastrel of a husband of hers, and so if I don't cooperate with you it's because I'm hiding her, is that it?' Suddenly he leaned towards me and showed me just how delicate those long, broad fingers were.

I was caught unawares. I stumbled back. Before I could

regain my balance Angry's thumbs were pressing into my throat, one either side of my neck, and I was fighting for breath and struggling to keep my feet at the same time, while my hands flailed vainly in the air between us.

'You're strangling me!' I gasped.

His face was so close to mine our noses almost touched. 'So I am,' he murmured nonchalantly. 'A little more pressure and I'll crush your windpipe.'

My knees were trembling and my eyes were straining to get out of their sockets. I tried to cry out but all I could manage was a feeble rattle at the back of my throat. There was a sound in my ears like waves crashing on a rocky beach. I began to feel dizzy.

Then I was on the ground, spluttering, coughing and choking, with one hand clawing at my bruised throat.

I lay groaning and shivering and willing my arms and legs to move so that I could get up and stagger away, out of the featherworker's sight. When I shook my head to clear it a wave of pain and nausea swept over me. I retched feebly, but nothing came out. I slumped on the hard earth of the court-yard, seeing nothing, but distantly aware that I could still hear Angry talking.

'No, Axilli, you don't understand.'

'But, Uncle, if he can help us find Marigold . . .'

The other speaker was a boy whose voice was on the verge of breaking. I twisted my neck cautiously until I could see them both.

'If only you were right!' the featherworker cried. 'But he can't. It's too dangerous.'

From where I lay Angry and the boy who called him 'Uncle' were dark shapes against the bright afternoon sky. Axilli, whose name meant 'Crayfish', was a slight figure beside his uncle's bulk. He looked down, as though dejected.

I levered myself upright. 'Dangerous?' I said hoarsely. 'Why? All we want is the costume back. Kindly will even pay for it. No questions asked.'

The big craftsman stared at me. 'And you think Marigold has it?'

Before I could reply, he had turned his back. I watched him step delicately over a heap of discarded feathers to stand in front of the nearest wall. When he spoke again, his voice was surprisingly soft: so soft that I had to make an effort to hear him.

'You see all these empty niches and ledges? She took all the idols with her, when they moved to Atecocolecan. She had to have them with her, you see.'

I scrambled unsteadily to my feet. 'I don't understand.'

'My daughter loved the gods, Joker, or whatever your name is. She feared them, but she adored them as well. Do you really think someone like that would steal the raiment of one of them?'

He gently laid one of his enormous hands on a ledge. Then a long, low sound escaped him: something between a sigh and a groan.

'It's funny. I used to think they were quaint, while she was here. A nuisance, even. Now I miss them.' He turned around, but not to face me: his eyes were fixed on the ground at his feet, while his hands hung loosely at his sides, as if he had forgotten what they were for.

'Marigold is my only child, she's all I have – can you understand that?'

When his hands moved this time, it was not to encircle my throat, but to cover his eyes and the rush of tears that threatened to flood them. Crayfish was at his side, but all he could do in the face of his uncle's torment was wring his hands helplessly.

Watching them, I had to force down the memory of what I had felt just that morning, tipping dismembered and desecrated remains out of those stinking jars by the canal.

'I understand,' I said. 'I had just the one son myself. He . . . I think it would help him, if I could find this costume. If it wasn't your daughter who stole it, maybe it was her husband – can't we work together?'

He dropped his hands. His glistening eyes widened. He looked at me for a long moment, frowning thoughtfully, as if he were making a decision. Then, gruffly, he asked what I wanted to know.

'You could start by telling me what it is between you and Skinny.'

Angry laughed, a short, harsh sound, such as one of his dogs might have uttered. 'Why don't you ask him?'

'I could,' I said. 'I might, except he isn't here.'

He sighed. 'We might have been friends, partners, instead of rivals, if it hadn't been for . . . well, never mind. Look, I'll show you something.' He turned to Crayfish. 'This is my nephew,' he said, by way of introduction, before adding, to the boy: 'Go and fetch me one of the dahlias, will you?'

'Dahlias?' I echoed, confused. The last dahlia I had seen had been killed off by frost at the end of autumn. Why would the featherworker want one now, anyway?

When the boy came back, I understood. He was carrying a picture of a flower.

It was a mosaic, made entirely of feathers: red feathers, on a background of black feathers. As Angry handed it to me, I admired the way it captured and reflected the light. The bloom in its centre had been built up in layers, to give it a depth of colour that a real flower could barely have surpassed. If there had been any bees around at this time of year, I thought, they would be swarming over it.

'See this?'

'It's beautiful.' I imagined a single bloom dropped on the lake, an offering perhaps to Chalchihuitlicue, the goddess who presided over the waters. I saw this flower drifting about the city at night, on its bed of water as deep and dark as the dense, shimmering black feathers – from a grackle or some other species of crow – and sinking slowly into it as it became water-logged, until it silently vanished.

The picture was snatched from my grasp and thrown to the floor.

'"Beautiful!"' Angry spat the word contemptuously back at me. 'Of course it's beautiful! It's just as beautiful as every other picture of a sodding dahlia that's come out of this workshop in the last thirty years. And you know why?' He whirled around, almost turning a full circle as he threw an arm out to encompass his courtyard. 'Because of Crayfish here and all the rest of my little army. Because everybody does one job, carding cotton, tracing patterns, mixing glue, hardening feathers, whatever, one job, the same, day in, day out, until they get so good at it they never even have to think about what they're doing. Not a real craftsman among us, but we can turn out anything you want – shirts, skirts, shields, fans, mosaics – any-thing, as long as it doesn't have to be unique, original, something none of your friends will ever have seen before.' He glared at me. He seemed to be daring me to ask the obvious question, and so I did.

'What if it does?'

'What if it does what?'

'Have to be unique, original, or whatever?'

He looked away. He was silent so long that I thought he had not heard me, even though I was standing only a couple of hands' breadths from him, but then I caught his almost inaudi-ble reply.

'Then you go to Skinny, of course.'

He stood with his shoulders hunched and his head bowed, as motionless as a tree stump, and his eyes were pale slivers against the dark flesh of his face. He was a larger man than I was in every way, and stood a head taller than I did, but I felt that to meet those eyes I would have to squat.

In the long silence that followed, I noticed that many of those sitting around me were making as if to go, laying aside their feathers, bone spreaders, paper and copper knives and creeping towards the exit from the courtyard with a furtive air and the bow-legged, hunchbacked gait people adopt when they are in plain sight and wish they were not. They did not want their employer to see them leaving, even though the sky was darkening and there was a chill in the air. I guessed that Angry drove his workers hard, but now he seemed oblivious to them.

'Uncle . . .' ventured Crayfish eventually, stretching out a hand which was brushed aside.

'It's getting late,' the big man muttered. 'It'll be dark soon. I'm going indoors.'

He turned and stalked off. I looked at the youth standing next to me, who sighed. 'Come on', he said.

I let him lead me towards the back of the courtyard and the kitchen, where I knew I would find the Old, Old God watching over three hearthstones surrounding a low fire.

3

The embers lit up Crayfish's face as he prodded them into life. The sight reminded me of sunlight falling on the bare hills beyond the mountains that ringed our valley, his cheeks, brow and nose picked out like the high places by an orange glow, while his mouth and eyes lay in shadows as dark as the deepest valley. The effect was to make him look much older than he was, and oppressed by his cares.

It was strange to watch a boy cooking, but with his aunt dead and his cousin gone, evidently there was no woman in the house to do it. Once the fire was going he set an earthenware pot on it, standing it over the flames on a tripod, and soon the room was filled with the appetizing smells of burning charcoal and maize gruel being warmed through.

Angry sat by the fire too, staring into it, letting the flames catch his eyes and make them glitter.

'You have to understand,' he began, while his nephew stirred the gruel with one hand and steadied the pot with the other, 'that most featherworkers don't live in Amantlan any more – not if they're any good, at least. Now I'm different,' he added unselfconsciously. 'So's Skinny, for that matter. We're private featherworkers, and always will be, but these days most of the best ones, especially the young ones, get taken into the Palace. Our youngsters go to the Priest House as part of their training. It's so that they understand the pictures they're making: who's in them and the stories behind them. Crayfish here is going later this year.' His nephew tested the gruel for warmth with his finger and went on stirring it. 'The Emperor's scouts come to the Priest House and pick the most talented ones out. They get lodged, fed, paid well, and they work for the Emperor, making fans and costumes and decorations for him to use as gifts or rewards for the valiant warriors. Isn't that stuff ready yet?'

As Crayfish reached behind him for three bowls I asked his uncle why he and Skinny were different.

The young man dipped a bowl in the porridge and passed it to me, after first sprinkling a little of the contents on to the fire, for the god. I accepted it gratefully, my stomach reminding me sharply that I had last attended to it before dawn, and then had promptly thrown up. While his uncle lifted his own bowl to his lips, Crayfish answered for him.

'My uncle could have gone to the Palace, but he wouldn't.'

I almost choked on my porridge. 'What?'

'It's hot,' Crayfish warned me belatedly. 'Do you want some salt or dried chillies?'

'No, thanks.' I turned to Angry. 'You turned the Emperor down?'

He regarded me through the steam rising from his bowl of gruel. When he spoke the steam vanished, blown away like cobwebs. 'The way I work wouldn't have suited them,' he said shortly.

'And Skinny? Did he turn the Emperor down too?'

'Skinny and I were the best featherworkers we had. Of course, we were great rivals, forever trying to outdo one another. I made the best feather mosaics ever.' The big man's tone as he said this was matter-of-fact, without a hint of conceit. 'Some of them looked so real you would have sworn they were real flowers and birds and maize cobs and fish and people, not pictures at all. Skinny used to make fans and costumes and insignia for warriors to wear on their backs. He didn't use glue much, he usually went for the frame and thread method, but he did incredible things – I can show you a fan of his that looks like water when a stone hits it, the feathers flying outward and the whole thing looking as if it's about to burst.'

'So what happened?'

'I got more and more commissions – from lords, great warriors, foreigners. I had more work than I could keep up with, even with my family working flat out. I got more and more of my relations in to help, and now, as you can see, I've a whole houseful. To be honest,' he added, lowering his voice, 'some of them aren't actually related to me at all, so I've had to bend the rules a bit to employ them all. Everybody does something different, and knows exactly how to do it.' He put his bowl down thoughtfully and stared into it. With the fire burning between us it was impossible to read anything into his expression. 'But you know what? I don't think there's one of us, maybe not even me, who could make a feather fan or a mosaic from scratch by himself, not now. And everything we do is flawless, but . . . Well . . .'

'But not original or unique.' I remembered that picture of the dahlia. 'But Skinny doesn't have the same problem. So what happened to him?'

'He didn't go the same way as I did. I don't know why. Maybe he didn't want to work that way. Maybe it has something to do with where he came from.'

'I'd been wondering about that. He's not an Amantecatl, is he? How come he ended up in featherwork?'

'Oh, you know that, do you? That's right, he started life in Atecocolecan. But he was born on an auspicious day for a craftsman, and somehow he got himself adopted into one of the families here. I don't know how. Someone must have decided he'd be wasted as a labourer. He certainly had talent, but he was always a loner – always insisted on working by himself, even when he couldn't sell what he'd made except at a huge loss. He couldn't compete with us, not when we were able to give our customers what they wanted, when they wanted it, and guarantee the quality.'

'Quality?' I cried, forgetting myself for a moment. 'But nobody ever produced featherwork like Skinny! Well, except you, of course.'

'Save your breath!' Angry said scornfully. 'I couldn't touch Skinny at his finest, and we both knew it. But most of the time, you see, Skinny wasn't doing his best work. A lot of the time he couldn't do anything at all. He'd just sit in the middle of a pile of feathers, just picking them up and staring at them all afternoon.'

I imagined the gaunt, hollow-eyed man I had seen earlier that day, idling away his life toying pointlessly with a heap of precious feathers.

'It's funny,' Angry went on. 'He could have turned out perfectly good fans or anything you wanted whenever he was asked, time after time, but it was as if he couldn't bring himself to do anything but his best and wouldn't trust anyone else to help him, even though what he earned from his work was all he had to live on.'

'You turned the Emperor down. You didn't tell me whether Skinny did too.'

'I'd have had to go and live in the Palace, making fans and costumes to the order of Montezuma and his nobles. That would have meant abandoning my set-up here, and to be honest, I wasn't sure I could work without it. The Palace may have thought this too, because they didn't insist. I don't know about Skinny. I'm sure he just didn't want anybody telling him what to make, even if it was the Emperor. Later on, his work dried up, and he started gambling and taking a lot of sacred mushrooms and peyote buttons, and after that the Palace wouldn't have wanted him anyway.'

'So what happened to him? How come he went back to Atecocolecan? To that hole he's living in now?'

Crayfish answered. 'I think it all started when he got married. That was about two years ago.'

'He left it late, then, didn't he?' I said. Most Aztec men married in their twenties, when they left the House of Youth. Skinny would have been considerably older than that.

'We all assumed it would never happen,' Angry said. 'He'd never shown much interest in girls as a young man. I don't know what changed his mind. But his wife seemed to have had some effect on him. You've met the woman.' He grimaced suddenly, as if his gruel had suddenly turned sour. 'I guess she inspired him. He started working again, and they both ended up here.'

'Here?' I stared at them both. 'But Skinny was your rival!'

'And what do you do with your competitor, when he's down on his luck? Bring him into the business and make use of him, of course. Skinny had just got married, he was working again but not making much and he needed help. So I hired him.'

I sat in silence, absorbing that along with the last of my food. 'I'd guess he wasn't here all that long,' I said at length.

'A year, maybe. But when they left, it wasn't really down to Skinny. It was his brother.'

The porridge was settling in my stomach, spreading its warmth through my veins, and with it the beginnings of a dangerous lassitude. I wanted nothing so much as to stretch out on a sleeping-mat somewhere, or failing that the bare earth. I had been struggling to keep my eyes open. Then, suddenly, Angry mentioned Idle, and I was wide awake again.

My son, I reminded myself. Idle was the man who would know what had happened to my son.

'I agreed to put Skinny and Butterfly up here for the sake of his reputation, and it seemed to work out at first. Skinny was off the mushrooms. He was putting his back into it. What he produced wasn't his best, not by a long way, but it wasn't bad. He just used to take his own supply of cotton and feathers and knives and squat in a corner by himself. His wife would fetch him food and water. I have to admit, she looked after him. He was that obsessive about his work: if she hadn't made him eat he'd have starved himself.'

'We used to gather round watching him,' Crayfish added. 'All the boys from around here – we all knew his reputation and we wanted to see how he did it, so we could be as a famous as he was.'

'So what went wrong?'

I had addressed the question to Angry, but his only answer was a little noise at the back of his throat, as though some of his food had got stuck there. Alarmed, I leaned towards him, but his nephew stretched out an arm and stopped me.

'His brother ran off with my cousin.' The young man's tone was apologetic.

'Oh.' I did not know what else to say. There was no need to ask what Angry had made of his daughter's deserting him to join his rival's family. The craftsman himself kept his eyes averted and said nothing.

'Idle wasn't like his brother,' Crayfish went on in a low voice. 'Skinny lived for his work. I don't think Idle knew what work was! My uncle never liked him. I heard him complaining about the way he hung around the courtyard, distracting everybody from their work, scrounging from his brother, chatting up the girls.' He glanced anxiously at his uncle, but Angry did not react. 'He wasn't meant to be living here. He still belonged to Atecocolecan. He still had his house in the marshes up there, and a *chinampa* plot at the edge of the city. His parish kept saying they'd take them both away if he didn't get on and work the land, but he still spent far too much time here.'

'He can't have been born on a good day for a craftsman, then,' I commented.

'I suppose not.' Crayfish looked uncertainly at Angry.

'Don't know,' Angry mumbled, staring into his bowl. 'Don't care either!'

There was a short, awkward pause before Crayfish continued: 'My uncle tried giving him work to do, but he'd always go and mess it up.'

'He did it on purpose,' growled Angry, looking up again. 'If I told him to harden feathers he'd let the glue boil until they disintegrated, and if he was supposed to cut out a pattern he'd let the knife slip and it would all have to be done again. He didn't care. He was only interested in Marigold. If he couldn't find an excuse to go and talk to her they'd just make eyes at each other across the courtyard.'

'So Marigold didn't do anything to discourage him?' I asked bluntly.

I regretted the question immediately as I watched the muscles in the man's face contort. What man could abide having his daughter accused of being a flirt? Once again, however, it was the nephew who stepped in, answering for his uncle before he could fly into a rage.

'You don't know what it's like here. Everybody lives for his work. It used to be . . . well, people used to chat and laugh and. . .'

'When your aunt was alive, you mean,' Angry grumbled. 'All right, you don't need to say it. She could bring me up short when I started throwing my weight around.' He squeezed his eyelids shut for a moment before going on. 'I know, we've been through this before. You know how often I've said it myself, especially . . . especially in the last few days. The poor girl started to see the walls of the courtyard closing in on her, didn't she? And she wasn't getting any younger herself. I can't pretend she's a beauty, and even with my money her prospects weren't that good. So what was she bound to do but fall for a layabout like Idle?' He sighed. 'If it had been his brother, now . . .'

'He was married,' I pointed out.

Crayfish said: 'I think Marigold was quite sweet on him, though. She used to talk to him a lot – about his work and religion, mainly. I'm not sure Butterfly was too happy about it, but I never heard her say anything. I doubt if Marigold and Idle ever spent much time talking,' the lad added ruefully.

'So what was Idle . . .'

'He wanted my uncle's money,' Crayfish said bluntly.

His uncle added: 'Idle tried it on with a few of the girls before he fixed on her. He's a bastard, but he's the sort who's so convinced every woman finds him irresistible that they end up believing it themselves. So I don't suppose he had to ask her twice.'

'They got married, though.'

'Of course they did,' said Angry bitterly, 'with a generous dowry from me. I kidded myself that maybe she'd calm him down a bit. He was causing too much disruption here. The women wouldn't stick to their work, and he seemed to have some sort of fascination for Skinny. I don't know what it was, but his work started going to pieces again, round about the time his brother got married.'

'And then they all left together?' I asked. 'When was that?'

'Near the end of last summer. A bit less than half a year ago.'

'I wondered if Skinny just got sort of homesick,' Crayfish

said. 'Being with his brother again after all those years reminded him where they both grew up.'

'More likely they both thought lying around in Atecocolecan living off my daughter's dowry was easier than working,' snapped Angry. 'I was happy enough when Marigold told me she and Idle wanted to leave. I thought they were going to make a fresh start and get a grip on that plot of land of his. She's a good girl, she'd have enjoyed doing that. And . . . well, I think she was . . . I mean, I'm pretty sure she was . . .'

'Pregnant,' his nephew added bluntly.

'You think?' I stared at them both. 'Surely you'd know – it ought to be obvious by now!'

'We've hardly seen any of them, since they left.'

I frowned into the fire. 'Skinny and his wife went at the same time.'

'Suddenly, no explanation. Not that I'd have tried to stop them – Skinny's work had more or less dried up by then anyway. But . . .' A tremor went through the big man's body. 'Do you know what I'm afraid of, Joker? I think they saw their chance. They had the money she took with her, but they didn't want her around any more. They've done something with her. It's that Idle – maybe he's lying low, hoping I'll forget about him before he reappears. But I won't!'

FOUR WATER

1

I was allowed to stay the night. I slept by the hearth, making the most of its warmth, luxuriating in it so long as I was awake and relishing the contrast with what I had undergone the night before. I could enjoy remembering the cold, the exhaustion and the numbness in my feet while I basked in the comforting warmth of the slowly subsiding flames. They still flickered when my eyes closed and I lost interest in them. By the time I woke again, to the distant sound of the pre-dawn trumpet, there was nothing left but glowing embers, ready to be blown into life again.

As soon as I was awake and able to move about, I left and headed back towards Pochtlan. I had no intention of trying Angry's uncertain temper any further than I had to. I thought I might find Kindly and tell him what I had found out. I was more than ever convinced that Idle held the key to his stolen property. Kindly knew his family and would be able to tell me things about him. And I was beginning to wonder how much the old merchant knew about the history of the costume. Who had commissioned the work, and how long would it be before he started making his own enquiries about it?

But my immediate concern was with Idle. He would know what had happened to my son. That thought hurried me along through the dark, empty streets. If my son was alive I had to find him as quickly as possible. If not then finding out what had become of him was the last service I could render him.

The weather had changed abruptly, as it was often apt to at this time of year. A thick layer of cloud had come down off the mountains and the city still lay in its shadow. As I made my way back towards the bridge leading to Pochtlan, I had to pick my way carefully alongside the canal. The clouds had unloaded a fair amount of rain in the night and the ground was damp and slippery. By the time the bridge came into sight, illuminated by a flickering light, my already frayed nerves were stretched so far that I did not even stop to wonder where the light might be coming from.

I found out the moment I stepped on the bridge.

'Not so fast, you! Stay where you are!'

I had imagined the orange flame at the far end of the bridge to be coming from an unguarded brazier, not a pine torch resting in the huge callused fist of a veteran warrior. When I heard his harsh challenge I froze, with one foot in the air, and I seemed to stand like that, poised at my end of the wooden structure, for an age before any of my muscles would give way in response to my urge to run. All that happened, as the warriors came for me, was that my whole body sagged and my suspended foot thumped the wood with the hollow sound of a rubber hammer hitting a drum.

'Well, well,' rumbled the man who held the torch. 'What have we got here, then?'

At first, all I felt was despair at the thought that my master and the Otomi captain had finally caught up with me.

It was too easy to imagine what would happen next. I would be dragged home, hauled through the streets by my hair, my scalp tearing and burning as pitiless hands tugged at it, the skin flayed from my heels as they scraped along the ground, leaving dark trails of blood, while passers-by watched my anguished throes with indifferent curiosity. I wondered what they had in store for me. Would the Otomi want to practise his way of knocking out teeth with a flint knife, or would he use a finer blade, a sliver of obsidian perhaps, the sort that could part a man's skin from his flesh and his flesh from his bones and leave him still alive?

Strangely, I found that I did not care much. All that mattered was that I had failed. I would never find out what had happened to Nimble.

Then I looked again at the two men striding towards me.

Both were seasoned warriors: even in the torch's unreliable light, their hard, glittering eyes, thin determined mouths and sleek, sinewy arms and legs were enough to tell me that, and had I doubted their status, the hair piled on top of their heads would have confirmed it for me. However, neither of them was an Otomi. As soon as I realized that I felt a twinge of hope. The captain would not have sent anyone to come looking for me: he was the sort to have wanted to see to it himself.

These men were locals: the parish police. Every parish in the city had them. Someone had to keep order within the parish boundaries, whether this consisted of moving beggars and vagrants along, arresting drunkards or thieves or rounding up anyone who thought he could shirk a work detail or a spell of military service. Officially, they went by a variety of names – *Calpixque*, *Telpixque*, *Calpolleque* – and unofficially they got called a lot of other things, especially by people with a history of falling foul of the law.

The chief policeman's name, I was to learn, was Yectlacamlauhqui – 'Upright' – and his deputy's Chimalli, or 'Shield'. They were from Pochtlan, as I assumed they must be since they had been at the merchants' end of the bridge. Naturally they could call upon the men of their parish to lend a hand when their own unaided efforts would not do, although I would have bet they did not need to very often. The wall of muscle, bone and sinew that separated me from where I was trying to go might as well have been a mountain range for all my chances of getting past it.

I took a step back, risking a swift glance out of the corner of my eye in case there was anyone behind me threatening to cut off my retreat. I could not help but notice the swords both men carried. Upright's in particular caught the light, the obsidian blades set into its edges flashing as he toyed with it. I thought he looked nervous, and wondered if it had something to do with being out after dark, at a time when a god was thought to be haunting the streets. Or were they worried about meeting a human foe: whoever had killed and cut up the person I had found at the Amantlan end of the bridge?

It was easy to see what these men were doing. After what had happened here lately they would want to question everybody they saw, and woe betide anyone who could not give a convincing account of himself.

I took another step but was brought up short.

'I told you to stay where you are!' Suddenly Upright thrust his sword in my face and there were razor-sharp blades hovering under my nose. 'Don't think I won't use this. I don't have to kill you. I can carve you up like something on a meat stand in the marketplace and still leave you able to talk, and believe me that's what you'll do, you'll be that desperate for me to put you out of your misery. Now keep your feet still!'

I shied away from the blades. I bent my neck first and then my back until I was looking up at the sky and the weapon still pressed forward until I was on the point of losing my balance. I fought the urge to take another step, knowing it might be my last, and then it was too late anyway as my legs were buckling under me. Squawking in alarm, with my short, torn cloak billowing around me and my arms flapping as frantically as the wings of a frightened turkey, I went over, striking the hard surface under me with a bone-jarring crash that left my ears ringing and my backside numb.

Something clattered on to the wood by my hip.

I tried to get up on to my elbows, and bent my leg in a vain effort to cover the thing up with my thigh, but Upright was already standing over me with the sword hanging by his side and one foot poised over my chest. His narrow mouth twitched with amusement while he watched my struggles, and then, without a word, he casually planted his heel on my sternum and forced me down again.

'Shield,' he said quietly, gesturing with his sword as the air erupted from my lungs.

His companion, following the direction in which the weapon was pointing, stepped around his chief and stooped to pick up my son's knife. When I had taken my tumble it had fallen out of my breechcloth.

'A knife.' Shield took it in his free hand and inspected it, sniffing at it as delicately as a well-bred girl smelling popcorn flowers. 'It's metal! What is it – copper?'

I said nothing, although the pressure on my chest increased.

'Covered in blood! I think we may have our man.'

Upright's heel was threatening to drive my lowest rib into my liver. I gasped and arched my back involuntarily, my head snapping up to bring my eyes into line with the knife. Its point was aimed at my head as directly as an accuser's stare.

I tried to cry out in protest but it was impossible to draw breath. With every gasp I took, the foot jabbed me harder. My head swam and my vision began to blur.

Faintly, as if from a long way off, I heard Shield's voice saying: 'You ought to take your foot off his chest now, boss, he's about to pass out.'

'Why don't you wake him up, then.'

Even if I had understood what Upright meant I would have been too weak to do anything about it. At first all I knew was that the pressure on my chest had gone. My lungs filled themselves with a great spasmodic whoop followed by a fit of explosive, racking coughs that left me doubled over. The next I thing I knew, I was falling. Shield had taken his superior's suggestion as an order to pitch me over the side of the bridge.

Hitting the surface of the canal was like falling flat on my face on to flagstones, except that it gave way immediately and then I was enveloped by icy water. My shout of pain and surprise turned into a silent explosion of bubbles. Water filled my already tormented chest. I was swallowing the stuff and coughing and retching at the same time, while my arms made frantic, futile swimming motions. I tried to lash out with my heels, but could not move my legs. Something held them fast by the ankles.

An instant after that my head was in the air too, with water streaming out of my nose and mouth and my body thrashing and twisting like an animal in a snare. My feet were caught but my hands were free. My fingers curled spasmodically as I tried to grab something, anything, to stop my wild, sickening gyrations and let me start trying to work out which way was up, but there was nothing within reach.

'Right, he's awake,' Shield rasped. 'What now, another ducking?'

I made a feeble noise in response. Hearing the deputy's voice, I began to realize what had happened. He was holding me upside down, with my head just over the water's surface, and my hair dangling in it, its saturated weight tugging at my scalp.

I willed myself to stop struggling. Slowly the twisting and turning began to slow down. The pain in my stomach and chest began to subside and the choking and heaving ceased.

'Better find out who he is, first.'

'Oh, we'll do that, boss! We'll soak it out of him, it'll be like getting blood out of a tunic after a fight – lots of cold water!'

The agonizingly tight grip on my ankles slackened suddenly and I fell, my face hitting the icy water just at the moment when Shield's hands caught me and yanked me upward again with a nauseating lurch.

I came up twisting and swaying once more. The moment I stopped, my stomach emptied itself once more, sending water and whatever else it contained spewing out of my mouth into my nose and eyes, blinding me momentarily and sending a violent shudder through me that my tormentor obviously felt, because it made him laugh.

'Shall we see if we need another rinse, or what?' He dandled me like a baby, letting me fall towards the canal and snatching me up again before the surface touched me. 'Perhaps you'd rather tell me your name!'

I groaned. 'Joker,' I managed to gasp.

He seemed to think about my answer for a long time before making his mind up about it.

'So what?' he said indifferently, and a moment later my head was under water again.

When he hauled me out there was a sneer in his voice. 'That's not a name that means very much to me. You'll have to do better than that!'

Instead of dropping me in, he yanked me towards him. For a moment I felt myself swinging through space with the air whistling past my ears until my shoulders caught the wooden edge of the bridge with a sickening crack.

I screamed.

'We can split your head open!' Upright roared. 'We can drown you and make it take all night! We can cut your balls off!' he added gratuitously. 'Now talk!'

I felt dizzy. I could not see. The red darkness that had threatened to engulf me when I had a foot driving into my chest had come back. There was a roaring in my ears and I could feel my stomach heaving again even though it was empty. I could not tell the truth but to say nothing seemed a certain way to get myself killed.

I could think of only one thing to say: a name.

'Kindly!' I gasped.

The grip on my ankles slackened abruptly, although not enough to send me plunging into the canal again.

'What did he say?' Shield's voice was suddenly hushed.

'Kindly!' I spluttered again. 'The merchant! Kindly the merchant! I was going to see him! He'll vouch for me!'

For a moment, as I hung upside down over the water, I did not know how the police were going to take what I had said. All I knew was that I was in danger of having my brains knocked out against the side of the bridge like a fish killed for bait.

Shield muttered slowly: 'Kindly the merchant?'

A moment later I was swinging slowly through the air and being lowered, surprisingly gently, on to the surface of the bridge.

As my head made contact with the wood and the rest of me was laid down like a piece of cloth being measured out for cutting, I heard Upright add: 'I don't think I'd trust anybody that claimed to know that slippery old bugger! Still, if he says he can vouch for him, we had better check, hadn't we? If he's lying . . .'

I did not hear what would happen if I turned out to be lying, because that was when I passed out.

2

'This knife.' The speaker was an old man with a voice so feeble I had to strain to catch his words. 'Bronze. Very rare. What I'd want to know is, how did he get hold of it?'

All of a sudden he seemed to be shouting so loudly that I wanted to scream and cover my ears. A man's voice laughed as I squirmed. The sound of it came and went with the throbbing in my head. It was as if my ears were still full of water.

Something hit me on the shoulder. 'Awake now, are we? Come on, get up!'

I lay face down on an earth floor. I rolled over, opening my eyes and promptly squeezing them shut against the glare of a clear morning sky.

'Up!'

I pushed myself slowly into a sitting position, with my eyes still shut because I thought the World would be spinning around me and I did not want to have to watch it in case it started my stomach heaving again. I tried to swallow but my mouth and throat were as parched as a dead cactus in the dry season. I thought that was strange, considering that I had nearly drowned.

When I finally dared to look around me the first thing I noticed was that I was naked. With a hoarse croak of horror I pulled my knees up and spread a hand over my loins. That set off more laughter from the men watching me.

'Told you he'd do that!' It was Shield speaking. 'All the trouble he's in and the only thing he can think of is, where's his breechcloth?'

I scowled at him resentfully. He stood to one side of me with his arms folded nonchalantly. When I turned my head towards the other side I saw Upright, who was squatting with a bowl between his knees. He surprised me by pushing the bowl towards me.

'Have some water,' he suggested. 'We took those rags off you to make sure you weren't hiding anything else. We probably did you a favour. They were about to fall to pieces anyway.'

I took a cautious sip while I looked past the two men flanking me towards a third, the man whose voice I had first heard.

He knelt on a reed mat, with his old brown knees tucked under him in the style of a woman, no doubt because they were too stiff now for him to squat comfortably. He was a merchant. I could tell that much by his hair, which was long, falling loose and unadorned over his shouders. His cloak was short but finely woven, and even at a glance I could see how much trouble had been taken over its embroidery. Heavy bone plugs pulled at his lower lip and earlobes. The workmanship that had gone into carving them in the shapes of little fishes could not have come cheap.

This man had my son's knife, grasping the hilt between the thumb and forefinger of one hand and balancing the point on the palm of the other.

I looked at Upright as I put his bowl down. 'Where am I?' I hissed. 'Who's that?'

Shield took one step forward and flicked a foot casually into the side of my neck. I flopped over, howling in pain.

'You're here to answer questions, not ask them! Understand?'

I picked myself up again, noticing a little smear of blood where my elbow had struck the ground. 'I get the idea,' I muttered.

'I am Ozomatl,' the old man informed me. 'You are in my house and my parish. I expect you to show a bit of respect! If you've forgotten your manners, I'm sure Upright and Shield here will be happy to help you recall them!'

Ozomatl: I had heard the name, which meant 'Howling Monkey'. I realized I had even seen him before, at Kindly's house. He was the man the merchants of Tlatelolco looked to as leader: the man whose voice carried most weight in deciding which trader would have the honour of buying, training and sacrificing a Bathed Slave at festival time, who had the ear of the military governor who ruled their part of the city, and who presided over the merchants' councils and their courts. The merchants, both because of their wealth and because of the information they brought back from every corner of the World, were immensely powerful; so much so that even men such as my master and the Emperor had to listen to them. And Howling Monkey was the most powerful of the merchants.

His eyes roamed over the weapon in his fingers the way another man's might have dwelt on a pretty girl. I had never considered how much the knife might be worth, because I had thought of it only as my son's sole possession. Suddenly I saw it through the eyes of a merchant. Bronze was almost impossible to get in Mexico. The knife by itself must be worth a fortune, and if there were any chance that there might be more bronze where that had come from, any merchant would jump at it.

I licked my lips nervously. 'You, er, you want to know where I got the knife? Listen, the man you need to ask . . .'

A sharp cuff to the side of my head silenced me. I looked up to see Shield glaring at me, with his hand raised for another blow. Out of the corner of my eye, though, I noticed the old man leaning towards me, as if eager to hear whatever I had to say next. He said nothing, however, and was clearly willing to let his policemen speak for him.

'Forget where it came from, you murdering little piece of coyote dung! You're here to tell us what you did with it!'

I looked at Howling Monkey, the chief merchant, and then hastily back at Shield, in case he was on the point of hitting me again. 'I don't know what you mean. I was just looking after it. Murdering?' Suddenly the import of his words seized me, shaking me like hands wrapped around my throat and leaving me just as unable to speak. 'Murdering who?' I squeaked, swallowing convulsively to hold my gorge down as I pictured my son's face, lying in the latrine in Amantlan, amid pools and piles of ordure, surrounded by his own dismembered remains, his strong features collapsed, his clear young skin grey and streaked with mire.

A moment later I was whimpering in pain as Shield seized one of my ears, twisting it until he had forced my head around and could stare into my eyes.

'I told you you're not here to ask questions!' he snarled. 'Now stop whining and answer me! What did you do to Idle?'

'Stop it!' I squealed, pain and fear and self-disgust pushing me out of the reach of any sort of sensible restraint. 'Do you think I'd kill my own child? Cut him up like a sacrificial victim? How could you . . .?' Then the name he had given the dead man registered at last. 'Wait a moment. What did you say? Idle?'

Relief and the abrupt release of tension do strange things. All of a sudden the savage, inimical face looming over mine took on a comic aspect. The deep lines in the puckered, frowning brow were like those of some constipated old man, straining over a pot. The narrow, grim slit of a mouth was a child's drawing of unhappiness, a straight line with the edges turned down. The threatening growl in the back of the throat was the sort of noise my stomach made when I had not eaten for a day or so. I started giggling, and once I had started I could not stop.

'Idle?' Shield was still twisting my ear but for some reason it did not seem to hurt any more. 'You mean Skinny's brother? It was really him?'

'Of course it was really him. Who did you think you'd killed?' The big warrior pulled my head about as he shook with rage. 'Think this is funny, do you? I'll show you how funny it is!'

The hand holding my ear jerked sharply upward. Whimpering with pain, I was forced to scramble to my feet.

The blow was perfectly timed. I saw it coming when I was about halfway towards standing up, my body unfolded and exposed, unable either to straighten up or, with the tight grip on my ear, to collapse and roll away to safety. I could only wait and watch while the fist described a short arc that ended in the pit of my stomach.

I tried to scream but all that came out was a high, almost voiceless whistling. I lurched forward, gasping in agony while I tried to tear myself away from the relentless grip on my ear and curl up around my wounded abdomen. I managed to totter a couple of steps before Shield let me go. He snatched his hand away from my ear as if it were red hot and watched as I pitched forward on to the hard floor.

'Do you need to hear any more?' he roared. 'We found the knife on him. It's covered with blood. Plainly he used it to kill the featherworker's brother and cut the body up. He came back last night and we got him. And now here he is, laughing at you!'

With difficulty I hauled my face off the floor and raised my eyes towards the wealthy, powerful man staring at me from his reed mat.

'You don't understand!' I gasped. 'I was given the knife – Kindly gave me the knife! Why don't you ask him, and ask him where I was the night before last?'

The old man peering down at me answered coldly: 'We have. No doubt as soon as he wakes up and gets over his hangover he will tell us all about you. I expect we'll give whatever he has to say as much weight at it deserves.' From the stress he laid on 'deserves' I gathered that he expected anything that devious old man came up with to weigh about as much as a handful of turkey feathers. 'But he isn't here. You are. Now you heard Shield. The brother of a featherworker is dead. Merchants and featherworkers – and Pochtlan and Amantlan, their parishes – go back a very long way, and we look after one another. So when we catch you with the weapon that might have killed Idle and you yourself admit that you were here on the night the deed was done, what do you expect us to make of it?'

'But I didn't kill him!' I protested. 'All right, I admit I found the body – you'd have to have been blind and deaf with no sense of smell to miss it. I had the knife because Kindly gave it to me – that's the truth!'

From where he stood next to me, Upright bent down to whisper confidingly in my ear. 'So convince him. Think of this as a trial and him as the judge.'

'You can't try me! I wasn't even in one of your parishes when these two picked me up.' Shield growled threateningly. 'I'm not one of yours, either. I don't come from Tlatelolco, I'm a Tenochca. Do you have any idea what will happen to you all if you don't let me go?'

From the knowing, shrewd look on Howling Monkey's face, I gathered I had made a big mistake.

The next thing I knew I was staring at the sky, or rather squinting at it through eyes narrowed with pain as Shield seized me by the scalp and jerked my head backward. 'Watch your tongue or I'll cut it out of your head, you worthless little pool of dog piss!'

He threw my head forward until I was looking at the chief merchant once more.

'Thank you, Shield,' the old man said smoothly. 'Of course, Joker may be right. We don't know what will follow from anything we do to him, do we? I could ask you to cut his throat and throw him in the nearest canal. I could take him at his word and tell you to carry him back to Tenochtitlan – hand him over to the Emperor, perhaps, or maybe the Chief Minister?'

He grinned at me, his teeth bared like a flayed skull's, as he watched the effect of his words flow over my face like floodwater, leaving devastation in its wake. I tried not to let my terror show but it was no good, and I could feel my eyes widening and my mouth growing slack at the threat of being handed back to my master. Howling Monkey surely could not know to whom I belonged, but he had obviously guessed that I was a runaway slave up to no good.

'I can tell you don't think that's a good idea. Well then, you'd better help us out, hadn't you?'

'Put it another way,' Shield hissed in my ear. 'If you don't tell him the truth, I'll scalp you!'

I did not know what to do. What could I say that would satisfy these men, especially if their chief thought he already knew what I was and was merely playing with me? Perhaps I could pretend to be a slave of Kindly's, and hope against hope that he would not disown me. Surely, I thought, he would not risk abandoning me where I might be forced to tell the World about the illicitly acquired merchandise he had asked me to find.

'You really ought to tell him, you know.' I gritted my teeth at the sound of Upright's voice: his helpful advice was beginning to annoy me, especially since I knew he would be just as willing to skin me alive as his deputy was. I wondered how they decided which of them was to bully the suspect and which to befriend him. Did they throw a bean in the air and see which side up it landed or just take turns? 'It's going to come out anyway, in the end.'

I stared at Howling Monkey and swallowed nervously as I finally made up my mind what to say to him. I was going to be Kindly's new slave, and then at least they would have a story that they would have to investigate, and in the time it took them to do that, I would try to think of something else, in case the old man failed to back me up.

'I . . .'

'You want to know who he is? I'll tell you!'

The voice came from behind me, from the entrance to Howling Monkey's house, and it rang across the broad space around me as loud and clear as a trumpet announcing the dawn. I recognized it, but could not believe my ears. I turned, scrambling on to one knee to get a better look, heedless of the risk that Shield would clout me for daring to get up without permission; in the event he was as fascinated by the newcomer as I was, and so were the other two. They all ignored me as their eyes tracked her uncertainly across the courtyard.

Lily had put on reed sandals to come out that morning. Their clattering as she strode towards the silent men had the sort of portentous, threatening note a warrior strives for when he beats his spear against his shield before a battle. They must have been the only sound any of us heard, because I was not breathing and I was sure that nobody else was either.

She looked magnificent. She had put on what must have been her finest clothes: a long shift over a matching skirt, in pale yellow and lilac in a jagged pattern like lightning bolts, both made of cotton, in brazen defiance of all convention and the law. Gold pendants hung from her earlobes, descending over her shoulders in sparkling cascades that were shot through with the green of jade or emerald. Her hair was unbound, as it must be while she was in mourning for her son, but she had not neglected it: it had been brushed until it billowed about her head and neck in a magnificent black and silver mane, waving in time to her steps.

She held her head up. Her eyes seemed to catch the sun and flare dangerously as she walked straight towards the chief merchant.

The woman acknowledged me with barely a glance. Suddenly recollecting myself, I hastily covered my groin with my hands again, but she had already looked away.

'He's mine,' she snapped, standing over Howling Monkey with her arms folded, the way a priest at the House of Tears might have done when about to reproach a novice for forgetting the words to a hymn. 'He's a slave in my household. What is he doing here?'

Howling Monkey struggled to get to his feet. I noticed with some amusement that, even drawn up to his full height, the top of the old man's head barely came up to the level of Lily's chin. 'He's under arrest,' he spluttered. 'We were trying to decide what to do with him. He didn't tell us he had anything to do with you.'

'If you left it up to those two clowns,' Lily snapped, with the briefest glance at Upright and Shield, 'I'm not surprised! I doubt if they could have got him to tell them his name!'

'We did, too!' cried Shield. A brief, contemptuous glance from the woman shut him up.

I marvelled at the change that had come over Lily.

When I had seen her and Howling Monkey in her own

house, not so many days before, she had been at his mercy, forced to listen to a humiliating harangue about her son's conduct at a time when her family was impoverished and barely able to fend for itself. Now her son was dead and she had recovered her wealth. It was hard to know whether the cause was the confidence born of being able to trade again or the belief that with her only child gone she had nothing further to lose, but for whatever reason she was plainly now in no mood to take any nonsense from anybody.

'Now where are his clothes?' she demanded. I felt my face heat up as another contemptuous glance swept over me. 'Where's his cloak, his breechcloth?'

Upright spoke up. 'Madam, they were just rags . . .' he stammered.

'By the time you'd finished with them, I expect so! What of it? Get him some new ones!'

'Now wait a moment!' Howling Monkey spluttered. 'A man's been killed, you know, and we have to investigate that.'

'No you don't,' she said brusquely. 'As I understand it he wasn't found in one of our parishes but next door, in Amantlan. What's it got to do with you?'

'This knife was found on him.'

Howling Monkey made the mistake of proffering the weapon, which was promptly snatched from him.

'Mine,' Lily asserted. 'That's it, isn't it? I thought as much when your messenger came to my house, looking for my father. I knew what you were about the moment I heard him mention the knife. You thought you'd happened upon a source of Tarascan bronze and you could help yourself to it. Well, sorry to disappoint you. This is the only one there is and it's been in my family for years, as a memento. Now, where's your evidence?'

'Evidence?' The merchant's voice had become an indignant squeak. 'My men found him near the body . . .'

'No they didn't! The messenger that came looking for my father said he was picked up this morning. The featherworker's remains were taken away yesterday. And besides, what do you mean, "your" men? I thought they worked for the parish!'

'But the knife!' Howling Monkey stammered desperately. 'It's covered with blood!'

'Our own,' Lily cried instantly. She must have had the answer to that worked out before she had come out that morning. 'Whenever we sacrifice our blood to Yacatecuhtli we always slit our earlobes and tongues with this knife. It's a family custom. What, you didn't know? It's how we remind the god where we got the knife, where our prosperity and his gifts come from.'

'What if I believe you?' Howling Monkey sounded genuinely puzzled. 'If this man Joker really is your slave, and he had some business with that knife, what then? How do you explain what happened to Idle?'

Lily snorted derisively. 'He didn't have any business with the knife at all! He was trying to steal it!' Then, as the predatory gleam flared up in the old merchant's eyes again, she added brutally: 'Of course, he was probably hoping someone like you would give him a good price! But he's my slave and I have the right to punish him for that. As for the featherworker's brother, I am sorry to hear about him but he really isn't my problem. Let the Amanteca find themselves a real suspect!'

With that, she turned her back on the chief of the merchants' parishes with as much haughty disdain as if he had been some disreputable foreign trader who had just offered her an insultingly low price for her earplugs. She strode between the silent, astonished policemen and stopped in front of me.

'Up you get, you! You have a lot of explaining to do!'

One hand still hovered uncertainly over my private parts as I blinked up at her. 'I haven't got anything to wear,' I whispered plaintively. It made no difference that the woman had seen me with no clothes on. She had seen as much before, although her manner towards me had been very different then. I simply could not contemplate being led naked through the streets of Tlatelolco, bent over, with my head bowed to avoid the astonished gaze of my fellow Aztecs.

Lily turned to Shield and snapped: 'I asked for someone to replace his clothes! It's not as if he needs anything decent. Go on, before I start getting angry!'

Shield slouched away, muttering to himself. A few moments later he was back with a breechcloth and a cape. They were plain, but better than anything I usually wore.

As I dressed I heard a step and, looking up, saw that Howling Monkey had relinquished his place on the mat to stand beside Lily.

'What are you intending to do?' he demanded.

'Take this slave home and punish him!'

'We haven't finished questioning him!'

'Questioning him about what? I told you where he got the knife from and what he was planning to do with it. That's nothing to do with you or anyone else!'

'But the body . . . Idle . . .'

Ignoring him, the woman bent forward and, encircling my forearm in a surprisingly strong grip, she dragged me to my feet. 'Come on, you! Now,' she added, glaring once more at the chief merchant, 'I am going to take my property home, unless anybody proposes to stop me.'

Howling Monkey looked sick. He was in a difficult position. He had clearly been ready to enjoy wringing the truth out of me, with the enthusiastic help of his policemen, but Lily's unexpected arrival and insistence that I belonged to her changed everything. I wondered at this, because where I came from, in Tenochtitlan, a woman's voice, while it might be law in her own home, would not have been heard among men in another's courtyard. Among the merchants of Tlatelolco, though, things were different. Women were left to run family businesses while the men were abroad, they decided what to bring to market and at what price, and women even served in their own right as directors of the marketplace. If I really were Lily's slave, then the merchants' chief would have no authority over me, unless he had real evidence that I had anything to do with Idle's death.

He turned away.

'All right,' he muttered darkly. 'You take him, then. But if I hear he's been seen in Pochtlan, or any of our other parishes, after today, I'll have Upright and Shield knock his brains out – and you'll answer for it as well! Just remember this, Lily. We have unfinished business. You may have got your family's money back again, but I haven't forgotten how your boy disgraced himself and his people. I still intend to get to the bottom of that!'

'Oh, don't worry,', said the woman softly. 'So do I!'

With another tug at my arm, none too gentle, she led me out of the courtyard.

3

Lily maintained a grim silence as she strode briskly towards the canal and a waiting canoe. Following in her footsteps, I felt like a small child caught stealing cactus fruit from the market and being dragged home by his mother to face a beating.

'Lily . . .'

'Shut up. Get in the boat!'

'I just wanted to say "thank you",' I said meekly.

'I told you to get in the boat.' She turned to me suddenly. 'And save your gratitude! I didn't get you out of there for your own good. Those two bears of policemen could have spent the rest of the day working you over, for all I care! And if you don't tell me what I want to know, then I'll take you straight back there and invite them to make a start on you. I might even watch!'

Her hands were clenched around the material of her skirt, bunching the cloth and crumpling it the way a cook might crush coriander leaves to squeeze the flavour out of them. When I looked in her eyes they were hooded as if with rage, but they glistened too, as if full of tears.

'Look, I know it can't have been easy . . .'

She hit me suddenly, swinging her open hand against my cheek with a ringing slap that left a hot streak of pain against my lower jaw.

I stared at her, slack jawed, until I became aware of the salty taste of blood and realized that the blow had made me bite my tongue. She said nothing but looked pointedly at the canoe. I climbed in meekly, settling myself in front of the boatman. He was Partridge, Kindly's slave who had brought me the knife, but he gave no sign of having recognized me.

'You know where to go,' the woman said sharply, as he pushed off from the side of the canal. 'And as for you,' she added, looking at me, 'you can start telling me the truth. I want to know what you did to my son!'

'Lion and I told you what happened,' I said blandly.

'You lied! You killed him – you and your brute of a brother!'

'How can you say that?' I felt the blood drain from my face, leaving it chill and numb, as if she had thrown a pitcher of cold water over it. If she had guessed the truth then there was no telling where that would lead.

She leaned forward and hissed into my face like a snake about to bury its fangs in my cheek. 'I know what Shining Light was doing on that boat. I know what he and Nimble had been doing between them. Now I want to know why you and your brother killed him. Revenge, was that it? Or was it because of what he and your son had been up to? Did you hate him for that? Or did you just want to spite me, because a few moments with you on a sleeping-mat didn't make me your devoted slave for ever?'

Partridge's eyes nearly fell out of his head at that, but he kept his face impassive and his gaze fixed on the water in front of him. I glanced anxiously at the Sun and realized, with a nervous start, that we were heading south, towards Tenochtitlan, and not towards Lily's home in Pochtlan. I gripped the side of the canoe tensely as it occurred to me that she might be intending to give me back to my master.

I wondered how she had guessed the truth, or whether perhaps Kindly had deduced it in the same uncanny way in which
he had worked out that Nimble was my son. I thought about
trying to escape. I could have leapt over the side and swum to
the shore of the canal, but the thought of scuttling away to
hide among the neighbouring houses with her taunts and
sneers ringing in my ears, like a cockroach dodging blows
from a furious housewife's broom, was too appalling to contemplate. The truth had to come out, but as I looked into her
eyes and saw the pain in them – the raw skin under the lids,
the spider's webs of broken red lines traced over the whites and
the dark furrows on her cheeks from night after night of weeping – I suddenly felt more pity than anything else.

'It wasn't any of those,' I heard myself saying. 'It was just
self-defence. We – Lion and I – wanted to make Shining Light
give up his sword, but he tried to kill me. There wasn't anything else we could do. We could have spared you the
truth . . .'

'You wanted to spare your son, and yourself from having to
explain what he was doing on that boat!'

'Well, that too,' I conceded.

'Who killed him? Who drove that sword into his skull – you
or your brother?'

'Does it matter? Lily, you know what Shining Light did.
Don't make me tell you all over again.'

Astonishingly, she laughed. It was a sort of laughter I had
not heard before, a thin, bitter sound that seemed to come
from high up near the bridge of her nose rather than her
mouth, and had no amusement in it whatsoever. 'Tell me? You
don't have to. I know what he was, but he was my son!' The
laughter shattered then, splintering into a shower of muffled
tears as she buried her face in her hands, and I stared hopelessly
at her bowed head and heaving shoulders. For an instant I

thought she might pitch forward into my arms. I even raised my hands, ready to catch her, but her pride and anger were too strong for that.

At last she looked up again. Her palms glistened damply as she lowered them into her lap.

'Just tell me who it was,' she whispered. 'I just have to know.'

'Lion,' I said reluctantly, because now there seemed no reason to lie. 'But Lily, Shining Light did have his hands around my throat at the time!'

'And what had you and your brother done to him? You goaded him into it, didn't you? What did you do, taunt him with your cleverness, just because you'd managed to find out where he was hiding?'

'It wasn't anything like that. Lily, he . . . he was desperate. He knew he would never have been allowed to live. My master would have killed him – he'd have had him burned alive. You know he could have done that. Shining Light hadn't just swindled the Chief Minister, he was a murderer, and he and Nimble were . . . well, you know the penalty for what they did together.' I found it hard, even now, to acknowledge the crime my son and his lover had committed. I understood, as well as any Aztec could hope to, what had driven the two of them into each other's arms, but nothing in my upbringing or teaching had equipped me to look at an offence against the gods with anything but disgust.

Lily would not meet my eyes. She looked over my shoulder, at something in the middle distance. When I turned around and saw what it was I felt as if my stomach were about to fall through the bottom of the canoe, because right up ahead of us, at the edge of a broad, traffic-choked canal, stood one of the tall stone cacti that marked the boundary between Tlatelolco and Tenochtitlan. I was being taken back to my master.

I turned back to her. 'Lily,' I said earnestly, 'you have to listen to me! I didn't want your son to die. He wanted it himself and he wanted to take me with him! Don't you understand?'

She kept her head up. Her eyes were dry and clear now, and her fingers lay still in the folds of her skirt without any trace of a tremor.

'I understand,' she said steadily. 'You and your brother killed my son.'

'Yes . . . no, wait, didn't you hear what I said?'

She looked at me then and gave me the thinnest of smiles. 'I've heard as much as I want to from you. Anything else you want to say, you can save for your master.'

I gaped at her in horror.

'What did you expect?' she asked coldly. 'You heard what Howling Monkey said – if you're seen in Tlatelolco again there'll be trouble. I'm taking you back to Lord Feathered in Black. No doubt he'll be fascinated to know what you've been doing during the last couple of days.'

'But he'll kill me!' I cried, and then, realizing that in her present state of mind that was unlikely to do me much good, I added: 'I could tell him about your son – how he cheated him, what he and Nimble got up to . . .' My voice tailed off as we both realized what I was saying.

'You'll tell him what your own boy did to him, will you? I don't think so. He can't hurt mine any more.' She lifted her eyes. 'Here we are – Tenochtitlan. Better start thinking about what you're going to tell your master, slave.'

Ahead of us, looming over the houses and public buildings fronting the canal, I saw the pyramids of the Heart of the World, dark, angular masses against the afternoon sky. Tallest of all was the double pyramid belonging to Huitzilopochtli the war-god and Tlaloc the rain-god. How long would it be, I wondered, before I was dragged up the bloodstained steps on its western face to have my chest slashed open by the Fire Priest's flint knife?

And that's only if you're lucky, I told myself, as I stared desperately into the indifferent faces of the men poling and paddling canoes along the great waterway, while our own boatman tried with some difficulty to get us into the thick stream of traffic. I looked over the canoe's side towards the bank, speculating on my chances of swimming to freedom.

'What are you waiting for?' Lily snapped, as if reading my thoughts.

'A gap,' Partridge said sullenly. 'All right, here goes!'

He dug his paddle into the water, driving us forward in a cloud of spray.

I could not see the space he had found. So far as I could make out the two vessels in front of us were nose to tail. In front was a big, scruffy barge, hacked out of the carcass of a whole tree. It lay low in the water, pressed down by the weight of its cargo of long, rough-hewn planks. The sweating labourer struggling to push it along with his paddle wore only a breechcloth and a surly look. Immediately following the barge was an entirely different sort of craft, small and well made, its wood carved into an elegant shape that tapered sharply at each end, smoothed until it almost shone and painted a rich green. Its middle section was shaded by a cotton canopy with bright parrot and hummingbird feathers around its edges and at its corners. The man paddling it was better dressed than most boatmen, with a short, netted cape billowing around his shoulders, as well as the obligatory breechcloth. He cursed impatiently as he tried to find a way around the great lumbering thing in front of him.

Suddenly he had something new to swear at, as Lily's canoe swung into his path.

'Look out, you clumsy sod! Where do you think you're going?' he screamed, as he sank the blade of his paddle into the water and twisted it frantically in an effort to slow his boat down and prevent a collision. 'This is a new paint job!'

All he got in reply was a grunt as Partridge deftly begun to swing Lily's craft into line. I had to admire his skill: he had timed the manoeuvre to perfection, leaving little more than a finger's breadth between his own charge and the cargo boat in front and the rich man's canoe behind. However, his calculations had not included the presence in his boat of a desperate slave.

As the stern of the big vessel ahead of us swung across our bow, I leapt up, ignoring the violent rocking this produced, and let myself fall over while I clawed desperately at the side of the other craft. At the same time I kicked, pushing against the bottom of Lily's boat with both feet as hard as I could. It worked. Suddenly we were no longer turning to follow the traffic. My kick exactly countered Partridge's efforts, leaving the canoe stopped in the water for the space of a heartbeat before the boat behind ran into it with a crash that sent Lily, her boatman and the man in charge of the vessel behind tumbling overboard.

I clung with both hands to the big boat. It continued on its way, unaffected by the chaos behind it, and all but wrenched my fingers out of their sockets as it plucked me bodily from the wreckage.

I fell into the water, suspended by one aching arm from the barge's side. For a few moments I was dragged along, spluttering and choking and gasping for breath, until at last I managed to get a grip on the damp wood with my other hand.

'Give me a lift up with your paddle!' I cried.

The boatman looked at me over the stern of his craft. He seemed oddly unsurprised. 'Why should I?'

'I'll give you my cloak.'

'It's all wet.'

'It'll dry out. Are you going to get a better offer?'

He thought about that for a moment, before dipping his paddle once in the water to push his boat along and then extending the dripping blade to me. 'All right, but mind you don't tear that cloak!'

The bargeman left me at Copolco in the west of the city, from where it was easy to get to the causeway in time to blend in with the crowd streaming across the lake towards their homes in Tlacopan or Popotla or any of the other towns and villages dotting the shore. With my cloak carefully folded and tucked away in the one clean and dry spot on the barge, my breech-cloth sodden and stained and my hair unkempt, I looked like any serf or slave or day-labourer returning home for the night.

I was tempted to rest when I reached the western shore of the lake, to find some quiet spot where I could simply sit and bask in the blissful realization that the body I had found had not been my son's. I wanted to laugh and weep for joy, but I could not spare the time. The Otomies might still be combing this countryside, looking for me, and I was convinced that if Nimble was still alive then he needed me and I had to get to him as quickly as I could. The only lead I had was still the costume. The task of finding that would not have been made any easier by Idle's death, since I had assumed that he had it, but I had to try. That meant going back into Mexico. In any event my son must be in the city somewhere. I was certain he had gone back there to retrieve his knife.

I knew he valued the weapon not for itself but for the last link it gave him with his former life, with the mother he had never known and with the man who had raised him and protected him out of love for her. I tried not to believe that he had killed Idle, either for the sake of the knife or for any other reason, but it made little difference.

Now Lily had the knife. I wondered what Nimble would do if he knew that. Would he try to take it from her too? The thought made me shudder as I realized how easy it might be for her to lay a trap for him. The way she had treated me showed what an appetite she had for revenge. Her son and his lover had duped her cruelly, and it would not be surprising if she hated the young man for it.

As I crossed the causeway, all of this passed through my mind, along with the practical problem I now faced: I was in danger not only from my master and the Otomies but also from the police in at least one parish, not to mention Lily. To return to the city, I concluded, I would need a disguise: a role I could slip into easily and convincingly. What might that be?

A sly grin spread across my face when I thought of the solution.

Once on dry land I turned aside from the jostling crowd and made my way up through the forests and fields into the low hills that edged the valley, the foothills of the mist-covered mountains that walled off the civilized world from the barbarians outside. I avoided the terraced fields and the houses scattered among them, climbing up under cover of the trees where I could, until I was far enough away from the lake shore to be reasonably certain that no one would recognize me. After that I took less care, scrambling up the bank separating a plot from the one directly above it, walking straight across a field freshly sown with spring flowers, squeezing between the tall fleshy leaves of the maguey plants that edged the field and skirting the wood above it.

Just beyond that I found what I had been looking for. The ground rose away from me towards the mountains. A track crossed it, a vague but clearly distinguishable line worn by generations of feet making their way between the woods on one side and the bare hillside with its cacti and clumps of coarse greenery on the other. About twenty paces in front of me and right in the middle of the track was a stain: a large round patch of dark grey ash that showed where many fires had been lit over the years.

I breathed a sight of relief, knowing that my memory had not failed me and I had indeed found the place again after all these years.

I did not think anyone would be using it now. All the same, I took the precaution of arming myself with a fallen branch from an ash tree before approaching the place. I brandished it in front of me like a club as I stepped out into the last of the evening sunlight, looking constantly from right to left.

No one disturbed me as I stood over the place, or as I knelt down and, laying the branch aside, plunged both hands into the black ash and started rubbing it vigorously into my face.

As soon as I was satisfied that my skin must be stained as black as a priest's I sat on a tree stump a few paces off the track and looked around.

A layer of cloud was rolling in, threatening to plunge the valley into darkness. The branches above and around me were vague dark shapes against a sky that was not much paler, as indistinct and threatening as the memory of a nightmare. Soon there would be no light at all.

Far away, something howled, a long, anguished cry that stopped as sharply as the scream of a man falling from a cliff. From much nearer I heard a rustling sound that I could not identify, except that whatever made it must have been bigger than a shrew and smaller than a jaguar.

Later, I knew, once the priests had sounded the midnight trumpet from the tops of the temples, an undeniably human noise would arise from the vast slumbering city at the centre of the valley floor and drift out across the lake and up to me in the hills: the sound of singing, as the boys and young men of the Houses of Youth raised their voices to show our neighbours and enemies that Aztecs never slept and were always alert. Until then, I had only the creatures of the night for company: weasels, centipedes, badgers, owls – every one of them, in Aztec eyes, a monster, a portent of death.

I shivered. It was getting colder. The clouds overhead meant there would be no frost, for which I was thankful, although they threatened rain, which would be almost as unpleasant for a man stuck out of doors with no cloak. I tried to reassure myself. As a priest I had been trained to venture into the darkness, to face the horrors that would leave most of my fellow Aztecs petrified, and defeat them. I had fought the spirits that haunted the night air while patrolling these very hills, and had survived, and taken pride in having kept them from the men, women and children sleeping in the valley below. I knew they could be beaten, and besides, they were essential to my plan.

I waited on my tree stump until my backside grew numb and the cold became so intense that I no longer had the energy to make my teeth chatter. I lost any sense of the passage of time. Unable to see the stars overhead, I had no idea how long it was until midnight, and then I found myself wondering whether I had passed out and missed the trumpets, for it would have been the easiest thing in the darkness for my eyes to close of their own accord for a few moments or half the night without my noticing.

I sat bolt upright, jerking myself awake.

There was a new noise among the rustlings and scamperings and snufflings filling the woods close by. I turned my head this way and that, listening intently to make sure I had heard it, and could catch it again. My wait was over.

Something was moving towards me. It was large, and proceeded more purposefully and less furtively than an animal hunting by night. As I heard the steady but cautious tread approaching, pausing and then moving away as it moved along the track, I knew that my plan appeared to be working. What I was listening to was a priest, making his rounds in the hills circling the city, walking a path so well known that he could find his way along it in the dark. Soon he would stop to make an offering to the gods, burning a bundle of reeds and censing the air with copal resin.

I walked slowly up the path behind the priest and stopped a few paces back from where I knew he would lay his reeds down and reach for his fire stick: the patch of ash I had found before nightfall. I was close enough to hear the scratching noise it made as he whirled the stick around to strike sparks from it, while my hand tensed around the knobby lump of wood I had picked up to defend myself with.

Suddenly the reeds flared into life, sending bright orange flames skyward, blindingly bright after the unrelieved darkness that had surrounded me since sunset, while the flames' roar and crackle filled my ears.

I turned aside, trying to blink away the ghostly green shapes that danced in front of my eyes. I forced myself to turn back again, to squint into the fire, knowing that reeds do not burn for long, and I had moments only in which to bring my plan off.

The priest was clearly visible, or at least his shadow was, a dark shape hunched before his fire.

I stepped forward slowly and trod on a large thorn.

I howled. I yelped and shrieked like a demon, jumping up and down on my good foot while my improvised club swung madly through the air.

The priest leapt to his feet with a shout of alarm. He spun around, brandishing his censer before him, and sending a sweet-smelling, choking cloud towards me.

'Who are you?' he cried. His voice trembled but he was a brave man and he was standing his ground. 'What are you? Are you a man, or a demon, or a spirit, or a god?'

I could not see his face with the firelight behind it. I hoped he could not see mine, although I was still hopping around so much that it cannot have been more than a blur.

'I am Ehecatl!' I cried. 'The Lord of the Night Wind!' I forced myself to stop hopping and planted the toes of my injured foot on the ground. I took another step forward, and walked into the cloud of incense. Suddenly to my troubles was added the urge to sneeze.

'M-my Lord?' The priest's voice was that of a young man, terrified but determined to prove himself. I felt a twinge of remorse for what I had to do. I felt as if I were hearing myself, twenty years before, and wondered what he thought he was confronting: a god indeed, or the transfigured soul of a magician, out for a night of mayhem, or maybe just a man, desperate enough to be here on his own and for all he knew as frightened as he was.

'Prostrate yourself!' I cried, lurching forward on my good foot.

He ignored my order, instead thrusting his censer towards me again and waving it about to send more waves of scent over me. Now the desire to sneeze was almost overwhelming and I had to clap my free hand over my nose and mouth as I swung my stick, catching the censer and sending it flying.

The effect was dramatic. The priest howled, and a moment later I had my wish as he threw himself to the ground, cowering before me like a beaten warrior inviting his captor to seize his hair in the ritual gesture of victory and so set him on the road all warriors were meant to desire: the road that led to the temples of Mexico and a flowery death at the hands of the Fire Priest.

His hair, greasy as priests' hair often was, since they were not allowed to wash it during fasts, glistened in the firelight. I was glad there was so much of it, as it would cushion the blow and make what I had to do next so much easier.

I brought the length of ash down on the top of his head with enough force to split the wood and send a jarring pain up my arm.

My victim slumped silently on to the forest floor.

I stood there for a moment, not daring to believe it had worked, until he had lain still at my feet for long enough to convince me. Then, with a long, loud groan, I collapsed next to him.

4

Ilay beside the unconscious priest for a while, enjoying the heat from his fire until it began to diminish and I realized that if I did not exert myself by gathering some more fuel it would soon go out.

When I tried to stand I remembered the thorn in my foot. I yelped, hopping about until I fell over again. I sat awkwardly, gritting my teeth as I delicately extracted the thing from my tender flesh. Holding it up to the fire, I heard myself grunt in surprised recognition. It was a long, thin cactus spine. My unwitting companion must have dropped it. It would have been an essential tool for him, for bloodletting, offering the gods one's own precious water of life, which was as much a part of a priest's life as sleeping and eating. I felt a twinge of envy as I looked down at the figure hunched by the fire, and then remorse as I bent my head to listen to his breathing and check that it was still smooth and even. I had been just like him, once.

I got to my feet again and hobbled about, collecting sticks and laying them carefully across the smouldering reeds. The flames gradually built up again, the roar and crackle subsiding to the duller, steadier sound of a well-made fire. It would burn till morning, I judged, or almost; in any event, long enough to keep the coyotes and the cold at bay.

I turned back to the felled priest.

'Now,' I said, as I proceeded to strip the man's clothes from him, 'I want you to understand that there's a good reason for this.' I lied. The less he understood the better. 'After all,' I added, as with some distaste I tugged at the loose ends of his breechcloth, 'it won't do you any good if you complain. Your friends will only think you've been at the sacred mushrooms!'

Fortunately the only answer I got was a loud snore.

I stripped my own breechcloth off and then, on impulse, tied it around the priest's loins so that he was at least no worse dressed than I had been. It is no easy matter dressing an inert body, and it took longer than I would have expected, but having been so recently left naked I could all too easily feel for a man forced to stumble back to the city with his face burning and his hands locked together protectively over his private parts. It was going to be difficult enough for him to explain himself as it was.

As I finished dressing myself in his clothes, pulling the cord of his tobacco pouch over my head and tying the ends of his black cloak over my right shoulder, I looked around me once more, squinting through the trees and up at the sky. I still had no clue as to how much time I had before dawn, and before the hunt resumed for my son. I could happily have wrapped the priest's cloak around me, curled up and gone to sleep by the comforting warmth of the fire, but I could not risk losing the time, not to mention the chance that the man I had hit over the head might wake up before I did.

I looked down at myself. My face itched under its coating of ash. My cloak fell about me like a black cloud. Suddenly, for the first time in many years, I felt that I belonged to the darkness, to the high, secret places the priests frequented, to the hills by night and the unlit niches at the backs of temples.

There was something missing.

It took me a moment to work out what it was, and then I knew, because I could still feel it, digging into my palm. When I opened my hand I could see it lying there, glistening faintly in the firelight: the maguey spine I had trodden on, with my own blood still drying on it.

Then I understood what I had to do, and it was right, not merely to perfect my disguise, but to give his due to whatever god the priest had meant to sacrifice his blood to. Without hesitation I drove the spine into each of my earlobes in turn, twisting it until I could feel the liquid warmth of my blood flowing down my jawline.

The pain was slight, nothing compared to the sensation that came over me in its wake: a strange contentment, as if I were making a kind of peace with the man I had once been. As I stared at the bloodied thorn in my palm I grasped the feeling and savoured it. For a morning, perhaps as much as a day, I could be a priest again, dedicated to the gods, my standing among the Aztecs secure and recognized, respected, even held in awe, by anyone I was likely to meet.

I held the thorn up by my thumb and forefinger, watching it glisten in the firelight. I did not know whether the man lying at my feet had made his offering or not. I knew that he would have kept the thorn, intending to return it to the Priest House, where it, along with many others, would be stuck in a ball of straw and placed reverentially in a stone casket. That was not going to happen now but I did the best I could. I looked up at the utterly black sky, towards the thirteen heavens, and prayed to the god I knew best, the one I had been dedicated to from birth.

'O Tezcatlipoca,' I whispered. 'O Lord, I was your servant once. Now I am again – for a little while. You know you could crush me like a beetle without an instant's thought. I'm asking you to save it till tomorrow, do you understand? I'm your man today. I've given my blood to you. Don't let me down now.'

I could hear my voice faltering. I was only too aware that the god I was praying to loved nothing better than letting people down.

I waved the thorn in a vaguely easterly direction, to scatter a drop or two of blood towards the Sun, on the assumption that he would be rising soon, and then, for good measure, threw it in the fire. The prone figure curled up beside it caught my eye. I looked down at him for a moment and then turned back towards the heavens.

'Oh, and say a few words to whichever god this poor bugger serves, won't you?'

There being nothing more I could do for my victim, I left him and headed downhill, back towards the city.

I had not gone more than a few paces before I began to feel a little less charitable towards the unwitting donor of my disguise. By the time I had come within sight of the lake and the unmistakable spectacle of my home city, the light of countless temple fires glowing steadily while their reflections danced on the surface of the water, I was cursing him.

'Bastard!' I muttered, my fingernails digging furiously inside my purloined breechcloth. 'Lousy bastard! I hope the sodding coyotes chew your balls off!'

The priest had been on a fast. I had no idea how long it had been since he had last washed, but it must have been many days. I could have sworn that some of his fleas were as large as small dogs, and they were clearly relishing their change of diet.

I had half a mind to give up the pretence of being a priest there and then, to discard my stolen costume and throw myself, naked, into the lake, but I restrained myself, gritting my teeth against the relentless itching and telling myself that I had been trained to endure worse than this.

Instead of taking the bath I craved, I sat down opposite my city and waited for the sky to lighten and the Sun to rise over its fields and temples and houses and the mountains beyond.

FIVE DOG

1

I returned to the city in the midst of the pre-dawn rush over the causeway towards Mexico's fields and markets. This time there was no question of blending invisibly into the crowd, but it did not matter. I basked at the centre of a respectful space, secure in the knowledge that anyone glancing at me would see only the soot on my face, the blood drying along my jawline and my black, soiled cloak. There were few anywhere in the valley who would look me in the eye or openly wonder what a priest was doing pushing his way into the city along with everybody else at this time of the morning.

It was an intoxicating feeling. As I strolled through the throng as fast as it could part around me, I kept my eyes on the floor to hide the incongruous smile that kept threatening to break out on my face. I mumbled to myself, not because I wanted people to think I was communing privately with a god or rehearsing a hymn, but to stop myself from giggling helplessly. I was happy. All the years that had passed since I had been thrown out of the Priest House seemed to fall away. I felt as if I were coming home; more than that, I felt, just for a little while, as though I had never left.

It was only when I set foot on Mexico's soil, with the lake and the waterlogged fields that bordered it behind me and the people around me scattering as they went about their business, that it occurred to me that, however impressive my disguise might be, it could not change the fact that I was exhausted and famished and had practically no idea what to do next.

I was standing in a little plaza with a short, stumpy pyramid at its far end. With its dozen or so steps and its single shrine, a thatched shelter at its summit barely tall enough for a man to stand up in, it might have been a baby of one of the mighty edifices that towered over the Heart of the World. In fact, there was every chance that this modest monument was older than they were. The great pyramids that towered over the city and could be seen rearing up into the sky from right across the valley had been rebuilt many times, and each time saw them rise higher than before. Not so long ago what had stood in their place must have been as crude as the one I was looking at, with a single scratched and cracked clay brazier in front of its shrine and a single priest with a conch-shell as large as his head standing behind it, glaring at me through its smoke.

This vision of how the greatest monuments we had thrown up to our gods had once looked was one more reminder of how far my people had come in the few bundles of years since they had found themselves on this island.

It also gave me an idea.

I hastened away, before the priest could accost me and demand to know what I was doing dropping fleas all over his parish, and made my sore feet take me back to Amantlan.

I soon found myself back in a familiar place: on the Amantlan side of the canal dividing the featherworkers' parish from the merchants in Pochtlan. As I neared the bridge where I had seen someone dressed as a god and the shelter where I had found Idle's body, I had to force myself to walk slowly, stand upright and look straight ahead, although what I really wanted to do was scuttle quickly from shadow to shadow in the hope that nobody would see me. Despite my disguise I felt horribly vulnerable. Both sides of the water were crowded, but nobody seemed to be paying much attention to me and there was no sign of any warriors.

I could just see the local temple, whose pyramid peeped above the roofs of the nearest houses. Seeing a narrow path that led that way, I made for it, after a quick precautionary glance over my shoulder. That was when I saw my son.

I glimpsed him only for an instant among the people milling about on the far side of the canal. If I had not been searching for him for three days I might not have recognized him, for the crowd closed around him again straight away. His skin was paler than I had expected. But I had no doubts.

'Nim—!' I bounded towards the bridge but stopped myself just in time, choking off my cry before anyone could wonder what had made a priest lose his composure. I walked as quickly as I dared. The crowd parted for me, out of respect for what they thought I was, but the bridge was crowded, and by the time I was in Pochtlan, Nimble had vanished.

I wasted half the morning hunting him among the streets and canals of the merchants' parish. Eventually I found myself back where I had started, beside the canal, leaning against a wall to catch my breath, with my eyes shut tightly to stop the tears of frustration flowing.

When I opened them again, the first thing I saw, on the far side of the water, was the top of Amantlan's pyramid.

It was hard to leave Pochtlan, knowing that Nimble had been here, but I decided that I might as well go through with my original plan.

The pyramid in the featherworkers' parish was not much taller than the one I had seen first thing that morning, but it was much more opulent. Its shrine was a solid-looking little house, and the steps leading up to it were smooth, sharp edged and clean, and showed signs of recent repair and daily attention.

About halfway up the steps a young acolyte was bent over a broom, sweeping away imaginary dust. His face, like mine, was stained black and streaked with blood, some of which was still fresh enough to drip on the steps at his feet and spoil his hand-iwork. As I watched him working his way down the stairway, always going backwards so as not to turn his back on the god at its top, I wondered whether he was destined for the priest-hood, or whether he was a featherworker in training, sent to the priests to learn the art and meaning behind the pictures he would make, as Angry's nephew would be before long.

Above the sweeper, in front of the shrine, stood a large earthenware brazier, a round vessel, half the height of a man, with the face of a god sculpted on its front and painted in daz-zling colours. I had seen the face before, in a niche at the featherworker Skinny's house. Now, presented for the first time with a more-than-life-size representation of the god, Coyotl Inahual, I could see properly how he looked, with his sharp, dog-like features and the feathers, needle and flattened bone for spreading glue in his hands. A lot of work had gone into making that face as lifelike as possible. Only real spittle dripping from its jaws could have made it more realistic.

I began to mount the steps. Their stone was cold and hard under my bare feet. The young man sweeping them seemed oblivious to my presence until I was standing next to him. Then I cleared my throat noisily and he dropped his broom in fright.

'Never ends, the sweeping, does it?' I remarked.

'Who . . . who are you?' he demanded, looking up at me fearfully as he bent down to pick the broom up.

'Just a visitor. A fellow priest.' I flourished my robes and fought off a violent impulse to scratch. I gestured towards the summit of the pyramid. 'May I?'

'Um . . .' The youth looked nervously into the plaza below us. There were one or two loiterers but I suspected he was hoping to see the parish priest, and there was no sign of him. 'I . . . I suppose it's all right. As l–long as you don't go inside the sh–shrine.'

'No chance of that.' As I mounted the rest of the steps I added, over my shoulder: 'What's your name?'

'El–Elmimiquini,' he replied, following me.

'Featherworker's boy, eh?' That seemed a safe guess: it was hard to imagine anyone being taken into the priesthood with a name that meant 'Stammerer'.

'Yes.' We had reached the top now and stood there for a moment in silence, while I surveyed the parish.

Amantlan and its neighbours lay below us. Through the shimmering heat of midday I could see gleaming white stuccoed squares, darker patches where the roofs were thatched and between them the black wells of deeply shadowed courtyards. Canals ran in straight lines among them, splitting the parishes one from another the way a cotton thread was used to cut maize cakes into portions. I could clearly see the waterway separating Amantlan from Pochtlan, and the bridge over it. I fancied I could see Angry's house, and Kindly's, farther off, on the far side of the canal, embedded in a jumble of evergreen trees and rooftops and small open squares.

Presiding over all of it, and looking down on us, so tall and solid that it might have been close enough to touch, stood the great pyramid of Tlatelolco. From here, with my view of it unobstructed by surrounding houses, it looked vaster and more imposing than ever, its summit bearing its two temples, to Huitzilopochtli and Tezcatlipoca, so high up that they had vanished into the low clouds.

'Nice view,' I observed.

'What do you want?' The boy gripped his broom tightly, as

if afraid I was going to snatch it from him.

'As I said, just visiting,' I said vaguely. If I could brazen this out, I thought, and let Stammerer think I was someone in authority – perhaps a Keeper of the Gods, an overseer at a House of Tears, a terrifying figure to a boy being trained by priests – then he might tell me anything. So far my disguise seemed to be working, and I was managing to hide the terror of being found out that was tying my guts into knots. 'You must be able to see everything that happens in the parish from up here.'

To my amazement, the youngster laughed. 'Oh, I . . . I see what you're up to! You want to know about the vi-vision!'

I stared dumbly at him for a moment, before remembering that I was supposed to be intimidating him. I frowned as sternly as I could. 'Now, listen to me, young man . . .'

'You . . . you want me to tell you if I saw anything, don't you? But you'll be just like all the others, you . . . you . . . you won't b–believe me.'

'Others?' I asked, to give myself time to think.

'You wouldn't believe the characters who've come through here the last couple of days. Sh-shady types, sorcerers and for-tune-tellers, ho-hoping for some omen they can make a big fuss about, I guess. And there was a r-right r-rough-looking crew doing the rounds yesterday. Warriors, and their b-boss was the meanest-looking character I ever saw – a big Otomi with only one eye. He looked horrible, but I found myself feeling more . . . more sorry for the man that put his other eye out . . . Are you all right?'

I must have shivered. I may well have turned pale as well, but he would not have noticed that beneath my coating of soot. 'Fine,' I said hastily.

'C-come to think of it, they seemed more interested in some runaway slave than the god. There've been lots of others, though. We've had n-nobles and their l-ladies wandering about down there, getting their slaves to crawl around on the ground as if they were looking for f-f-feathers or scales, or whatever else they expected the Plumed Serpent to leave behind. And there were some boys from the H-house of Y-youth who want . . . wanted to show how brave they were, but they made so much noise it would have scared even a god away.

'The police have obviously got fed up with it all, because they've taken to posting guards lately. I watched a c-couple of them from the other side' – he evidently meant Pochtlan – 'picking up some drunk the night before last. They gave him a ducking to sober him up before dragging him home!' I tried not to let my embarrassment show as he chuckled at the memory.

Then he looked at me with the corners of his mouth turned down, as if from disappointment. 'They . . . they all want to know if I saw Quetzalcoatl, of course, but when I tell them what I saw, they don't listen. It's not what they w-w-want to hear, you see.'

I reappraised the lad hastily. He did not seem to be scared of me after all, but he obviously thought that what he had to say was important and was keen to talk about it. 'Suppose I prom-ise to believe you?' I suggested. 'You saw Quetzalcoatl . . .'

'No!' he groaned. 'That's just what I didn't see!' Seeing my baffled frown, he went on patiently: 'Look, you were right. You . . . you can see everything from up here. Even at night you c-c-can see a lot, and s-sound travels from down there too.' He indicated the canal and the bridge I knew so well. 'I'm up here every night, keeping vigil. That's how it is in this parish – the p-p-priests make us stand watch for them while they're safely curled up on their sleeping-mats.

'So the night when everyone says they saw the g-g-god, I

was here, and I saw the whole thing. I saw him running – well, staggering – along the P-pochtlan side of the canal, and crossing the bridge. I lost him then. Then two nights later, on Two Deer . . .'

'Hold on. You just told me you didn't see the god!'

'I saw what everyone else saw! And it had me fooled, too, for a couple of days. But then I saw him come back.'

Suddenly I felt as if the blood were freezing solid in my veins. Two Deer was the night I had met Quetzalcoatl – or thought I had. 'Go on,' I said weakly.

'This time he came by boat. I mean "they" – there were t-two of them.'

'Two gods?'

'There were no g-g-gods! The people I saw were f-flesh and b-blood! One of them was wearing a costume, though. He got out of the boat first and started running back and forth along the bridge, ob-obviously to scare off any passers-by. The other one pulled some . . . something heavy out of the b-boat, and then shoved the boat under the bridge, out of sight. The one in the costume kept scampering about while his friend dragged whatever they'd brought with them into the latrine – well, everyone knows what th-that was. It was that f-featherworker's b-brother.'

'I heard about him,' I mumbled.

'The one behind the screen was there for a long time. I couldn't see what was going on, but I guess the body was being c-c-cut up. All the while the one dressed as the god was roaming about, but no one came along until the end, when his friend had got back in the boat. Then someone stepped on the b-bridge. Maybe he wanted to use the latrine, but he took one look at the man in the cost . . . costume and f-fell over. By the time he got up the other one had . . . had d-ducked into the boat.' He grinned at the memory. 'When the stranger had got up he was running about like a headless quail, obviously look-ing for the god, but I guess he didn't th-think to look in the canal!'

I wanted to slap my forehead in self-reproach for my stu-pidity. The boat had not been visible from the bridge, although I remembered thinking how loud the lapping of the water had sounded. I must have heard it splashing against the boat's sides.

'I don't suppose you recognized either of the people you saw?' I asked.

'It was too dark, too far away, and one of them was dressed up.' Suddenly the boy's expression changed into a fierce scowl. 'If . . . if I knew who those . . . those bastards were, do you think I wouldn't have said?'

'Did you know Idle?' I asked sympathetically.

'I don't c-care about Idle. Everyone says he was a waste of skin. But there's someone out there wearing the r-r-raiment of a god, prancing around in it as if it was his breechcloth, des . . . desecrating it. You know what that means. They teach us about it in the House of Tears.

'That isn't just a c-costume. It's powerful. It's like an idol. It should be prayed to, handled with care. That's what I keep trying to tell people. Everyone wants to believe this is an omen, but it's worse than that. Using the costume like that, it'll bring the gods' anger down on the city. We could all be k-k-k-killed.'

I opened my mouth to reply, but before I could speak, a heavy footstep behind me told me we were no longer alone.

The parish priest of Amantlan was a curious specimen. The men I had known in the days when I had served the gods, the men who lived under the watchful eyes of the chief priests in the great temples at the Heart of the World and set an example of self-mortification and self-denial to their students, had been gaunt and skeletal, as if they belonged as much in the afterlife as in this world. This man's concerns were plainly with the living. The skin under his coating of pitch was soft and fleshy, and he did not smell. He obviously spent as little time as he could exposed to the privations of the House of Tears, where poverty, squalor, the reek of scores of unwashed male bodies and relentless discipline ruled.

I swallowed nervously, momentarily lost for words, but when the newcomer spoke, it was his young acolyte he turned on, rather than me.

'Stammerer!' he growled. 'You've not been telling tall stories again, have you?'

The lad looked at his feet.

The priest sighed. 'He has this silly obsession about our vision,' he told me. 'People come up here, expecting to hear about Quetzalcoatl, and they get some nonsense about a man dressed up in a fancy suit. Now you and I know,' he added in a confidential tone, 'that that isn't what they leave offerings for. Turkeys, fruit, honeyed tamales, tobacco . . .' He looked reproachfully at the boy as he listed things that were given to placate the gods but which mostly ended up being consumed by priests.

'But I'm forgetting my manners!' he said suddenly, turning back to me again. 'You must have come a long way. You look tired and out of breath. You need something to eat and a place to rest.'

On this occasion the customary greeting was true. I mumbled a polite denial but was heartily relieved when he ignored it, and I let him usher me down the steps and to his quarters, for something to eat and drink.

We left the youngster standing alone on top of the pyramid, staring silently at the scene of the crime he had witnessed two nights before.

The priest was as well provided for as I would have expected. He had a house at the corner of the precinct of his temple, which he shared with his fellow priests and acolytes when they were not praying or sacrificing or keeping vigil on top of their neat little pyramid, or teaching or officiating at Tlatelolco's Priest House.

'Now, I know what you're thinking,' the old priest said as he steered me through a room draped with rich cloth wall-hangings into a small, neat courtyard. 'This isn't much like your place in . . . where did you say you came from?'

'Xochimilco,' I said quickly. I had already decided that it would be best if I pretended to be from out of town. To name a temple or Priest House within the city would have been too risky.

'Really? You sound as if you come from Tenochtitlan.'

I stared at him, momentarily dumbstruck, before I found the presence of mind to laugh. 'Oh, doesn't the whole valley, these days?' I said casually. 'Since Montezuma and his predecessors started sending their armies everywhere, we've all ended up talking like Aztec warriors. Let's face it, half of us are probably descended from them by now! Now, what I came to ask was. . .'

'It's those robes, that's what it is!' he cried suddenly, as if he had just managed to put his finger on something that had been troubling him for a long time. 'They look just like the ones the priests of Huitzilopochtli wear!'

'They . . . they . . . they probably do. Where I come from, we have to send a score of these robes to the Heart of the World every year as tribute, so we end up dressing our own priests in seconds that look just like them.' If nothing else, I thought, as I looked down at my clothes, I had found out which god the man I had ambushed had served. 'Now, as I was saying . . .'

'Oh, that explains it!' He laughed. 'Forgive me, but the bloody Tenochca, they think they own the World. I expect you know that down in Xochimilco. You know what they did to Tlatelolco? Some petty squabble broke out between some of their merchants and the women in our marketplace and the next thing anybody knew there was an army in here.'

This was for the benefit of the ignorant foreigner I was pretending to be. No one from either part of Mexico would have needed reminding that Tlatelolco had once been an independent kingdom until Montezuma's father Axayacatl had conquered it, less than forty years before. Even now, Tenochtitlan ruled with an unusually heavy hand. Most tributary towns were allowed to keep their own kings, but our emperors had never dared take that risk with Tlatelolco: it was too close and too powerful, and so had a military governor instead.

'It's the same for us,' I said. 'The Emperor says "frog" and we end up jumping around after the slippery little buggers so that we can send to him as tribute.' I had no idea whether live frogs, or for that matter priests' costumes, were part of Xochimilco's tribute, but then I was sure the priest had no idea either and it sounded plausible enough. 'One of these days someone will come along and teach them a lesson.'

A short, uncomfortable silence followed. We were a lowly priest raging powerlessly against a force his elders had long ago come to terms with and a slave pretending to be a foreigner and denouncing his own people, and not much liking it. Neither of us was particularly keen to prolong the topic.

Suddenly my host slapped his thigh. 'But I'm being so rude! I haven't given you anything to eat or drink, or asked you your name or why you're here!'

I opened my mouth to answer, but he was on his feet before I had time to think of yet another pseudonym. A moment later he was back with a dish of the steamed maize cakes called tamales, which he placed carefully in front of me.

'Thank you,' I said, as I reached quickly for one of the little round cakes. 'This looks splendid.' As my fingers brushed the food I reflected that this was as true of the dish as of what it contained. It was an oval plate, standing on three little stubby legs, which a craftsman had fashioned so that one half formed a bowl for the sauce, and which he or another equally skilled had finished off with an intricate, many-coloured pattern that followed the contours of the vessel exactly.

'The plate's from Chalco,' my host confirmed, as if he had read my thoughts. 'A gift from a grateful parishioner.'

'I envy you.' I spoke between mouthfuls. 'My people can't afford to give me anything more than lizards and grasshoppers.'

'The featherworkers do well for themselves. Now, you were going to tell me . . .'

'I've been touring the city,' I said hastily. 'We wanted to learn more about how you Aztecs worship the gods. We thought you must be doing something right, since they have made your city the most powerful in the World. So I've been sent to look around some of your temples, talk to priests like you . . .'

I watched him carefully, trying to penetrate his pitch-black mask with my eyes in case his face gave any clue as to whether he believed me or not.

To my surprise, he laughed softly. 'You would have learned all you needed to from the priests of Huitzilopochtli, the Tenochcas' war-god! His people have conquered the World in his name. Why bother coming here? Still, I suppose our crafts-men here in Amantlan do well enough. People will always need feathers, and men and women who know how to work with them, won't they?'

'Exactly!' I cried eagerly. 'Now, that is just what I wanted to know about. We know that no one will ever beat the Aztecs in war, and so we don't hope to learn much from the priests of their war-god. But if your god has helped your people to riches, that's something we would definitely be interested in.'

I took another of the tamales, swirling it thoughtfully in the sauce before taking a bite, while I studied my host and pondered the questions I wanted to ask him.

'The featherworkers are very attentive to Coyotl Inahual,' he acknowledged proudly. 'We do our best to anticipate their wants. We're always on hand whenever a sacrifice has to be made and the god's wishes interpreted. It's important to keep a close eye on your parish, I always think, and understand the people whose god you serve.'

'So,' I said casually, 'you know the people around here pretty well. You must be in and out of their houses, and so on.'

'Of course.' Suspicion made his voice gruff and his manner formal. He looked away from me and pulled his hands inside his cloak as if to protect them. It made him look as if he were huddling against the cold, although his courtyard was sheltered and warm. Plainly I was asking too many questions for his liking. 'Why?'

'Oh, it's nothing. It's just that you must know all the feather-workers. The famous ones, I mean. We're great admirers of your featherwork in Xochimilco, you know. We can't make anything like what your people make in Amantlan, of course, but that doesn't mean we don't appreciate it.' I tilted my head up in a gesture that I hoped conveyed the right mixture of admiration and pride, as though I wanted him to know that we poor rustics were capable of recognizing quality when we saw it.

'I know everybody,' he admitted grudgingly. 'Everyone in the parish comes here, and I have to go to their houses from time to time, to consecrate a feast in the name of Coyotl Inahual.' I had to bite my tongue to stop myself laughing. Consecrating a feast was a good way for a priest to ensure he got a square meal at someone else's expense.

'So,' I said eagerly, 'you must actually have met men like . . . well, like Skinny and Angry?'

'I have,' he said. 'What of it?'

'What of it?' I echoed. 'Two of the greatest artists that ever lived? You know it's said they're really Toltecs, come back to life to teach us how it should be done?'

I was playing the role of the naive tourist for all it was worth. It was a wild claim I had made. The Toltecs were an ancient race who had died out many bundles of years before we Aztecs had settled in the valley, but we clung to their ideals: their buildings, their wisdom, above all their art. I had never been altogether sure what it was about Toltec art that made it so untouchable, especially by featherworkers. The loveliest plumes, including the matchless feathers of the quetzal, had never been seen in the valley of Mexico until the merchants had begun bringing them back when I was a child, and so I knew the Toltecs had never used them, but I supposed they must have had the skill to turn heron and turkey feathers into something magical. All Aztecs took it for granted that this ancient people had achieved things that we could never aspire to.

'I dare say people say that. What's it to you?'

'What are these men like?'

He stared at me for a long time. It was impossible to tell what he was making of my enquiries. I could see his cloak billowing as his hands moved underneath it, perhaps clasping and unclasping nervously while he tried to make up his mind whether my questions had a point or whether I was just a harmless lunatic.

At length he decided, and his hands emerged from the cloak, one of them reaching automatically for the last maize cake, which I had diplomatically left on the plate between us, as he relaxed. I had, after all, been dismissed as a madman. I felt pleased with myself. I had counted on one of the few things that, for all our differences, the Tlatelolca and the Tenochca had in common: the conviction that all foreigners were stupid.

'Angry's a mosaic man, probably the best maker of screens and shields we ever had. Skinny mainly works with thread and frame. Warrior costumes, headdresses, fans, banners, and so on. Worked, I should say,' he added, correcting himself. 'Skinny hasn't been heard from much in the last few years.'

'Why's that?'

The man shuffled uncomfortably, obviously wondering whether he had said too much. 'Steady on! You really expect me to share my devotee's problems with a stranger? Look, I don't how it is with the priests where you come from, but men and women come to me in confidence. I may not be quite like the priests of the Filth Goddess, hearing confessions and sworn to secrecy and all that, but if I'm to intercede with the god and make offerings then I have to know what the trouble is, and people have to be able to trust me. I don't know what you're about, but I think you're asking too much.'

I lowered my eyes. 'Sorry,' I muttered. 'You're absolutely right, of course. It's the same with us. I should have realized. It was just that when you said Skinny hadn't been heard of in years I was curious about what happened to him.'

He seemed to relax a little. 'I suppose you would be. But what can I say? It was always difficult for him. Do you know – I don't think this is a secret – he isn't an *Amantecatl* by birth at all?' I raised my eyebrows in what I hoped was an expression of surprise. 'He comes from some filthy bog at the northern edge of the city. He was adopted into one of our families.'

'Is that usual?'

'No, not at all. But his mother – sorry, his mother here, I mean – she was barren, and her husband had no one to pass on his craft to – no son, and as it happened no brothers or nephews either. He was in despair at one time because he thought his work was going to die with him, but then this lad turned up, with his ideal day sign and a god-given gift for craftsmanship.'

'That was lucky,' I said sceptically.

'It was. I gather it was some merchant who sorted it all out, because he happened to know both families. That's not uncommon between merchants and featherworkers – we're neighbours and do a lot of business together and go back a long way. A pity he couldn't have done something with Skinny's brother, too . . . well, never mind. I don't know what the connection with Skinny's real parents would have been.'

I kept my face very still. I could guess exactly what the connection might have been, and for that matter who the merchant was, but once more it would not have done to say so. 'You said it was difficult for him?'

'Skinny wasn't exactly a baby when he was adopted. He picked the craft up easily enough, but he struggled at the Priest House. A loner, had trouble mixing with the lads who'd grown up here and known all their lives what their future was going to be. Sensitive type. He took setbacks and criticism hard, especially after he came out of the House of Tears. It ended up that he wouldn't talk about his work or show it to anyone unless he thought it was perfect, and in the end I suppose it just got too much for him. He couldn't go on.'

'Which meant he had nothing to live on, I suppose,' I commented.

'True. He got more and more desperate. He tried everything. At one time I had him up here almost every day, sacrificing to the god, pleading with him for inspiration. He was drinking a lot of sacred wine, although he knew the penalties, and he tried mushrooms, and he even got married!'

I just stared.

He looked up then. 'Look, I don't know why I'm telling you this. If you're off back to Xochimilco or whatever desolate hole you say you come from, then I don't suppose it matters anyway. But that's how desperate Skinny was. He never showed much interest in women – I don't mean to say he was interested in men or boys or anything else, in that way – he lived for what he did. But something made him think marrying that girl would help.'

'You mean . . .' I had to choke back her name. So far as the priest was concerned I had never heard of Butterfly.

'He came to me once, with tears in his eyes, and asked me if he was doing the right thing, if I thought the gods would restore his abilities to him. He thought maybe Tezcatlipoca resented him for spurning the chance to become a father.' Tezcatlipoca, the Lord of the Here and Now, was the god who chose whether to grace a woman's womb with children. 'What I could say?' The priest laughed once, briefly, a sound like a small dog with a bone stuck in its throat. 'I'm a priest – well, so are you. You know how much use we are where women are concerned!' I could only agree: my own experience with women, both when I really had been a priest and afterwards, had been less than happy.

He sighed. 'The girl's family had already hired a soothsayer to check that their birthdays were compatible, of course, as anybody would, so there wasn't much I could tell him about that. I just said treat her well and hope for the best. And told him not to let her know why he was marrying her, if he valued his sanity!'

'And did it help?' I asked.

'What, my advice? I doubt it!'

'No, I mean the marriage – did it help him to work?'

'Oh.' He pursed his lips thoughtfully. 'I suppose it must have done, in the end. Something did. I know he was working on something big the last time he came to see me, anyway. Some private commission.'

'Who from?' I asked automatically, and regretted it instantly: from the parish priest's point of view this was clearly none of my business.

But he grinned in response. He could not resist answering my question, because it gave him a chance to utter the one name that he knew would register, even with a foreigner, because it was known and feared throughout the World.

'Montezuma.'

2

After I left the priest's lodging I stood in the plaza of his temple for a few moments, turning over in my mind everything I had seen and heard that morning and trying to decide what to do next.

I was tempted to go straight back to Pochtlan and spend the rest of the day scouring the parish's streets for any sign of my son, but I knew it would be futile. The Otomies were looking for us both. If Nimble stayed in plain sight for long enough for me to find him then the captain would be sure to get to him first. The only way I could hope to reach him was to trace his movements, starting on the night the costume was taken and the knife used. Reluctantly, I admitted to myself that Kindly had been right: I had to find his property, because it was the key to finding my son. That task would be easier now: thanks to the priest of Amantlan and his acolyte, I now knew for certain that Skinny had lied when he denied all knowledge of the costume, and that whoever had taken it was involved in Idle's murder. I resolved to confront the featherworker, overawe him in my disguise as a priest, and force him to admit the truth.

Fear gripped me as I set off for Atecocolecan, and I could not shrug it off. I could deal with Skinny and his wife, but now I knew there was someone else in the background whose terrible presence was going to overshadow everything I did until the work he had commissioned was returned to him.

Sweat broke out on my forehead, threatening to make my sooty disguise run as I thought about the most powerful man on Earth, a man who could end my life as quickly or slowly as he chose with a casual word: the Emperor of Mexico, Montezuma.

'You stupid, greedy old bastard,' I muttered, imagining Kindly chortling over the costume he had bought. 'What have you got us into now?'

If Butterfly was at all disconcerted by the sight of a strange priest in her doorway, asking for her husband, she did not show it.

'He's not here,' she said shortly. 'I don't know when he'll be back.'

Her hair was unbound, as it had been when I had seen her before. It fell over her shoulders and bare arms in dark, glossy waves, and had certainly been combed that morning. Her eyes shone and her skin had the pale yellow tinge of ochre. It looked so soft and deep that I felt a wild urge to stretch a hand towards her cheek just to see if its surface yielded to my touch. For a moment I was too taken aback to speak. A woman whose brother-in-law had died just three days before should be in deep mourning. I would have expected red-rimmed eyes and tangled, split and matted hair, not the glow of skilfully applied cosmetics.

'What do you want?'

'I have to talk to him about his brother.'

Suddenly she giggled. She took a step back, reaching for a door post for support as laughter threatened to overwhelm her. Her teeth flashed at me. They were as perfectly white as when they had first broken through her gums.

'I know your name! You're that slave, Joker, who was here a couple of days ago! You're from what's-his-name, the

merchant, Kindly.' She puckered her forehead with the innocent curiosity of a little girl asking her mother how it was that
embroidery threads came in so many colours. 'Why are you
dressed like a priest?'

I wanted to swear. My disguise obviously fooled no one
who had met me even once before. I toyed with the idea of
simply running away, hoping to get clean out of the city before
she raised a hue and cry, but then I forced myself to think.

If the girl had thought I had killed her brother-in-law, she
would be screaming her throat raw, not laughing. Probably, I
reasoned, nobody had bothered to tell her I was suspected of
the murder. There were some households – my parents' was
one, and I had no doubt that Lily's was another – where you
kept the women in the dark at your peril. In most, though, a
woman's world was bounded by the walls of her courtyard and
her interests and knowledge were expected to begin and end
there. There was no reason to suppose that Butterfly, a young
girl whose husband had apparently only married her because
of some whimsical notion that she would bring him inspiration, would be let into men's talk.

'It's a long story,' I began lamely.

'Oh, well, you'd better come in, then. I love stories!' She
swung on the doorframe, tilting her body forward so that her
breasts pressed against the fabric of her blouse. 'I'm sure yours
will be fascinating!' she added in a throaty voice, before
detaching herself from the doorway. She spun around so that
the hem of her skirt flared around her calves and tripped
lightly back over her threshold.

I followed her through into the courtyard, feeling a little
dazed. Having been a priest from childhood and then a slave,
I was unused to this sort of invitation.

The place did not appear to have been swept since my previous visit. I looked briefly from the scattered maize cobs,

squash seeds and tortilla crumbs to the spotless beauty who presided over them and tried to make sense of it, but I could not.

'Sorry it's a mess,' the woman said carelessly. 'We keep meaning to do something with it, but with Idle's burial rites and everything, well, you know . . .'

I looked for a clean corner of the courtyard to squat in, despaired of finding one and then reasoned that it hardly mattered since my stolen mantle had not been clean in the first place. Lowering myself to the ground, I said: 'Surely, at a time like this, it's all the more important to attend to the sweeping?' I regretted the words as soon as they were out of my mouth. There was no need to stay in character, and I thought I sounded sanctimonious.

She clucked impatiently. 'You sound like my sister-in-law! Marigold was like that. The gods this, the gods that – well, just look at this place! I don't mind a few little statuettes round about, they can be nice, but you can't move for the things, and it's just as bad indoors.'

I gaped at her. For a moment I seemed to have mislaid all the words in my head, and then when I managed to muster a few I struggled to find the breath to say them. 'You can't . . . you can't really . . .'

That drew a peal of laughter, swiftly hushed with a slim hand over her mouth. 'I'm sorry! Have I shocked you?'

'You don't fear the gods,' I gasped. This was unheard of. The gods ruled our world, not in the remote way of an emperor governing a subject town and saying who should be in charge of it and what tribute it should pay, but immediately and directly. We could drink because Chalchihuitlicue made water flow through the aqueduct. We ate because Tlaloc made rain fall on our fields and Cinteotl and Chicome Coatl made the maize cobs ripen. We did not freeze to death because our own

Huitzilopochtli made the Sun rise. We were born only because Tezcatlipoca put us in our mothers' wombs. Nobody could be expected to love the dangerous beings that governed our affairs. Sometimes desperation drove people to do things that the gods might disapprove of, and we expected to pay for them afterwards. Not to fear them, however, smacked of insanity.

She was still laughing. 'Of course I'm afraid of the gods. If I want something I'll be up at the temple with flowers or quails or tobacco or whatever else the priests tell me to bring, and maybe it'll work or maybe not, but let's be realistic. The gods don't care about us, and we can't make them do what we want. I'm quite sure no god cares one way or the other whether this place is swept out or not. You know what I think? I think the only reason we're told sweeping is a sacred duty is because it's women's work and all our priests and rulers are men!'

I shivered. A cloud had passed over the Sun. Its shadow caught my eye and prompted me to look up at a sky that was rapidly filling up with grey. 'Looks as if Tlaloc might have heard you,' I muttered. 'It's going to rain soon.'

'The roof doesn't leak. Now, you were going to tell me why you're dressed like that.'

I had had time to think of an answer to that one. 'I had a row with my master. He wasn't happy that I came back empty handed, the last time I was here. In fact . . . well, it's not the first time, and he was on the point of having me sold as a sacrifice. So I ran away. You can see why I didn't want to be recognized.'

'What are you doing back here, then? It's nothing to do with my brother-in-law at all, is it?'

'I thought if I could get my master's stuff back for him anyway he might forgive me. I haven't got anywhere else to go, you see.'

Butterfly stood with her back to the wall of the room she and Skinny had emerged from during my previous visit, leaning nonchalantly against it next to the doorway, which was screened off as before by a cloth. There was something unwomanly about her pose. She had one leg drawn up so that the knee strained the thin fabric of her skirt and the foot rested against the plaster behind her. She plucked one-handed at a loose thread in the hem of her blouse as she looked down at me, her eyebrows raised speculatively.

'What makes you think we can help? Skinny and I told you, we don't know anything about this costume your master's supposed to have bought, let alone what might have become of it.' She spoke mildly, like a young mother chiding a small child. 'I'm sorry you didn't believe us.'

'I didn't believe you because you were lying!' I snapped, suddenly goaded out of civility. 'I have it on the best authority that the Emperor himself ordered Skinny to work on the raiment of Quetzalcoatl. The Emperor! Montezuma! Now, you didn't just happen to forget about him, did you?'

I had to admire the woman's composure. She looked at me steadily, her only reaction to my outburst being to form a silent 'O' with her lips.

'Are you going to tell me the truth, now?' I added. 'Or should I take my enquiries up with the Palace?'

'You wouldn't dare!' she sneered.

Since she was absolutely right, I tried something else. 'Your brother-in-law was murdered – did you know?' I said brutally. 'Whoever killed him has the costume. Doesn't that matter to you?'

'I know about Idle,' she replied matter-of-factly. 'The parish police told us about it three days ago – just after you left here, actually. We'd reported him missing and they came on the off-chance that the body might be his. Skinny went to

Amantlan to see if he could identify it. I expect you know what he found. You heard his brother was cut to pieces and stuffed in. . . Oh, it's too nauseating to talk about! His face was unrecognizable, of course, even after they'd cleaned it up. I was surprised Skinny agreed even to look at it, but he thought it was his duty.'

'How did he know it was his brother?'

'They'd found a charm of his, a little figure of Tezcatlipoca. It was in his left hand. Idle always carried it with him for protection when he played Patolli.'

I remembered the object I had seen in the body's hand. Patolli was a game, a race around a cross-shaped board on which a vast fortune could easily be lost on a single bad throw of the beans we used to reckon moves. This was where Tezcatlipoca, the Enemy on Both Sides, belonged, rolling the beans one way or the other or, once in a lifetime, standing them on end out of sheer caprice, just so that he could amuse himself watching the consternation on the other players' faces as the man who had made the freakish throw gathered up their stakes and left with them.

'So he was a gambler?'

'And a lot else besides!'

'What do you mean?'

'You asked whether Idle's death mattered to me. Aren't you wondering why I'm not in mourning? Look!' She detached herself from the wall and stood with her back to me while she lifted her hair with both hands and let it fall, cascading over her shoulders as softly as falling oak leaves in autumn. When she turned back towards me her eyes blazed defiantly. 'See? I washed it just this morning! And do you think we sacrificed a dog for him to take with him? No way! He can find his own way through the Nine Hells!'

'What did he do?'

'He brought us down to this, that's what!' Her gesture, a furious sweep of her arm, took in the courtyard, the house, and somehow the whole run-down district beyond the walls. 'My husband's work went to pieces all over again, because of him.'

I looked nervously up at the sky, where dark clouds were swelling and swirling about each other in a stately dance. A downpour was going to begin at any moment. I thought anxiously of the thin coating of ash on my face. A real priest would have worn pitch, which was waterproof. What I had would turn into a mess of muddy grey streaks as soon as a few fat raindrops hit it, and that would be the end of my disguise.

'His brother stopped him working?' I asked absently. 'How did he do that?'

She hesitated. She took a couple of quick steps away from me and then a couple back and sighed, and then, at last, knelt in front of me, sweeping her skirt under her knees with a brisk gesture.

'Skinny went to Amantlan when he was a boy. It was his fate, you understand? He had the right birthday, and he had the talent. He grew up there, with this old couple who were never going to have any children of their own. When my husband was the sort of age when most boys are out fishing or hunting frogs on the lake or larking about in the fields pretending to learn how to use a digging-stick, he was being taught how to mix glue and trim feathers. He went straight from there to the Priest House. I don't know if you can imagine what that place is like.'

'I know. This wouldn't have been a disguise, once.'

'Really?' That made her raise her eyebrows. 'How interesting! You must tell me all about it! But Skinny, now, he never forgot his time at the House of Tears. He didn't talk about it much to me, and it wasn't as if he surrounded himself with idols, like his sister-in-law, but it was always there, at the back of his mind.'

'You're telling me he never had any youth. He grew up under the influence of the featherworkers and then the priests. Let me guess what happened then. He met his brother, who showed him what he'd been missing all these years.'

She looked down, peering long and hard into her lap. It was as if she were searching for the loose thread she had been playing with earlier, as her fingers strayed towards it again.

'He was working for Angry then,' she informed me in a low voice. 'His work hadn't been going well. To be honest, it hadn't been going at all. He had nowhere else to go: the couple who adopted him were both dead and he had always refused to work with anyone else, so he was on his own. But it was hard for him. As hard as anything could be, throwing in his lot with his rival. I don't suppose he would have done it if he hadn't had me to support.' To my surprise she sniffed loudly, and brushed a hand swiftly across her face as though sweeping away a tear.

'But he did it. He went to Angry, and Angry gave him work, and he just sat there meekly in the corner and got on with it, and I kept telling him that it didn't matter, that one day things would be better and he'd be able to make something of his own again – something to astound them all, the way he used to. It would have happened, you know. It would, except . . .' She ended there on a little choking sound, but I could guess the rest.

'Except,' I suggested gently, 'that his brother turned up.'

She looked up. Her eyes were not glistening but she blinked several times, as if something were pricking them behind their lids. 'I don't know why he came when he did. He'd had nothing to do with Skinny and I'd never met him. I think it must have been getting difficult for Idle here. He'd been neglecting the family plot.'

'I guess he hadn't realized you'd fallen on hard times yourselves.'

That provoked a bitter laugh. 'Of course not! And he wouldn't have believed it if we'd told him. My husband was a featherworker, so naturally he was rich.' She sighed. 'Idle was the worst kind of beggar, the kind that thinks you owe him whatever he asks for because you've got it and he hasn't and you're family. In the end Skinny got so fed up with his demands for food and drink, and even cloth and cocoa beans that we knew he was going to use for gambling, that he made Angry take him on as hired help, as one of his conditions for going to work with him himself.'

'And the arrangement didn't work.'

'Skinny just found it impossible to work with his brother around. It would have been easy enough for him just to squat there all day stitching feathers on to a frame, but that bloody man just wouldn't leave him alone, always asking him to try some mushrooms or have a crafty nip of sacred wine or join his friends for a game of Patolli. For a man brought up the way my husband was, frustrated in his work and with nothing to look forward to but mindless toil in someone else's workshop, it must have been impossible to resist.'

'Skinny came back here,' I recalled. 'Whose idea was that? Did Angry throw him out, or what?' I dismissed that idea as soon as it occurred to me, remembering then that Idle had become more to Angry than a hired hand. By the time he left the craftsman's house, Skinny's brother was Angry's son-in-law.

'Oh, no. Throw his own daughter out? What kind of father would do that? Especially one like Angry. He used to go around as if the air she breathed was perfumed. No, he wouldn't have thrown Idle and Marigold out. It was her idea: she told her father the best thing for her and Idle was to get away. She persuaded him they should come back here. She said honest toil in the fields was what they needed – it was what Idle had been born to, it was what his father and grandfathers had done, and the only way of life for an Aztec was the one his ancestors had known, plying their trade or walking around up to his ankles in shit in their fields or whatever, and honouring their gods. Above all, honouring their bloody gods!'

I looked around at the statuettes peering down at us from their niches in the walls. 'She was the devout one.'

'Oh, wasn't she just! It was never going to work, but try telling her that. Try telling her her husband didn't know one end of a digging-stick from another and couldn't care less anyway. So they ended up here, with nothing to live on except what her father gave her as a parting gift, and no means of earning a living.'

'So how come you and Skinny followed them?'

It took her a little while to answer. She frowned and looked away, as if she were nervous about the weather too. I waited.

Eventually she said: 'All right. You wanted the truth. You know most of it anyway.'

'It had something to do with the costume?' I prompted.

She sighed. 'It was just before Idle and Marigold left. Skinny had disappeared. He slipped away, just before dawn, without telling anyone where he was going, and was gone all day. I thought he'd gone on a binge, but Idle wasn't with him, and when he did come back he was stone cold sober. Excited, though – almost feverish.

'He told me what had happened that night. He'd been summoned before the Emperor himself! Montezuma had told him what he wanted, and asked him lots of questions about how he'd set about the work. I don't think I'd ever seen Skinny so enthusiastic about anything – by the time he got home, he was really fired up. It was . . . well, you know what it was. The biggest thing he'd ever done – probably the biggest thing any featherworker ever did.

'But it had to be kept secret. Montezuma told him nobody, especially the other featherworkers, was allowed to know about it. Not even Angry, although Skinny was working for him.'

'So you left.' It made sense: by returning to Atecocolecan Skinny could escape the prying eyes of his own employer and the rest of his fellow craftsmen. I doubted that the field hands and day-labourers of his home parish would take much notice of what he was up to. 'And Skinny worked on the costume here, in the peace and quiet. All right, how did Kindly get hold of it?'

She laughed mirthlessly. 'How do you think? He stole it!'

I stared at her, speechless.

'Your master lied to you, slave! He didn't buy it from us. He must have got wind of it somehow – maybe Angry found out and let something slip – and thought it was too good an opportunity to miss.'

'No,' I protested, 'that can't be right! Remember, he sent me here to buy it back from you . . .'

'Because someone stole it from him! Funny, isn't it, a thief's house getting burgled? But your coming here was the first we knew of where the costume had gone. Now can you understand why we weren't exactly keen to talk about it?'

If what she said was true – that the work Montezuma had commissioned and sworn her husband to secrecy about had gone missing twice, once from his own house – then I had to agree that it was not something they would want the whole World to know.

'What about Idle?' I asked. 'And his wife? He's dead, and I know whoever has the costume is connected with that, and she's missing . . .' I let my voice tail off as I worked out the answer to my own question.

'Well, it's obvious, isn't it?' Butterfly sniffed. 'He found out where it was and stole it from Kindly. Then Marigold killed him and fled. You want to find the raiment of the god? Find my sister-in-law!'

A peal of thunder sounded overhead. Tlaloc was making his presence felt.

I looked up at a sky that had turned the colour of slate. A large raindrop hit me in the eye. A moment later they were falling all around us. Little dark discs were forming and spreading in the dust at our feet and moisture was streaking and spattering the whitewashed walls.

'Better go in,' I muttered, rising and automatically heading for the nearest room, the one I had seen Butterfly and Skinny emerge from on my previous visit.

The woman was there before I was, barring the doorway.

'No! Not in there! The other room – go in the other room. Please.'

I froze, astonished.

She had turned her face up towards mine and was staring at me, her eyes still unblinking despite the rain whose stinging blows I could feel even through the hair on top of my head. Her cheeks glowed with something more than make-up and her breathing was suddenly quick and shallow. Her teeth were bared and her fists clenched and there was something in her voice I had not heard before, the kind of tremor you hear from the throat of a person fighting to master rage or terror.

'Sorry,' I said mildly. 'The other room, then.' I turned back, towards the room that led through to the street, and added, because I felt I ought to add something, 'I didn't know.'

I barely heard her let out a long breath, like a sigh of relief,

and then she was by my side, hurrying as I was to get in out of
the rain. 'No, it's my fault.' Her tone had changed again. The
moment of tension had gone now, releasing in its wake a flood
of words as hasty as a small bird's chirping. 'It's just that that
room . . . well, it's a terrible mess. Much worse than this
courtyard. It was my brother-in-law's room, the one he shared
with Marigold. He never let us clean it, you see, and there are
things in there I wouldn't want anyone to see. Do you understand what I mean?'

'Um, yes,' I said, with a quick glance over my shoulder. The
already sodden cloth over the doorway flapped lethargically
under the beating it was getting from the heavens. I did not
understand what she meant, except that beyond that scrap of
material lay something she would fight to keep me from
seeing. Perhaps whatever Idle had kept in there was enough to
spell disaster for the remaining members of his household if it
were found. I was going to get to the bottom of that later, I
decided, but I had other questions for now.

'Tell me about Idle and Marigold.' As we ducked into the
shelter of the house's front room, I had to raise my voice to
make it heard over the rain hammering on the thin stucco
roof. 'What makes you so sure she'd have killed her husband?'

She rolled her eyes as if in despair at my ignorance. It was
the kind of gesture I might have seen on the face of one of my
teachers at the House of Tears while he explained to me, for
the third time, that the plant for curing leeches was Amolli,
not Yiamolli, which was good only for dandruff. 'What do
you think? It wasn't just drink and mushrooms and gambling
with him. He couldn't keep his hands off the girls – or any
other bit of him, for that matter! For some reason she managed
to turn a blind eye to it. I suppose she was flattered when Idle
started courting her and didn't want to believe what she must
have been able to see for herself. Getting married didn't

change him – it never does. He tried it on with half the women in Angry's household before he came here. Maybe that had something to do with why Marigold wanted to bring us all here, to get him away from temptation. If that was it, it didn't work! Almost the first thing he did after we arrived was to proposition me!' Her voice became shrill with outrage and she had to pause and take a couple of breaths before going on. 'Of course, I told him what would happen if he didn't behave himself.'

'Naturally.'

'But what I think is, Marigold caught him with some local lass. That wouldn't have been so very difficult for him, you see. He's been boasting so much about his connections with the featherworkers over the years that he's made himself quite famous, in a pathetic, parochial sort of way. And it's not as if the men around here . . . Well,' she concluded primly, 'it's a pretty rough sort of place.'

'So you think Marigold finally had enough.'

'I think she had too good a chance to miss! She found out about the costume, somehow, and suddenly there was her opportunity – to get rid of her bastard of a husband and get all the money she could ever need, in one go!'

I frowned. 'Angry told me he thought she was pregnant. Would she really kill her child's father?'

Butterfly laughed.

'Only a man would ask that!'

3

The shower did not last long. The sky was brightening already by the time Butterfly had finished speaking, and a few shafts of sunlight were falling on the cloth over the doorway, converting its darkness into a dirty mottled brown.

She got up and glanced through the doorway. 'It's stopping.'

I could still hear tapping and creaking sounds from above me. I wondered how well made the roof was, although a brief, anxious look up at it showed no suspicious cracks or bulges. I tried to remember whether any trees had spread their branches directly overhead, to take over shedding water when the clouds had finished.

'You may as well go.' She tried to sound regretful even as she reinforced her words by crossing the room to look out of the street entrance. 'I doubt if Skinny will be back today at all. He was meant to be going to Tlatelolco market, but he said something about seeing some friends in Amantlan as well.'

I was tempted to argue, but there seemed little point. I had a lot of questions, some of whose answers, I thought, must lie in this house, but I could see I was not going to get them by pestering Skinny's wife. I believed practically nothing she had told me. I was convinced that the key to everything – the whereabouts of the costume, the identity of Idle's killer and whatever had become of my son – lay in the room across the courtyard. If she was not going to show me what was in there then I would have to find out for myself.

All the same, I could not help admiring her, not just for the elegant silhouette she made as I watched her in the doorway but for her command of herself. There was no way I was going to get her to tell me anything she had not already decided I should know.

Besides, those curious, alarming sounds were still coming from the roof. They were not loud and the woman seemed too intent on ushering me quickly out of her house to notice them, but they were undeniably real. I wondered whether the moisture had got into the beams and swollen them, or whether there was some other explanation.

As I left the house, I looked around me quickly. Directly to my front, running alongside the path I stood on, ran a narrow canal. At its end I saw the labourers I had noticed when I had first come here, still toiling over the plot whose edges they were reinforcing. They had finished their joyful, rhythmic hurling of hammerheads against wooden piles and were were now silently engaged in the back-breaking work of heaving rocks and tumbling them into place to form the foundations of their artificial island.

Skinny's house abutted straight on to the deserted property on its right-hand side, a poor-looking thatched hovel surrounded by tall, dripping weeds. Around the corner on the other side was a little open space. A stumpy-looking willow grew there, one or two of its polled branches ending just short of the edge of the roof, so that I could see they had not been dripping on it.

After a quick glance in both directions I decided to go for the willow.

Keeping my back pressed against the outside wall of the house, I edged towards it, slithering around the corner like a snake winding itself around a rock. I put myself between the house and the willow's trunk and looked up.

A branch made a fork in the wood right over my head. It was perfectly placed, and so was I. When I heard the scraping noise from the roof I moved without even waiting for the foot to appear.

I leapt upward and had the ankle in my grasp before whoever was up there had got so much as a toehold on the branch. I did not need to pull. I just let my weight drag us both down, and with a shocked howl my victim tumbled from his perch and crashed in a heap at my feet.

He was up in an instant, snarling at me like a cornered ocelot, too furious for a moment even to think about running away. This was just as well as I could see straight away that he was a youngster and I would have had trouble catching him. I took the opportunity to lunge towards him, to seize him by the arm or the hair and get him on the ground and subdued, but two things made me stop with my arm hanging in midair.

The first was that the fight went out of him. As he stared at his assailant I saw his eyes widen and his jaw drop and his hands, which were raised and clawed for self-defence, fell limply to his side. An instant later he was on his knees in the mud with his head bowed, whimpering with fright. It took me a moment to realize what had happened and then I nearly ruined it by laughing. Probably for the last time, my pathetic disguise had worked, and the fake aura of a priest had overcome him.

The second thing that stayed my hand was that I recognized the lad.

I could not have said who I might have expected to find skulking around on Skinny's roof, but one of the last names to occur to me would have been that of Angry the feather-worker's nephew, Crayfish.

★

'You'd better tell me what you thought you were doing,' I said sternly.

'Please, sir,' the boy snivelled, his face averted so that he seemed to be talking to my feet, 'I didn't mean any harm. I was just looking for . . . just looking for . . .' He was a poor liar. In his place I would have worked out my story in advance.

I looked down at him speculatively. The temptation to carry on acting as a priest and bully the lad into confessing everything was strong, but I knew it was not going to work. Once the shock of being plucked from the roof had worn off he would have no more difficulty in recognizing me than Butterfly had. Besides, I was not anxious to draw a crowd, and the sight of him cowering on the floor might well do just that.

'"You were just looking for",' I repeated. 'Fine. Up you get. You can explain it all on the way back to Amantlan. And mind you do if you don't want me telling your uncle where I found you!'

That made him stare. 'My uncle? How do you know. . . Oh!'

I reached down and seized his arm, not roughly but firmly enough to get him on his feet. 'Now each of us knows who he's talking to, shall we go?' I turned to leave, keeping hold of the boy with my arm outstretched in case he was tempted to fight me after all.

He hesitated, biting his lip, his head darting about as if looking for somewhere to run. 'I don't understand. You were at our house – why are you dressed like that? What are you doing here?'

'Just move,' I hissed, 'unless you want us both to get caught!'

His eyes widened again at that. Then he seemed to relax, as though catching the sense that I might, after all, be a fellow conspirator.

'You promise you won't tell my uncle?'

I made a threatening noise and tugged his arm. He started walking.

'Are you going to let go of me?'

I did. 'Just remember where I'll go if you try to run away. Now, are you going to tell me what you were up to? The truth, mind.'

'I was looking for Marigold.'

He was still a growing boy. As we walked the top of his head came to the level of my chin, but he was watching the ground in front of him, so that he seemed shorter. As I looked down at him I wondered how old he was: eleven or twelve, perhaps. I had thought him older when I had met him before, in his uncle's presence, when he had seemed to show the sort of care for the older man that I might have expected of a wife or an elder sister. Angry's wife was dead, however. I wondered how great a void Crayfish's cousin had left in her father's household.

I also remembered another young man who had seemed to me old beyond his years. My son was older than this boy, but not by much. I had not seen him grow up, and suddenly the vision I had of us walking and talking together like this, as we never had, brought tears to my eyes and made me break my stride.

'What's the matter?'

'Nothing.' I swallowed once, blinked a few times and turned back to Crayfish. 'You were fond of your cousin.'

'We all were.' The boy sighed. 'After my aunt died she took over the household. She cared for the idols – she loved doing that – and made the tortillas and swept and made clothes for my uncle, just the way a wife would have. She was kind to me. She looked after me when I first came to my uncle's house. She was really more like a sister to me than a cousin – even after she met *him*.'

There was no need to ask who he meant. 'You know Idle's dead.'

'Good riddance!' the boy spat.

'Careful what you say, lad,' I cautioned him quietly. 'People might think you had something to do with it!'

'Me and everyone else he ever met!' he cried with spirit. 'The only person I ever knew with a good word to say about him was his wife! Only the gods know what she saw in him.'

'Did you hear any of what Skinny's wife said to me?' I asked. 'She thought your cousin killed her husband because he was . . .' I wondered how worldly the youngster was. 'He was treating her badly.'

'Screwing around, you mean.'

I rolled my eyes in disbelief, wondering whether all young boys were like this and my upbringing had been unusually sheltered.

'I didn't hear what she said. I don't believe it. I know her – even if she'd finally realized what her husband was like, she'd never commit murder. It would be a crime!'

'Obviously,' I said drily, but I understood. He thought someone as pious as his cousin incapable of any transgression. 'But the best of people can do terrible things when they're desperate.'

'Anyway, why would she need to kill him? She could just have gone back to her father. Uncle Angry would have taken her back, and she knew it. They'd have divorced eventually, and that would have been that. Why would she risk killing him and getting caught? What would have happened to her then?'

I cast my mind back to the law I had been taught in the House of Tears. 'If she wasn't put to death she'd probably have been handed over to Butterfly as a slave.'

'So she'd be worse off than ever!'

'Someone would have to find her first.' I looked at him thoughtfully. 'I take it she and Butterfly didn't get on?'

The youth grimaced. 'It didn't help that Marigold's husband kept making eyes at his sister-in-law – who didn't do anything to put him off! And Butterfly would go making snide comments about the idols, which upset my cousin.'

'She may not have been too happy about your cousin's cosy chats with her husband either,' I reminded him.

'I'm sure they weren't doing anything wrong!' he said hastily. 'It's just that, well, I think Marigold told him things he needed to hear. Do you know what I mean? About how important his work was, how much the gods valued it. Butterfly wouldn't have understood any of that.' He paused. 'I don't know what to say about Butterfly. She seemed to look after her husband well enough, but none of us ever liked her much. My uncle seems to think she's up to no good, but I can't get him to say what.'

'He didn't know you were going to Atecocolecan.'

'No. He thinks I'm meeting a friend who's at the House of Tears, another featherworker's boy.' I suspected he meant Stammerer. 'Going to Idle's house was my idea, just to see if I could find anything out. To tell you the truth, Uncle Angry has hardly spoken to me in the last couple of days. He's been hiding in his workshop, not talking to anyone, not letting anyone in, only coming out for his meals. I know he's brooding over Marigold. It would help him so much if I could find out where she was.'

Crayfish and I parted company at the border of Amantlan. Just before he set off home, he suggested I lose my disguise. He told me my soot was starting to flake off. When I looked down I saw that my hands and legs were beginning to look grimy rather than sinister and I was shedding flecks of dark ash the way fruit trees shed blossom in the spring.

Deciding to take the boy's advice, I looked for a secluded spot, a quiet, narrow canal where I could wash unobserved. Thinking I had found just the place, I turned a corner, only to discover that someone else had had the same idea.

He had just finished relieving himself into the water and was straightening his clothes. He was dressed from neck to ankle in green cotton, and his feet were clad in broad sandals with over-long straps. A sword and a shield lay beside him, and his hair stood up upon his head and flowed in a dark mane down the back of his neck. He had his back to me, but before he turned around I knew who he was: an Otomi warrior.

I stood quite still while he looked me over. I wanted to run, but all my legs seemed able to do was tremble violently, and I knew I would be caught before I had gone five paces. All I could do was trust in my disguise.

I recognized him as one of the captain's entourage. I was thankful that he was not the captain himself, or Fox, either of whom I was sure would have recognized me. I wondered where his monstrous, one-eyed chief was.

'What are you doing here?' the warrior demanded eventually.

I remembered to disguise my voice, mumbling the way priests sometimes did, owing to having drawn so much blood from their tongues. 'The same as you, by the look of it.'

He bent down to pick up his sword and shield. 'There isn't a latrine near here. It always feels better to go in the canals in this part of the city, anyway!' He was obviously from Tenochtitlan, besides having a warrior's contempt for the merchants and craftsmen who lived in the surrounding houses. He looked at my robes. 'What's a priest of Huitzilopochtli doing in Tlatelolco?'

'Official business,' I said casually. 'I might ask you the same question, though.'

He made an impatient gesture with his sword. 'We're look-ing for a couple of runaways – a boy and an escaped slave. Seen anything like that?'

'No.'

'Well, report it if you do. My captain is very keen to get hold of the slave in particular. He led us a merry dance over in Tlacopan, and he's going to be wearing his own guts for a breechcloth when we find him!' Suddenly he was look-ing at me intently. 'Don't I know you from somewhere?'

I gulped. 'I don't think so. I serve the god at his great temple in the Heart of the World – maybe you've seen me at a festi-val.'

He frowned. 'No, it's not that. I don't know, your face just looks familiar, that's all.'

I summoned up a nervous laugh. 'Hard to say under all this black stuff, isn't it?'

He peered at me for a long moment, while I fought to control my terror. Then he seemed to make up his mind.

'Can't stand here all day,' he said briskly, stepping around me. 'Got to get after those bastards. It's a year's supply of tobacco for the man who catches them!'

Then he was gone, and I was on my knees at the water's edge, being violently sick.

It was only when the last uncontrollable spasm had passed through me and I squatted, gasping and shivering, by the canal that the full import of what the Otomi had said began to sink in.

He had told me he and his comrades were looking for a slave – me – and a boy. But when I had left him in Tlacopan, the captain had still been convinced that he was pursuing a third person. The boatman he had been torturing would not have known any better.

So how had the Otomies learned the truth?

I stayed where I was for the remainder of the afternoon, trying to rest. Once night had fallen, I finally abandoned my disguise, washing the soot off in the canal and hiding the cloak behind a patch of nettles. Then I made my way back to the house in Atecocolecan.

I scrambled up the willow that had got Crayfish on to the roof earlier in the day and crawled around the edge, as the boy must have done, for fear of falling through the insubstantial plaster in the middle. Then I paused, looking around me and hesitating while I thought about what I intended to do. The sky overhead was brilliant with stars, although luckily the moon had not risen yet. When I looked over my shoulder I could see the faint, flickering light of the brazier at the top of the parish temple, but it was too far away to shed any light on me. There was no sound except the wind stirring the willow by the house and the trees and rushes that lined the parish's plots out on the lake.

What I intended to do here was to find Kindly's featherwork for him, because it was the only thing I could think of that might lead me to where my son was. I was convinced that the place to look for it was the room Idle had shared with Marigold. There was something concealed in that room, I was certain of that: why else would Butterfly have been so desperate to keep me out of it?

As I shifted my weight and prepared to drop into the courtyard as quietly as I could, sudden dread made my stomach cramp painfully. What I was about to do, trespassing in a house at night, was a serious crime, but it was not that which frightened me. I had committed capital crimes before and got away with it, one way or another. What terrified me was the conviction that whatever Idle had died for, it had something to do with what I had come here to find, and whoever had killed him would not hesitate to kill again.

I took a deep breath and jumped.

As soon as my feet were on the ground I darted into the shadows. From there, after a quick look around me to ensure I was alone, I crept towards the forbidden doorway. I had to hold my breath as I lifted a corner of the cloth that covered it, in case I missed any sound that might betray the presence of someone in the room: a cough or a footstep, a grunt or a snore or the faint rustle of someone turning over under a blanket. Butterfly had told me that this had been Idle's and Marigold's room, and I assumed from this that it was unoccupied, but if Skinny and his wife had moved into it since the afternoon then I intended to be out of the front doorway before they could stir.

Hearing nothing, I slipped into the room and let the cloth fall back behind me.

Now there was no light whatever. I would have to do all my searching by touch. I cursed under my breath. The last thing I needed to be doing now was blundering about in a strange room with my hands groping the air in front of me in the hope that one of them would connect with something important, but I had no choice.

I took a single step forward, and a moment later was in agony, with my tongue clamped between my teeth to stop me screaming and my legs buckling with pain and shock.

I had stubbed my toe.

Tears sprang to my eyes as I tried to work out what I had walked into. Whimpering, I dropped to one knee, curling the leg with the injured foot protectively under me as I felt for the thing. It was a piece of rock, rough hewn and jagged, or so I thought until I managed to turn it over and discovered that parts of it had been polished smooth. As I ran my fingers over its curves and ridges I realised that it was a carving, although there was no way of telling by touch what it was meant to be.

'I wonder how this got broken?' I mused. 'Maybe some other clumsy moron bumped into it before me.'

I got up, grimacing as my sore toe touched the floor. Edging around the place where I had left the stone, I found another piece, as rough as the first, when my heel brushed against it.

Butterfly had not lied when she said the place was a mess. Working my way along the room towards the back of the house, I soon found a pile of rubbish. Somebody appeared to have made a loose heap of all Idle's possessions and just left it in the middle of the floor. Fishing around in it with my hands, I found stale tortilla crusts, broken pottery, cloth, thread, something sharp that I thought must be an obsidian razor and feathers. There was a surprising number of feathers.

The pile spilled across the whole width of the room, so that I had to clamber over it to find out what lay beyond it. I started nervously as something fell off the top of it, and rolled across the floor with a loud clatter. I froze for a moment but heard no other sound.

The room turned out to be smaller than it had looked from the outside because I found the rear wall of the house imme-diately beyond the heap.

I ran my hands over it briefly. There seemed to be no shelves or niches, just plain plaster. The surface had a rough feel as though it had been hastily finished. There was a draught around my feet, which made me think mice from the fields behind the house must have eaten their way through the adobe from the outside.

An unpleasant smell filled this part of the room. It was

vaguely familiar, but for the moment I could not recall where I had come across it before. It was not difficult to guess where it emanated from, however: somewhere in the mass of garbage behind me. I sighed, realizing that I had no choice but to rake over the heap. I had already decided why it had been left there. It was the obvious place in which to have concealed the costume.

I clambered back over it, meaning to search it from the other side where there was more room to work.

I was stooping over the pile with my back to the doorway when I heard something behind me. It sounded like a light, stealthy footstep.

I tried to stand up but I was an instant too late.

Something crashed into the back of my head, and before I even hit the floor I was plunged into a darkness even murkier than the room around me.

4

A snake danced in front of me. It was not the venomous kind. When it raised its broad, flat head and opened its mouth to send its tongue darting silently towards my face, I saw no fangs. It was the sort that killed its victim slowly, squeezing until he could not draw breath, until ribs cracked and organs split and burst. With every movement I made, I knew its grip would tighten further. I kept as still as I could, taking short, shallow breaths until the strain on my lungs and the sensation in my head, a feeling that it was whirling and rocking even while the rest of me was pinned to the ground, became too much and I gasped and coughed.

The snake did not react. Its eyes watched mine. As I gazed into them I realized that they looked wrong: their pupils were not thin elliptical slits but perfectly round black beads and their irises were a warm brown that I knew from somewhere.

I kept my eyes on the snake's because I could not look at the flickering light that illuminated them. It seemed to swing back and forth like a censer in the hands of a priest, looming towards me until it threatened to fill my head up and then shrinking to a shimmering point the size of a star.

I could hear a voice. It seemed to come from far away and I was not sure whether it was uttering words or inarticulate cries. The sound was so faint that when it stopped I could not decide whether I had really heard it, but when it resumed, the snake seemed to respond to it.

'Can you hear us?'

I blinked. My eyes were shimmering, misty. It was becoming harder to focus on the creature's face, on those unsettling eyes, the scales that glistened where they caught the light, the lipless smirk on its mouth. I shut my eyes but somehow the snake was still there, its head now moving from side to side in a slow, sinuous dance. I felt its coils moving over my body, and terror convulsed me, making my hands clench and snatching my head up off the floor, but the choking, suffocating pressure did not come. I lay still again, wondering at the sensuous caress of the snake's skin against mine, its tongue flickering over my throat and chest.

It reared up then, as if to strike.

'Can you hear this?' it asked, more loudly than before.

It had a woman's voice, throaty, compelling, thrilling. It was a voice to fill a man with yearning even when on the point of death, or perhaps particularly then, when all he has left is the desire for life and what creates life.

I groaned.

It seemed to me that the voice was not speaking to me. The distant voice answered it with a sound like sobbing.

'Oh, we can do better than this. We can make much sweeter music than this, can't we?' purred the snake.

Then it seemed to shed its skin, letting it fall away the way a snake will, leaving last year's scales draped over a rock or a cactus to dry and shred and blow away in the wind. In the moment before it moved towards me, blotting out the light, I caught a last glimpse of the creature's body, of the play of shadows over its pure, smooth new flesh, and I thought it was most beautiful thing I had ever seen. The yearning stirred in me again, stronger than before when I had merely heard the creature's voice, and when it slithered over me again, curling itself slickly around my manhood, for all my fear I could not find it in me to struggle. Instead I found myself trying to writhe in time with the snake, to match its own undulations with my own, and when I found myself still pinioned too tightly to move it was frustration, not pain or terror, which made me groan again.

'Oh, this is good!' The voice had changed, becoming wilder, higher in pitch. 'Can you hear how good this is?' Again its words seemed directed somewhere else, despite the intimacy with which its flesh was engaging mine.

A pain, tiny at first but growing and getting more insistent, started to gnaw at the back of my head, even as I heard my own moans of pleasure beginning.

'You're loving this, aren't you?' The words were definitely meant for me now, whispered from lips that brushed my ear in time to them.

I groaned again. I had to get out but there was nothing I could do, and the urge to let this continue was too strong.

'Why don't you tell me who you really are?' The lovely caresses slowed almost to a stop. 'If you don't, I might stop. Do you want me to stop?'

I could manage only a gurgling noise.

'I didn't think so. I gave you some of those little black seeds of Idle's. Now you can't let me stop, can you? We use them ourselves, so I know.' An unpleasant, snickering little laugh stirred the hair around my ear. 'Even if this didn't tell me!' She squeezed me once, making me gasp. 'What are you doing here?'

Something other than fear or sexual desire jerked the reply from my throat, something that seemed to have overridden my will and produced answers to her questions without my thinking of them. 'My name's Cemiquiztli Yaotl,' I gasped, 'a slave of Lord Feathered in Black. I was looking for my son.'

She was still for a moment. Then she rose, still gripping me, to look down at my supine figure. She leaned slightly sideways so that the light, the flickering yellow glow that I could now see came from a pine torch, fell over her face, and, reflected in the light, I caught the glint of a bead of sweat on her cheek.

'Why did you think he'd come here?' She was still whispering.

'I thought he and Kindly's featherwork might be in the same place.' Her movements had ceased. Part of me willed them to resume. Part of me wanted to scream at her to stop. The pain in my head was intensifying.

She bent towards me again and I felt her hair and her breath on my face. 'I don't have to lie to you about this,' she murmured. 'There's no featherwork here and I don't know anything about your son. If we ever let you go, you can tell Kindly that. But now . . .'

She moved again suddenly, her hips grinding against mine with a new urgency, her hands kneading the bare skin of my chest and little cries bursting from her lips.

The pain in my head seemed to expand with her excitement, making me feel that my skull was about to explode. Nausea seized my stomach and the breath stopped in my throat as if I were being choked. I groaned aloud, making a sound like ecstasy even at the moment when my manhood began to shrivel.

The world spun around me, sucking me back down into the darkness. The last thing I heard was her scream.

It was more than a sound of pleasure. It was a war-cry, the vaunting boast of the victor, a triumphant shout.

I drifted in and out of my dreams and from one dream to another.

Fantastic creatures danced in front of me. I thought I saw

nests full of snakes, their glittering skins patterned with stripes and whorls and painted in glorious colours, scarlet and yellow and blue and green and colours I had never seen before and never would again, colours that I could taste on the tip of my tongue and whose sounds were like flutes or falling rain or laughter. Sometimes I could not see the snakes but only the patterns on their skins, growing and merging and dividing and wavering before my eyes.

I thought I was in a room filled with birds. Their wings darkened the space around me and their beat filled my ears until it drowned out my own heartbeat. Their feathers seemed to fill my nose and mouth, making me sneeze and gag.

Then I found myself in a world peopled by gods.

A single, brilliant light shimmered through my tears. It seemed to pulse in time with the throbbing at the back of my head. Was this what the Sun looked like, I wondered, when seen from the Thirteen Heavens, above the sky and the clouds? Or had night fallen and the Sun dropped below the western horizon, parting from the souls of dead mothers who formed his guard of honour before making his return journey through the land underneath the Earth? I felt a chill come over me as I realized that I might be in one of the nine regions of Mictlan, the Land of the Dead.

I wanted to move then, to run away or beat my fists on the ground or curl up into a ball around my terror and the pain and the sick feeling in my stomach, but something held me flat on the ground, at the mercy of any creature or demon that might come for me.

At that moment I knew I must be dead or dying, because I heard a woman's voice.

It seemed to me that I had heard it not long before but had not known it for what it was, but now there was no mistaking it. It had no words for me, but that did not matter. Racked with bitter sobs, each one torn out of a throat tormented by pain and hunger and reproach and regret and flung at me through the icy darkness of Hell, it could only belong to Cihuacoatl, Snake Woman, the goddess whose cries were the most terrifying sound an Aztec could hear, foretelling utter disaster, death and the ruin of the city.

'No,' I wanted to cry out, but all I could manage was a husky whisper between dry lips.

A large, irregular shadow filled my vision. Its shape was strange, but familiar. As it dawned on me what I was looking at, I felt all my fear renewed and redoubled.

I had seen every detail of the figure before. From the long, graceful plumes that towered over his head and flowed down his back to the sheen of obsidian on his sandals and, more than anything else, the blank, terrifying, gaping face of his serpent mask, I could not fail to recognize the god. I was in the presence of Quetzalcoatl: the Feathered Serpent himself.

I dared not make a noise. I lay, paralysed with fear, watching him as he knelt over me.

The black pits that served him for eyes seemed to roam speculatively over my helpless, bound body. I squirmed, my buttocks clenching as my bowels threatened to turn into water.

Then the god advanced upon me, with a small, glittering object in his hand. I could not help a squeal of fright as I recognized a copper knife: an implement fine enough to prise feathers apart, or peel a man's skin away in layers. I was a gripped by a fear of something worse than death: if I truly was in Hell, could the god go on torturing me for ever?

'No . . .'

The god stood over me. He raised his free hand, extended his finger, and held it up in front of his mouth. He was motioning me to silence.

As he knelt over me, reaching towards me with the knife, I

could not have found my voice even if I had wanted to. I merely lay trembling silently as he tugged at the ropes that bound me, slicing them cleanly one by one until I was free.

He straightened, but put his empty hand on my chest, pressing gently but firmly in a gesture that meant I must not get up. He might have spared himself the trouble: my limbs were too numb and leaden to move.

Against the light there was less expression than ever in the serpent mask, but something told me that the mind behind it was troubled and perplexed, as though he had come across something unexpected and could not decide what to do about it.

In the end he mumbled: 'Why are you here?'

His voice sounded as though it were coming from the bottom of a clay pot. It also sounded young, but then I supposed gods were ageless.

I felt compelled to answer. 'I . . .'

'Quietly!' he hissed. 'She'll hear you!'

His warning had come too late.

Something stirred at the far end of the room. A sound like a yawn came to us, and then her shape appeared, uncurling itself from where she had lain, rising and stretching as naturally and gracefully as a jaguar waking from its midday nap, while the shadow cast by the wavering torchlight on the wall behind her danced suggestively.

Quetzalcoatl was on his feet in an instant, turning with a rustle of feathers and a tiny grating noise from the heels of his sandals.

'You're back at last!' Hearing her speak was like having my ears stroked with down. Her voice was soft and seductive, but there was something about it, some quality or feeling or memory it evoked, which made me shiver. She walked towards the god with her arms outstretched, and in the instant when the light fell directly across her body I saw that she was naked.

'Come here,' she said huskily.

In the instant he saw the woman Quetzalcoatl had seemed rooted to the floor. As her fingers stretched towards him, their tips brushing the hard skin of his jewelled mask, he seemed to waken. With a muffled cry he threw his arms out in front of him as if to push her away. He stepped back. The sole of one sandal trampled my ankle. I howled in pain and the god nearly fell over me. He stumbled, caught himself in time and backed towards the doorway.

'What's the matter?' cried the woman. 'Don't you want to . . . Come back!'

He blundered into the edge of the doorway. For a moment he seemed a blind, billowing confusion of cloth and feathers and sparkling jewels, and then he was gone, his inarticulate cries echoing around the courtyard.

'Wait!' she screamed. Still naked, she ran after him. 'Don't go! Tell me what's wrong!'

I forced myself to raise my head so that my ears could track her voice through the courtyard, and beyond it. I heard it dip as she ran through the other room and rise again as she reached the street outside, and I marvelled at how shrill and ugly it sounded, and how desperate she must have been to have run clear out of the house without anything on.

My head started to spin. I forced myself to concentrate, thinking I had to stay awake, I had to get up and get away before the woman came back, but the pain and the sick feeling were too strong for me, and I blacked out.

SIX MONKEY

1

I woke to an angry buzzing. It came from one side of my head and then the other, as though its source were moving in circles around my head, and it was only when it settled on my nose and made me sneeze that I realized that I was being inspected by a fly.

My eyes snapped open.

It took me a moment to recall where I was. My head was still full of the sights and sounds of the night, and the strange, disjointed dreams that had come upon me while I slept. I shook my head briskly, dislodging the fly and creating a spasm of pain at the back of my skull.

What had happened to me, and what had I seen? Vague images of the god Quetzalcoatl and a beautiful woman filled my head.

I remembered a tale of Topilztin, the infinitely wise and good last king of the Toltecs. He shared the attributes of Quetzalcoatl, the god whose high priest he was and whose name he bore. He had fallen prey to the malice of Tezcatlipoca, his divine patron's enemy. Tezcatlipoca had visited him in the guise of an old woman, a healer, and urged sacred wine upon him, saying it was for the good of his soul. Try just a drop on the tip of your tongue, the old woman had wheedled. He had refused; he knew that the taste would lead to a drink, and a drink to another, and so on until his soul was drowned in the stuff and lost for good.

At last he had assented to having a drop of it placed on his forehead, and from that moment he was lost.

Gourd after gourd he had downed, and then he had called his sister to him and had her taste the stuff too, and then, in a drunken frenzy, they had lain together.

Afterwards, consumed with remorse, he had left the city of Tollan, fleeing to exile in the East, never to be seen again.

Did this, I wondered, give meaning to the vision I had seen? Until that day, Quetzalcoatl had been celibate as well as temperate. Had the god, tempted by what had brought the man down, chosen to run away rather than risk the same fate?

I had come looking for the raiment of Quetzalcoatl, convinced I would find it in this room. Instead, I had seen the god himself. Or had I seen a man dressed as the god? Had I seen Idle's killer?

I began to understand Stammerer's fear and anger when he had described what he had seen from the top of the pyramid in Amantlan. Perhaps I had seen a man wearing a costume, but there was a power invested in the raiment of a god that belonged to the god himself and must not be misused, and I had felt it.

Daylight fell as a bright oblong across the floor and bathed the rest of the room in twilight. Still, it was not easy to see. My vision was blurred and it took a conscious effort to get my eyes to focus. With some difficulty I managed to lift my head off the floor. It came away with a sticky, tearing noise and an instant of blinding agony. I squeezed my eyes shut against the pain and slapped my palms against the floor to brace myself and stop myself falling back. I took several deep breaths until the throbbing and nausea had diminished and I felt able to move again.

'Got to get out, Yaotl.'

I got to my knees and then, gingerly, to my feet, watching

in puzzlement as several lengths of severed rope fell about me. Swaying a little, I looked down, noting the rope, the large patch of freshly dried blood where my head had been, and the fact that I was naked.

'Where are my clothes?'

Fortunately I did not have to look far: my breechcloth and cloak had been discarded next to where I had lain. Something on top of them glittered. Ignoring the renewed dizziness that it caused, I bent towards it and recognized a small copper knife.

That explained how the ropes had been cut, I thought, as I tied the breechcloth. Once I had wrapped myself in the cloak and knotted it over my right shoulder I felt able to look around me and make some effort to piece together the things I could see and the vague, disjointed memories that they stirred up.

I noted the pile of rubbish by the back wall. I could see now that it had not grown out of a year's worth of detritus thrown casually into a corner. Some effort had been made to sweep it all together. I stepped over to it and began sifting it experimentally.

As before, I was surprised by the number of feathers, and much else connected with the featherworkers' craft: knives, needles, glue spreaders, and so on. As I stirred the rubbish with my fingers the air around me suddenly filled with feathers and I had to hold my breath to stop myself sneezing.

Something fell off the top of the pile as I disturbed it, a round, lightweight object that struck the floor with a hollow ringing noise and rolled a little way across it until it reached the opposite wall. When I picked it up I saw that it was a bowl. I put a finger inside it and found that its surface was moist, and a few hard little grains still adhered to its sides. By putting the finger cautiously to my tongue, I could tell that someone had been drinking an infusion of Morning Glory seeds.

I threw the bowl back on the heap and spat on the rubbish to get rid of the taste. I knew it from my time as a priest. We had drunk a little of it, on occasion, to induce visions, but we knew that if anyone had too much, the demons he saw would take both his soul and his life. I wondered how much I had had, and how many of the fantastic things I had seen and heard in the night had come out of that little bowl.

I surveyed the heap of rubbish again. This had been Idle's and Marigold's room, according to Butterfly, but it looked as if she and Skinny had taken advantage of their disappearance to dump all the debris from his workshop in here. It did not take me long to satisfy myself that there was nothing underneath the pile. If the costume had ever been hidden there, it was long gone.

There was little else to be seen in the room except a cheap, frayed sleeping-mat and an old cloak or blanket on the floor beside it. However, as I stood over them, I noticed something I could not see.

I sniffed the air and frowned.

By far the strongest smell in the room was the smoky, resinous odour of a pine torch that had been left to burn itself out. There were others that it did not quite mask.

Clinging to the air over the sleeping-mat were faint hints of musk and sweat and stale perfume. A woman had lain there most of the night. I gathered the discarded blanket up in my arms and buried my nose in it. Then I threw it away violently, because there was something familiar in the complex of smells that it bore, something horrifying, a reminder of things I did not want to think about. I thought of snakes, hissing and writhing and threatening me with their stifling coils.

Shuddering, I turned to go. Then I caught another smell.

This one was fainter than the others, but once I noticed it I could not avoid it. It was the smell I had noticed when I had first come into the room, before I was knocked out, but now I remembered what it reminded me of: all the things I instinctively shied away from, the smell of my worst nightmares – a mixture of putrefaction, decay, filth, piss and blood.

It was the stench of the Emperor's prison, and for a moment my nose was filled with all the things that had assailed it in my time there, in my tiny, cramped, unlit cage, squatting, because there was no room to stand or lie down, and listening to the hoarse, rattling breaths of my neighbours while I waited for my turn to come.

I stumbled towards the doorway, gagging.

Something snagged my foot and sent me sprawling.

I scraped my knee painfully on the floor as I fell. The shock helped, reminding me that I was not in prison but free to blunder about and fall over things. I lay still for a moment while I repeated this to myself a few times, and then I turned to look at what had tripped me.

I realized it must be the same thing that I had stubbed my toe against in the night. It was a carved stone, one of a pair, because another, identical in style, lay next to it. When I picked them up I could see that they were two halves of the same piece. It had split, perhaps when someone had dropped it.

I rubbed my knee and then stood up, holding the broken sculpture. I could feel that when the pieces were fitted together there was a jagged surface left, where they must both have been joined to something else.

That gave me an idea. After a quick glance out of the doorway to make sure it was empty, I took the pieces out into the courtyard and carried them over to the broken plinth.

They fitted.

Holding the broken idol in place on its mounting, I was able to see it properly for the first time.

I knew it at once. It had a dog's face, wrinkled and furrowed with age. Its ears were misshapen rags, covered with sores, and its hands and feet were shrivelled and bent, so that had it been an animated, breathing creature, it could have done nothing but lie in the dust, howling for release from its agony. It was Xolotl, who represented disease, deformity and those feared and ill-omened beings, twins, whose presence could bring disaster on a household by draining the life out of the fire in the hearth.

I put the idol's two pieces on the floor carefully, so as not to make a sound. I wondered why it had been here: whether someone had been ill, or whether Marigold had acquired it because she felt she needed Xolotl to complete her collection. I wondered, too, why it had been desecrated so. Perhaps the god had been placated to get rid of an illness that had, in spite of everything, proved fatal. The smell in the room I had just left came to mind.

Or had Xolotl been venerated here for some other reason? It suddenly crossed my mind to wonder whether Skinny and his brother might have been twins, and what it might mean if they were. But if so, I thought, then why had the idol been broken?

I would have to think about that later. Now I had more pressing problems. The first was how to get out of the courtyard without having to go through the room leading to the street, where I might run into Butterfly or Skinny or both. Then I had to find a way of avoiding the Otomies. I tried not to think about what came after that. Kindly's property and my son were still as elusive as ever.

I thought the best thing I could do would be to clamber up one of the walls and leave the way I had come in. A stout climbing plant, like a mature gourd vine, would do, just something to give my hands and feet some purchase.

I had a quick look at the walls at the back and sides of the courtyard but found nothing. I turned to the front, but could not see anything there either, because there was someone standing in the way.

He was tall. My eyes were on a level with his chest. As they travelled upward, I tried very hard not to believe what they were telling me. Unfortunately there was no mistaking the short, plain, functional cloak tied at the throat, the grim mouth with its lips pressed firmly together, and the hooded eyes, the piled-up hair and the sword whose handle projected over one shoulder, ready to be seized and brought into use in an instant.

I took a step back. 'Up . . . Upright?' I spluttered. 'This . . . this isn't your parish. What are you doing here?'

'No. But it is theirs.' The policeman jerked his head once across his shoulder to indicate the men behind them. At the same time all three of them stepped forward. One was his own deputy, Shield. The others, judging by their thickset forms and harsh faces, were policemen too: at a guess, the parish police of Atecocolecan.

'I . . . I was just leaving,' I said.

'Quite right, you were.'

In one fluid movement Upright reached behind him, plucked his sword from its harness and had it poised over my head. Quick glances to the left and right told me his companions had done the same, and moreover that the two local men had stepped forward so that I was effectively surrounded.

'Now, Yaotl, we can do this the easy way where you come with us on your feet, or we can do it the hard way . . .'

'Where you have to carry me because I can't walk with both legs broken. Right.' I sighed. 'Look, you don't understand . . . No, wait, what did you call me?'

'We don't need to understand,' growled the bear on my

right. 'Look, Upright, we're here, it looks like you've got your man, why not just bash him over the head and get going? We've got work to do.'

'But my name isn't . . .'

'We know perfectly well what your name is, you murdering little bastard! The woman went and reported you to the local lads here.' Shield suddenly jabbed me with the blunt end of his sword, not hard enough to hurt but with enough force to make me stagger. 'And this time there's no wealthy widow to back your lies up with her own. You didn't think my boss was joking, did you?'

'No,' I cried hastily, as the sunlight flashed off four sets of cruelly sharp obsidian blades. 'No, but you said . . . you called me a murderer – I had nothing to do with Idle, I tell you. I swear it, I will eat earth. . .'

'Idle?' To my amazement Upright laughed. 'You don't think we still care about Idle, do you?'

'You mean there's someone else?'

'Oh, this is pathetic!'

The end of the sword hit me just below the rib cage, knocking the breath out of me so that I could not cry in pain but only collapse, doubled over and gasping vainly for air.

I barely heard what Upright said next, but I managed to follow it somehow.

'You're such an idiot, Yaotl. If you'd stopped with Idle I don't suppose anyone would really have given a toss. Certainly I wouldn't. I gather his family might even have paid you for getting rid of him. But you had to go on, didn't you? You didn't seriously expect the Amanteca to overlook the death of someone like Skinny, did you?'

There was an argument over whether or not to search the house. Upright wanted to, but the local men wanted to leave and were not prepared to let the men from Pochtlan have the place to themselves. It was not a prolonged or heated discussion, since Upright and Shield were convinced they had got their man. It would be easier and more fun, they assured their colleagues, to get any evidence they needed by beating it out of me rather than breaking up the courtyard or rifling through wicker chests full of old skirts and breechcloths.

By the time this was settled I had got my breath back enough to be frog-marched through the empty front room to the canoe the two men had brought with them. At least, I told myself as I was bundled into the swaying craft, I would be spared the walk back.

Shield took up the pole. As he pushed us away from the shore he let his eyes linger on his two local colleagues as they turned their backs indifferently and walked away along the side of the canal.

'Get a warm welcome around here, don't you, boss?'

Upright grunted. 'We wouldn't like it if a couple of strangers turned up on our patch and started telling us what's what.' He leered at me. 'Maybe we should have told them our suspect was from Tenochtitlan. They wouldn't have minded then. Round here I don't suppose they like Southerners any more than we do.'

'We didn't know . . .'

The constable shot a warning glance at his deputy but it was too late to stop me from picking up his meaning. 'You weren't out looking for me, then?' I asked innocently.

Upright looked suddenly sick. 'Mind your own business!'

'Only, if you weren't, then who were you after? What made you connect me with whatever's happened to Skinny?'

'The fact that you did it!' rumbled Shield dangerously. He was taking out his annoyance and embarrassment on the pole, stirring up the muck at the bottom of the canal and cleaving a dark wake through the weeds and scum on its surface. I hoped he might be furious enough to capsize us or run us hard aground and give me a chance to run, but he was too skilful for that.

'We just came here to tell Skinny's wife the bad news,' his superior said. 'Of course, we called on the local police on the way, and what did we find? The newly widowed Butterfly tearing her hair out and babbling about finding you, of all people, trying to burgle her house. Wouldn't you say that's a bit suspicious? Especially since you've never answered for what happened to Idle. And we know the story you and Lily came up with was a pack of lies.'

'Did you ask Kindly about it?' As soon as I posed the question I realized it was pointless. Whatever Kindly may have said scarcely mattered since the truth, at least about who I was, had come out anyway. I had a vision of the merchant's daughter striding into Howling Monkey's courtyard, her skirt flowing around her and the sound of her sandals striking the floor, and was suddenly aware of the risk she had taken and the fact that, for whatever reason, it had not come off. 'And what about Lily?' I asked, in a small voice.

'What about her?' Upright grimaced. 'Like father, like daughter, aren't they? And she had a son who was just as bad. If any of that family told me my own name I'd have to run home and ask my mother, to check!' He laughed shortly. 'Don't worry, she set the record straight. After you did a runner – wasn't I surprised when that happened! – she went and told your master what had happened.'

'*What?*'

Shield gave an unpleasant chuckle. 'Old Black Feathers himself! The Chief Minister!'

'Of course, there wasn't much for us to do once we knew whose slave you were. He's got enough men of his own to send running around after you without needing any help from us. If we'd wanted to get you for doing Idle, we reckoned we might as well wait and see what was left after they'd finished with you.' He gave me what may have been a pitying look. 'And from the look of some of them, you're bloody lucky we found you first!'

I wondered what had possessed Lily to go to my master, but I had more urgent worries on my mind now. 'So where are you taking me now?' I asked in a low voice. 'Back to Lord Feathered in Black?' I could guess what would happen after that. My master would gloat over me for a while and then hand me over to the captain's tender mercies.

'Oh no. Not now. You're going to the Governor.'

'Itzcohuatzin? Why him?'

'Why do you think? I told you Skinny was a mistake. As soon as we knew who the dead man was, every parish police-man in Tlatelolco was told to bring whoever did it to the Governor. Now I don't know whether Lord Feathered in Black has any other ideas, seeing as you're his slave, but since I've had no orders to the contrary, it's to the Governor you're going.'

'What happened to Skinny?' I asked.

Shield groaned. 'Here we go again!'

Upright snorted. 'You might tell us. We know you attacked him on the Pochtlan side of the canal, right near the bridge with Amantlan. Why so close to where we found his brother? I suppose you were unlucky, though. I don't reckon you hit him hard enough to have killed him outright, but of course he drowned. You could have pulled him out, though.'

'Maybe he thought he was doing him a favour, letting the poor bugger die like that,' Shield suggested. People who died by water were spared the terrors and misery of the Land of the Dead; instead they were destined to spend the afterlife in

Tlalocan, the rain-god's paradise, where the seasons never let you down and there was always plenty to eat.

'I didn't kill him,' I said, for the sake of saying it.

'Well, you can tell that to the Governor and whoever else asks you,' Upright said indifferently. 'I'm curious, though. Why'd you do it? What were Idle and Skinny to you?'

'He fancied getting up the widow's skirt!'

Shield's crude jibe jolted some memory, a dream I thought I had once had, or rather a nightmare, and suddenly I was in a dark, cramped space, and a great snake was wrapping its coils around me, its woman's voice cooing softly in my ear, saying things that should have been beautiful and arousing and were all the more grotesque and sickening because of it.

I struggled. I tried to cry out, to stand up, to flee, and then there was a massive hand on my shoulder, driving me back down into the bottom of the boat.

'Don't even think about it!' Shield snarled.

I sat, shivering, while Upright looked at me thoughtfully. 'Interesting,' he said at last.

'Look,' I said, mustering all my self-control to keep my voice steady, 'I didn't kill Skinny because I wanted his wife or for any reason. I didn't kill Idle. I was asked by Kindly the merchant to look for some property of his that he thought they had. That's why I was at their house.'

Why had I found Shield's words so disturbing? More of the visions of gods and serpents that I had had in the night were coming back to me. I wondered why the images were so enduring. Dreams, even those induced by the seeds of the Morning Glory plant, were fragile, evanescent things, usually dispersing like mist as soon as the Sun came up, but these would not go away. They were like the memory of a real event rather than something I had had to travel to the land of dreams to see.

'We know why you were at their house.' Shield's voice, outlining his theory, dragged me back to the present. 'You'd got rid of Idle and Skinny so there wouldn't be anyone to get between you and Skinny's wife. I bet you also got her sister-in-law out of the way too, didn't you? We haven't found her body yet, but we will. So now you thought you had everything nicely set up and it was time to go and enjoy yourself.' He gave a raucous laugh. 'You must have been really looking forward to that. I've seen Butterfly!'

Upright looked at me again. 'Why'd you bring up Kindly again? We know you aren't his slave. What's this lost property you were talking about? Why would you have been looking for it?'

I thought quickly. There was one thing I knew I could never reveal to the policemen or anyone else, my search for my son, because I could not risk giving anything away that might help Lord Feathered in Black to guess who he really was or that he was still in the city. That was my secret, I decided, but other people's, including Kindly's, were none of my business.

'I was running away. I needed cash – something I could carry, like a few quills of gold dust or some copper axe heads. The merchant said he'd pay me quickly if I did this job for him. He'd bought some featherwork from Skinny and . . . well, we were pretty sure he'd stolen it back again. Skinny himself told me he knew nothing about it but I didn't believe him, so I went back to look for myself.'

'Balls,' muttered Shield.

Upright curled his lip. 'Well, either way, the Governor will have to make up his own mind about you. We're nearly at his palace.'

I looked up in surprise. I had not noticed how far we had come, but there was no mistaking the shape of Tlatelolco's great pyramid towering over the buildings in front of it. The

Governor's palace faced the sacred precinct at its base, imitating the palaces of the Emperors in Tenochtitlan. Also next to
the sacred precinct was the world's largest marketplace, a huge
open space surrounded by colonnaded walls where up to sixty
thousand people came every day to buy, sell, cheat, steal or just
pass the time. I could hear them from here, the constant background rumble of an uncountable number of unraised voices.

The canal we were on now was a wide one, as were the
ones it crossed, and the large, blank-faced buildings and sturdy
landing-stages around us told me that this must be where the
merchants unloaded and stored goods ready for the market.

'Not the most direct route,' Upright explained. He was
looking forward to getting rid of me and passing the responsibility on to someone more senior, and his sense of relief
made him positively chatty. 'But it's easily the quickest. Hardly
anyone uses these canals except merchants going to their warehouses, and they only travel at night. At this time of day,
everywhere else will be jammed solid.'

Sure enough, it was quiet, with no traffic beside our canoe
and little sign of life apart from a few weary-looking sedges
growing up between the wooden reinforcing posts at the
canal's edge.

We were not quite alone, however.

Shield saw him at the same time as I did: a lone figure
standing beside one of the warehouses, in the centre of the
path running between it and the canal, with his legs braced
slightly apart and his head turning slowly from side to side, as
though scanning the area around him. 'What's he up to?'
Shield asked suspiciously. 'Doesn't look like a porter or a merchant – off he goes!'

The stranger had vanished around a corner, leaving only a
blurred impression of a cloak flapping behind him as he ran. I
blinked, thinking he must be extremely fleet to have covered

the distance that quickly. 'I thought he looked more like a warrior,' I said slowly, suddenly filled with foreboding.

'Around here?' Upright replied. 'I doubt it. Some of the merchants hire muscle to guard their property, sometimes. He was probably one of them.'

'More likely a lookout man for a robbery,' his colleague suggested. 'Once we've dropped our little friend here off we ought to come back and check.'

Either of them might well be right, I thought, but hired guards tended to sit or lounge, dozing peacefully, against a handy wall, rather than standing, alert and ready for action, in the centre of a path. And robbers and their lookout men did not run like a jaguar after a deer when there was no one pursuing them. They did not wear their hair piled up on their heads and flowing over the backs of their necks, either, but neither of my escorts seemed to have noticed that.

They caught up with us just short of the Governor's palace.

Shield poled the canoe slowly along a broad waterway in the shadow of one of the marketplace's outer walls. The distant rumble I had heard before had become as loud as thunder over the mountains, or perhaps a waterfall: a continual babbling, a sound made up of many smaller sounds that caught the ear a thousand different ways without ever increasing or diminishing.

'Hold your noses,' he advised us. 'This is where they moor the dung boats.'

Upright and I both looked ahead. We were passing scores of vessels filled with the contents of the city's privies and brought here for sale to parishes, landowners and makers of dyestuffs.

'Not surprising there aren't many people about, is it?' Shield went on nasally. It was nearly the warmest part of the day. I was breathing through my mouth and I thought the air even tasted foul. I did not want to dwell on what it must be like in high summer.

'Look out!' Upright shouted suddenly. A canoe had appeared in front of us, blocking our way. It looked as if it had been launched from the side of the canal straight into our path.

'What's he doing? Move that thing, you idiot!' yelled Shield, but the last word died in his throat as he had a clear look at the other craft's only occupant.

This time there could be no mistaking his occupation. If his green costume and his hair had not given it away, the deft, familiar way he handled the sword in his fist would have done. He was using it to motion us towards the bank with a curt, slashing gesture.

The captain and his men stood in a semicircle by the side of the canal.

'What do we do?' Shield whispered.

'What he says,' Upright muttered tensely. He glared at me. 'You know anything about this?'

I said nothing. I was speechless with terror.

'Well, hello, stranger.' The living half of the captain's face twisted into a lopsided grin as he caught sight of me. 'I was afraid we wouldn't meet again!'

'Now look . . .' Upright began.

'Shut up. Out of the boat, the lot of you.'

Upright swore under his breath, but complied. Shield and I had no choice but to follow him. The captain and his men formed a semicircle around us as we scrambled ashore.

I stood at the very edge of the canal, with the policemen on either side of me. At that moment they felt like my only protection.

'What do you want?' Upright demanded.

'Him, of course.'

'On whose authority? He's going to the Governor. If his Lordship tells us to hand him over to you, you're welcome to him, but. . .'

'This is my authority.' The captain lifted the wicked, four-bladed sword I had seen him with earlier and jabbed Upright in the stomach with its blunt end, just once and not hard, and then raised it further so that the blades glittered in front of the policeman's eyes. 'You do what it tells you, see? Sod the Governor!'

What Upright did then was instinctive. If he had thought about it, even for a moment, he might have lived, but it all happened instantly, and by the time I saw what he was about it would have been too late to intervene even if there were anything I could do.

He raised his right hand towards his shoulder, where he wore his sword slung over his back.

He was dead before his fingers could so much as brush the weapon. Fox's blade took him with a casual backhanded slash across the stomach. For a moment Upright just stood, watching, with a bemused look on his face, while his guts spilled out in front of him, and then he made an odd belching noise, blood gushed from his mouth and he fell over.

Two warriors had Shield's arms pinioned behind him before he could move. He seemed unable to speak. He stood staring down at his chief's body, open mouthed, the colour draining from his face even as I watched.

'Fox,' the captain said, 'you are so clumsy. Who's going to clear up that mess?'

Shield was still struggling to find his voice. 'You. . .' he gasped.

'Forget it.' The captain thrust his brutal, ravaged face into the policeman's. 'Sorry to hear about your colleague's unfortunate accident. The Chief Minister sends his condolences. It's important you remember that. "Accident" and "Chief Minister" – got it?'

Shield made a noise that the captain was obviously willing to take as assent, as he turned to me.

'Now, as for you.'

He raised the four-bladed sword. I watched the glittering black razors set into its edges, one by one, as they swept past my face on the weapon's upward swing. I felt my stomach lurch and I squeezed my eyes shut to spare myself the sight of the blow coming.

Nothing happened.

I opened my eyes again.

The handle of the weapon ended in a heavy wooden knob. That was the last thing I saw, filling my vision as it was driven down between my eyes like the head of a mallet, before everything went dark.

2

My head was an ear of maize. The back of it lay on a grinding-stone and someone was bearing down on my forehead with a stone roller. My skull was the husk they were going to split as their hard surfaces scraped against each other.

I screamed, rolling over to escape the stones' relentless pressure, and my face came up against a sandalled foot.

'Ah,' said a voice I knew and hated, an old man's voice that I had somehow hoped I might never hear again, 'he's awake.'

'I said he was, my Lord. I know how hard I hit him. He was shamming.'

'Well, perhaps.' The old man heaved a regretful sigh. 'So hard to get reliable slaves, these days.'

'Would you like me and my boys to teach him to behave himself?' The sound of a man with not much more than half a mouth smacking his lips with relish is not one I would wish to hear again.

'Thank you, Captain.' The old man paused, no doubt wanting to let the Otomi's suggestion work its way through my brain and down into my guts before continuing. 'However, I think I would just like you to get him on his feet for now. Then why don't you and your men have something to eat? You must be tired and hungry after your search. I'll send for you if this slave needs . . . well, if I want anything further.'

'Thank you, my Lord. You're too kind.'

The captain's way of getting me on my feet consisted of grasping me around the throat, which he could easily do with one massive hand, and yanking me upright. I made a strangulated noise while my feet danced about, looking for the floor. My eyes opened but everything was a blur, slightly tinged with pink.

'If you don't stand up,' the big warrior hissed, 'you'll choke.'

I managed to get both feet on the ground. They could just about reach it, but it took some of the pressure off my neck. That felt stiff and sore, even when the hand released it to leave me standing, unsupported, swaying slightly but still upright.

My stomach made an unpleasant sound.

'I advise you not to throw up in front of Lord Feathered in Black, Yaotl,' said another voice portentously. 'You're in enough trouble already.'

I turned my head slowly towards the speaker and forced my eyes to focus on him. My master's steward, Huitztic the Prick, was squatting a few paces away, his eyes respectfully downcast in our master's presence. He looked strange, and after a moment I saw why. Partly faded, yellowing bruises covered his arms and legs, and the ear I could see was badly swollen.

I remembered how I had left him, surrounded by a hostile crowd of Tepanecs. 'You look a bit rough,' I said. 'Been in a fight?'

'Yaotl,' my master said evenly, 'shut up.'

As I swivelled my head towards him I heard him admonish his steward. 'When your advice is needed I will tell you. In the meantime, perhaps you would care to show the captain and his men where they can rest, and find them some food. Now, as for you. . .'

The old man's high-backed, fur-covered wicker chair had been placed in one of his favourite places, on the raised patio on the roof of his palace, beneath the magnolia tree that his father had planted. From here he could look towards the Sacred Precinct of Tenochtitlan, the Heart of the World, its temples soaring towards the sky just beyond the canal at the front of his palace. He was looking that way now, probably indulging himself with a vision of me being dragged up the steps of a pyramid towards the sacrificial stone at the top.

I squinted painfully, forcing my eyes to focus on his face so that I could try to judge his mood now. To look a great lord in the eyes was the kind of impudence that would normally have got me a severe beating, but I felt as if I had had so many of those lately that it scarcely mattered. The back and front of my skull were still competing over which hurt most, but the bruises the Otomi's finger had raised on my neck were catching them up fast.

His Lordship was dressed casually, for him, in a pale green cape with a border of shells, a matching breechcloth with golden tassels at its ends and real shells dangling from his ears. A mother-of-pearl lip-plug completed the ensemble. I thought it a little vulgar but I knew he would change if he wanted to go out anywhere and he would almost certainly never wear any of it again. The plumes in his hair were only heron, but they were the longest, whitest heron feathers you could get.

He looked me over slowly. His fingers, long swollen and crippled by arthritis, lay in his lap. He had no tobacco tube or chocolate bowl by him, but the moment he needed either he would have it almost before he could ask. All I wanted then was a drink of water, but I did not expect any graceful serving girl to slip a gourd into my hands at the merest gesture.

'I don't suppose,' he began heavily, 'that there's much point in my asking you for an explanation, is there?'

I swallowed. 'My Lord, I . . .'

'I could ask you to give me a good reason why I shouldn't just take the Otomi up on his suggestion. I gather he has a talent for dentistry that any curer would envy.' I shuddered at the memory of what I had seen in Tlacopan. 'But what's the point? You'll only lie to me, and anyway, I know perfectly well what you've been up to. So I'll tell you what I'm going to do instead.'

I tensed, feeling my mouth go dry with fear as I waited to learn my fate. A flicker of something that may have been amusement crossed my master's face, and he moved a cracked, leathery hand once in a barely perceptible gesture.

A moment later a girl was at his side, presenting him with a steaming bowl. The aroma of chocolate and vanilla filled my nostrils, and a sudden sharp pain in my stomach reminded me how long it was since I had eaten or drunk. As his Lordship sipped delicately at his drink I tried to take my mind off my fear by wondering how they managed to serve him freshly whipped chocolate at just the right temperature so quickly. I supposed a drink must be kept just outside the room, to be poured away and replaced if it was not called for, but what if he had wanted a different flavouring – honey or green maize or pimentos instead of vanilla?

I got so absorbed in this nonsense that it took me a moment to realize that my master had started speaking again.

'Of course, you have run away. Whatever happens, you know I can't overlook that. I shall have to admonish you. That will be for the second time. Once more and you know what will happen.' Of course I knew: I could lawfully be sold, and having been marked out as obviously useless, could expect to be bought for only one purpose.

But at that moment the prospect of being sacrificed barely entered my thoughts. All I could understand was that I was being reprieved. My master was giving me another chance.

I swallowed, I gaped, and then I fell to my knees, less out of gratitude and deference than because my legs had buckled. I flopped forward in front of his Lordship, prostrating myself, with my arms flung out towards him.

'My Lord! Thank you! I . . .'

My words ended in a scream as something hard slammed into the top of my head. I heard a crack like a fir branch full of sap bursting in a fire, and there were pieces of pottery on the floor and scalding liquid all over my head and neck. Unlike most Aztecs, my master liked his chocolate piping hot, and the contents of his bowl seared the tender, bruised flesh of my scalp, making tears spring to my eyes and my hands snatch convulsively at my hair.

'Don't start thanking me, you worm! Why do you think I didn't just give you to my steward and the captain and let them take turns breaking every bone in your body, one by one? Eh? Look at me!'

I raised my head towards my master. A pathetic sight he must have thought me, with fragments of pottery in my hair and chocolate running down my face and over my eyes, forcing me to blink.

'I'm going to let you live – for now – on one condition.' Disgust twisted his mouth, as though I were the corpse of some verminous thing found rotting in one of his storehouses. 'You tell me where the boy is.'

'The . . . the boy?'

He leaned towards me slightly, probably as far as his ancient back would allow. 'The boy, Yaotl. Don't play dumb. You know who I mean. Shining Light's accomplice, the one I want for cheating and humiliating me. Your son, Nimble!'

'My son? How can you . . . How . . .?'

'How do I know? How do you think? His boyfriend's mother told me.'

'Lily?' I asked, incredulously. I remembered Upright telling me how she had gone to Lord Feathered in Black after I had escaped.

'Yes, Lily. He only had one mother, as far as I know. And she told me everything you told her. So I know what her son did, and what your son did.' Suddenly his Lordship laughed, a cackling sound followed by several dry, shallow wheezes. 'Have you any idea how much that woman hates you? She thinks your boy led hers astray! That's why she was bringing you back to me. She thought you'd get what you deserved here. If you didn't, she told me, she'd take your skin off you with her fingernails!'

I said nothing but my mind was in turmoil. I understood, now, how the Otomi I had met by the canal the day before had known who he was looking for. After she had snatched me from Howling Monkey's house Lily must have come straight here and passed on everything I had told her. But had I told her that much?

I tried to remember what I had said to the tense, bitter woman sitting opposite me in the canoe. I had not intended to mention Nimble. Where had I gone wrong?

'I know what you were up to in Tlatelolco.' The Chief Minister's voice had become soft, and years of experience told me that there was no more dangerous sound in the World. 'You were looking for him, weren't you? You convinced that meathead of an Otomi to go blundering into Tlacopan after him and then went to Tlatelolco because somehow you knew that was where he'd really gone. So where is he, Yaotl?'

I looked down and squeezed my eyes shut against the tears that threatened to overwhelm them. 'My Lord, I don't know,' I muttered truthfully. Then I took a deep breath and looked up again, straight into my master's startlingly clear brown eyes. 'But you may as well send for the captain now, because even if I did know, I couldn't tell you.'

3

'And then what happened?'

Handy, the big commoner my master retained as his general dogsbody, was following my story with a look of frank amazement. I was no less astounded to be looking at him. In fact I was surprised to find myself looking at anything at all: by now, I calculated, my eyes ought to be dangling out of their sockets like a couple of dead flowers drooping over a wall.

'He said he'd give me a day to think about it.'

I still marvelled at the changes that had come over my master's face in the moments after I had defied him. It had darkened with fury, its lines deepening and bunching together and his lips drawing back over his teeth in something like a snarl. Then, abruptly, it had cleared. His hunched shoulders had relaxed a little and he had sat back, letting his fingers caress his chin while he thought over his decision.

I could have one day.

'Mind you, he told me not to let you out of my sight,' Handy pointed out.

'Could have been worse,' I said. 'I might have had the Prick for an escort!'

A day during which I was at liberty: no duties; go where you like, Yaotl; start by having a bath and a good meal. Remind yourself how sweet life can be, and ask yourself if you really want the captain to part you from it.

I was not that naive and his Lordship knew it. If I was lying, a day would make no difference. If I was telling the truth, he expected me to look for Nimble again as soon as he set me free. And he had given me Handy as an escort knowing that I thought of the commoner as a friend and would think twice about slipping away and leaving him to face the Chief Minister's fury.

I had had the bath and the meal, and now Handy and I sat in one of the Palace's many courtyards while we brought each other up to date on our exploits.

'I saw Lily when she came to see his Lordship. Angry? She was spitting. I wouldn't have wanted to be on the receiving end of anything like that, I can tell you, and I'm used to Citlalli at her worst.' Handy's wife had a tongue like an obsidian flake: it had scratched me in the past. 'I couldn't work out what she was doing here, mind you. You say she told Lord Feathered in Black her own son had duped him? What would have been the good of that?'

'She probably thought she had no choice. She was in deep trouble for spiriting me away from her parish chief the way she did. I suppose she thought the best way out of it was to bring me back here once she'd got what she wanted from me. The merchants could hardly complain about her restoring the Chief Minister's slave to him, could they, even if she had a funny way of doing it?' I sighed regretfully as I realized that what Lily had done probably had a simpler explanation than that. I could not see her handing me over to the Chief Minister in cold blood, just to spare herself a confrontation with her parish elders. She was too proud to have stooped to that. If she really had intended to deliver me to my master, then she had been prompted by anger and a desire for revenge. 'When I screwed it up for her by escaping there was nothing for it but to come here anyway and tell his Lordship what she'd learned from me, and hope that would be enough. Which apparently it was.' My master had by all accounts been more than happy with the woman's tale. He had even rewarded her with a load of cotton that had gone back to Pochtlan in her canoe.

But how had she known so much? I kept asking myself what I might have said to enable her to guess the truth about Nimble, but I still had no answer.

I asked Handy what had happened to the steward and the captain in Tlacopan after I had fled.

He grinned. 'They got roughed up a bit. The trouble with people like your captain is they depend on people being so shit scared of them they won't fight back. But even the Tepanecs were able to work out eventually that there were far more of them than the Otomies. It's probably just as well that the local version of the Chief Minister turned up eventually, before things started getting really bloody. By the time I got back there with your brother and his warriors, there wasn't much going on except a lot of snarling and swearing. It didn't do me any harm – the Prick even thanked me for going to get help.'

And the boatman had, in the event, escaped with his life. He would be living on maize gruel and mashed-up squashes for the rest of his life, but having bolted and left Lord Feathered in Black stranded he might consider himself lucky. I almost envied him. He had taken his punishment. Mine was yet to come, and it was probably going to be far worse.

'So, it looks like you're the boss for a day,' Handy reminded me, 'since I have to follow you everywhere. Where to now?'

I looked up at the sky. There were no clouds. It was beginning to darken, a deeper blue washing over it from the East, with a star-studded indigo to follow. My stay of execution ended at noon the next day: I had a night and a morning.

I dismissed any thought of going to look for Nimble. Even

if I could find him in the time I had, it would only be to deliver his death warrant. I doubted that I would live long after that, whatever my master might have said.

Desperate as I was, there was only one place I could think of going. When I thought of it, I realized that that was where I might find the only person who might conceivably be able to help me.

'I think,' I said, unexpectedly having to squeeze the words past a sudden lump in my throat, 'I'd like to go home.'

By 'home', I meant my parents' house in Toltenco.

The name meant 'At the Edge of the Rushes' and it fitted the place well. It was in the south of Tenochtitlan, about as far as you could get from Skinny's and Idle's home in Atecocolecan without leaving the island altogether, but the two parishes had much in common. Each of them managed to give the visitor the impression that this was a place where the land could barely be bothered to stay above water: canals and streets blending into waterlogged fields and many of the houses crudely built, thrown up in obvious haste after the last flood to give their dispossessed owners a roof over their heads before the rains came again.

None of this had struck me while I was growing up. In the short time I had had between being old enough to take notice of my surroundings and being taken to the House of Tears, I had known only that we had space and clear air, unlike people who lived in the middle of the city, whose houses were all crowded together and permanently wreathed in the smoke of their neighbours' cooking-fires. It was only later, on my rare visits to Toltenco as an adult, that I had learned to sneer at the place. Later still I had done my best to forget all about it.

Prior to my last visit to my parents' home, I had scarcely set foot in the parish in ten years. That last visit had been only nine days before, though, so my surroundings were more familiar than they might otherwise have been.

'It's not that bad,' Handy said. 'Our place in Atlixco isn't much better than some of these.'

'Maybe I'm not doing it justice. I left under a bit of cloud, after all. Still, if you're that easily impressed, you'll like my parents' place. It's on slightly higher ground, so it hardly ever floods.'

Handy dug his pole into the bottom of the canal and shoved the canoe in the direction I showed him. My master had very generously lent me a boat. I wondered where he expected me to go in it. I had spent most of the time it had taken to get to Toltenco checking to see whether he was having me followed, or was relying on my escort to keep me from straying. If I had a shadow, then he was very good at keeping himself hidden, since none of my anxious backward glances revealed anyone other than the occasional incurious passer-by.

'That's never it there?' Handy cried suddenly. 'The one with the tall pole in the courtyard?'

I had to smile in spite of myself. 'Oh yes,' I said, without troubling to follow his stare, 'that'll be it. The tallest tree in Toltenco.'

The tree was a shorn trunk, dragged across the lake from where it had been felled on one of the hillsides on the mainland, and stood upright in the middle of my parents' home. It was there for the annual festival of the Coming Down of Water, when we honoured the mountains that surrounded our valley, on account of the dark clouds that gathered around them, and the other gods who brought rain, such as Quetzalcoatl Ehecatl, Lord of the Wind, and Chalchihuitlicue. The coming night and the next day, I recalled suddenly, would see the climax of the festival. The pole would be pasted with banners made of rubber-spotted paper and offerings made to

the gods. There would be a vigil, followed by a feast. Most of
my family would be at home and there would be many guests
the following morning. This was one of our more enjoyable
festivals, especially if you could afford to celebrate it in style. In
the morning there would be food and drink in abundance, and
even sacred wine, which at other times commoners were forbidden to touch.

Organizing all this was no small undertaking, and it was not
cheap either. I was sure my mother would claim it was all on
account of my father's bad leg. It was especially important for
the lame to placate the mountain gods. No doubt the fact that
none of her neighbours could afford to put on such a show
had something to do with it, though.

'Tie up at the landing stage here,' I said.

'Your people do all right for themselves,' my companion
remarked as the canoe glided to a stop. 'We couldn't afford to
set up our own pole, not when it means having to feast the
singers and musicians as well. We always go to a neighbour's
house.' There was a wistful note in his voice, no doubt because
he would be missing the next day's celebrations.

'That's on account of my brother. Lion sends enough home
for my mother to be able to make a big splash and spend the
rest of the year complaining about the mess.'

I heard my family before I saw any of them. There were not so
very many of us – my parents and their grown-up children,
five besides myself, and my nieces and nephews – but put
them all together within the walls of a small courtyard and they
could sound like a busy day at Tlatelolco market.

'It'll be worse tomorrow, after the guests arrive,' I assured
Handy.

'I'm sure. What are we waiting for?'

We were still standing on the landing-stage, to one side of

the entrance, so that we were not visible from the courtyard. I pretended to inspect an imaginary crack in the smooth, newly whitewashed plaster on the wall beside me while I pondered Handy's question. Why was I hesitating?

On my previous visit here, my father and my brothers, apart from Lion, had been away. All commoners, except slaves whose labour belonged only to their masters, could be made to work for their parish or the city, and it had been their turn. However, their task would be done by now, and they would probably be here this evening.

It had been many years since my father and I had been able to meet without practically coming to blows. Each of us had too much to resent ever to have been able to let it drop. He begrudged the price he had paid to get me into the Priest House, which had all gone to waste when I was thrown out. I blamed him for the ridicule and petty insults that had been heaped on me at home for failing in a way of life I had not chosen but had grown to love, and the bitterness and humiliation that failure had caused me.

No doubt that was it, I thought, not wanting to dwell on the alternative explanation: that when I stepped through the doorway, it would be to say goodbye for ever. Even if I tried to save my life – if, say, I were to paddle my master's canoe to the edge of the lake and run clear out of the valley – I would surely never be back here again.

'Nothing,' I muttered. 'Better go, I suppose . . .'

The final decision that it was time to face my family was taken out of my hands by a shrill but strong voice.

'Who are you?'

I looked about me, startled. 'Who said that?' The voice seemed to have come from nowhere.

'Me!'

'Try looking down, Yaotl,' suggested Handy. 'I can tell

you're not used to children!' He crouched down next to me. 'What's your name, then?'

I would have put the newcomer's age at about three. He was naked apart from a short cloak that barely covered his loins. He took no notice of Handy but looked curiously up at me and sucked nervously on a finger. 'What did you do to your face?' he mumbled.

I opened my mouth and then shut it again when I found myself unable to think of a sensible answer. I looked hopefully at Handy, who was standing up. 'He fell over,' he said.

For some reason this struck the child as funny. He started giggling.

'Well, he seems to like you,' the commoner said. 'One of your nephews?'

'Possibly. Or a great-nephew, even.'

'His name,' said an icy female voice, 'is Quiauhtli. Quiauhtli, this is your great-uncle Yaotl. What are you doing here?' she asked me. 'It's no use scrounging for food, you know – the fast doesn't end till tomorrow!' In a slightly milder tone she added, 'And who's your friend?'

My elder sister Quetzalchalchihuitl, 'Precious Jade', had come looking for her child. I noted with some amusement that she had obviously run out of the courtyard in a hurry, and in the middle of washing her hair, since it was still plastered wetly to the back and sides of her head and her blouse was sodden where she had pulled it hastily back on.

'Hello, Jade,' I said wearily. 'Meet my friend Handy. He's working for my master. Aren't you supposed to be fasting before the festival? How come you washed your hair?'

Those households that had the means and the inclination to set up a pole and make offerings for the festival of the Coming Down of Water also committed themselves to a fast over the four days preceding it. During the fast it was permitted to wash your face and neck but nothing else, and no soap was allowed.

My sister looked at me as if I had just asked her why tortoises could not fly. 'Because obviously there won't be time tomorrow before everyone gets here,' she said shortly, before turning her attention to my companion. The modest angle of her head belied the blush that darkened her face and the hint of a sparkle in her eyes as she greeted him formally: 'You have come a long way, you are tired. Please come and rest. I am sorry we can't offer you anything to eat . . .'

I felt a grin creeping unbidden across my face as I stepped carefully around my sister and the child who was now clinging to her skirt. 'I'll leave you to it,' I said, knowing they would be quite safe. Jade did her best not to act her age, but she would not be able to keep the pretence up for long with her own grandson by her side. Besides, Jade's husband, Amaxtli, would be in the house somewhere. And I felt sure Handy would jump in the canal rather than have to endure whatever Citlalli would have to say to him if he misbehaved.

'That can't be the musicians already? It's too early! The Sun hasn't set yet, we're not ready, where's Jade got to? One of you . . . Tlacazolli, stop staring at that pole like a cretin, go and fetch your father! Are those paper streamers ready? Neuctli, the streamers, I said . . . Oh.' The old woman's head had been swinging sharply from side to side as she rapped out orders to her children as if they were eight-year-olds. When it finally came to rest, with her clear eyes narrowing as they finally took in the appearance of the man standing in front of her, the squawking tailed off into a kind of nasal drone comprised of disappointment, chagrin and something like resignation. 'It's you.'

'Hello, Mother.'

'What are you doing back here?'

My mother's piety ran deeper than my elder sister's: either that, or she had not had time to wash yet. She was dressed in a plain blouse and skirt of coarse, undyed maguey cloth, and although her grey hair was bound in the manner of a respectable Aztec matron, swept up and gathered into two long tufts that projected over her forehead like horns, it had a greasy, frayed look that told me it had not been washed for a while.

'I am your son, you know,' I said, reproachfully.

'I suppose so.' She sighed heavily. 'But I wasn't expecting you. I thought you were from the House of Song. Oh well. What with it being a fast, it's not as if you're another mouth to feed. What your father will say, I've no idea.' She glanced over her shoulder at my brother Tlacazolli, or 'Glutton', who had been shambling across the courtyard in response to her order. For a moment I thought she was going to call him back before he reached the room where my father evidently was, but she was just too late. My parents had named the elder of my two younger brothers Glutton for a reason, and his speed matched his bulk. On a good day he could just about beat a snail, provided he stayed awake long enough to finish the race, but he had managed to cover the distance and was disappearing through the doorway to deliver my mother's summons.

I followed my mother's glance nervously. 'How is my father?'

'Same as ever,' she said shortly. 'I take it you are here for the vigil?'

'Um, yes.'

I took the opportunity to survey the courtyard. Piled up beside the pole that dominated it was the wood and kindling that would keep the household warm during the long winter's night to come, and in front of the bonfire, sitting in a circle on tiny reed mats, were the dolls that would be the focus of the vigil and the next day's festivities.

'You've made a real effort,' I said. 'That looks like the full set.'

'It is.' My mother could not keep the note of pride out of her voice as she recounted their names: 'Popocatepetl, Iztaccihuatl, Tlaloc, Yoaltecatl, Quauhtepetl, Cocotl, Yiauhqueme, Tepetzintli, Huixachtecatl – that's all the mountains, then there's Xiuhtecuhtli, Chicomecoatl, Chalchihuitlicue and Ehecatl.' I imagined the labour that she and my sisters would have lavished on these figurines, these images of the mountains that surrounded the city and the gods that protected it, fashioning each one out of amaranth seed dough and giving it beans for eyes and pumpkin seeds for teeth. Of course, it was a wonderful excuse for them to sit around and gossip and it made a pleasant change from weaving, making tortillas and beating bark into paper, but I could still admire their handiwork.

One of the workers came up to me now.

'Yaotl?'

I stared dumbly at a slim, lively-looking young woman, trying to work out who she was. She would be about twenty, I thought, but I could not remember any female relative of mine who was that age. Jade was a year older than I, and my other sister so much younger that when I had last seen her she was still too young for the House of Youth, still at home, being taught by her mother to cook and spin maguey fibre into thread.

I stared from her to our mother.

'Neuctli?' I said, incredulously.

'Honey' was her name, and as far as I remembered it reflected the little girl's nature. She smiled sweetly at me now. 'You didn't recognize me, did you?'

I continued staring stupidly at her. 'You, er, you weren't here last time I came,' was all I could manage to say.

'Why should she have been?' snapped my mother. 'You chose to drop in unannounced for the first time in I don't know how many years, so what did you expect? The whole family lined up to greet you? You were lucky any of us remembered your name!'

'But I'm back again now,' I replied defensively. I looked around once more, concentrating this time on my family. I recognized Jade's husband Amaxtli, a short, wiry man in a one-captive warrior's multi-coloured breechcloth and a cloak embroidered with scorpions, squatting against the wall with his sons around him; and kneeling near by, Glutton's wife, Elehuiloni, a plain-looking woman with a weeping infant on her knee and a harassed look. Other children of varying ages milled about, filling the courtyard with their voices, but I could not have said whom any of them belonged to because I could not remember having seen any of them before. I saw no sign of my youngest brother, Copactecolotl, or 'Sparrowhawk', but that was no surprise. I would never have looked for him in a household that was fasting. Fasting included abstaining from women, and from what I remembered, that would not suit Sparrowhawk at all.

'Besides, I really had no choice.'

'Nonsense! You had a home here. And all I told you to do was go to the market and sell some paper, not drown yourself in sacred wine and get yourself thrown into prison!'

'I didn't mean . . .'

'Anyway, I'm not going to argue with you.' My mother stepped aside, and I saw my father, standing about four paces away, glaring at me with his arms folded and his teeth bared like an angry dog's.

He looked like an older, heavier version of my elder brother

Lion, thicker around the waist and neck and with most of his hair long since turned ash-grey, but still hard and strong. He still proudly wore the orange cloak and piled-up hair of a two-captive warrior. Had he been as lucky on the battlefield as his first son was to be, no doubt I would have grown up as the child of an exalted commoner, not exactly a great lord or a noble but the next best thing, and my precarious and ultimately doomed existence among the nobles' offspring in the Priest House might have been very different. In the event, each of us had had to make his own way in the world, and if I were ever tempted to hold that against my father, I only had to look at the jagged white scar left by the javelin that had shattered his left knee to remind myself that he was as much the victim of his fate as I was.

Unfortunately he was less philosophical about it.

'I heard you'd been here. What are you doing back again? Have you come to pay your mother back for the paper you stole? Fine. Pay her and go.' He lurched towards me, balancing himself on his good leg. 'If it's food and shelter you want you can forget it. I'll throw you in the canal first, and don't think my knee will stop me!'

I glanced at my mother. She looked down, her face darkening, although whether this was from embarrassment or anger I could not tell.

'All I've got,' I started to say, 'is what I'm wearing. I'm sorry . . .'

My father almost fell on me, stumbling forward and striking me on the chest with both hands. Surprised, I staggered back, almost losing my footing. The old man followed me and screamed in my face.

'You're sorry! You useless, lying, drunken, filthy, thieving, whore-mongering little excuse for a shit-smeared dog's arse!'

'Mihmatcatlacatl!' my mother cried, reproachfully.

He ignored her. He hit me again, but this time it was a real punch, aimed at my shoulder and with all the force of his strong right arm and a decade or more of bitterness behind it, and the numbing force of the blow sent me crashing to the floor with my cloak flapping around me in a tangle of billowing cloth.

'How dare you show your face here! I'll give you "sorry"! If you knew what I gave up for you!'

He aimed a kick between my sprawled legs. Fortunately kicking was no longer one of his strengths. His wounded knee gave way and he stumbled, momentarily off balance, and I took the chance to roll to one side and get on my hands and knees.

I scuttled away. A small circle of spectators, mainly my curious nieces and nephews, had gathered around us, and I made for its edge. He caught me before I got there, grabbing the hem of my cloak and jerking at it until I heard the cloth tear. 'Come back here, you coward! I've not finished with you yet!'

I let him have the cloak. I managed to undo the knot with one hand and help myself to my feet with the other. I whirled around, just in time to see my father collapse, screaming with rage as the cloak fell away in his hands.

My mother called his name again as she ran to help him up. She shot me a reproachful look.

'Get him away from me.' The old man was suddenly in tears. 'I can't bear to see him here. Just get him out!'

I watched and listened, mystified. 'I don't understand you,' I gasped. 'You won't even let me tell you why I came.'

'He's probably looking for me.'

The newcomer spoke in a self-confident drawl that I knew very well. I turned in time to see him stepping forward from among the spectators, the red border of his rich yellow cotton cloak swirling about his feet and the white ribbons at the nape of his neck flowing behind him. His sandals had big loose straps which slapped the ground as he walked.

The Guardian of the Waterfront stopped to survey the scene in front of him, a knowing smile spreading across his face as he watched my mother helping my father to his feet and me rubbing my sore shoulder.

'Looks as if I got here in time. I see you two have met at last!'

'Lion!' My father limped towards my brother with his arms outstretched and his eyes sparkling with joy. 'I didn't think you'd come! Are you here for the festival?'

Lion's reception could not have been more different from mine. While they embraced, clapping each other on the back, I looked around. The little children and their parents were beginning to move away to resume their seats at the edges of the courtyard. I saw Handy among them, looking self-conscious. I hoped my elder sister had not teased him too much.

When he had managed to disengage himself Lion said: 'I can't stay. I'm sorry, I'm needed at home.' Lion's family was housed in a mansion near the city centre, and if he intended to celebrate the festival he would have a pole of his own standing in the biggest of his courtyards. 'I came to find him.' He looked at me.

'How'd you know to look here?' I asked suspiciously.

'Just a lucky guess. I gathered from that evil little scorpion of a steward your master employs that you'd gone out. He claimed to have no idea where you'd gone, so I thought I'd try here first. It's where I found you last time, if you remember. You seem to be making these reunions a habit!'

My father gave me a disgusted look. 'Well, you've found him,' he snapped. 'Now will you please take him away with you.'

I groaned, realizing that I was about to get the blame for my brother's not being able to stay. 'Look,' I began, 'I only wanted to say . . .'

'Come on, then,' said Lion briskly. 'Don't forget your cloak.' He turned to my mother. 'I'm sorry about this. Duty calls — for both of us. But I'll send him back later.'

My mother said nothing. My father stepped towards me, then turned on my brother. 'Bring him back? That's the last thing I want. I don't want to see him again!'

Lion had started towards the doorway, gently brushing away the small crowd of admiring children who were trying to feel the hem of their hero's cloak. Now he stopped and looked back.

'I'll send him back,' he repeated coolly. 'What you do with him then is up to you. But it looked to me as if you two had some unfinished business and I would hate to interfere!'

He walked away. The only sound was the flapping of his sandal straps.

I looked at my parents. My mother looked back at me. Her face looked as if it had been carved in stone. My father merely stared wistfully after his favourite son.

'Well?' my mother said eventually, in a cracked voice.

'You heard what he said, Mother. I'd better go.' I turned away.

'Do you want your cloak?'

'No,' I said, without looking around. 'Keep it. In return for the paper!'

4

I left Handy in the midst of my family. If my father could for-give him for being associated with me, I knew they would make him feel welcome.

I ran down to the canal and caught up with Lion just as he was about to climb into a canoe. There were three of them, moored in a line: one for Lion and me and two for his escort of powerful warriors.

'I've learned from experience that whenever you're involved I've got to be ready for anything,' he explained. 'Now, in you get!'

'Aren't you going to tell me where we're going?'

'When you're in the canoe, yes.' By which time, of course, I would not be able to bolt. Ignoring my misgivings, I climbed into the canoe. It was either that or go home again and get beaten up by an old man.

'I have to hand it to you, Yaotl,' Lion continued as he settled himself behind me, 'when you get yourself into trouble, you do it in style. After all, if you're going to piss people off, why not go straight to the top?'

'What are you talking about?'

He chuckled. 'Can't you guess? This is the second time in a matter of days you've managed to earn yourself something most people don't get once in their entire lives.' He leaned forward to add, murmuring into my ear in a confiding tone: 'Your very own private audience with the Emperor himself!'

Night was falling. The canals and streets around us were almost empty. The evening rush home from the city's places of business, its marketplaces, courts, palaces and temples, was largely over, and it was too early yet for the merchants and their secretive, nocturnal traffic, or for any revellers on their way to dances or banquets, which usually began at midnight. The trumpet calls that announced sunset had faded and there was little sound other than the lapping of water against the sides of my brother's boat.

'My favourite time of day,' Lion mused.

'Me too,' I said eagerly. 'I liked watching the Sun go down over the mountains when I was a priest. I used to tend the temple fire on top of Tezcatlipoca's pyramid sometimes, even when I didn't have to, to get the best view. On a good evening it would make the surface of the lake shine like gold.'

My brother stared at me. 'What are you on about? I just like the fact that the canals are empty and I don't have complete strangers bumping into me!'

'What does the Emperor want?' I asked.

'Don't know, but I guess it has something to do with whatever you've been up to in Tlatelolco. Are you going to tell me about that?'

He listened to my account in grave silence. In the gathering gloom it was hard to read his features, but I thought I could see a frown forming and deepening as I neared the end of my tale.

'So what actually happened to you last night, at Skinny's house?'

'I'm not sure,' I confessed. 'I thought it was all a dream, brought on by the Morning Glory seeds, but now . . . well, some of it must have happened. I mean, there really was a woman there. I found signs of her when I woke up this morning. And I had been tied up and someone had come and cut my ropes. But the rest I don't know about.'

'I never get dreams like that,' my brother remarked ruefully. 'Still, if you're telling me it was another case of you not being able to keep your breechcloth on, I can believe that!'

'That's not fair! I was drugged!'

'So you say. Still,' Lion went on soberly, 'your problem right now comes down to this, doesn't it? Old Black Feathers wants to tear Nimble limb from limb. He's given you until tomorrow to produce him, failing which you'll suffer the same fate, but you don't even know where he is.'

'I thought that if I found the featherwork, I'd find him. That's what Kindly as good as told me.'

Mention of the old man's name drew a derisive snort from my brother. 'From what little I've seen of Kindly, I wouldn't place too much reliance on that!' He sighed regretfully. 'But as for your master . . . I don't know, brother. I'd do what I could, you know that.' I believed him. At one time, not so long ago, it would not have surprised me to see him in the audience at my own execution, visibly gloating over my fate, but a good deal had happened to both of us recently. 'It's not as if old Black Feathers is any friend of mine! The trouble is that he's the Chief Minister and I'm just an officer. So long as the Emperor is minded to let him, he can do pretty much what he likes.' He rubbed his chin thoughtfully. 'I could probably stop him from doing anything too flagrantly illegal. Even for a man in his position it would be awkward if the Guardian of the Waterfront started asking what had become of his brother, and he couldn't come up with some sort of explanation. But he has a perfect right to admonish you, especially since you've run away twice already, and no power in Mexico can prevent him. And we both know what's likely to follow if it happens a third time.'

At the entrance to Montezuma's Palace we were directed towards the Zoo.

The Emperor shared the vast, rambling complex that was his residence when he was in Mexico with many other creatures, both human and animal, and some that might have been said to be something in between.

At any one time Montezuma would give house room to enough servants and guests of varying ranks, from the Emperor of Tetzcoco to the most newly admitted of the Eagle Warriors, to fill the ranks of a small army. Some three hundred of the Palace staff worked full time looking after a select group of their fellow residents: the inmates of the Zoo and the aviary. Here, in stout cages that in many cases were bigger than most houses in Mexico, the Emperor kept specimens of every kind of bird and animal he and his subjects could get their hands on. Everything with feathers on it from eagles and vultures down to finches and sparrows had a perch here. There were ponds for brilliantly coloured ducks and flamingos to paddle in, whole trees full of fruit for parrots and toucans to destroy and avocados to keep the resplendent quetzal happy and encourage him to grow his magnificent long green tail feathers. What the eagles and vultures ate scarcely bore thinking about, but it was probably the same as the jaguars, cougars, bears and coyotes, who lived in another section of the Zoo with smaller meat-eaters such as foxes and ocelots. Their diet included man: the torsos of sacrificial victims.

There were snakes here too, kept in pots that had been lined with feathers so that they could lay their eggs in them without breaking them.

'You can tell where we're going,' my brother remarked.

'You can hear them from here!' The birds twittered, cawed or screamed, the jaguars and their cousins howled and roared, and I could imagine, even though I could not hear it yet, the hissing of the snakes.

Not all the specimens made a noise. There was no sound at all from the humans. For another section of the Zoo held its most curious exhibits: men and women born with the wrong number of fingers and toes or their joints reversed or no eyes in their heads or some other deformity that marked them out as someone the gods had noticed and decided to have some fun with.

'I hope the Emperor isn't looking at those brothers joined at the hip,' Lion said glumly. 'They bother me, I don't mind admitting. Twins are unlucky enough, but those two . . .' He shuddered.

'Not this evening, my Lord,' our escort assured him. 'He's with his newest guest. Please come this way.' The growling noise from where the meat-eaters lived was growing louder, and now it came with a rank animal smell, like a cross between a temple, just after a victim's blood has been smeared on the door posts, and a dog kennel.

'Change your cloak in here, if you will, my Lord,' our guide said. He ignored me. My brother could not appear before Montezuma in his fine cotton cloak and his sandals. As I had neither cloak nor sandals of any description, I simply waited for him to reappear, barefoot and in an old, patched and frayed piece of maguey fibre that ended almost indecently far above his knees.

'I don't think I want to know what happened to the last person who wore this,' he muttered, as we waited to be admitted. 'I just hope his end was quick!'

Something was fluttering about in my stomach. I tried to calm it. The last time I had been shown into the Emperor's presence, I had been threatened with death.

Our escort motioned us forward.

'Remember – don't look at his face!' he hissed.

Between us and the room where Montezuma was waiting stood a single guard, a Shorn One, an elite warrior who blocked the entrance and our view of what lay beyond completely because he and the doorway were about the same size and shape. He stepped aside, at the same time hissing: 'The Guardian of the Waterfront and a slave, my Lord!'

As I prostrated myself on the floor, I wondered why the announcement had been delivered in a whisper.

Out of the corner of my eye, I could see that the room gave directly on to a garden. Pale evening light flowed through a wide opening, and made a striped pattern on the floor that puzzled me until I realized that the entrance to the garden must be barred. Against what, I could not tell, but I thought I heard something out there making a rustling noise.

Montezuma the Younger sat in front of the opening, looking out. Almost all of his body was hidden from me by the tall back of the wicker chair that had been placed there for him, and most of what I could see was an irregular shadow against the pale background of the garden. However, where the light fell on his face, with its delicate features and neat little beard, and on the hand resting on the arm of the chair nearest to me, it picked him out eerily, as though he were outlined in silver thread.

A man stood beside and just behind the chair. He must be the interpreter, I thought, since Montezuma was not given to speaking directly with any but the most exalted of his subjects.

Suddenly sound erupted from my brother.

'My Lord!' he cried ritually. 'O Lord! My great Lord!'

Absolute silence followed him. Even the rustling in the garden stopped.

A small noise came from Montezuma. I was not sure

whether there were any words in it but its meaning was clear enough for the interpreter to turn to us and say: 'The Emperor says shut up!'

Lion gulped audibly.

I knelt, with my face pressed to the floor and wondering whether I could breathe more quietly if I somehow managed to use just one nostril at a time, until a faint creaking noise from the Emperor's chair told me he had relaxed a little. A moment later I thought I heard the rustling sound I had noted earlier. It was louder now, somehow more confident, as though whatever made it had decided to push its way into the open rather than skulking cautiously in the bushes.

'Ah.' The voice was undeniably the Emperor's, and to hear it so full of contentment was such a relief that I could not help risking a peek at whatever was happening out in the garden beyond him. It took me a moment to spot it.

'Here he comes.'

I twisted my neck awkwardly, so that I could look up without meeting Montezuma's eyes if he should chance to look round.

The garden looked as if no one had tended it in years. The plants were tall and unkempt and, except for an area just on the far side of the bars that was empty apart from a few artfully placed tree trunks and branches, so densely crowded together that if anybody had wanted to weed the place, they would have had to do it by starting a fire in the dry season. Foliage and ornament were not the point here. There was something else: something that I could just make out as a pale shape among the dark stalks and leaves beyond the clearing.

It moved. It became a long, white form, sliding along the ground so smoothly that I took it for a snake until I saw that it moved upon feet. One foot was advanced at a time, the paw put deliberately and silently in place before another was lifted, and the legs were bent as tensely as a bow, keeping the body as close to the floor as it could be without scraping along it. It was stalking something. Its sharp-pointed, triangular ears were erect and its eyes, strangely pale against its white face, were wide open.

I saw its prey only in the instant of its death.

It was a small dog. The keepers had tethered it by a long rope to a peg in the middle of the clearing, although they need not have bothered. It was one of the little fat hairless creatures we kept for food, born and bred for the pot, and any instinct that it might have had to survive, to run away or turn and fight for its life, had been lost many generations before. It simply had no idea what was going to happen until the moment when the jaguar sprang.

The creature became a white streak. Only when its great claws clapped together around it did its victim at last react. The dog let out a single yip and shot into the air, escaping momentarily until it reached the end of its rope and was cruelly snatched back to earth. Before it landed a paw swiped it out of the air, slamming into it with a blow that knocked it sideways and snapped its neck at the same time.

The great head stooped and picked its meal up. It held it aloft, and for a moment those strange pale eyes looked straight into the Emperor's. It seemed to know that it was the only creature in Mexico that might do that and live.

It growled surprisingly softly. It shook the dog once and dropped it contemptuously.

As it began to feed, I heard a long sigh from the man in the chair.

'You may watch,' the interpreter said solemnly. 'You may never see this again.'

I could not have taken my eyes off the animal in any case. My brother exhaled loudly. I guessed he had been holding his breath for a long time.

Then we heard the Emperor's voice again. When he was speaking half to himself he did not seem to mind being over-heard.

'A white jaguar. Such a perfect creature. The most noble of beasts, and the colour of the East, the direction of light, and life!'

'It is a beautiful animal, my Lord,' ventured my brother.

There was a pause. Montezuma mumbled something and his interpreter translated it: 'Indeed. They come from the country around Cuetlaxtlan, near the shore of the Divine Sea. When he was Chief Minister it amused the great Lord Tlacaelel – your master's father, Yaotl – to punish the people of that city for rebelling against us by making them send white jaguar pelts in tribute in place of spotted ones. He thought it would take up so much of their time to find anything so rare that they would never be able to foment another revolt!' There was more mumbling from the chair. 'I told them I would remit some of their annual tribute if they could furnish me with a live specimen. And here he is!'

Hearing my own name fall from the Emperor's lips – or at least his interpreter's – shocked me into speaking up. 'My Lord, why have you shown us this?'

There was another long pause, during which the figure in the chair showed no sign of movement. Then he began to speak again, his interpreter picking it up before he had fin-ished: 'This white jaguar is surely the emperor of all beasts. He fears nothing, and nothing is his equal. Yet he is almost blind! If you saw him in daylight you would see that his eyes are pink. He cannot bear the Sun, and can only come out at night.

'I could have you killed as easily as that dog, Yaotl. You know that. Even your famous brother – I only have to com-mand it and you will both be dead on the floor before me. But that power – without understanding, without knowing what is to come, what is that power? I am as blind as the white jaguar, who for all his strength would be dead if he had not been captured as a cub and brought here!'

There was a long silence. 'My Lord,' I asked eventually, 'what do you want?'

Neither Montezuma nor the interpreter spoke at first. The Emperor seemed engrossed in watching his favourite pet devouring his food. Only when the contented growls and sounds of grinding teeth began to diminish did he start mumbling again. What he said was as indistinct as ever, but there was one word that I understood: the name 'Skinny'.

'Last night,' the interpreter said, 'a man named Skinny, a featherworker, died in the canal between Pochtlan and Amantlan. This morning two of Pochtlan's parish policemen found you at his house. I am told that their canoe capsized while they were taking you to the Governor of Tlatelolco and you took advantage of the confusion to escape.'

I could not restrain myself. 'I didn't escape! I was kidnapped!'

My brother groaned. The interpreter looked uncertainly at the figure in the chair, and then leaned towards me.

'Interrupt me again,' he advised me in a confidential tone, 'and you're likely to end up like that dog!'

'Sorry . . .' I swallowed. I had forgotten myself, but at least I could see what had happened. Shield must have taken the Otomi captain's warning to heart.

'Now,' the interpreter went on, 'the Emperor requires you to tell him what you know about Skinny and his work.'

I told them the same story I had told Upright and Shield. It took a little while, because I kept hesitating, afraid that some mistake or inconsistency might prompt a question that would reveal what I had really been up to in Tlatelolco. I did not want Montezuma to know about my son. I had no idea what he might do if he did know but I thought Nimble, wherever he was, probably had enough to contend with, without coming to the Emperor's notice.

As darkness gathered, even the animal noises and bird calls from the other parts of the Zoo came to an end, and apart from my own voice the only sounds were the soft padding of the jaguar's paws as he left the remains of the dog and a faint creaking as the Emperor shifted in his chair.

After I had finished he asked me, through the interpreter, what I thought I had seen, on the night I had gone to meet Kindly and encountered an apparition in the form of Quetzalcoatl.

'I saw a man dressed as a god,' I said confidently. 'The costume he was wearing had gone missing from Kindly's house two nights before, and that was when the vision was first seen.'

'Why was the thief wearing it?'

'It's a good disguise. Most people who saw it would run away rather than challenge what they thought was a god.'

The Emperor and the interpreter were now only indistinct shadows, and the mumblings of one and the other's speech had become harder to distinguish as well, so that they seemed to blend together, as though the two men shared a single voice. I was not sure whether it was the Emperor's voice or the interpreter's that replied to me.

'You are wrong. The thief wore the costume because he wanted to. The raiment of a god has power of its own. The man who wears it takes the form of the god, and his attributes. He becomes the god.'

I tried to remember what Stammerer, the featherworker's apprentice from the temple in Amantlan, had told me. The costume was like an idol, to be prayed to and handled with care.

'My Lord, may I ask – did Skinny make the costume for you?'

I could easily tell where the reply came from this time. The Emperor's high-pitched giggle was unmistakable. 'For me to wear? No. At my command – yes.' There was a pause, and then it was the interpreter's voice again. 'What I will tell you now is not to be repeated, not even within the walls of this palace. If it is, both of you will die, and your families will die, and your houses – your parents', and that mansion of yours, Lion – will be demolished. It will be death to mention your names. Nobody in Mexico will remember anything about either of you. Is that understood?'

It seemed reasonably clear to me. I glanced at my brother, but he had not dared to lift his face off the floor since we had been shown in here. I heard a muffled 'Yes' from him and hastily said the same.

'You know how the city has been disturbed in recent times. You know of the omens that have been reported. Some I have seen myself: the fire in the sky, the lake boiling over and flooding on a day when the air was still, the temple that burned for no reason, the men . . .' Both the Emperor and the interpreter seemed to hesitate at this point. 'The pale men, riding on the backs of deer, that I saw in a vision.

'You know that these men exist.'

I had heard the rumours – some of them from the Emperor himself, on the last occasion when I had been in his presence. From the lands of the Mayans on the eastern shore of the Divine Sea had come tales of bizarre and sinister happenings: the appearance of creatures like men with pale skins and hair all over their faces, accompanied by other, still more fearsome monsters with four legs and great savage brutes of dogs like tame coyotes. I had heard something of the tales that had pre-ceded their arrival too: the stories from the islands in the Divine Sea, of how the people there had been hunted and enslaved by the pale men and fallen victim to strange and horrible diseases that had come with them. I had even seen something of the newcomers' magic myself, things that had been washed up on the coast a few years before: cloth finer and stronger than the best cotton and a marvellous sword made of a metal harder than bronze.

'We do not know who or what these men are. We do not know that they are men. Perhaps they are gods. We have heard it said that one of them is our predecessor, Topiltzin Quetzalcoatl, the last King of Tollan. Quetzalcoatl, who fled his realm hundreds of years ago,' the interpreter added, to emphasize the obvious: that for the ancient ruler to have returned after all this time, he must be divine. 'We had to prepare for the possibility that there are gods among these strangers, or that they are emissaries of the gods. We caused gifts to be prepared for them. Among them was the finery that a god would array himself in.'

So the costume had been made for Quetzalcoatl himself! I said nothing, but my mind was running ahead of the interpreter's words now. Even while he was explaining the measures that had been adopted to keep the making of the costume and the other gifts secret, I was working out why such pains had been taken, and why I had been summoned here, into the Emperor's presence, to learn about a piece of lost property.

If the Emperor truly believed that one of the pale-faced, bearded strangers might be Topiltzin Quetzalcoatl, then he knew what that must imply: that a power higher than his own, no less than the King of the Toltecs, the semi-divine race from whom he claimed descent, might soon be among us. Then his own rule would be on sufferance, subject to the strangers' scrutiny, to be judged and pronounced upon. How Montezuma might view such a prospect I could only guess, but I did not need to be much of a politician to understand

how damaging the mere rumour of it might be to his authority, not just in Mexico itself but throughout the Empire.

'We caused other costumes to be made,' the interpreter was
saying. 'The finery of Tlaloc and of Tezcatlipoca were made
here, in our own workshops, and we swore the seamstresses
and embroiderers and lapidaries and featherworkers who
worked on them to secrecy on pain of death. But palaces
breed rumours the way a battlefield breeds flies. We could not
take such risks with the raiment of Quetzalcoatl.' That, then,
was Montezuma's greatest fear: that word would get out that
he thought his ancestor might be coming to supplant him. 'We
gave the work to the finest featherworker in Amantlan to
finish.'

'But my Lord – didn't you know that Skinny had not made
anything in years?'

My brother hissed at me out of the side of his mouth. 'Don't
ask any more questions, you idiot!'

The Emperor, however, seemed disposed to answer me.
'We did. We interviewed him personally. He would not refuse
our command, of course.' No sane person would. 'But we
judged that he was genuine. He spoke about his vision of the
work. It pleased us. He spoke well about his devotion to the
gods, and to their servant on Earth.' By that, Montezuma
meant himself. In Skinny's position I would have come out
with the same sort of sycophantic nonsense, but it was puzzling to hear of the failed craftsman apparently volunteering
details of his plans, as though he wanted the commission.
What I heard next was still more puzzling, however, for the
interpreter added that one of the Emperor's chief councillors
had been sent to inspect the work twice, in conditions of the
utmost secrecy, and had pronounced himself satisfied.

What had come over Skinny, in the end?

'Now the featherworker is dead,' the interpreter went on,

'and the piece we commanded him to make has disappeared into the hands of a thief. It has been worn by a thief, who has assumed the raiment and power of the god. Is that in itself an omen of what is to befall us?' The question was left to hang in the air for a moment before he went on: 'It does not matter. The costume must be found.

'You will find it.'

I spluttered into the floor. 'My Lord! Why me? How can I . . .?'

'Silence, slave!'

The Emperor himself spoke. He had almost never been known to raise his voice but he did so now, and his ringing shout echoed across the garden outside.

His chair creaked loudly. I heard him get up, his sandals slapping the floor as he came around the back of it and stood over me and my brother. I pressed my nose to the ground and prayed silently to Tezcatlipoca for deliverance.

'I remind you,' he said, 'that this costume has been stolen once before.' His voice was quieter now. He spoke almost under his breath, and his words were the more menacing because of it. 'It somehow came into the possession of Kindly the merchant, who by your own admission asked you to retrieve it when it was stolen from him. I do not know what possessed you to agree, but it does not matter.

'You will do for me what you were to do for Kindly. You will find and bring me the costume. You will do it by tomorrow. If you do, I may be disposed to be merciful.'

He stopped. There was a long silence, during which I was aware of his brooding presence above me, the most powerful being in the World looking down upon a cowering slave.

I resolved to keep silent, but it was my brother, of all people, who blurted out the one question I did not want the Emperor to have the chance to answer.

'And . . . and if he does not, my Lord?'

'Then he will suffer the slowest and most excruciating death we can devise.'

Lion barely spoke to me after the Emperor dismissed us from his presence. I could hardly blame him. I had no idea what I might have said in his place: 'Now look what you've done!' would have been quite inadequate.

'My boys will take you home,' he said shortly, waving me towards one of his canoes.

'But . . .' I started to protest.

'Just get in!' he snapped. 'I don't know what you're going to do about finding this costume of the Emperor's. I don't know how you're going to find your son, either. But there's not much you can do now till morning, so go and see our parents. Sit out the vigil in their courtyard.' He hesitated before adding, in a voice that had suddenly become hoarse, 'We both know it's likely to be the last visit you ever pay them. Do whatever you have to tomorrow, but for tonight' – he grinned weakly – 'well, you can always tell Father that he doesn't have to kill you after all. It looks as if your master and the Emperor between them are going to spare him the trouble!'

5

The house had fallen silent by the time the canoe bumped up against the wooden landing-stage, but nobody in it was asleep. As I approached, the smell of wood smoke filled my nostrils, and looking up, I saw embers and the tips of flames dancing over the top of the courtyard wall.

Suddenly an astonishingly loud noise, a trumpet call, split the air around me. A moment later the whole neighbourhood seemed to reverberate to the sound of singing, accompanied by drumming and the squeaking of flutes. The vigil had begun.

I stepped through the doorway to be greeted by the sight of a small crowd squatting or kneeling around a bonfire. Those nearest to me were just black lumps against the light of the flames, but I could see that most of my family were there, apart from Lion and the errant Sparrowhawk. My nieces and nephews were gathered in silent, solemn groups around their parents. My father and mother were on the far side of the fire, so that its orange light flickered over their faces. They squatted together, but with a deliberate distance between them that implied that words had been exchanged, and from the way my father glowered at me, his eyes glittering under lowered brows, I thought those words might well have concerned me. Perhaps Mother had told him that he would have to put up with me for one night, at least. He did not speak, but his eyes tracked me suspiciously as I took my place next to Handy.

On my other side was a little party of musicians and singers from the House of Song, led by a young priest with a conch-shell trumpet.

Cautiously, and with my eyes on the old, inimical face glaring at me across the pool of firelight, I squatted in my place and prepared to join in the vigil.

I picked up the song easily. It was an old hymn to Tlaloc:

> *In Mexico*
> *God's goods are borrowed*
> *Among paper flags*
> *And in the four zones*
> *Are men standing up*
> *And also it's their time for tears . . .*

I looked at Tlaloc himself, the rain-god who was also one of the mountains that my mother and sisters had modelled out of amaranth seed dough and placed on his own little mat, among his divine companions. His teeth and eyes glowed like embers in the firelight and the paper vestments that the priests had made for him shone. Strange, flickering shadows played on the paper: the shapes of his instruments, the tiny drum, the gourd rattle and the turtle shell that lay on the mat before him. Also there were his food and drink. He had a plateful of miniature tamales, and a green gourd containing a shining pool of fortified sacred wine. It was his first meal and his last, for along with all the other gods and holy mountains around him, he was due to die in the morning.

> *But I've been formed*
> *And for my god*
> *Of bloody flowers of corn*
> *A festive few*

I take
To the god's court . . .

'Do you think it will rain?' Handy hissed, between verses.

I looked up. The paper streamers hanging on the pole moved sluggishly in the updraught from the fire. There was no sign of any wind, and through the light and smoke it was hard to tell whether there were any clouds overhead or not. 'I don't know. Still, the rains have been good so far, this winter.'

You are my warrior
A sorcerer prince
And though it is true
That you made our food
You the first man
They only shame you . . .

I opened my mouth for the next verse, but shut it when Handy started whispering to me again.

'Got something for you.'

I looked anxiously at the young priest on my other side. I might have expected him to disapprove of our chattering instead of singing but he seemed too intent on not losing his own way in the song to take any notice.

'What?'

'Here you are. No idea what it is. A slave delivered it just after you and Lion left.'

'Whose slave?' I asked suspiciously. I took the thing. It was a parcel, wrapped up in the kind of cloth bag field hands took their lunch to work in.

'He didn't say. He spoke to your brother, Glutton. He said it was for you, or if you weren't here, it was to be given to

Lion. He ran off before Glutton thought to ask him where he was from. . .'

'Trust Glutton!'

'Your father wanted to open it but your mother gave it to me. She thought I'd be able to get it to one of you. . . What's the matter? Aren't you going to open it?'

I hefted the parcel in my hand. It was heavy for its size. I could feel something hard and unyielding through the cloth. When I turned it over I caught a brief bright gleam, a sliver of something shining in the firelight.

It was so sharp that it had cut its own opening in the bag, almost as if it wanted to escape.

The parcel, the fire, the priest on one side of me and the commoner on the other all suddenly became blurred. In that moment I could not have said whether the tears in my eyes were tears of joy or unspeakable sadness.

'I don't need to,' I whispered. 'I know what it is.'

> *Whoever shames me*
> *Knows me quite ill*
> *You are my fathers*
> *My priesthood*
> *My jaguar serpents . . .*

Of course, I did look in the parcel. I waited until the next song was about to begin, when my young neighbour raised his trumpet to his lips and produced a blast of sound that made all the grown-ups clap their hands over their ears and screw their faces up painfully and sent some of the smaller children scurrying for safety behind their mothers' backs, and I was sure no one was paying attention to me.

I did not bother unwrapping it. I just worried at the hole the knife had made until it slipped out into my palm.

It shone. Someone had cleaned and polished it, removing all trace of the dried blood and bringing up the blade's dull glint until it was as bright as the moon. I tested it with my thumb and grimaced when I felt how sharp it was. Whoever had been looking after this knife had known what he was about.

The song began. I barely heard it. I looked from the gleaming blade in my hands to the fire and from the fire, with the flames' glare still in my eyes, to the faces of my family, some solemn, some frowning in concentration, one or two bobbing as sleep threatened to win through in spite of the singing and the trumpet calls. I raised my eyes, following the glowing sparks and tendrils of smoke as they rose into the sky, hiding the stars in imitation of the clouds we were trying to encourage.

My son was alive, I thought, gripping his knife fiercely. No one else in Mexico would know how to maintain a bronze knife so well.

The first thing I felt was a pang of terror. To know Nimble was alive was to know how much danger he was in. For a moment, all I could see was a vision of the Otomies stalking the boy, drawing the net of my master's vengeance around him.

Then I pushed the vision aside. I told myself that my son was alive, and he must have sent the knife to me as a message. But what kind of message?

Then it occurred to me to wonder how he had got the knife back. It had passed through several pairs of hands since he had last possessed it: to my knowledge they included his deceased lover, Shining Light's, Kindly's, my own, the chief of the merchants' parish, Howling Monkey's, and Lily's.

How many of the lights I could see in the air above me were stars and how many floating embers? I found myself wondering this, even while I was trying to guess what chain of events might have worked to reunite my son and his most precious possession, and leave him with the freedom to send it to me. Sometimes, I knew, it helped, when you had a difficult problem to solve, to turn your mind to an easier one, and so I made myself watch the little dancing orange lights and try to spot the still, pale, flickering points among them.

I went on counting sparks, listening to the singing and feeling the weight of the knife in my palm, until I passed into the land of dreams.

While I was there, it all seemed to come together: all the little things I had seen and heard, in the days since the knife had first been passed to me, all bloody and wrapped in its bundle. By the time I woke up, I thought I knew everything: who had killed Idle and Skinny and why, where the costume was, where Marigold had gone, and the solution to the most important mystery of all – what had become of my son.

It all seemed so simple and so obvious then that I hardly knew whether to laugh or weep with frustration at my own stupidity, for not working it all out sooner.

As it turned out, I got some of it right. If I had only paid closer attention to what Kindly the merchant and Angry the master featherworker had told me, and been a little less susceptible to Morning Glory seeds, I might have got it all.

'Wake up!'

A slap struck my cheek and forced my head sideways.

'Come on!' snarled a voice, very close to my ears. 'Wake up!'

I blinked, clearing the fog from my eyes and bringing my father's face into focus. It was twisted with rage.

'What's happening?' I asked groggily. I found I was lying down. I propped myself up on my elbows.

'You fell asleep during the vigil,' my mother told me reproachfully.

'I told you we shouldn't have let him stay,' rasped my father. 'Now look what he's done. What will the gods do to us all now? Suppose the whole city is plunged into drought, or the crops are blighted, or the lake floods or nobody can light their fires, and it's down to us?'

'Oh, shut up,' replied my mother. 'It's not the gods I'm worried about, it's him!' She glanced at the young priest, who was looking intently at his conch-shell as if he were wondering how he could get it to blow louder next time. 'We're really sorry about this,' my mother continued, her tone somewhere between threatening and wheedling. 'It's never happened before. We didn't know our son was going to be here, you know.'

'He's not going to be here any longer, either,' my father added.

The young man muttered something about how it did not matter, it happened all the time.

I thought it was time I said something. 'I'm sorry I fell asleep. If you knew what had happened to me yesterday . . .'

'I don't care what happened to you!' my father snapped. 'I'd rather see you being eaten by vultures than littering my court-yard!'

'Oh, thanks!'

My family had gathered around me the way a crowd of stall-holders in the marketplace might surround a suspected thief. As I looked from one to another, the thoughts that had assembled themselves in my head while I had been asleep came back to me, and I felt a broad grin starting to spread itself, unbidden, across my face.

That earned me another open-handed blow from my father. This one was so hard it left my ears ringing.

'Think this is funny, do you?' he shouted. 'You miserable slave, get out of my house! Get out, now!'

I stood up. My legs wobbled a little but in a moment I was towering over my father, who was still stooped in a position from where he could deliver repeated blows to the face of a man lying in front of him. His knee would not allow him to kneel.

As he straightened himself, moving slowly to spare his elderly spine, I realized what an advantage I had over him. His back was to the fire. One good shove and he would be in it.

I took one step towards him and held out my arm.

He was plainly used to having something to grab hold of while he pulled himself upright: one of his other sons, presumably, or perhaps one of his grandchildren by now. He took my arm instinctively before he remembered who it belonged to.

I seized his wrist with my free hand, pulled hard and twisted, and spun the old man around until he was facing the fire, tottering on his good leg while his bad one was doubled uselessly and painfully under him. He squawked in alarm.

'Yaotl!' my mother screamed. 'What do you think you're doing?'

'Let me go!' the old man cried. 'Glutton, the rest of you – get him off me!'

'Don't move!' I shouted. 'Remember how you used to hold us over burning chillies and make us breathe the smoke for the smallest thing, Father?' I took another step forward, shoving him towards the fire while taking great care not to let him fall in it. 'Care to find out what it was like?'

He started to cough. 'Help!' he cried hoarsely.

It suddenly seemed to occur to my brother Glutton that he ought to do something. He got up and started to lumber towards me, but he had to circle the bonfire and sidestep the hired priest first, and by the time he had done that, Handy was in his way.

'Wait a moment,' Handy said.

'But he's my father!'

'And the other one's your elder brother. I'm sure he knows what he's doing,' the big man added, with more conviction that I could have managed.

My brother-in-law Amaxtli was on his feet as well, but to my amazement Jade put out a restraining hand as he passed her. I heard her hiss at him: 'Mind your own business!' Then she turned to me. 'Yaotl, have you gone raving mad?'

'Of course he's mad!' cried my father. Desperation made him sound like a wild pig squealing. 'What's the matter with you all? Get him off!'

'All right,' said Handy mildly. 'Yaotl, let go of him. What's all this about?'

I took two steps back from fire, dragging the old man with me so that he was out of the smoke, although I was not ready to release him. 'I'm sorry,' I said, 'but I don't seem to have had much luck getting your attention up until now. If you'll listen to what I've got to say, I'll make it as quick as possible, and then I'll go.' I looked at Jade and Handy. 'Is that all right?'

Neither of them said anything, but neither of them moved either. I seemed to be surrounded by life-sized statues, Handy and my brother on one side, Jade and her perplexed husband on the other, and just next to me the priest, who looked on the point of tucking his conch-shell under his cloak and going home.

'You won't come back?' my father muttered.

'Not if you don't want me to, no.'

He grunted something that may have been assent. I relaxed my grip, and he did not at once turn around and try to kick me in the groin with his good leg, and so I decided I was safe for the moment.

'Now, I'm going to tell you all a story,' I began.

The young priest interrupted me. 'Excuse me, but this is supposed to be a vigil!'

'So we're awake,' growled Handy. 'You can still blow your trumpet, if it makes you feel any better!'

'May the gods forgive us,' my mother whimpered fearfully.

I looked from one to another of them in bewilderment, before deciding I might as well carry on. 'As I was saying . . .'

'You probably heard most of this from Handy, while I was away with Lion.'

'I told them everything you told me,' the commoner replied. 'They know about your son, and the business with Kindly, the featherwork.' He shot a brief, nervous glance at Jade. I grinned sympathetically. Jade was capable of extracting gossip from an oyster.

'All right. So most of the story you know already. Here's the rest of it.'

I told them about Skinny and Idle; how their father had done some service for Kindly and how the merchant, in return, had arranged his talented son's adoption into a family of featherworkers from Amantlan. I told them how the lad had prospered at first, and how it had all started to go wrong.

'He dried up. He tried all sorts of things to get himself working again – which to him must have meant making something every time that was better than his last effort. Nothing worked, of course. All he was doing by joining in with his rival, Angry, following his brother around into drinking and gambling dens and getting married, was taking his mind off the fact that the task he'd set himself was all but impossible.'

'So what about this suit he was making, the one that was nicked from Kindly's house?' Handy asked.

'Yes,' my elder sister Jade added, 'what was so special about it that Skinny suddenly managed to remember what he was supposed to be doing for a living?'

'It may not have been the costume itself, although it was something special.' Mindful of the Emperor's threats, that was as much as I was going to say about Skinny's last commission. 'I think he finally managed to find what he'd been looking for for so long: a source of inspiration. I think he fell in love.'

Glutton frowned deeply. 'He was married, Handy said. He and his wife . . .'

'Forget his wife! It was his brother's wife he fell for – Marigold!'

All of my family stared at me, wordlessly. I had lost them, I could tell, and I was not surprised. It had been a pure guess on my part, but it made sense to me.

'Skinny spent a large part of his youth in the House of Tears, being taught by priests. All featherworkers' children do. They don't become priests themselves and I'm sure they're spared the full rigours of a priest's training, but at the sort of age they are when they're there, all that sacred lore is bound to get under their skins. Judging by what his own wife told me, it made a big impact on Skinny. And then, years later, when he was at his wits' end, with his skills having deserted him, close to despair, who did he meet but the most devout woman in Mexico?

'There are more idols in that house in Atecocolecan than there are in the Heart of the World. Marigold brought them with her when she dragged her husband back to his home parish. According to Butterfly, she thought the move would do him good, but I'm not sure it was Idle she was thinking about at all. I bet what she really wanted was to get him away from his brother. She was the sort to sacrifice herself for the sake of Skinny's art, so he could go on honouring the gods.'

'It didn't work,' my mother pointed out. 'Skinny followed them.'

'He couldn't work on the costume in Angry's house. It was too secret. Marigold may not have known that.'

'Maybe he couldn't bear to be away from her,' Jade suggested.

'That too. If I'm right, and she was his inspiration, then maybe he couldn't work if they were apart. Angry told me Skinny's work started going to pieces again around the time his brother married, and the two things may have been connected. Somehow he had got over it by the time he started working on the costume . . .'

'I'll say he got over it!' Jade cried. 'How do you think Marigold came to be pregnant?'

I stared at her. 'You don't think . . .? No, she'd never . . .'

'Don't be so simple, Yaotl! Nobody's that pious! Besides, if she really thought sleeping with her brother-in-law would enable him to finish the work, I bet she'd do it. Don't you think so, Mother?'

I was always amazed by my female relations' ability to put the most prurient interpretation on anybody's actions. All the same, my mother, perhaps catching the troubled look on Jade's husband's face, settled for a prim frown and a comment that there really was no way of knowing.

'Well, anyway,' I said, 'Skinny got to work on the costume, and it went well – in fact, he finished it. Unfortunately, it was never delivered.'

'He sold it to Kindly,' Handy pointed out. 'Why would he have done that?'

'He didn't. His brother did.'

'Idle?' Handy said. 'No, that can't be right. Kindly told you Skinny sold the thing to him. He wouldn't have made a mistake over which brother he was dealing with. He'd known their family since they were little boys.'

'Not quite,' I corrected him. 'He knew the family *when* they were little boys. I don't suppose Kindly had much to do with the brothers after they grew up, particularly after their father died. Idle would have been too feckless to be any use to him and Skinny was in another line altogether. But even if he did come across them over the years, it would still have been an easy mistake to make. They were identical twins. I found an idol of Xolotl at Idle's house. It had been knocked off its plinth and hidden. I thought maybe someone had been ill, and the idol desecrated after he died. But I'm sure Xolotl was worshipped because there were twins in the house. Maybe Skinny was angry with the god after his brother died, and broke the statue in a fit of pique.'

There was a long silence before Handy said: 'Let me guess. Idle sold Kindly the costume, pretending to be his brother. Why? And what made Kindly buy it?'

'Idle was a mushroom-head and a gambler with no money of his own. He saw something in his brother's workshop that he thought he could barter with. And I don't know how things were between the brothers just then. Maybe Jade was right about Skinny and Marigold. Perhaps his main motive wasn't profit, but spite. As for Kindly, he may have wondered why the man he thought was Skinny was so keen to sell something so valuable, but he's too greedy to turn down a bargain. He wasn't about to ask any awkward questions.'

Jade, as shrewd as ever, told me what happened next. 'The featherworker found out, and stole the goods back.'

'That's what must have happened,' I agreed. 'Skinny wouldn't just have known what his handiwork was worth. He also knew – as I'm pretty sure Idle didn't – who had commissioned it. And let's just say he would have been seriously scared at the idea of having to explain that it was missing.

'Skinny planned the theft well. He seems to have known where to look, and that there would be a lot of people about who'd be in no real state to recognize him or work out what he was doing or stop him doing it. He just had one piece of bad luck. There was one other person in the house who was wide awake and alert, because he was there for the same reason as our featherworker: my son, Nimble.'

At the mention of my son's name, something rippled through my audience: a kind of restlessness, a shuffling of feet and one or two sighs. Even my father, who had ignored me ever since I had started speaking, looked up sharply. None of them had ever set eyes on Nimble, or even known of his existence until a few days before, but nobody could fail to respond to the idea of a long-lost grandson, nephew or cousin. Perhaps, I thought, they were all able to take one look at his father and feel sorry for the lad. It saddened me that they would probably never meet him.

'He wanted to get his bronze knife back. He knew his . . .' I looked at the eager faces around me and hastily amended what I had been about to say to avoid offending their sensibilities. 'He knew his associate, Shining Light, had taken it to Kindly's house and left it there. The knife wasn't all he found, of course.

'Only the gods know exactly what happened when our two thieves surprised each other. Obviously there was a fight: I saw the bloodstains, on the floor and in the courtyard outside, and on the knife itself, and I saw what looked like a knife wound on Skinny's hand. I don't suppose Nimble tried to stop Skinny taking the costume. He just wanted to grab the knife and run. Maybe Skinny found it first, and the fight started when Nimble tried to take it off him.

'I'm afraid Nimble came off worse. In fact, for a while, after

I found the body at the bridge, I thought he'd died.' A groan came from several throats. 'It didn't occur to me at the time that the blood I saw on the bridge couldn't have anything to do with what I'd seen at Kindly's house, because there was no trail connecting them.

'As for Skinny – I don't know whether he'd planned what he did next or whether it just occurred to him on the spur of the moment. Instead of carrying the costume home, he put it on. It didn't slow him down any more wearing it than it would carrying it, and he knew that if he was dressed as a god anyone he met would run away rather than try to stop him. It worked so well he wore it again a couple of nights later, when I saw him. Then he was trying to scare people off while his accomplice disposed of his brother.'

The fire was burning down rapidly: it was little more than a pile of ash harbouring a few stunted flames, although there was still plenty of smoke. There was a chill in the air, even though the sky was brightening and the mountains were appearing in the East, their peaks and ridges dark and jagged against a pale pink background. The Sun would be up soon, heralding the end of the fast and the start of the festivities as well as, for me, the day I had to satisfy both my masters – the Chief Minister and the Emperor – or perish.

'I think Skinny and Idle had their last argument when Skinny got home. He'd have been spoiling for a fight. He'd got involved in one brawl already that he hadn't been ready for, and then had a terrifying journey home. Maybe Idle had words to say about how close Skinny and Marigold had been getting. It's hardly surprising they came to blows. Idle died. I don't know whether Skinny meant to kill him or whether things just got out of hand, but the next thing they knew, they had a body to dispose of.'

'They?' Glutton had been frowning in puzzlement for much

of the night, but he had been following the story well enough to ask the question.

'Skinny, of course, and his wife, and for all I know Marigold. None of them had any reason to love Idle. For all I know they were all in it together.'

'Why did they choose that latrine to dump the body in?' Jade asked. 'It was taking an incredible risk, carrying it all that way. Why not just bury it in the marshes at the back of the house?'

I frowned. She had a point. 'They're working on the chinampa plots up there,' I said. 'Perhaps they were afraid of someone finding it so close to the house. It would have been too easy to connect it with them.'

Jade's husband thought he had spotted a flaw in my account. 'I thought it was Skinny who identified the body after the police found it,' he pointed out. 'That doesn't figure, if he'd hidden it in the first place.'

'The police knew his brother was missing. There can't be a lot of unidentified corpses in Amantlan at any one time. That's why they came and asked him to help identify the body, and when he found his brother's charm, he had to own up to who it was. It wouldn't have mattered that much. There was nothing to connect him with the killing, after all.'

'So the featherworker got his piece back, and killed his brother, and all the stories about people seeing visions of the god Quetzalcoatl were down to him.' Handy was motioning with his fingers, as if he were trying to count off all the unsolved mysteries one by one. 'All right, so what happened to him? And his . . . well, whatever was going on between them – to Marigold?'

'Oh, that's simple,' I said airily. 'Butterfly killed them both.'

'What?'

'Well, who else? She hated Marigold. Whether her relationship with Skinny was innocent or not, I'm pretty sure I

can guess what Butterfly made of it all. It was simple jeal-
ousy. She killed Marigold, probably shortly after Idle died,
and later she killed her own husband. Perhaps he'd been
fretting over where his girlfriend had got to, and it started to
get on her nerves. I think she did it just before I went to her
house the second time, when she told me Skinny had gone
out. She didn't make nearly as good a job of dumping the
body as her husband had: she just left it floating in a canal
and it was found almost immediately. That may be why she
took more care over Marigold's body. Nobody's found that
yet.'

'You went to that house a third time.' My mother's unblinking stare and sneering tone told me Handy had told her what
had happened the night I tried burgling the featherworker's
home.

I sighed. 'I don't know what to say about that. You know
about the woman, and the god.'

'Who was wearing the costume then?' Jade asked. 'Both
brothers were dead, weren't they?'

I looked at her seriously. 'I don't think there was a costume
then. Maybe it was the Morning Glory seeds, or . . . I don't
know. But that time, I think it really was the god.'

Nobody had an answer to that. A long silence ensued. Even
the crackling of the fire had ceased.

Eventually Handy asked, hesitantly: 'So, where's the featherwork?'

'Butterfly's house,' I said quickly, relieved to have a question
I could answer sensibly. 'Where it had been all along. You see,
there was one place I didn't know about – although I should
have realized it was there at the time . . .'

'Featherwork?' My father's voice, heard for the first time
since I had begun, silenced me and made everyone sit up.
'Forget the featherwork, who cares about that? What about

your son?' He looked at my mother. 'Our grandson. Where is he? What are you going to do about him?'

'Oh, that's even simpler,' I said.

Then I did one of the most stupid things I have ever done. I told him.

SEVEN GRASS

1

The young man with the trumpet seemed eager to be off as soon as the Sun came up. He could not decently leave until the parish priest arrived to perform the sacrifices and formally end the fast, and he even managed to sound a few half-hearted notes, but he kept staring at the eastern sky, as if willing the Sun to get a move on. Every so often he would look nervously at me, but I could hardly blame him for that. For a priest, accustomed to long fasts and sleepless nights, the office he had been expecting to perform at my parents' house would have seemed like a holiday. The last thing he had needed was a madman turning up uninvited and throwing the whole carefully planned ritual into chaos.

Eventually, he got his wish. It was dawn, and the parish priest was at the doorway.

'I'll be on my way, then,' the young man said, gathering up his conch-shell and his flute.

'Won't you stay?' my mother cried, alarmed and upset. 'There's food and drink. You must be hungry.'

'No, that's all right,' he said, although the food and drink were his due – payment for his role in the household's celebrations. The other musicians and the singers shuffled anxiously, no doubt wondering whether they were going to have to go without as well. 'The others can stay, but I'm not hungry, to be honest. Or thirsty. Have to go!'

He almost ran past his colleagues, whose faces had all broken into relieved grins, and past the parish priest, who turned and watched him go speechlessly from where he was waiting, just outside the gateway.

'This is all your fault,' my mother hissed at me.

'Why? I didn't tell him his conch-shell sounded flat, or anything . . .'

'Don't try to be funny!' my father snapped. 'You know you upset him, falling asleep and talking all night when we're supposed to be honouring the gods. These young priests, they can be very temperamental . . .'

'Look, don't tell me about priests. I was one, remember?'

'I remember. I'm surprised you can, with all the sacred wine that's been sloshing about inside you over the years. . .'

We were squaring up to one another, our chests puffed out like turkey cocks', my father stooping slightly as he leaned forward on his good leg so that his face was just on a level with mine. At any moment, I thought, yesterday's fight would resume, and either I would be driven bodily out of the house or I would have to do the old man some serious harm.

I was not going to let that happen. I felt myself begin to relax as I resolved to turn around and walk away while both of us could still stand.

I heard a loud cough from the direction of the gateway.

'Excuse me.' It was Imacaxtli, the parish priest. 'May I come in?'

Imacaxtli was an institution in Toltenco. He had served our little temple on top of its stumpy pyramid for as long as I could remember. He had watched me and my brothers and sisters grow up, and I suspected he had been instrumental in getting me into the Priest House, something for which it had taken me a long time to forgive him. Now, watching his bent figure and wizened features as he stood, strangely diffident, on my parents' threshold, I wondered what this old man thought of his position. Did he hanker after the honour and glory to be found at the top of the Great Pyramid, or would he rather serve in a place where he knew everybody's business and everybody knew him?

'Of course!' my mother gushed. 'Please, you've come a long way, you must be out of breath. Have a rest, have something to eat.' The formal greeting sounded faintly absurd when addressed to someone who lived only two streets away.

'Not at all, not at all. Now, who do we have here – why, it's Yaotl, isn't it?' He walked straight up to me. 'I haven't seen you since . . . now, let me think . . .'

'I was just going,' I said hastily.

'Oh no you aren't,' my father snapped, seizing my arm in a painfully tight grip.

'But you said . . .'

'You've probably done enough to offend the gods already,' he snarled. He looked at my mother. 'Not to mention her. So you can bloody well stay for the sacrifice.'

'You don't understand. I have to . . .'

'I know perfectly well what you have to do. You're going to need all the favours the gods can spare you, and you won't help yourself by running out now. So you stay for the sacrifice,' he repeated, in a low but determined voice, 'and then you go and find your son!'

While the priest inspected the little dough figures they had made, my mother, Jade and Honey looked on, as proud and anxious as parents presenting their children for the first time to the masters at a House of Youth.

'These are beautiful,' the old man said. 'You have all done very well. The gods are honoured to have such devoted servants.'

'We did our best,' my mother simpered. A slight flush coloured her cheeks. 'We know what is right in this household, and try to live by it.' She glanced reproachfully at me for a moment before turning back to the priest. 'Here is the weaving-stick.'

The priest took the implement she handed him, murmuring a few words of thanks as he turned it over in his hands. It was nothing more than one of the flat, curved weaving-sticks that all Aztec women learned to use as little girls, but once a year, in those households that observed the festival of the Coming Down of Water, it served another purpose.

Bending down, he picked Tlaloc up from his tiny reed mat, looked lovingly into the god's shiny little bean eyes for a moment, and then drove the weaving-stick into his breast.

He twisted the stick this way and that, not so hard as to break the figure up, but with the kind of ferocious expression that I had seen on the faces of Fire Priests digging the hearts out of real, living men and women on the sacrificial stone. He bent the god's head back until it was at an angle that would have snapped a human being's neck. Then he put the stick down and pulled a tiny lump of dough out of the figure's chest. He held his prize up towards the East, presenting it triumphantly to the rising Sun, before dropping it into the god's own tiny bowl of sacred wine, just as the Fire Priest would have cast his victim's still-beating heart into the Eagle Vessel.

He did the same to each of the other little statues, one by one, until all the gods were dead and their decapitated, eviscerated bodies lay in the courtyard among their offerings, while their hearts floated and softened in their own bowls of sacred wine. Then he gathered up the bowls and the plates with the tiny tamales and the paper clothes that had adorned the gods, and threw them all on the bonfire.

My family cheered. The ritual had been performed flaw-lessly, and no doubt they were relieved that the fast was over and the guests were about to arrive and there would be food and drink in plenty.

'Thank you!' my mother cried. 'You don't know what it means to us, having this ceremony performed here.'

'My pleasure,' said the old man. He was already gathering up the reed mats, the little instruments and the remains of the dough figures, all of which would go back to the temple with him. The mats and the instruments were too expensive to burn every year, while the dough was the delicious kind, flavoured with honey, that we made sweets out of, and was part of his payment for performing the rite. 'My best wishes for the rest of the day.'

As the first of the guests began to flow through the doorway, bringing with them their offerings, ears of corn, grains of dried maize and paper banners for the children to hang on the pole in the middle of the courtyard, he suddenly turned to me.

'You too, Cemiquiztli Yaotl. I hope you find what you're looking for.'

He left then, with his offerings gathered in the folds of his cloak, and me staring dumbly after him.

My mother gave me my cloak back. I might need it, she told me.

'I'm only going to Tlatelolco, not the summit of Mount Popocatepetl,' I pointed out. 'Anyway, it's day now, it's starting to warm up – the time I'd have needed it was last night! Look, I told you, it's yours. . .'

'Well then, bring it back when you've finished with it.'

I winced. For all my confidence that I had solved the mys-tery of Kindly's featherwork, I knew full well that there was no guarantee I would ever be back. Being able to satisfy the

Emperor was one thing, but the Chief Minister was another matter, and his demand was one I could never give into. So Montezuma probably would not have me killed, but unless he exerted himself to save me from my master I might yet die.

'Look, Mother, I might not see you again . . .'

'Oh, nonsense,' she snapped. 'You always come back. Now go and do what you have to, and if you could manage not to get that cloak too dirty, I'd appreciate it.'

She turned away quickly. I began to stretch a hand towards her, but I hesitated too long, and she was out of reach, lost among the crowd of her guests.

I headed for the doorway, but Handy was in the way.

'What about me, then?' he asked plaintively.

'What?'

'What about me? Look, I know what you're about. You're going to warn your son old Black Feathers is after his blood, and once you're sure he's safely out of the city, you'll go to ground or run away yourself. Well, fine, I'd do the same, but where does it leave me? The old bastard's bound to blame me if you get away – and I can't run. I've a family to think of.'

I looked at him blankly. 'Um, right.' His dilemma had never occurred to me. 'You have, yes. Er, well, can't you just tell him you couldn't stop me? No, I suppose not.' Handy stood a head taller than me and had muscles conditioned by his time in the army and years of hard work in the fields and on the city's building sites. He could have picked me up and carried me back to the Chief Minister's palace if he had wanted to.

Glutton, Amaxtli and Jade came up to us. 'Come to see you on your way,' Jade said. 'We wanted to make sure you were really going! What's up?'

'Handy's worried he'll get the blame if I manage to find Nimble and help him escape,' I explained.

'Oh, that's no problem,' said Jade's husband sourly. 'Bash him over the head, tie him up and shove him in a ditch somewhere – preferably a long way away from here!'

'Just a moment,' said Handy.

'You can't do that!' cried Jade.

'What, like this?' said Glutton.

My brother was even bigger than Handy. Before any of the rest of us knew what he was doing he had stepped up behind him and clouted him on either side of the head with his fists.

We heard a soft thump. Handy's eyes rolled into the top of his head and he fell forward on to the floor.

Jade screamed and rushed towards him.

'I didn't ask you to do that!' I shouted. 'You might have killed him!'

'I didn't feel anything break,' my brother said defensively. 'Anyway, it was for his own good, wasn't it?'

I stared at him.

'Are you going, or not?' Amaxtli asked testily.

I looked down at the prone figure of my friend. As far as I could see past my weeping, hysterical sister, he appeared to be breathing normally. I looked at the crowd in the courtyard. Every back was turned towards me, as if telling me I had no further business here.

I did not answer my brother-in-law. I just went.

'Where is he?'

Kindly's slave Partridge took a step back through the entrance to his master's house. He had to, to avoid being run through by the bronze knife I was pointing at his throat.

'Where's who? No, you can't come in. The mistress's orders . . .'

'Get out of my way. Or have you learned how to breathe without a windpipe?'

The man stumbled away from me and then turned and fled, shouting for help. I followed him, letting the knife dangle from my fingers.

The fleeing slave almost bumped into his mistress. Lily was standing in the middle of her courtyard, beneath the fig tree that dominated it. In the tree's shadow, against the base of one wall, squatted her father. The old man had a drinking-gourd in his hands, as always, but he was wide awake and staring at me with a quizzical expression.

'Hello, Yaotl,' said Lily coolly. She ignored her slave, who was cowering behind her. 'We were expecting you last night.'

'I got held up,' I said drily. 'I want to see my son.'

'He's probably asleep.'

'So bloody well wake him up, then!' I snapped, waving the knife in front of me furiously.

If Lily found my gesture threatening she did not show it. The corner of her mouth twitched in amusement when she looked at the gleaming blade.

'Why don't you put that thing away before you cut yourself? And you, Partridge, stop whimpering and do something useful. Go and see if the boy's awake . . . Ah, no need.'

Nimble stood in a doorway, blinking as his eyes took in the sunny courtyard.

I stopped waving the knife and gazed at him.

I could see immediately that he had been in a bad way. His face was gaunt with shadows around the eyes. I thought he seemed old. He had always appeared older than his years, but now the lines etched in his forehead by pain and fever made him look almost as ancient as his father felt. It was hard to say whether he now looked any better than the pale figure I remembered glimpsing across a canal, two days before. Nonetheless he stood up straight and his eyes were clear and alert.

'Nimble,' I said. It was difficult to speak. My mouth was dry and the sides of my throat seemed to have stuck together. Eventually I managed to add: 'I brought your knife back.'

I ought to have been more careful. As we ran into one another's arms, winding each other in an ecstatic, breathless embrace, I nearly stuck the weapon's point in his shoulder by accident.

'I knew you'd come. I thought if I just sent you the knife, you'd know where to find me. I couldn't think of any other sort of message I could send that would be safe. I was afraid that if I had Kindly or Lily write anything down it might fall into the wrong hands.'

'You mean old Black Feathers', or one of his minions'.' I kept looking at the lad and grinning like an idiot. I had thought I would never see him again, I had thought him dead, more than once. It was hard to accept that we were squatting together in the middle of Kindly's courtyard, talking, having a conversation, behaving, just for the moment, at least, like a normal father and son. 'It worked,' I added. 'I knew you could only have got the knife from Lily. But I should have guessed where you were anyway, because she'd told my master who you really were, and she didn't hear that from me – did you, Lily?'

The woman knelt next to her father, with her plain skirt tucked under her knees and a plate of small honeyed maize cakes nestling in its folds. They were the kind of token food offering that was always presented to a guest, but I noticed that this did not stop Kindly from reaching across his daughter's lap and plucking one from the plate every so often.

'No,' she conceded. 'Your son told me. Not that he meant to, but he was pretty feverish the day after he was wounded. I think I heard just about everything.'

'Including who he was, and . . .' I looked directly into her eyes as I continued: 'And how your son died, and why.'

She met my glance steadily. 'That's right. Everything. But I had to know for sure, you see? I couldn't trust . . . sorry, Nimble, but I couldn't rely on what you said when you were delirious.' She smiled at the youth and reached out and touched his arm, as if to reassure him. He lowered his head and said nothing. 'That's why I took you from Howling Monkey's house,' she told me. 'I needed you to tell me what happened, to confirm what I'd heard from your son.'

'And then you told my master.' At one time it would have been an accusation, hurled in her face with all the force I could muster, but with Nimble sitting by us I found I could state it calmly.

'I'd no choice,' she said. 'I'd taken you – not to mention that knife – from the chief of my parish and then you'd escaped. I had to protect myself. Going to your master and telling him what had happened seemed the best way of doing it.'

'So you told him you'd got his runaway slave and had tried to bring him back.' I sighed. 'All right, I understand that much. Why tell him Nimble was my son?'

'He asked what you'd been up to, so I told him. And why not? It didn't make any difference to the boy whether your master knew who his father was or not. It's not as if I was about to tell old Black Feathers where to look for him! I know it won't have made life any easier for you – but let's face it, why should I have worried about that?'

It was my turn to look down, to stare at the floor while I made sense of what she was saying. There was no spite in it, I realized. I wondered how it had come about that we were able to speak to each other so dispassionately about things that, to anyone else, would have represented betrayal and the deepest kind of wound. I had not killed her son but she knew I had

had a hand in it. It was hard to believe that neither of us cared any more.

'We . . . we slept together, once,' I mumbled.

That produced an explosive guffaw from Kindly, swiftly stifled by his daughter shoving another maize cake into his mouth. She glared at me. 'Once,' she said, pointedly.

'Is that why you sheltered my son?'

She laughed. 'Forget it, Yaotl! My father found him lying in the middle of the courtyard, with the bronze knife in him, and the other thing that had been kept in the same room as the knife was missing. So he was the only witness to the theft. What would you have done?' She turned to Nimble. 'I'm sorry, but . . . well, we didn't know you then.'

'Besides,' Kindly said, 'you may have forgotten, but my daughter wasn't at home that night. She was messing about on the lake with you and your brother and old Black Feathers. By the time Lily came home in the morning he was stretched out on a sleeping-mat with his chest strapped up and covered with ground pedilanthus stalks. When the fever started the doctor gave him watered-down peyote juice. Myself, I'd have watered it down a bit more: I think that's why he started raving.' Kindly had clearly not forgotten all the medicine he had had to learn as a merchant, journeying unprotected among barbarians.

'I was here two nights later. I heard you crying out,' I said to my son. I turned to Kindly. 'Why didn't you tell me? You knew what he was to me by then, didn't you – and it wasn't a clever guess at all, because he'd told you himself.' I answered my own question before he could. 'You didn't tell me because you wanted me to look for your bloody featherwork, and you thought you could use my son as a lure. That was it, wasn't it? No wonder you got me out of the house so fast. Why, you . . .'

'Oh, save your breath. I've been called enough names over the years, I've heard them all.' The old man inspected his daughter's lap but the maize cakes had all gone, most of them down his own throat. He sighed and picked up his gourd instead. 'Look, if you'd known where he was, what would you have done? The lad wasn't fit enough to remember his own name, let alone go anywhere, so you'd have ended up hanging around here like a lovelorn youth haunting the house where his favourite pleasure-girl lives. Your master would have been on to you both in no time. This way, you were able to stay one step ahead of the old bastard – at least for a while.' He grinned wryly before putting the gourd to his lips. 'And I really thought you might be able to find that bloody costume, but I suppose you can't have everything!'

'I did find it.'

Sacred wine exploded in all directions like water when a large stone is dropped in a pond. The gourd fell on to the old man's lap, its contents soaking his breechcloth, and he did not notice.

'You what?'

'I found the costume. I mean, I know where it is. Shouldn't be a problem going to get it.'

He coughed. I looked at Lily and Nimble and was gratified to see them both staring at me.

I told them what I had told my family during the night.

Kindly forgot his gourd. It lay beside him, slowly leaking its contents on to the surface of the courtyard. Once or twice he closed his eyes and muttered to himself, and I thought I heard him say: 'No, that's wrong.' However, he did not interrupt until I had finished.

I leaned back, feeling the warmth of the wall through my cloak, and waited to be congratulated.

The old man picked up his gourd again. He hefted it, sniffing disgustedly when he realized it was empty.

'Well?' I demanded.

'Well what? It's the biggest load of old bollocks I've ever heard!'

I felt my jaw drop. 'What are you talking about? Look, can't you see, it all makes perfect sense . . . Nimble, Lily, listen . . .'

They both looked away in embarrassment.

'It makes no sense at all,' snapped Kindly. 'Where's that slave? Ah, you – fill this up, won't you? Right. Now, for a start, you don't seriously believe I can't tell Skinny apart from his brother, do you?'

'But if you only knew them as children . . .'

'Who told you I only knew them as children? Skinny lives in the next parish! Or at least he did until recently. I can't recall ever meeting Idle, I grant you, and if they're twins then I dare say they look pretty much alike, but with my eyes that would scarcely have mattered, and I can tell you for a fact that I know who I was dealing with.'

If Kindly was right, then the story I had told him and my family must be wrong. But how could that be? If Idle had not stolen the featherwork from his brother, then why had he been killed?

'You're telling me,' I replied, 'that Skinny sold you his own work? But that's impossible! Never mind what it was worth – do you know who commissioned it?'

'Oh, sure,' he replied casually. 'Montezuma.'

'You knew that? How?'

'Well, I didn't actually know, but it wasn't hard to guess.'

I turned to Lily, who had set the empty plate down beside her and now knelt placidly next to her father. 'Did you know about this?' I demanded. 'He guessed the piece belonged to the Emperor and he still let the featherworker sell it to him. He's crazy! He's not safe to be allowed out on his own!'

'It's not that simple, Yaotl.' She seemed concerned, with her brows drawn together and her eyes narrowed, but not shocked.

There was no sign of the things I had seen her do when she was stressed, when her hands would tremble and wring and pluck at the material of her skirt.

'I didn't buy the costume from Skinny,' her father said.

'You told me you did!'

'No, I didn't. I said I wasn't likely to get him and his brother mixed up, and I didn't, and I'll tell you why there's no way I could have made a mistake. He didn't sell it to me. He gave it to me, for safe-keeping.'

'But . . . but you said . . . when I came here five nights ago, with the knife, you told me. . .'

My voice tailed off as I thought back to the conversation we had had then. I was sure I remembered Kindly telling me he had bought the costume from Skinny, but for some reason I could not seem to recall the exact words he had used.

'What I told you,' the old man said, in a deceptively patient tone, 'was that I had got the costume from Skinny. You seem to have assumed that I'd bought it, though what you thought I'd have wanted with something like that, I can't imagine. It's not as if I'd have been able to sell it anywhere!'

I looked away, feeling suddenly foolish and a little ashamed, because I realized that he was right. It had been so easy to see Kindly as party to some crooked deal that it had never entered my head that his actions may have been honest.

'All right,' I muttered eventually. 'Who were you keeping it safe from?'

'If I knew that, I'd have told you at the time. I suspect it would have made your task a lot easier! But Skinny didn't seem to know himself, or if he did, he wasn't telling. He claimed nobody else knew about the costume. He said he was sworn to secrecy. If it was Montezuma who commissioned it, then I'm pretty sure Skinny would've had more to worry about than just his oath if he didn't keep his mouth shut.'

'He did,' I confirmed. 'The Emperor told me as much himself.' Yet I knew Skinny had told at least one person – the priest at Amantlan, who was not the most discreet person I had ever met. And his wife had obviously known as well. Who else had he told – his brother, Marigold? Did his reticence with Kindly arise from a misguided desire to protect them, even though he knew one or all of them would steal from him if they could?

'Do you see why I know it was him and not his brother I saw?' Kindly asked. 'Idle might well have sold me the featherwork, if he could, but there's no way he'd have parted with it for nothing.'

'But why give it you, of all people?'

'The costume was almost complete, and Skinny would have delivered it in the next few days. Skinny seems to have been afraid that if he kept it at home it would disappear.

'Now, I know what you think of me.' He took a swig from his gourd and glanced at his daughter as if he expected her to share my opinion. 'But I'm not totally without principles. Skinny's father was with me in Quauhtenanco.'

Lily's husband had been there too, but unlike his father-in-law he had not come back. She stared impassively into the middle distance as she listened to her father telling the tale.

'I took him along as a porter, but he turned out to be a real fighter as well. Whenever we were hardest pressed he was always there, next to me. He was wounded three times, and I thought we were going to lose him once. I came back without a scratch! So when we parted after we were back in the city I told him if there was ever anything I could do for him or his sons he only had to name it. I meant it as well.'

'You got Skinny into an Amanteca family,' I said.

'Yes. That was the only time he asked me to make good on my promise.' He sighed. 'He never asked me to do the same for Idle. I think he'd already given up on him.'

'So when Skinny asked you to look after the costume, you felt you couldn't refuse?' I made no effort to keep the sceptical note out of my voice. I was having difficulty getting used to the idea that Kindly had a conscience, even one apparently so intermittent and selective; but then, I had not been at Quauhtenanco.

'I wasn't very happy about it, but no – how could I? And it was a simple enough proposition, just to keep the thing for a few days until Skinny was ready to deliver it. But we had to throw this bloody party, didn't we? And somebody seized their chance. From what you tell me, that may well have been Idle.'

'Who got himself killed,' I reminded him. The more I thought about this, the more worrying it became. If Skinny had stolen the costume back from Kindly and killed his brother, as I had thought, then he would have taken it straight back to the house in Atecocolecan. Even if Butterfly had later killed her husband, I thought there was a good chance it would still be there. However, if it had been Idle who had burgled Kindly's house, then there was no telling what he might have done with it. I could only hope that Skinny had caught him, killed him and taken his goods back. I shuddered, as an alternative explanation occurred to me: what if Idle had sold the costume and the buyers had decided to eliminate him, and so save themselves a lot of money and cover their tracks at the same time?

I turned to my son. 'You were here when the costume was taken. What did you see?'

'I don't remember much,' he confessed. 'He got here before me. I found him looking at the knife. I didn't think – I just asked him for it. He went for me. We fought over it – I was desperate to get it off him, and I nearly did. I think I cut his hand, but he didn't let go of it, and the next thing I knew I was stumbling around out here. Then I was lying on a sleeping-mat, in there' – he gestured towards the room he had emerged from – 'with Lily leaning over me dripping water on my forehead.'

I looked at the woman. She looked away.

'Why didn't you tell me?' I asked. 'Kindly I can sort of understand, but you? How could you be so. . .?'

'Harsh? Cruel? What do you expect? You thought I could just forget about my son? I know you didn't kill him, but you were there, and if it hadn't been for you none of this might have happened – he might still be alive.'

'It's not my fault he hated me!' Her words stung me into raising my voice more than I wanted to, but as my cry of outrage echoed around the courtyard I saw the pain crossing my son's face, and that calmed me. 'Lily,' I said, 'that's not fair.'

'Who said it had to be fair?' she hissed. 'You asked me why I kept what had happened to Nimble a secret, and I told you. Anyway, for once my father was right. He was in no fit state to go anywhere and you would just have come blundering in here and led your master straight to him.'

'Did you hate me enough to turn me over to Lord Feathered in Black? Is that really what you were going to do?' I asked.

There was a long pause.

'I don't know,' she admitted, at last. 'Once you'd escaped, I knew what I had to do, just to save myself, but before that . . . Yaotl, don't ask. I can't tell you.'

'None of this,' Kindly reminded me, 'gets us any closer to finding the costume, does it? Would I be right in thinking you're as anxious as I am to get it back now?'

'Yes,' I said. 'But I don't see how we're going to do it. From what you tell me, the only person who would have known for certain what happened to it is Idle, and he seems to have met his death pretty soon after the theft. We can try his house again, but there's no certainty we'd find anything there.'

We all squatted or knelt in brooding silence. I believe we must all have been thinking the same thing, that there was nothing for it but to go to the house in Atecocolecan, but none of us could bear the thought of going and coming away empty handed, with the Emperor's threats still hanging over our heads.

Then Nimble spoke. He was quiet and diffident.

'Father, there's something I don't understand.'

'What's that?' I beamed at him. I had not got used to being called 'Father'.

'When you went to see Skinny, on the morning after you came here, you as good as told him you thought he'd sold Kindly the featherwork and stolen it back again.'

I frowned. 'That's right.'

'Why didn't he just tell you the truth, instead of claiming he wasn't working any more?'

'Why, because . . .' I stopped in mid-sentence. I had been about to say that Skinny and his wife had no idea who I was, and naturally did not trust me, but then I saw what my son was getting at. 'Because,' I went on slowly, 'the man I saw wasn't Skinny.'

But the man I had seen was the thief. Nimble had confirmed that for me, describing the struggle over the knife and how he had wounded the other man's hand. I had seen the wound for myself.

For a moment I found myself wrestling with the implications of this. If Nimble was right, then the mystery of who had killed the man I had found in the privy was solved. It took me a moment more to work out why he might have done it, but then I saw that, too, and it was so obvious that I had to groan at my own stupidity.

'What's the matter?' Lily asked.

'I just realized what this is all about,' I said. 'And how stupid I've been. If I'd only listened to what Angry said four days ago . . . No, that's wrong. It's not what he said that's important – it's what he didn't say!'

They all stared at me, faces slack with incomprehension.

'Let me explain . . .'

2

'Now, you both know what you're meant to be doing?'
Partridge looked doubtful. 'Your brother . . .'

'My elder brother, the Guardian of the Waterfront. And as many of his bodyguards as he feels like bringing. . .'

'And a sledgehammer. Got it.'

I would sooner have sent my son to fetch Lion, but it would have been too hazardous. I could not be sure old Black Feathers did not have men watching his house, or for that matter his quarters in the Emperor's palace. Besides, I had another job for him to do.

'You want me to fetch Angry the featherworker. What if he refuses to come?'

'Tell him it's about Marigold. He'll move so fast it'll be all you can do to keep up with him!'

Lily came out into a courtyard with a rabbit's-fur mantle which she insisted on tying around the boy's shoulders. 'Are you sure you're going to be up to this?' she asked, anxiously. 'You've only just got back on your feet. Why don't you rest, have something to drink first . . .'

'There's no time, Lily,' the boy said. 'Look, I'll be fine. I was up and about two days ago, remember?'

'So it *was* you I saw, down by the canal,' I said.

'Stretching my legs. Lily wasn't happy about it, though. She made me promise not to go out of the courtyard after that.'

'You could have got yourself killed!' Lily protested. 'If those Otomies had seen you . . .'

'He won't come to any harm,' I assured her. 'I'm not expecting any trouble, you know.' As my son and the slave left, I wondered at my own words. The woman had grown fond of the lad, I could see that. Did he remind her of her own child? I hoped not, considering what Shining Light had done. But I realized with a pang that she had probably seen more of Nimble – and learned more about him, listening to him speak with the candour of delirium – than I had. I knew so little. Perhaps I was fortunate, to have been presented with my son almost full grown and known none of the anxiety, frustration and self-reproach of a parent watching his child grow up. I had been spared the kind of pain my father must have known, and the fear of becoming an angry, bitter, disappointed old man like him. All the same the realization of what I had lost was like looking down and seeing a gaping wound in my flesh that I had somehow failed to notice.

'You'd better go, too,' Lily said. 'It wouldn't do for them to get there before you.'

'No,' I agreed. I started to leave, but turned back again. 'Lily – I'm sorry about Shining Light. I mean it. If I could have done anything . . .'

She hesitated. She looked over her shoulder at her father, but he appeared to have nodded off over his last gourd full of sacred wine. We might as well have been alone.

She walked towards me, stopping only when she was so close I could see my own eyes reflected in hers.

'My son,' she said in a brittle voice, 'was vermin, worse than a rattlesnake. The World is better rid of him!'

I blinked, confused by what I was hearing. 'But . . .'

Suddenly she let out a huge groan and threw herself forward, and then her head was on my chest, jerking up and down against it as the sobs racked her body. 'Why do we do it, Yaotl?' she cried in a muffled voice. 'Why do we risk everything for them? You could have got yourself killed, defying your master, and I took a stupid chance with the merchants just to find out what had happened to my son. Why?'

I held her awkwardly. 'I don't know,' I murmured.

I could have added that I knew an old man who might have told us. His love for his daughter had induced him to take terrible risks as well, and dragged him into an unspeakably vicious plot. I pitied that old man because I could imagine the anguish he had been through already and the horror he was about to witness, on account of that love.

But that was not going to stop me using it to destroy him.

The labourers working on the plot at the back of the house in Atecocolecan had started hammering again, raining blows upon the wooden piles around its edge more fiercely than ever. It looked as if the weight of the rocks and mud they had piled up in the middle of the plot had made some of the piles collapse, and now they had had to pull some of them out of the bottom of the swamp and reset them. I grinned at the thought of the curses and arguments that must have started flying about when that had been discovered.

I was still grinning when I entered the house.

Butterfly knelt in the courtyard, alone. On the ground beside her was a plate, empty but for a few crumbs. On her other side were a jug and a small bowl half full of water. Her hair hung loose and tangled over her shoulders and she wore no make-up. The courtyard had been tidied and swept, as though she had belatedly remembered her obligations to the gods.

I noticed that Xolotl's statuette was still missing from its plinth. I wondered whether Butterfly had got rid of the broken pieces yet.

She did not get up when she saw me. She smiled thinly. 'Hello, Yaotl. I thought you'd come back. I was told you were dead, but I didn't think I'd seen the last of you. You're just like me, aren't you? You'd live through anything.'

'Who told you?'

'Why don't you sit? That policeman from Pochtlan – what's his name, Shield? He told me about the Otomies. He was upset about what happened to his colleague. He didn't mean to tell me about it, but I got it out of him.' She giggled. At one time the sound would have enchanted me; now it seemed grotesque. 'Men usually end up telling me everything I want to know! He seemed to think it would help him if he found some featherwork that he thought I was hiding. Of course, he didn't find it.'

'He wouldn't,' I said. I jerked my head in the direction of the narrow room, the one that had been forbidden me, and which I had tried to search, on the night when I was knocked out and had that strange dream, which had hardly been a dream at all. 'Did you let him look in there?'

'Oh, no. I just told him, very sweetly, that he could look at anything he liked.' She giggled again. 'He was out of the house in no time!'

Even now, just looking at the innocuous-looking, curtained-off doorway was enough to make me break into a sweat. 'All the same, I think we might go in there now, don't you?'

She yawned and stretched so that the cloth of her blouse and skirt flowed and tightened suggestively across her body. Then she looked at me, wide eyed, and deliberately curled her tongue around the outside of her mouth.

'Why, what did you have in mind?'

My patience snapped. I stepped towards her, bent down and seized her by the arm.

'You know why I came here, Butterfly, and it wasn't to play games! There are three people dead, maybe four, because of your scheming, and if I don't get what I'm here for there will be a lot more by nightfall, and you'll be one of them! Now, we're going into that back room and you can show me what it is you've really been hiding in there all along!'

I hauled her to her feet and began to drag her towards the doorway. She did not resist. She smiled, as if convinced that, whatever it was I thought I knew, nothing I could do or say would hurt her.

For the moment, at least, she was right.

The cloth had been hung over the doorway again. I had just got a corner of it between my thumb and forefinger when a strong, harsh voice called out, 'Stay there!'

Angry strode through the entrance to the courtyard. A sword swung from one massive fist, an old one, with some of its blades missing, obviously not used in years but still deadly. His nephew trotted behind him with the nervous air of a small dog unsure whether it was about to be petted or put in a cooking pot.

Nimble was not with them. I realized they must have been on their way here already, even before I had sent him to fetch the featherworker.

I dropped both the door covering and Butterfly's arm. The woman sprang away from me, and then hit me, slapping me across the face with enough force to send me staggering into the door post.

In two steps Angry was next to me, with the sword poised under my chin. 'Move away from her,' the old man growled, 'or I'll cut your throat. Are you alone?'

'Yes.'

He looked about him. 'I don't believe you're that stupid.' He turned to his nephew, who was looking at each of us in turn with a baffled expression that made it plain he had no idea what all this was about. 'Crayfish, go out and watch the street. Yell the moment you see anything!'

'But, Uncle . . .'

'Shut up and do as you're told!' the big man roared, and the sword twitched in time with his words. The boy jumped, and then, without a word, turned and ran through the front room and out of the house.

His uncle turned back to Butterfly and me. For a moment he seemed unsure of what to say, or, perhaps, which of us to say it to. When he spoke his voice was surprisingly soft.

'You know why I'm here.'

Butterfly said nothing.

'I heard a rumour in the marketplace, and I checked with the parish police. They told me Skinny was dead. Discovered floating in a canal, yesterday morning. They found nothing with the body – nothing. I came here the moment I heard.'

The woman maintained her silence. A hint of a smile lifted the corners of her mouth. She seemed to be enjoying herself. I knew why: she had something the featherworker wanted, and that gave her power over him.

'Now, where's my daughter?'

Still Butterfly had nothing to say. I jerked my head in the direction of the second room, the one she had tried to keep me out of. 'In there,' I said.

Angry's jaw dropped. Then, without a word, he reached towards me with his empty hand, seized the knot of my cloak and yanked me towards him until my face was pressed against his and I could smell his breath.

'I don't have to cut your throat straight away,' he hissed. 'Do you think I don't know how to use this sword? I could skin you alive. Any more jokes about my daughter and I'll make a start right here!'

'Angry,' I gasped, 'I'm not joking!'

'I've been in that room! There's nothing there but garbage!'

'I'm telling you, I know where she is!'

'Angry,' Butterfly said, in her most reasonable tone of voice, 'this is a stupid charade. You'll get your daughter back, but listen to me – there's something we have to do first. The costume is missing! We have to find it now. What do you think Montezuma will do to us if we don't? We daren't waste any more time on this slave. He knows too much anyway. Just kill him!'

Helpless in the big man's grip, I could not react, but my mind was reeling. If the costume was missing, how was I going to get it back to the Emperor?

For a moment Angry seemed to have no idea what to do. He and Butterfly were not friends. Only terror, desperation and blackmail had made them temporary allies, and it would not take much to set them at one another's throats.

'Missing? But Idle . . .'

'It's like the police told you – there was nothing with the body! Now get rid of the slave, and then we have to talk.'

Droplets of sweat glistened on the featherworker's forehead. Out of the corner of my eye, I saw his sword blades flashing in the sunlight as the weapon shook in his hand. The grip on my cloak tightened convulsively, and then loosened a little.

'No,' he muttered, 'I want to find out what he knows.'

He shoved me away from him, at the same time raising the sword. He could have struck down either me or Butterfly in an instant, but instead he gestured with the weapon towards the forbidden doorway. 'In there, you say? Go on, then, both of you. If you're lying, slave, you know what to expect!'

We crammed ourselves into the room, which was so much

smaller than it looked from the outside. I looked around me quickly, wondering whether Angry was really so stupid that he could not see what I could, before reminding myself that I had missed it myself at first. The unpleasant mixture of smells still hung in the air, the nastiest of them, the blend of blood and putrescence, stronger than ever. Even that was not enough to tell the featherworker what he so badly wanted to know.

'Angry, listen, the costume . . .'

'Shut your mouth, woman!' He waved the sword in front of my face. 'Now you, talk, before I cut your nose off!'

I opened my mouth to speak, but hesitated. I could tell him what he wanted to know straight away. I wanted to, out of revulsion for what Butterfly had done, and pity for her victim, but I did not know what the featherworker would do after he had learned the truth. Would he just kill both me and the woman out of hand?

Too clever by half again, Yaotl, I told myself. I had sought this confrontation, but it had got out of my control. I had hoped to face Angry with Lion and a squad of warriors beside me. The featherworker had thwarted me by arriving early. All I could do now was to spin this out for as long as I could, and pray that Partridge had convinced my brother of his mission's urgency.

I looked at the wall beyond the pile of rubbish. Angry followed my glance but its significance seemed lost on him. 'You remember the first time I came here, don't you, Butterfly? I met you and your husband, Skinny, and asked you if you knew anything about Kindly's featherwork. Of course, you told me you didn't, and that Skinny's workshop was closed.'

'It's true. It was. Look around you – this is all garbage, it'll be gone as soon as I can get around to clearing it out.'

'Oh, don't worry,' I said hastily. 'I believe you!' I could not help smiling at my next thought. 'It's funny, though. If you've spent your whole life telling lies you forget how easy it is to be fooled by the truth. I assumed you were lying about Skinny's workshop being closed, but strictly speaking you weren't. It was bound to be closed, since he was dead.'

She laughed.

'Don't be stupid! You met him!'

'No, I met his brother.'

Her expression froze. 'Angry,' she said deliberately, 'I told you he knew too much! You've got to kill him. Do it now!'

I flinched as the sword jerked towards my cheek.

'I'll kill him after he tells me about my daughter,' the man growled. 'You hear that? You're going to die, but how I do it depends on whether you tell me the truth. Fast or slow, it's your choice. Now get on with it!'

I spoke quickly. 'Idle stole the costume from Kindly's house and killed his brother. He'd planned the murder all along, of course. When Skinny asked the merchant to look after the costume, Idle probably realized his brother was on to him, and that would have made killing him more urgent. It was such a simple, obvious thing to do. Get his hands on the single most valuable piece that would ever come into his twin brother's workshop, get him out of the way, take his place and collect his money from the Emperor. It would never occur to Montezuma that there was anything wrong, provided the costume was delivered in pristine condition. And who would have seen through the deception, out here in Atecocolecan, where Skinny hadn't been seen in years?'

'What's this got to do with Marigold?' rasped Angry.

'Everything,' I said, as coolly as I could, 'because she *would* have seen through it.' I looked at Butterfly. 'And so, naturally, would she. But you were in it from the beginning, weren't you? And after the murder, you helped Idle hide the body.'

'Who told you they were twins?' Butterfly snapped.

'Nobody. But I found an idol of the god of twins in this room. I misread it: I thought someone must have been praying to Xolotl to relieve sickness. That was stupid of me, wasn't it? I should have realized there was a reason why Idle was so eager to identify his brother's body, and even provide his own charm as the evidence. Come to think of it, why else would the killer have gone to so much trouble to dispose of it in such a way that nobody would be willing to examine it too closely?

'You tried to throw me off the scent by hiding the idol. That was silly of you, you know – I might have overlooked it if it had been with the others!' I turned to Angry then. 'But it was what you said that really put me on to the trick.'

'What do you mean?' His voice was a threatening rumble, like a sleeping volcano's.

'When's your son-in-law's birthday?'

'Seven Flower,' he rapped out, automatically. 'If you think I'm playing some kind of guessing game with you . . .'

Keeping my voice as even as possible, I went on: 'When I talked to you and Crayfish at your house, you told me you didn't know when it was and didn't care. But of course you knew! Before your daughter and Idle got married, you'd have hired a soothsayer to check that their birthdays were compatible, as anybody would.' Unconsciously I echoed the words the priest at Amantlan had spoken to me when he told me about Skinny's wedding to Butterfly. 'If I'd picked up on it at the time I'd have realized you were lying to me for a reason. You didn't want to tell me when Idle was born, because then I'd have known he and Skinny were twins. When I finally got my head around that, I could see what had happened, and how you were involved, and why. And that's how I know where your daughter is.'

'I knew I should have killed you after I knocked you out.'

Butterfly sighed. 'Couldn't resist it, though. You looked so tempting, lying there . . .'

'Shut up,' Angry hissed. 'You,' he said to me, 'get on with it!'

Where was my brother? I strained to catch some sound from outside. Occasionally a muffled thump would come from the work gang labouring behind the house. I had not noticed the noise to begin with but it seemed to be getting louder, and occasionally the walls would shake a little.

'You got involved because your son-in-law's plan went wrong. He had to be able to deliver the featherwork in the same state as it would have been in if Skinny had just finished it. The trouble is, it wasn't. He was surprised while he was trying to steal it, by my son, of all people, and it got damaged in the fight. I know he left at least one feather behind because Kindly showed it to me. So he had a big problem. He knew nothing about featherwork himself, and there was no way he could fix it. He needed a featherworker to sort it out. His brother was dead by then, so he came to you.'

'What's that noise?' the woman cried suddenly.

I could not decide whether she had been reacting to something real or just wanted to change the subject. Surely the sound of hammer-blows outside was getting louder, coming closer?

Were those dust motes I could see dancing before my eyes?

'But you wouldn't cooperate, would you? I'm not surprised – it must have been galling enough to learn that Skinny had landed such an important commission when he was supposed to be working for you, but then to be asked to finish it so your despised son-in-law could take the credit in your rival's name – that was too much.'

'I told that slug Idle where to go,' the big man confirmed. 'So he came back the next night with . . . with . . .' He faltered before going on, in a small voice: 'He told me to get on with it if I wanted to see my daughter again.'

The sound from outside was becoming undeniable, thuds and crashes and muffled cries and a shaking that I could feel through the floor.

'What are they doing out there?' Angry cried, momentarily distracted. 'Are they trying to knock the house down, or what?'

'So I was right!' Despite my fear it was hard to keep my glee at my own cleverness out of my voice. 'Idle and Butterfly were holding her hostage, weren't they? And you lied to me because you were afraid that, if I knew the brothers were twins, I might work out what Idle had done and manage to recover the costume for Kindly. And there would go your daughter's ransom.'

Angry's response was a howl of anguish: 'So where is she, then?'

Butterfly screamed.

Suddenly she, Angry and his sword all vanished in a thick cloud of white dust and I was on the floor. From somewhere very close came a crash so loud that I did not so much hear it as feel it, as if the ground had grown legs and kicked me hard in the small of the back, and then the World exploded into a frenzy of flying masonry chips and plaster.

The dust around me glowed as light poured into the room. Men shouted and cursed. Pieces of timber and fragments of what had been the back wall of the house creaked, cracked and clattered as they fell. A woman shrieked.

I got to my feet, coughing and sneezing and spitting dust. I staggered blindly towards where I thought the doorway must be, away from the light, and into the courtyard of the house.

Voices were all around me, all talking at once, yelling orders or demanding answers to questions I could not make out, or merely swearing. There was a lot of swearing.

As the dust cleared in the open air I began to take in the scene around me. The courtyard was full. Soldiers stood all around, swords drawn in a gesture of battle readiness that their owners' baffled expressions made a nonsense of. My brother's bodyguards' eyes swivelled left and right as they looked for someone who could give them orders, or anything that might give them a clue as to what they were meant to do now. One or two recognized me and looked at me expectantly, as if they thought I could sort this out for them.

I saw my son, standing among the warriors. I realized he must have come here as soon as he found out that Angry and his nephew had already left. Crayfish was next to him, held in the unbreakable grip of a huge armed man.

'Nimble . . .' I croaked. Then, at last, from behind me, I heard the one voice I had been longing to hear since I had arrived at the house that morning.

'Yaotl? Anybody seen my brother? He'd better have a bloody good explanation for all this . . . Ah! Right, you come here. I want you to see what we've found. You won't believe it!'

Dust billowed out of the doorway into the ruined back room. Through the cloud strolled Lion, coated in the stuff from head to foot so that he looked like a chalk-whitened captive on the way to his one and only meeting with the Fire Priest's flint knife. A large flat piece of plaster decorated the top of his head. A hammer swung easily from his right hand.

Behind him, moving as slowly as cripples, came two of his warriors. They were supporting a woman between them. They had to support her because, judging by the way her head hung and her feet dragged apathetically across the ground, she would not have been able to stand unaided, let alone walk. At first I thought she was unconscious, but she was clutching something in both arms. I could not see what it was, because it was swaddled in cloth that had evidently been torn from her skirt. Both the bundle and the woman were caked in dried blood.

My sigh of relief turned into a groan of horror when I guessed what the cloth concealed.

'Found her in that hidden room at the back, behind the false wall,' my brother was saying. 'Lucky the wall didn't fall on her. Poor creature! You wouldn't keep a dog like that . . . What is it?'

I struggled to find my voice. 'What's she carrying?'

Lion turned and walked over to her. 'Here, let me look . . .'

The woman made no sound, but my worst fears were confirmed by the way she recoiled, snatching the little bundle out of my brother's reach, and the look of revulsion and disgust that crossed his face as he glimpsed what lay inside the pathetic wrappings.

A loud moan and a bout of convulsive sobbing burst out behind me.

Marigold, Angry's daughter, turned away, hiding her face and her burden from us all. But her father and her cousin had both seen as much as I had.

I hoped the child had not been born alive. In any event his soul would be happy now, sucking at the heavenly milk-tree until it was his turn to be born again; but there had been enough anguish here, without adding his suffering to it.

3

The warriors found a sleeping-mat in the front room of the house and lowered the silent woman on to it with surprising gentleness. They kept away from her bundle, on Lion's instructions. She lay down passively, seemingly oblivious to their attentions.

One of my brother's men ran to fetch her a doctor while the others stood up to watch as Angry and Butterfly were led out into the courtyard, surrounded by more warriors and a small crowd of curious labourers.

'We only brought the one hammer,' my brother explained, 'and they were so sick of driving piles into the lake bed that they were happy to help.'

'Watch Angry,' I warned. 'When he gets over the shock . . .'

I was almost too late. The featherworker suddenly roared like a trapped animal, and then, as a trapped animal sometimes will, he found a reserve of strength that was probably unknown even to himself, and burst free.

As the warrior holding him stumbled, he threw himself first forward, towards his daughter, then sideways, then back, turning and barging his bemused guard out of the way as he went for Butterfly.

'Stop him!' my brother bellowed.

Butterfly's guard was faster than Angry's had been. Shoving her aside, he lunged at the berserk old man. They crashed into one another, and for a moment the force of the impact locked their bodies together, still and upright, until they both collapsed. The collision winded the guard, who flopped and gasped for breath where he lay. Angry screamed hoarsely and tried to rise, but by now his own guard had recovered and others were running towards him, and they buried him under a pile of muscular bodies.

'Careful!' I said. 'I need to talk to him. Her too.' If Butterfly had had any thoughts of escape they were short lived. Two men held her fast. I caught her smiling at one of them, but he might as well have been made out of granite for all the good that was going to do her. They had all seen her sister-in-law by now.

'I suggest you keep them far apart.'

'Really?' said Lion heavily. 'I'd never have thought of that! Now, is anybody going to tell me what's going on?'

'Bring Crayfish over here.'

'You mean the lad blubbing by the doorway? Right.'

As his guard dragged him, still sobbing, towards us, the youth turned his head, so that his eyes stayed fixed on his cousin.

My son came after them, frowning anxiously. 'Father, don't let them be too rough with him!'

'I won't,' I promised, 'so long as he cooperates. What happened out here, anyway?'

'When I got to the featherworker's house they told me he and his nephew had already left. Angry didn't want Crayfish to come, but he followed him anyway. So I ran all the way here and found Crayfish outside. He said I couldn't go in, but he didn't seem to know why.'

'Then we turned up,' added Lion. 'I couldn't see the point of standing out here arguing with the boy or barging in through the front room and alerting his uncle. I got your message about breaking into a secret room at the back, so we just went straight to it.'

In spite of everything I grinned. 'I didn't really mean from the outside, Lion! But thanks, anyway.'

Lion's answer was a non-committal grunt. 'So what do you want done with the boy? Do I let him go, or what?'

'He doesn't know anything about this,' my son said. 'Look at him. All he cares about is his cousin!'

'Hold on to him for the moment,' I said. 'There's still the matter of the costume.' I had had a thought about that, since hearing Butterfly say it was missing. It was only a possibility, but the more I considered it, the more convinced I became that I had the answer.

First, however, I had Angry and Butterfly to deal with. I walked over to where they stood, each firmly pinioned by their guards. The featherworker was staring at the woman, his expression a mixture of fascination and loathing. He did not look at his daughter. Perhaps, I thought sadly, he could not bear to.

Butterfly returned my gaze with wide-open, defiant eyes.

'I suppose you expect me to confess all now,' she snapped.

'You may as well.'

'Fuck you!'

One of her guards growled at her but I motioned him to be quiet.

'What is really so bizarre about all this,' I said eventually, addressing both her and Angry, 'is that neither of you has actually killed anybody. I thought you had,' I added, to Butterfly, 'but I realize I was wrong. So I don't know how all this is going to turn out, but I guess that if you both make a clean breast of everything, you may escape with your lives.'

'I told you,' Angry muttered. 'Idle came to see me. It was on One Death. He brought the costume to me and asked me to repair it. I didn't want anything to do with it. I could see what it was and it didn't take a genius to work out who must have ordered it. And Skinny's style was all over the thing. I told him to give it back to his brother. Then, the next day, he came back. He told me Skinny was dead, and how he was going to impersonate him. I thought it was the most stupid thing I'd ever heard, and I told him so. That's when. . .' Suddenly a deep, broken sob broke from him. 'That's when he showed me the finger.'

'*What?*'

'Oh no,' my brother whispered. 'You,' he ordered one of his men, 'check the girl's hands – gently, mind!'

I closed my eyes and clenched my teeth against the wave of nausea that threatened to overwhelm me. I decided then that I did not care whether Butterfly talked or not. She was going to get whatever the law said she had coming to her, regardless.

'Little finger, left hand, missing, sir!' the soldier barked.

'It was deformed,' the old man whimpered. 'She broke it when she was a little girl, and it healed funny. That's how I knew it was hers.'

'So you did what you were told. You shut yourself in your workshop – your nephew told me about it – and worked on the costume night and day, to get it finished before he brought you any more.' I looked at Butterfly, whose expression had not altered. 'But you'd walled her up by then, hadn't you? Did you hate her that much? Just because your husband finally found what he needed, and it wasn't you? Whose was the baby, Butterfly – his or Idle's?'

'You don't know what you're talking about!' she spat.

'I think I do.' I took a step towards her. I was going to grasp her chin and force her to face me, so that I could look straight into her eyes and see whether there was anything I could learn from them, but then I changed my mind. She was straining restlessly against the hands that held her, and there was a ferocity about her staring eyes and bared teeth, the desperation of a trapped beast, that made me want to keep my distance. 'How old are you, Butterfly? How old were you when you were married – fourteen, fifteen? Only just out of the House of Youth, I bet. Your whole life ahead of you, and you the most beautiful girl in Amantlan.' As she must have been, and still was, even with her features contorted with fury. 'So you ought to have had the pick of the men of your parish, at least; or even some of the others – think of all those rich, exciting young merchants from just the other side of the canal, and maybe even the chance of some freedom: running the family business while your husband was away, your own pitch in Tlatelolco market – I can see that that would have suited you. It wasn't to be, though, was it? The matchmaker came to see your parents with an offer they couldn't turn down. How much did Skinny pay for you? How much would Amantlan's most famous son have needed to pay?'

Her answer was a growl.

'Well, never mind. There you were, hitched to a failed craftsman more than twice your age. Still, you're a practical girl. You made the best of it. You tried to support him while he was working with Angry.' I remembered Crayfish's description of how Skinny's wife had made him eat and drink, fetching him food and water while he was working. 'It must have hurt so much when he and Marigold started getting close. All that attention, all you'd given up, and what it really took to get him interested was something you couldn't offer him, something you couldn't even understand.'

I was goading her, taunting her with what I was almost sure had happened in the hope of making her own up to it.

It worked. She finally met my eyes: not scowling at me from beneath lowered brows, in the manner of a person

reluctantly facing her accuser, but raising her head to look me
full in the face. When she spoke, her voice was clear and confident.

'You've no idea what happened. Why, my husband never
even screwed her! He wasn't capable. He never managed it
with me! But she wanted to. He never saw through all that
crap about the gods and their gifts to us and all our labour
going to pay our debts to them. But I did. Everyone thought
she was so pious, so innocent, so correct she would never tell
a lie or do anything dishonourable. You know what she did?
She lied to her own father! She told him that fairy tale about
needing to move to Atecocolecan, so that we could get Skinny
back here where nobody would know any better when his
brother took his name.' Out of the corner of my eye I saw
Angry tense, but his guards held him as fast as Butterfly's held
her. She saw it too, and laughed. 'What, you didn't think your
beloved daughter was involved? She was in as deep as the rest
of us!'

I glanced past her, towards what had been her sister-in-law's
prison. 'Then why that?'

Butterfly tossed her head. 'She found out about me and
Idle. Bound to, once we were all living together in such a small
space. She went hysterical. Maybe it was knowing I was getting what she wanted, and with her husband! She threatened
to go back to Angry and tell him everything! We weren't
going to let that happen, were we? And then when the suit got
damaged and we needed a featherworker to mend it – well, it
was the obvious thing to do.'

I had been wrong about looking into this woman's eyes, I
realized. There was nothing in them that gave me any clue as
to how immurement, extortion, mutilation and murder had
ever become the obvious thing to do.

Perhaps it had been just as I had said. She was a practical girl.

I turned back to Angry. 'You saw the scratches on Idle's face, and you guessed from that that she'd put up a fight. I suppose that helped convince you she was alive, didn't it? That they hadn't just poisoned her or knocked her over the head.'

'It wouldn't have mattered,' he mumbled. 'I'd have done anything if I thought I might get her back. You can understand that, can't you?'

I sighed. 'So you mended the costume. But it still went wrong, didn't it?'

'It wasn't my fault!' the man cried, ridiculously defensive. 'I did my bit! The bastard came and picked it up and that was that – he even bloody well thanked me! I should have got her back then. He told me he'd send her, as soon as he got home. I believed him!'

'I know.' I looked down, unable to meet the broken old man's eyes. I forgot how he had threatened me earlier. I just prayed silently to the gods to preserve me from ever being that desperate. 'But he never got home, did he? And the next thing you heard was this rumour that Skinny had been found dead, and there was no sign of the costume.'

'But she didn't kill him?' Lion asked. He had come to stand next to me and was looking at Butterfly with an expression of mystified awe. I guessed he had never met anyone like her before.

'No,' I said. 'She'd no reason to. Quite the opposite: she needed him alive, to keep up the pretence of his being Skinny. And anyway, they were lovers. She's in mourning – look at her hair – and it's not for her husband.'

'So who did it?' my brother demanded. 'And what for?'

Angry kept his face hidden behind his fingers. They trembled slightly. Enclosed in his own world of remorse and grief, he seemed oblivious to what we were saying. It was Butterfly who responded to Lion's question, letting out a little gasp and looking sharply from him to me and back again.

What had Montezuma said to me? *The thief wore the costume because he wanted to. The raiment of the god has power of its own. The man who wears it takes the form of the god, and his attributes. He becomes the god.*

It's like an idol, someone else had said. *It should be prayed to.*

'He would keep wearing the bloody thing,' I muttered.

'Who?'

'Idle, of course. That's why he died.' I turned towards the doorway leading out of the courtyard. 'Let's go, shall we? It's nearly noon. I want to get that costume back to Montezuma before my master turns the Otomies loose again!'

'Hang on!' cried Lion. 'What do I do with this lot? What about the boy? What about . . .?'

From behind my brother's back came an animal noise.

Lion stiffened. It took him a moment to turn around; about as long as it took me to look over his shoulder and work out what was happening, and almost long enough for it all to be over.

Angry had freed himself. Where he had found the strength, and what combination of pain and fury had released it in him, I could only guess, but his guards were on their knees, clutching their brows and looking dazed. The featherworker had banged their heads together and launched himself at Butterfly.

The men guarding her took a moment to take in what was happening: the big man rushing towards them with murder in his eyes. Then they both let their captive go, and she ran. She dashed towards the interior of the house, the room where Marigold had been held, or rather the mass of rubble and broken timbers that was all that remained of it. Seeing there was no escape that way, she checked herself, and turned.

Angry crashed into her guards. Still bemused, they made

only a half-hearted effort to stop him, and he knocked them aside as if they were children. As they staggered away from them he seemed to stumble, but when he straightened up there was a piece of masonry in his hand, a large flat stone.

Butterfly waited for him. The last expression I saw on her face was oddly calm, serene even, and a slight, knowing smile played across her lips.

Lion was moving by the time Angry hit her, but too late, and nowhere near fast enough. I took one step, and stopped because I had heard the blow, and from the sound of it there was going to be nothing for me to do.

Nothing for anyone, except the vultures and coyotes.

4

'We have to go,' I said gently.

I had rarely seen my brother at a loss, but he seemed so now, as he surveyed the scene. In front of him lay a once beautiful woman, her face mercifully turned away as her blood soaked into the dust around her, while a broken, weeping old man huddled nearby with his nephew kneeling by him, a consoling hand resting vainly on his uncle's shoulder. A moan from somewhere behind us may have meant that the maimed girl Lion had dragged from her cell had broken her silence, or it may just have been one of his men nursing a sore head; I did not bother to look.

'We can't do any more here,' I added. 'Leave a couple of men to look after Angry and his daughter. That's all they'll need: they aren't going anywhere. Bring the rest.' I stepped over to the boy. 'You too, Crayfish. We may need you.'

He looked fearfully up at me, and then turned to my son, as if he expected him to intercede for him. 'But I don't know anything about this costume!'

Nimble answered before I could speak. 'I think my father knows that,' he said sympathetically, 'but he thinks you can help. It's for your uncle's sake, as much as anybody's.' He extended a hand. Crayfish looked at it for a long time, but at last he took it, and let my son help him up.

'Lion!' I called out. 'Come on!'

My brother roused himself from his reverie then. 'Let me get my men together,' he muttered. 'Where are we going, anyway?'

'Amantlan.'

'It was those Morning Glory seeds,' I explained. 'I should have remembered what that stuff is like, back from when I was a priest. Morning Glory, sacred mushrooms – the food of the gods, and others like them – peyote buttons, water lilies – all these things, they don't just open up the world of dreams to you when you're asleep. Sometimes they send you visions when you're awake, and change the way things that are happening to you seem, so you have to sort out what's real from what isn't, or at least what belongs here on the Earth from what belongs in the heavens.'

Lion, Nimble, Crayfish and I were in Lion's canoe. The boy sat in sullen silence between my brother and me, where we had taken the precaution of putting him, although I was sure he would not try to run away. One of my brother's bodyguards propelled us with firm, sure strokes of his paddle, and the rest of his men rode in boats ahead and behind. The little flotilla churned up the surface of the canal as it sped long, sending waves slapping against the banks to splash the occasional passer-by on the canal path. I did not hear any complaints about a soaked cloak or breechcloth: one look at our escort would have been enough to quell any protest.

I had been going through my account of what had happened, trying to reconstruct it all. I had reached the night when I had returned to the house in Atecocolecan to look for the costume, and Butterfly had surprised me and knocked me out.

'She could just have stuck a knife in me while I was unconscious, but I suppose she wanted to know exactly what I was doing there, and how much I knew. So she tied me up and drugged me to loosen my tongue. After that – well, she was waiting for Idle to come home, and I have the impression they made love a lot in that room, on purpose so that Marigold could hear them, so I suppose she was ready. And perhaps she saw me lying there at her mercy, and the feeling of power went to her head. I think that's what she liked, feeling powerful, and it's not a feeling many women in Mexico get to indulge in very often.'

'Power, eh?' my brother said. 'Well, that makes sense. If sex had been all she was after there'd have been no need to drug you!'

I shut my eyes with embarrassment. 'I can assure you it wasn't my idea, and it wasn't pleasant. I kept thinking she was a snake!' I opened my eyes again in time to see Lion shudder. When I looked at Nimble, though, he returned my gaze frankly, without a hint of embarrassment or self-consciousness. My heart went out to him then, as I recalled the things he had seen and been made to do in his short life, which made my experience seem ordinary. 'I thought I was seeing the feathered serpent, or . . . well, I don't know. It was all very confused. Gods and goddesses. At one point I heard a woman's voice, and I thought she must be Cihuacoatl crying in the night, the way they say she does when the city is in real peril. It was only a lot later that I worked out that I hadn't been dreaming: it was your cousin I heard, Crayfish. I'm sorry I didn't think of it earlier, or notice there was a false wall, but at the time I was just too befuddled. I didn't even think of it the next morning, when I found the place smelled a bit like a cross between a temple and a prison. It didn't occur to me until I realized that Butterfly and Idle needed your uncle to finish off the featherwork for them, and that they must be using your cousin to force him to do it, and that meant they'd found somewhere to keep her.'

I had to pause for a moment, because the thought of it was threatening to overwhelm me. To be sealed up for good in a tiny cell with no access to the outside world but a little hole at the bottom to pass her rations through – the hole I had thought was made by mice – that was horrific enough; but to have borne a child there?

Alone, in the dark, with no curer or midwife, no one to help deliver the child or grieve with her over his death. I wondered whether Butterfly had been on the far side of the wall at the time, gloating over her sister-in-law's agony. I wondered whether Marigold would ever speak again.

During most of the journey Crayfish was as silent as his cousin, staring morosely at the bottom of the canoe and seemingly becoming more withdrawn the closer we got to his home parish. Suddenly, however, he looked up.

'Was it true, what that woman said – about Marigold lying to my uncle, and being involved in stealing the costume? Did she really only pretend to be Skinny's friend so he would work harder, when all along she knew they were going to kill him?'

I was on the point of saying I had no idea, but then I saw the boy's expression. He was pleading with me, the way a captive might as he looked into the Fire Priest's face, and the wrong word from me could be like the blow of the flint knife.

Once again it was my son who answered for me while I struggled to come up with a reply. 'No, of course not,' Nimble said, leaning forward to lay a hand lightly on Crayfish's arm. 'She was too good for that, and too devoted to the gods to lie. Isn't that right?' The question was for me, and in his tone were both deference and defiance, as if he were daring me to contradict him.

'That's right.' After all, I thought, it was not as if Marigold herself was ever likely to say anything to the contrary.

'And the baby?' Lion asked. 'Was it her husband's, or the featherworker's?'

'Oh, I should think Butterfly told the truth about that,' I said. However, as Crayfish relaxed, I found myself wondering whether she had or not. Poor old Skinny, I told myself, it wasn't just your featherwork they took from you, was it?

'You still haven't told us', Lion reminded me, 'where the costume is. Nor, come to that, who killed Idle. You seem very sure it wasn't Butterfly.'

'The costume's in Amantlan, of course, where we're going. But as for Butterfly killing Idle, remember they were lovers. Besides, she had the perfect alibi – me! She must have been with me when he was killed, although I couldn't have sworn to it not all being a dream. But what clinched it for me, once I'd got my head back together, was the fact that she obviously thought Skinny was alive and well and roaming around dressed as the Feathered Serpent.

'There was another thing I saw that I thought was a vision, you see: the god comes into the room and a woman tries to embrace him, and the god runs away. I had some idea that Quetzalcoatl was trying to avoid a repeat of what happened when Topiltzin was driven out of Tollan, all those bundles of years ago, but it was much simpler than that.

'What I really saw was what I'd seen once before: a man dressed in the raiment of the god. Butterfly thought he was Idle, back from Angry's house with the costume, which he would have worn partly to scare off inquisitive passers-by and partly out of vanity. But she was wrong. Idle was dead, and the person wearing the costume was his killer.'

The canoes brought us to the bridge between Amantlan and Pochtlan, the bridge I knew so well, where I had seen Idle dressed as a god and found his brother's body and been arrested. We leaped out of the canoes within plain sight of the parish's temple, which made me nervous. I was urging Lion to get his men moving as quickly as he could when my son called out: 'Who's that?'

Dodging the men scurrying around me, I followed his gaze, and let out a groan of despair.

A lone man stood on the bridge. He started walking towards me as soon as I saw him, hailing me grimly. 'Didn't Howling Monkey once tell you you'd have your brains knocked out if you were ever seen in Pochtlan again?'

'Hello, Shield,' I said lightly. 'I'm not in Pochtlan. I'm in Amantlan. Look, we don't want any trouble . . .'

'Who is he?' my brother demanded tensely.

'The local police.' I looked at the newcomer uncertainly. His face was grey and drawn, as though he had not slept since the morning, two days before, when we had seen his colleague killed. I felt sorry for them both. They had only been doing their job. 'Look, we can't afford to waste any time. If he tries to detain us, your men will have to take him, but don't hurt him any more than you have to.'

'All right. You!' Lion called out to the man stepping off the bridge. 'We said we didn't want trouble. Now just go home, like a good lad, eh?'

Shield did not hesitate. He came straight towards me, even though I was now surrounded by armed soldiers, the smallest of whom stood a head taller than he did. 'Yaotl,' he began urgently, 'I've got to tell you . . .'

That was as far as he got before the flat of a sword fell on his head. His words tailed off into a moan, a sound as soft as a breeze through sedges, and he sank peacefully to the ground, smiling like an idiot.

'There you are,' said my brother proudly. 'That wouldn't have hurt a bit! Wonder what he wanted? Didn't sound like he was about to arrest you, did it?'

'Never mind,' I said. 'Let's go!'

★

As we entered the little sacred plaza of Amantlan, the parish priest, no doubt alerted by the unaccustomed sound of so many sandals clattering over the flagstones, came bustling out of his house. I was certain he did not recognize me, but his jaw dropped when he saw who I was with.

'Grab him,' I muttered to Lion, and before he could speak the man was seized and swept along by the advancing warriors like a piece of driftwood picked up by a wave. We surged forward to the base of the stumpy pyramid and on up its short flight of steps.

Stammerer, the apprentice featherworker, stood at the summit, in front of the temple, holding his broom. At the sound of our approach he twisted his head around, so that he could watch us without turning his back on the idol at the top of the steps.

He recognized Crayfish first. Angry's nephew was just behind me. I saw shock register in Stammerer's face, his eyes widening and his mouth opening in a gasp, and then his stare fixed on me.

So much for my disguise. He knew me at once.

He stepped past the idol into the doorway of his temple, turning as he did so and brandishing his broom over his head like a weapon. 'Get . . . get . . . get out of here!' he shouted. 'This is a s-sacred place! Only priests . . .'

I kept going until I stood one step below the top, and my eyes were level with the boy's. 'Forget it, lad. Look at all these warriors. If you break that thing over my head, what are you going to defend yourself with?'

His eyes jerked left and right, as if looking for a means of escape, and then he took the obvious course and darted through the doorway.

I made as if to follow, but something made my cloak twitch.

I looked down. Crayfish was standing on the step below mine, plucking timidly at the edge of the cloth.

'I was right, wasn't I?' I said. 'Stammerer is the one you mentioned, your friend at the House of Tears.'

'Let me talk to him,' the boy offered. 'It's what you brought me here for, isn't it?'

I looked from his anxious, upturned face to the open doorway, and stepped aside.

He did not go in, because the shrine was forbidden to all except the priests of Coyotl Inahual. He stood on the threshold, and spoke softly to the lad inside. I did not hear what passed between them, but after a few moments Crayfish turned to me and said: 'It's in there.'

'I know.'

It took some time for Stammerer to bring the raiment of Quetzalcoatl out into daylight. It came in many pieces, each wrapped in a cloth cover, and many of them were heavy.

The youth laid them at my feet, like the king of a subject town presenting gifts to the Emperor's tribute collectors. I waited until he had finished before kneeling and reverentially unwrapping just one item whose shape had caught my eye.

As I peeled back its binding, the face of the god stared up at me. In the early afternoon sunlight every scale of its turquoise skin flashed, each one its own colour, some blue, some green, some almost black, each seemingly perfect and irreplaceable.

'The serpent mask,' I breathed. 'And look at those feathers! Angry did a good repair job on his rival's masterpiece. . . Skinny's monument.' And all that was left of him. It crossed my mind that perhaps it had been all he really wanted.

'How . . . how did you know?' Stammerer asked.

'Where else would it be?' I stood up and turned, looking at the view I had taken in the last time I had been here: the houses of Amantlan and Pochtlan, and the canal that separated them, and the bridge across it.

Lion and Nimble had joined us on the summit of the pyramid.

'The night before last, when he came back,' I continued, 'were you waiting for him? Or was it a lucky chance?'

'I . . . I . . . I guessed he'd be back,' Stammerer mumbled. 'I didn't know when. I've spent every night up here, the last few nights, watching that canal, just in case. And then he came along, on the Amantlan side this time, but the same as before – st-strutting about in the raiment of the god like it was fancy dress!'

'So what did you do – run straight down to the bridge and tell him to take it off? What happened then?'

'I didn't want to kill him!' the youth cried. 'He . . . he had a knife – one of those copper blades the featherworkers use – it was him or me! And it was an accident, anyway. He shouldn't have tried to f-fight in the costume. He lost his balance and hit his head on the side of the bridge.'

'You pushed him in after you'd got the costume off him,' I pointed out.

'He'd profaned it! The god was angry with him. So was I. But I didn't mean to kill him, I told you – I just kept hitting him until he fell off the bridge. I d-didn't do it really – it was the god!'

Montezuma's words came back to me again. Idle had enjoyed parading around as a god, scaring people. This youth had really believed he would become the god, and be the instrument of his will, and in the end the featherworker's brother had died as a result of an excess of piety.

That was his story, anyway. Remembering what Idle had done, I decided it was good enough for me.

'What made you go to the house in Atecocolecan?' I asked.

'I . . . I w-wanted to help Crayfish. He'd told me about his c-c-cousin, how she'd gone missing and how his uncle seemed to think her husband and B-Butterfly had something to do with it. I knew he'd been to the house to look for her. I'd been on the lookout for that man every night, and so I hadn't been able to go myself . . .'

'But now you had your chance, and thought you'd have a go at playing god yourself?'

'It was d-different!' the boy protested. 'Can't you see – Crayfish, you understand. . .'

'It's true,' Angry's nephew told me. 'I did tell him all about Marigold.'

'Oh, never mind,' I said wearily. 'Let's just get this lot wrapped up and returned to the Emperor, shall we?'

'Why did you cut his ropes?' Nimble asked.

'I thought I was going to find M-marigold. I found him instead, and I thought if Butterfly and Idle were holding him prisoner I should let him go. And then that w-w-woman . . .'

'You really were re-enacting the story of Topiltzin Quetzalcoatl and his sister, weren't you?' I mused. 'Only this time, you resisted.'

5

'What's going on down there?'
My brother was looking at the bridge, where we had left a couple of men standing over Shield. Some sort of commotion seemed to have started, and someone was shouting. It was hard to catch the words but it sounded like a warning.

'Looks like the policeman's coming round, that's all. We'll know in a moment – here comes one of your boys to tell us all about it!'

As we watched the warrior racing towards us, Lion asked: 'What now? I've got . . . let's see, counting the parish priest down there and not counting Shield, five prisoners – what do you suggest I do with them all?'

'Let them all go, of course.'

Lion almost fell off the top of the pyramid. 'Let them go?' he spluttered. 'Are you joking? We're talking about two deaths, or is it three? One kidnapping, theft, blasphemy, and probably a whole load of other crimes there aren't even words for, and you want me to let everybody go?'

My brother was not stupid but he saw the world in very simple terms. I reminded myself that executing miscreants was one of his functions, and to him every crime was followed by retribution, as surely as night followed day. 'Think about it, Lion. Who else would you have to arrest – Kindly, Lily,

Nimble, me? We're all caught up in this one way or another.'

'Yes, I know, but . . .'

'As for the theft – the stolen property is here. The Emperor will get it back, and as long as nobody blabs about it, no harm will have been done. Of course, it's been handled a bit roughly and will need mending and checking over. Now who's going to do that, with Skinny dead?'

Lion said nothing. It was my son who volunteered the name: 'Angry.'

'Right. You want to punish him? Go back to Atecocolecan and look at him and his daughter, and ask yourself if there's any need.'

Lion sighed. 'All right, point taken. But what about Stammerer here?'

'He got the raiment of the god back for us, in the end, even if he didn't mean to, and as for killing Idle – be honest, Lion, do you really care?'

'I suppose you're right,' he admitted reluctantly. 'I'll have to give the Emperor some sort of report, but it's the costume he's concerned about.' He looked sternly at the two youths and the priest. 'Just remember that none of this ever happened, do you understand? Your lives depend upon it! Now, what do you want?'

The warrior bounding up the steps two or three at a time was almost black in the face with exertion and could scarcely draw enough breath to deliver his report. Fortunately, it was a very short report.

'That policeman, sir – came round – wanted to warn your brother – his master's at the merchant's house! He's got a bunch of Otomi warriors and they're holding Kindly and Lily!'

Shield met us on the bridge. He was rubbing his head as he fell into step beside my brother, my son and me.

'Look, I'm sorry about this,' I said. 'I didn't know.'

'Forget it,' he said roughly. 'Compared to those animals, your brother's boys are like wet-nurses.' I had no need to ask what animals he meant: his frown, the set of his jaw and the way he spat the word out, as if it were snake venom sucked from a wound, were enough.

'You're sure old Black Feathers is there in person?' my brother asked. 'How many men has he got with him?'

'Nothing happens in this parish without me knowing about it,' the policeman assured us. 'They turned up about midday – the Chief Minister, twenty Otomies and a priest.'

'A priest?' I asked. 'Why would he have a priest with him?'

'How should I know? He was a youngster, that's all I can tell you. Looked as if he'd come straight from a vigil – he was still carrying a conch-shell around, like he hadn't had time to put it away and wasn't sure what to do with it.'

'Idiot!' I cried, slapping my own forehead. Now I knew why my master had been willing to give me only Handy as an escort, and why the young man my mother had hired to lead my family's devotions had left in such a hurry.

'Forget the priest,' said my brother. 'What about the Otomies?'

'Like I said, twenty. And don't kid yourself that I might have made a mistake. I'm not likely to forget what that little squad of lunatics looks like – especially the big ugly one-eyed bastard in charge of them! Mostly they're in the house. They've got a few posted outside as lookouts, and a couple of the others on the roof. They don't take any trouble to keep out of sight.'

Lion halted. 'We need to work out how to play this,' he said.

His bodyguards drew up behind him as he looked at my son and me.

I said: 'It's easy enough to see what the old man's after. He wants me and Nimble. He probably hoped to catch us in Pochtlan. Now he's got Kindly and Lily as hostages, and he's just sitting there, waiting for us to come back.' I turned to Upright. 'How's he going to get away with it, though? Surely the merchants won't stand for this?'

Tlatelolco's merchants had their own laws and their own courts and policed their own affairs. They bitterly resented any interference from outside, and could afford to make their resentment felt – so long as they remained the Emperor's obedient subjects and kept the Palace supplied with exotic foreign goods and intelligence from abroad.

'They won't,' the policeman confirmed. 'They'll complain to the Governor, and he'll complain to the Emperor, and your master will have to explain himself. He's supposed to be the Chief Justice of Tenochtitlan, among other things, and we all know what happens to corrupt judges.' Strangulation was the usual penalty.

'Yes, I can just hear it,' said my brother drily. ' "All a silly misunderstanding. Just paying a call on some old friends. Of course I had my guards with me, I always do, I'm a great lord, what could be more natural?" No one will believe a word of it, of course, but it won't matter if the right people get paid off. And by then it'll be too late anyway. What do we do in the meantime?'

'You mean, besides busting in there and freeing Lily and Kindly?' It came out more sharply than I had intended. Nerves had added an edge to my voice. What was the captain doing now? I wondered. Was he content to squat in Lily's courtyard and wait, or had he found some other, unspeakable way to pass the time? My teeth ground together in anger and frustration.

Lion went pale. 'Now listen, if you think I'm afraid of a bunch of thugs with silly haircuts . . .'

'Relax,' I said hastily. 'I know you're not. I only meant . . .'

'We'll go in,' he went on, ignoring me, 'but we need to know where they all are first. I'll get a couple of lads to spy out the land.' He looked at Shield. 'How well can you see the house from the parish temple? I could send someone up there for a recce.'

'No you won't,' I told him.

He rounded on me. 'Mind your own business! This is war, Yaotl, not some game you can win with a bit of luck and a fast mouth. Now leave it to me!'

'Lion, will you listen?'

'Shut up!'

'Please! Father, Uncle!'

The tremor in Nimble's voice made us both pause. I looked at him and understood, from his wide-eyed and fearful expression and the way his lower lip trembled, that he must be as afraid for Lily as I was. More so, perhaps, since she had nursed him back to health, treating him for a few days as if he had been her own.

I stretched out a hand and put it on his shoulder, gripping it the more firmly as the knowledge of what I had to do became clearer, along with the certainty that this was the last I would ever see of him.

'I'm sorry, son. You too, Lion.' I turned back to my brother. 'Nobody doubts your courage, or your men's. But face it, you're wrong: this isn't a war. This is the middle of Mexico, not some frontier province. If you go charging in, half your men are going to get killed, at least, and even if you get Lily and her father out alive, the chances are old Black Feathers will twist the whole thing around afterwards so as to make it look as if it was you who started it. As you said yourself, as long as the right people get paid off . . .'

'But what can we do?' cried Nimble desperately.

I looked silently into his face for a long time. I wanted to speak, but the words would not come, and I could not have forced them past the lump in my throat. Nonetheless he understood. I could tell as much from the way his eyes filmed over with tears and his lips parted, silently forming the word 'No'.

'It's . . . it's the only way,' I whispered at last. Tears were clouding my own vision. I swatted them away furiously, not wanting to lose sight of him a moment before I had to.

'What are you talking about?' my brother demanded, his head darting from side to side as he stared at each of us in turn. 'What's the matter?'

I forced myself to look away from my son and towards Lion, whose puzzled frown might have struck me as comic in other circumstances. 'Lord Feathered in Black wanted me to tell him where Nimble was.' I spoke deliberately, bringing the words out one at a time because I knew that if I did not, they would all come at once in a desperate, incoherent, unintelligible rush. 'But he knows perfectly well that I wouldn't betray my own son, no matter what he did. He hoped to catch one or both of us at Kindly's house, but he missed us. So now he'll be ready to work out his anger on whichever of us he can get his hands on. If I give myself myself up to him, he'll let Kindly and Lily go. He's taking too big a risk holding them not to. But Nimble – you have to run away. Now, before he sends the Otomies after you!'

'You can't go!' the boy cried. 'I'll go instead!'

'No – look, you don't even exist, as far as the law's concerned.' Having been brought up among barbarians and crept back unnoticed into the city, Nimble had no parish and, apart from me, no family. 'Even if you did, he could charge you with complicity in Shining Light's crimes.' I saw him wince at my brutal reminder of his dead lover and the vicious cycle of deceit and murder he had been drawn into. 'I'm a slave, remember? There's not much he can do to me, except sell me. He'll have enough to do covering up his activities today, without breaking the law further by ill-treating a slave. Look, I'm not really taking a risk.' The illogic of my own words was painfully plain to me, and I could see from the look in my son's eyes that he saw it too, but my brother and the policeman took it up.

'He's got a point,' Shield said. 'The merchants will be all over him for what he's doing now. If I were him, I'd be treading very carefully for a while.'

'You're young and your father isn't,' Lion said harshly. 'You've got more to lose!'

But what convinced Nimble in the end was not words but force. He suddenly bolted, springing forward and darting off in the direction of the merchant's house, but Lion was ready for that. He caught him before he had gone two steps, and held him fast, ignoring his struggles, his cries and the knife waving impotently in the air in front of him.

'If you're going,' Lion grunted at me, 'I suggest you go. Now!'

Nimble suddenly stopped writhing in his arms.

I got one last look at him before my eyes misted over completely.

'Sorry, son,' I mumbled brokenly. 'I wish I'd . . . Goodbye!'

It was a short walk to the merchant's house, but long enough.

Twice I stopped, standing still in the middle of the street, while canoes sailed past on the canal beside me, their occupants going carelessly about their daily business, until I had mastered my fear enough to carry on. Both times I made myself imagine Lily at the Otomi captain's mercy, the four-bladed sword at her throat.

What are you worrying about? I asked myself, as I prepared to turn the last corner. The worst he can do is sell you. And the Emperor will have the raiment of the god back, he'll be grateful for that . . .

I could not make myself believe it.

I was going to be sold for an offering to the gods. What then? I wondered. Would my flesh be charred and blistered and split in the Fire Sacrifice, or pierced and lacerated in the Arrow Sacrifice, when my blood would start from so many wounds at once it would fall like the rain the priests would pray for as I died?

As I walked through the entrance to the merchant's courtyard, the grins on the faces of the waiting warriors told their own story.